Killing David McAllister

The McAllister Series

Book 4

L. V. Gaudet

ISBN 978-1-9992823-0-1
Library and Archives Canada
First edition published October 2019
By IngramSpark

Cover Photo by
Lenka Sluneckova on Unsplash

Discover other titles by L.V. Gaudet:

Garden Grove
The Gypsy Queen
Old Mill Road

The McAllister Series:
Where the Bodies Are
The McAllister Farm
Hunting Michael Underwood
Killing David McAllister

"Day-vid," little Cassie whispers in a taunting sing-song.
"Day-vid.
Why did you hurt me David?"

She stares at him with vacant eyes, the light of life extinguished.

To sleep more deeply is to dream more deeply.
In the darkness, where the nightmares live.

Table of Contents

Part One
Safety

1   Promises

"Did you mean what you said? That you are going to kill him?" Kathy asks, looking at Cassie.

Kathy still feels the shock. It fills every fiber of her being, numbing her and pushing the world away to some distant place. She feels like she is trapped in a bad movie.

"Did I mean what?" Cassie does not look at her. She can't. Every time she looks at Kathy she is filled with anger.

"At the farm; you said you are going to kill him. Did you mean it?"

"I meant it." Cassie glances at her and quickly looks away.

Kathy swallows, thinking.

Do I ask? What will she do, kill me? Isn't that what I want? To die? To get this all over with? The only way out of this is death.

"Who did you mean?" she asks, hesitating. "Which one of them are you going to kill?"

"Does it matter?"

Kathy feels nauseas. *I don't know who I want it to be,* she thinks.

"I feel like this is unreal," Kathy says. "I thought you were dead."

"I'm not. No thanks to you."

"That's harsh."

"You deserve it."

Kathy's throat constricts and her eyes burn with the tears that threaten to come.

"It's time to go." The voice has the raspy tremor of age.

They look up at Anderson's intrusion. Kathy is anxious he somehow knows what they are talking about.

Cassie gets up and walks away without looking back.

Kathy watches her go. "She hates me," she says softly.

"She has good reason to," Anderson says.

He reaches one age-gnarled hand down to help her up.

She reaches up, taking his hand and letting him help her up, surprised at the strength in his withered muscles.

They walk to the vehicles together, where everyone is waiting.

Anderson moves to walk next to William.

"We have to drop off your Mrs. Bheals somewhere at the first chance," Anderson whispers to him. "We have too many people involved in this already. I don't think I can do anything for that woman David brought, but we can get rid of the old woman before it's too late for her."

William nods.

"I couldn't leave her there. You saw the place. What it's like; the patients. She doesn't belong there. There is nothing wrong with that woman's mind. I don't know why she was in that place."

"Family probably wanted to put her where she can't trouble them," Anderson says. "It happens when you get old."

"What about the kid?" William asks, his eyes shifting to look at the kid following Jason.

"I don't know. I have to find out." Anderson's face is grim.

I don't want to tell them the kid is probably going to have to be disposed of, he thinks. But, William probably already knows that.

2   Open Doors

Jim McNelly is sitting at a small battered table in a very unpleasant run-down motel room. The ugly wallpaper has stains he would rather not try to identify. The carpet is a worn down shag that never should have happened, and the décor a nineteen thirties thrift store match. The room has a decidedly disagreeable odor reminiscent of the curious stink of death.

His cell phone rings.

"McNelly," he gruffs into the phone.

I pulled some strings and got those DNA samples pushed through."

Even distorted by the bad connection, Beth's voice is a ray of sunshine in the dreary room.

"Beth, I could kiss you right now."

"Jim, that's sexual harassment."

She is teasing, of course. Beth knows he does not mean it as anything more than a metaphor to express his thrill at the news.

"Save it for internal," he jokes back. "What are the results?"

"We have confirmation," Beth says. "The match came back. There is a ninety-nine point six percent chance Donald Downey is the father of the Jane Doe."

Jim blinks back the tears that suddenly come to his eyes. He feels stupid for it, even with no one here to witness it. He swallows. His voice has just the hint of a tremor when he speaks again.

"What about the other one?"

The silence waiting for Beth to respond is torture. Finally she speaks, hesitantly.

"Michael Underwood is Donald Downey's son."

The rest of her words come from far away, hollow and empty while Jim's world drops out from under him and he stiffens with a slow smoldering anger. Her voice grows more distant with each word.

"Michael is Brian Downey. Jim, you did it. You solved the cold case of the disappearance of Brian and Stephanie Downey. I don't know if we will find anything confirming if they are also David and Cassie McAllister."

When he does not respond, she says his name into the silence of the phone, waits, and repeats his name.

"Jim."

"Jim."

"Jim."

He snaps out of it, shaking off the shock enveloping him to focus on the phone call again. The shock is as pointless as the crimes he investigates. He knew it was coming, the DNA would confirm what they already know, but hearing that confirmation is still jarring.

It's not closure, he thinks. There will be no closure. Not until I find Michael Underwood and take him down.

"Beth," he manages into the phone.

"Jim, if you can find Jason McAllister and get him to confess, or get Michael to give you a statement, you will have this. You will have Jason McAllister on kidnapping Madelaine Downey and her children, and the murder of Madelaine Downey."

"Have you had any luck tracing any of them?" Jim's voice still has an edge to it.

"No. Sophie and William McAllister have vanished off the grid. There has been no action on their bank accounts and credit cards."

"You aren't telling me something. I can hear it in your voice. What are you leaving out, Beth?"

Jim is met by silence.

On the other end, sitting at her desk in their shared office at the small precinct, Beth's red-nailed fingertips go nervously to her mouth. She starts chewing her lacquered nails, a habit she never had before.

The discovery of a massive multi-generational hidden graveyard in the woods brought out a host of new nervous ticks for her as new revelations are revealed.

I can't tell him, Beth thinks. He will completely lose it. He already lost it over finding out Michael played him; that his partner, Michael Underwood, is a fictitious identity; a clever con.

"Beth, don't hide it from me. There is more. What is it?"

"Jim," her voice is hesitant, her mouth open to make herself keep breathing, and her eyes anxious.

"Marjory McAllister vanished."

"What do you mean she vanished?"

"She is missing from the nursing home."

"How? What happened?"

"There was a commotion at the nursing home. One of the patients got up and pressed the emergency release on a fire exit in the lockdown wing for Alzheimer patients. When the alarm sounded it was chaos. The alarm sent an automatic signal to emergency and fire trucks were dispatched. There were fire crews coming in and out of every door clearing the building. When they finally sorted the patients all out and put them back to bed two patients were missing."

"Marjory." Jim's voice is definitive. He pauses. *It's probably irrelevant*, he thinks. "Who else?"

"A Mrs. Rose Bheals. She has no relation to the McAllisters."

"Probably an accident or a diversion," Jim decides.

"You don't think Marjory vanishing is an accident, do you?" Beth asks.

"No. William visited his wife very day. He is not going to vanish without taking her with him."

"He kidnapped his wife." Beth's voice still holds the strain of the shock she felt when everything fell in her lap.

She taps her gnawed on red-painted fingernails on a thin closed file on her desk.

"He broke her out," Jim says.

Jim remembers the care home with its very un-charming attempted false Southern charm. The frightening Miss Krueger, Director of the Bayburry Street Geriatric Home, and the cold mental ward hospital feel of the lockdown ward with the moaning and wailing patients wandering in states of confusion and distress.

"Beth, remind me to never get old."

"What?"

"Never mind."

"Jim," Beth's voice is hesitant again, unsure.

"What is it?"

"There is something else."

The line goes silent. Jim is just about to speak when Beth's voice comes back. She speaks quickly, in a hurry to get the words out before she changes her mind.

"I ran the DNA through some database searches with other departments in other jurisdictions."

I don't like where this is going, Jim thinks.

"Jim, I got multiple hits."

Lawrence Hawkworth scans the dark alley. The two streetlights in the long alley are not working. One shows the jagged teeth of broken glass, the other looks burned out. Litter is strewn haphazardly, spilled from an open refuse bin nestled against the back of one building.

Old brick buildings back onto both sides of the alley like mismatched brick segments of tunnel walls. Their back doors are solid steel and windowless, leaving no windows to be broken. There are no windows on ground level, and those in the second and third floors above are reinforced with wire mesh.

Some of the doors have doorknobs, and others have only the steel reinforced plate meant to prevent the door from being pried open, making them accessible only from inside.

One building, taller than the others, has a fire escape that zigzags down the windows of the sixth to fourth floors. These dirty windows are missing the mesh reinforcement. The fire escape ladder hangs from the fourth floor landing, above the heads of anyone walking below.

Lawrence steps into the alley, walking down it to the soft sound of his shoes. His posture reveals his lack of confidence.

He stops below the fire escape ladder looking up at it, judging the height he would have to jump to grab the bottom rung and pull it down. He might almost be able to make it with his height and the long reach of his arms.

A breeze gusts down the alley, picking up a discarded page of newspaper and skimming it along the concrete with a soft rattle that whispers to him.

Lawrence goes to the back door of the building.

The doorknob is slightly off kilter. The strike plate protecting the door frame is bent with the telltale mark of a pry bar.

He steps closer, studying it. He reaches out and grasps the knob. It turns. The lock is broken. He frowns at it.

"Someone got in."

Entering the building, Lawrence walks down the poorly lit hallway into the interior in search of the elevator.

Taking the elevator up, he gets off and walks down the hallway. The sounds of life that never totally sleeps in an apartment building echoes down the hall.

Lawrence stops at a door that has multiple locks and glances up and down the hallway. Fishing in his pocket, he produces a ring of keys and starts unlocking them one at a time in an order that matters only to him. He uses the same order every time, reversing it to lock them when he leaves.

Opening the door, Lawrence quickly glances up and down the hallway, steps inside, and closes the door, locking only one lock to secure the door for a faster exit. He starts his search of his apartment to make sure there are no intruders hiding inside.

The apartment is not large, consisting of a single bedroom, bathroom, living room, and a small kitchen. It is tidy except for the banker boxes in the living room with some of their contents laid out on the floor. More stacks of files and papers fill the coffee table and the floor around it. Piles have slumped over on both ends of the sofa, leaving a space in the middle for someone to sit.

Satisfied the apartment is clean, Lawrence starts securing the locks on the door in his particular order.

Inside the door is a stack of three more banker boxes with fat large manila envelopes piled on top. Each box and envelope is carefully sealed with tape. The envelopes are unremarkable; however the boxes are yellowed and stained with age and water damage. The bottoms and sides are reinforced with more tape to hold them together. The cardboard looks rotten with age and is splitting apart. They are older than the other boxes stacked in the apartment.

Minutes before, when he arrived at his apartment door to find the three boxes and fat manila envelopes sitting outside it, Lawrence was sure he felt that unnerving sense of being watched as he stood in the hallway looking down at them. Looking up and down the hallway for any sign of who might have delivered them, he had thought he heard the quiet dull thud of the stairwell door.

That is what prompted him to leave and circle the apartment building, searching for how an intruder got in and re-entering through the broken back door after depositing the boxes inside.

Lawrence goes to the window and looks down. Headlights move along the street in the darkness below. Somewhere a dog is barking. A couple walks arm in arm down the sidewalk.

He returns to the door, looking down at the boxes. Picking up one of the fat manila envelopes, he looks at the address. The handwriting is identical to the labels on the other banker boxes whose lids are set aside and contents are pulled out, and the others filling his closet.

"I know you are dead. So, why are you playing this game? Who do you have sending me these files and why a few boxes at a time? They are labelled by your hand. You planned to send these to me. You knew you were going to die."

He looks at the opened boxes, the files piled around them.

"It's time to get back to work."

Lawrence gets a sharp knife from the kitchen, sets the envelopes aside, and cuts the tape sealing the first box, removing the lid. It is filled with files, their edges age-stained to match the box.

Pulling out a file, he flips through it, scanning its pages. The type is old manual typewriter. The kind you had to press each key with enough force to swing the arm up to strike the symbol on its end hard enough against the ribbon on paper sandwiched with carbon paper and additional sheets of paper to create duplicates, leaving imperfect ink and carbon imprints.

He scans the clunky lettering of the old manual typewriter used to print the report; the Ks only half there, each faded on the right to make them look like Ls wearing a small faded bowtie.

The photo of a middle-aged man clipped to the first page is small, sepia-tinted, and not well focused. The fading of the photo shows it is as old as the typewritten pages.

Placing the folder on top, Lawrence picks up the box and plunks it on top of the papers on the coffee table.

He goes to the closet and pulls out a laptop bag, pulling the laptop out and setting it on the papers next to the box before sitting down.

Lawrence frowns at the laptop, picking up one end and tipping it. Then he remembers and lays it down again, opening the lid and pressing the power button.

After a moment struggling to use the unfamiliar device, he gets his file open and picks up the file off the box, reading it.

"What is special about you, Mr. Grant Cormer? Why are you in these files? You have been missing for a very long time. Everything about your file is unremarkable."

Holding the file in one hand, he starts one-finger typing information into the database file, struggling to figure it out.

"Beth, you probably saved me a lot of work making this database for me, but I wish you were here to tell me how it works."

Lawrence's cell phone warbles. He answers.

"Hawkworth, InterCity Voice. You bury 'em, I dig 'em up."

"Lawrence, I have a story for you."

The voice on the line is his editor, Paul Giovanni.

"I don't know Paul; I'm really busy on this big story I'm working on."

"Don't give me that. I know you are still trying to dig up those bodies in the woods. That's old news. This is new. A nursing home lost two Alzheimer's patients. I want you to go talk to the staff."

Lawrence groans.

"I'm an investigative reporter, Paul. You have other reporters for that kind of story."

"I wouldn't be giving this to you, except I know it's right up your alley. Another nursing home lost a patient the same night."

"What's the angle? Nursing homes lose elderly patients? Aliens are abducting our old and infirm? Infirmaries go nuts, patients on the lam?"

"Very funny, Hawkworth. Just check it out."

"Why me? This is not investigative journalism."

"Like I said, it's right up your alley, literally. There is a possible witness right around the corner from you."

Lawrence sighs.

"There is no way I can get out of this, is there?"

"Not if you don't want me to fire you."

"You threaten me with that at least once a week. When are you going to get on with it?"

"Next week. I'll fire you next week, after you bring this story home."

"What are the nursing homes?" Lawrence sighs, unhappy.

"Bayburry Street Geriatric Home and Cranbrook Nursing Home."

A sudden chill goes through Lawrence.

"What are the names of the missing patients?" he asks stiffly.

There is a pause before Paul speaks again.

"Mr. Richard Andrews, Mrs. Rose Bheals," he pauses again, "and Marjory McAllister."

Lawrence almost drops the phone.

"I'm on it."

"I thought so. I'll send you the information on the informant." Paul hangs up, leaving Lawrence staring ahead with the dead phone still to his ear.

Lawrence lowers the phone slowly. He looks at the open file box on his coffee table.

"I will find you. I will find you and I will discover what you were looking for."

3   DNA and Fingerprints

"You got multiple hits." Jim's grip on the phone tightens. "Which DNA sample?"

"Michael's."

He hears Beth's voice, that single word, but feels like he did not hear it. The name is a whisper in his head; a foul utterance coming from someplace that is not here.

It feels like Jim's world is turning slowly off kilter. So slowly you sense it, but are not sure it is real.

"Jim? Did you hear me?"

"Yes. Beth." Jim pauses, still trying to figure out what to say, what he wants to know. His mind is blank. The unending questions filling it before about who Michael is and where he came from are gone.

He says the only thing he can manage.

"Tell me."

"He's good," Beth says, realizing as she is saying it that Jim won't take the compliment well. "I mean, he's good but-."

"You are better," Jim finishes for her.

"You are not the first in the force he duped."

"That doesn't make me feel any better."

"Michael seems to have a preference for rescue services. I got some of the requests for prints back too. He comes up in a few different police forces, firefighter, search and rescue. There is a stint in the military too.

"Any thoughts to why he likes the rescue services?" Jim asks.

"At first I thought that maybe he likes the sense of power. But then I thought there has to be more to it. It's about access."

"Access to what?"

"Information. He knows what the first responders know. He has access to do background checks and to question people. What better way to know when to cut and run?"

Jim is silent.

"Jim; what better position to be in to make people disappear?"

"What else do you know?"

Beth is hesitant. Oh God, I really liked Michael, she thinks miserably. Of all the people to work with, he was just so darned likeable.

Beth had no romantic notions towards Michael. He was too smooth for her. He is the kind of guy every girl falls for. Not her kind of guy. He was just a genuinely likeable person.

"Tell me more about the DNA hits," Jim says.

He can hear her breathing into the phone.

Beth takes a moment, expecting Jim to explode with the information she is about to give him.

"Michael has been busy. I got multiple fingerprint and DNA hits on Michael placing him as the unknown person of interest in a number of missing women cases. His description matches persons of interest too, although the witness accounts were all sketchy. The descriptions also are vague enough to be almost any man in the age range and a spectrum of physical characteristics. I'll send you a list."

Jim's hand starts to shake with the surge of anger.

"Get me everything you can on him and every instance he shows up, no matter how irrelevant."

The cold tone of his voice sends a chill down Beth's spine.

She hangs up the phone, looking down at the file on her desk.

"There is also this, but I don't think you are ready for it yet Jim."

4   Motel One

The extended cab pickup truck and car pull into the lot of an old out of the way motel, parking out front. Both vehicles are full with five adults, four elderly people, three kids, and one medium sized brown dog.

"Stay in the vehicle, I'll rent the rooms," Anderson says, getting out of the driver's seat of the car.

He motions Sophie to stay when she moves to exit the truck, and she settles back to wait.

Minutes later he returns from the motel office.

Behind the wheel of the truck, Sophie rolls down her window.

"Park around back," Anderson says, motioning to go around.

He gets back in and they both drive to the back of the motel.

Getting out, he starts handing out room keys.

"We are going to have to double up some. We were not expecting the extra bodies." He gives Jason and David a sour look.

He gives one key to David and Kathy, the two youngest adults except for David's younger sister Cassie.

"You are bunking with them," he tells Jason.

A look of fear flashes in Kathy's eyes and she glances quickly at David, avoiding looking at Jason.

Billy looks at them uncertainly.

"You are with us, kid," Jason says, motioning Billy to come.

Relieved to not be getting separated from the person he is most familiar with, Billy saunters after them, trying to look as if it is all completely irrelevant to him.

Anderson gives a key to Sophie.

"You and Cassie and the kids are together."

She nods and they start collecting their bags from the truck, the two younger kids looking around in bewilderment at the less than ideal motel.

"This place doesn't even have a pool," Ethan complains, looking at his mother sulkily.

Younger, his sister Lauren just follows their mother, Sophie, as if it is all very ordinary.

"Get the dog, Ethan," Sophie says.

Ethan sullenly moves to do as told.

Marjory is standing around looking at their new surroundings and William is still helping Rose out of the car.

"That leaves us old farts sticking together in the last room," Anderson says.

"How long are we here?" William asks.

"Two days and we move on and swap the truck. Next stop after that we trade in the car."

"Why are we here?" Marjory asks. "Are we on vacation?" Her eyes are still clouded with the drugs in her system from the home.

"Yes Marjory, we are on vacation," William says.

He takes her hand, leading her to their room.

Their rooms are all in the front of the motel.

"Why did we park all the way in the back?" Ethan complains.

Billy glances at Jason.

"So nobody knows we're here," Billy says.

"Help Mrs. Bheals," William says to Anderson.

Anderson scowls.

"I don't need your help," Rose grumbles, waving him off. "Get the bags."

Anderson unhappily goes to get the bags.

"Tomorrow we have to get some proper clothes," Rose complains. "And some wigs. We need disguises."

Moving more slowly than the younger people, the four geriatrics follow the others to the front of the motel.

Kathy feels like screaming. She feels like bolting out the motel room door and running as far away as she can. She is filled with the unsettling urge to look at Jason, but she is trying to hide it. It fills her with desperation.

I can't do this, she thinks. I just can't. How can I go with these people? With him?

She is pulled back in time to the memory of the first time she saw Jason McAllister.

I did not see Jason that first time he came to the farm. Cassie did. Cassie was looking out the window while I was trapped in a fresh moment of hell. He . . . Michael, David, he didn't even have a name then . . ., brought another woman home. Connie. I was furious. I was heart sick. He didn't need anyone else. He already had me. He had her. He believed Jane Doe, was his sister Cassie. He had no reason to kidnap and torment, kill, another woman looking for her.

I snuck a peak when he came back. After Cassie and Connie ran away, Michael came back after searching for them, and then he was there; this man, Jason McAllister. Michael was slipping into one of his black rages. He was talking to him for so long and I could tell from his posture he was ready to tear him apart, to beat him to death.

The next time I saw him was when they brought me in for a police line-up. I was so confused. He was there, the man who kidnapped me, only he was pretending to be a police detective, Michael Underwood. I was expected to point to Jason McAllister and say he kidnapped me, but that was a lie. I could tell; they both expected it, Michael and that other police detective, Jim McNelly.

They grilled me for hours about Jason McAllister, the farm house Michael kept us in, and about Michael's other victims. They kept calling them Jason McAllister's victims. The police, psychologists, psychiatrists; they all wanted me to say Jason did it. I couldn't, and I couldn't tell them the truth either. I said nothing. Then I saw Jason McAllister in court when they brought me in and put me in the witness stand. They said he killed so many people. It was more than the women Michael killed that they were blaming him for, hundreds of bodies. How can one man kill so many?

The things they said he did, Jason is a monster. He terrifies me.

Kathy feels sick with it, memories also filling her of being Michael's prisoner in the root cellar, starving and cold and terrified.

He made Michael what he is. He raised Michael to be a killer just like him. Michael did those things, to me, Connie, Cassie, others. I don't know how many others, but I know there are more. I am sure he was kidnapping and killing girls, teens, women, over the years he searched for Cassie.

Michael is crazy. Scary crazy. He talks to someone who is not there and I think he is talking to Cassie, the ghost of the little girl he lost. I am afraid. I have a feeling Jason came to kill Michael.

Michael. Should I call him Michael or David? He said to call him Michael, but they all call him David.

I am afraid of Michael, Jason, and of these other people. They must know that Michael, or David, and Jason are killers. Who can these people be that they would protect them? Family? Jason's maybe. Not Michael's. Would family protect someone who killed so many?

"Hey, are you all right?" David asks.

Kathy starts, looking up at him with a startled look.

"I'm fine," she manages.

Jason is not oblivious to the tension filling the room. It is not coming off just her. David has been pacing the room with it. It is fraying on everyone's nerves.

He sits there, flipping through channels, none of which are coming in very well, and finally gives up.

"I'm going to find something for us to eat," Jason says, getting up. "Kid, are you coming?"

Eager to escape the confines of the room and the stress oozing out of every person in it, Billy is at the door faster than he can answer.

"Coming."

As soon as they are gone and the door is closed, David stops pacing and looks at Kathy.

"I know this isn't ideal," he starts.

"Not ideal?" Kathy's voice is high with a tremor. "He's a serial killer. I don't care if he raised you. I don't feel safe here with him."

Standing up to him like this, at this moment when she is feeling so uncertain about him, fills her with a cold dread sitting hard in her stomach she has not had since she was a prisoner in the root cellar under the McAllister farmhouse.

"Do you feel safe with me?" David's voice is cautious.

Kathy looks away quickly. She is afraid he will see what she is feeling in her eyes.

David sees the uncertainty and fear in her eyes before she can look away. It slices him through like a knife to the heart. It is the same fear he saw in her eyes when she stared up at him from the darkness of the open trap door to the root cellar he kept her in.

"Are you saying I shouldn't feel safe with you?" Kathy's voice is small.

"No. Of course you are safe with me. You are safe here, with him, with all of us. Jason is . . . like my father. He is the only father I remember."

A small voice whispers in David's mind. A voice only he can hear. Distant. Small. Little Cassie.

He kidnapped your mother and murdered her. He kept you and your sister. You grew up in fear of him. You hate him.

David ignores the voice, although he cannot make it silence.

"I am just saying that he won't hurt you," David says.

He might hurt me, he thinks. Jason might kill me. He found me to kill me.

Kathy looks at him again.

"Are we changing names again, Michael? Are we getting new identities all over again?"

"Probably. I don't know. We still have to sort all that out. Anderson will tell us what to do."

"What do I call you? David? Michael? What do I call myself?" The pain in her eyes is a low ache inside him.

"Michael Underwood is dead. As far as the world is concerned he never existed. Everyone else here knows me as David McAllister, the name Jason gave me. Call me David. You can go by your real name for now. I like it. Kathy. Katherine Kingslow."

Kathy looks down, swallowing a knot of pain in her throat.

He gave up, she thinks. He isn't even trying. He hates the name David. Does that mean we are as good as caught? He will go to jail forever for the things he did.

"Michael-," she starts, correcting herself, "David, where are we going to go from here?"

"I don't know."

"That detective, the one you worked with, your partner. He won't give up looking for you, will he?"

David shakes his head.

"Jim McNelly. No. I don't think he will ever give up. Not until one of us is dead or I am in jail. It's too bad. I liked Jim."

Alarm flashes in Kathy's eyes.

"You aren't going to kill him, are you? I mean, he's a police detective."

"Not if I don't have to."

"How could you do it?" Kathy asks.

"Do what?"

Kathy cannot bring herself to say the question in her mind.

You were a police detective, but at the same time you were kidnapping and murdering women. You kidnapped and hurt Jane Doe, Cassie, and left her for dead. You kidnapped me. I almost died in that root cellar beneath the old farmhouse. And all that time, while I was starving, dying of thirst, you sat at the hospital guarding your Jane Doe, your Cassie, as a police detective, and plotted to kidnap her again. You kept me prisoner in that cold cellar and nobody had any idea who you really were. Who you really are.

Instead she says this.

"Pretend to be a police detective and never get caught."

David smiles.

"I learned to pretend I was someone I wasn't very young."

His smile falters.

They hear the voices of his sister, Cassie, with Jason's sister, Sophie, and her kids, Lauren and Ethan, going by outside their door.

"They must be looking for something to eat too," he says.

Jason walks quickly across the lot. There is a small cluster of buildings across the highway with a gas station and a couple of fast food restaurants.

Billy has to half jog to keep up. He glances back at the closed motel room door then up at Jason.

I still can't believe I'm with this guy. The creeper from the creep factory rooming house full of jail house rejects. Maybe he isn't a creeper. He hasn't tried anything. Or he might just be waiting. Everyone tries something sooner or later. When he does I will stick a knife in his stomach.

That last thought fills Billy with a rush of false bravado rising in his gut that dies and evaporates just as quickly as it came on, leaving a faint sick feeling behind.

As they walk, Billy studies their surroundings, memorizing possible escape routes in case he needs one.

When you have been running as long as I have, you always have an escape route planned.

They stop on the edge of the highway, waiting for a break in traffic, and run across.

"What do you want to eat?" Jason asks.

"How about that one?" Billy points at a burger restaurant. He feels uncertain about making any kind of decision that involves someone else spending money on him.

"Good choice. Let's go."

They enter the restaurant and place an order to go for them and for Kathy and David. They stand aside, waiting for the order.

A woman comes in with two small children and a baby. She goes to the counter, studying the board with the menu on the wall behind the bored cashier.

Jason's eyes follow her the moment she enters and stay on her.

The car pulls up outside with William alone. He gets out, looks around, and enters the restaurant.

The moment William walks in the door, he spots Jason and Billy. He follows Jason's look, resting his eyes on the woman with the kids.

He scowls, staying back by the door. Jason has not seen him yet.

The woman is placing her order now and Jason is still looking at her. Billy is fidgeting next to him, looking anxious to be moving on.

"Sir. Sir, your order. Sir."

Billy nudges Jason.

Jason pulls his attention away from the woman to look at Billy.

Billy indicates the teenager behind the counter trying to get his attention with his head.

Jason smiles, taking the food, and thanks the teenager. He hands one of the bags to Billy and turns, leading him to the door.

He makes it three steps before he notices William standing there, his grizzled old face in need of a shave, white stubble roughening an already weather-roughened face. William's worn clothes hang on his thin frame, accenting his emaciated boniness. Clothes he has not replaced in decades, since he was not so old and thin.

Jason hesitates. He forces a smile on his lips and meets William's eyes; tries to meet his eyes. He never could manage to look his father in the eyes.

The old fear he always had of his father sours his stomach, reminding him of the resentment his father always harbored towards him. They have to pass close enough to William to rub shoulders to get out the door.

"Dad." It is on his lips, his mouth opening to speak.

William cuts him off with a look and Jason only nods greeting to him instead, quickly looking away.

Behind Jason, Billy is taking in every nuance of the exchange, finding it very curious.

"I see you looking," William hisses so only Jason and Billy can hear. "You just never mind and keep to yourself. Don't bring attention on us with your nonsense."

Jason has the urge to say something in his defense, but cannot come up with any words to say.

He just keeps walking past William without a word, fighting the flush that is creeping up his neck, the shame he always feels under his father's hard stare, and the embarrassment at being caught.

"Behave yourself," William hisses a parting shot as Jason escapes out the door with Billy on his heels.

Billy looks back at William's scowling face and feels a surge of fear of the old man.

"What was that about?" Billy asks when they are outside and out of earshot.

"Nothing. The old man always hated me."

Billy looks incredulously at him.

"Is he your dad?"

"Unfortunately, yes."

Jason stares straight ahead, his fear turning to anger.

"What does he think I am going to do? Talk to some woman with kids? If anyone is making anyone take notice of us it's him with that ugly scowl and suspicious hate-filled look. He thinks he can scold me like I am some child. I'm past forty. I'm older than he was when he was still playing farmer and raising Sophie and me."

He looks at Billy and back at the path ahead.

"I don't know what kind of dad you had, what kind of history you have, but my dad wasn't around much. He was always out of town on business. His business; not the farm business. McAllister business."

Jason flushes and clenches his jaw, stopping at the edge of the highway to wait for cars, realizing he said too much.

I know all about fathers hating their kids, Billy thinks. He pushes the thought away. He does not want to think about it.

"You don't want to hear about all this," Jason says, his voice still bitter and sulky. "It's in the past; ages ago. He is still a jerk though. Let's go."

Jason darts off across the highway, Billy following and wondering what all that was about.

William watches them go from inside the restaurant, still scowling. Finally, he turns and approaches the counter to place an order of food.

"Where is William?" Marjory asks, looking at Anderson.

She hesitates uncertainly, and then moves towards the door.

Anderson moves to block her.

Marjory stops and looks at him.

"If you don't think I don't know who you really are Mr. Richard Andrews, then you are a bigger fool than you think I am." She puts an extra emphasis on his name. Marjory's eyes are lucid and alert. There is no questioning whether or not she is in there.

"I know that you know very well who I am," Anderson says carefully. He considers her. "You are not the same nervous hand-wringing young lady I met all those years ago."

"You are not as scary as you used to be," she says with a little smile.

"Ah, there's the shyness," Anderson says. "There is the Marjory I know. William went to find us something to eat. The authorities are looking for you two ladies, so we thought it best that you stay out of sight as much as possible. At least until we are further away."

"When are we getting our disguises?" Rose asks. "I want a blond wig. I always wanted to be a blond."

"Mrs. Bheals, we will be just fine as long as you don't bring any attention to yourself."

Rose sits on the bed, easing herself onto it.

"Can't move this old body like I used to," she complains, adjusting herself stiffly.

"You just needed to get out of that old bones home. At our age, once you stop moving, your body forgets how."

"It's all those crazy old people in that hospital they call a home," Rose says. "They are all loose up here if you know what I mean." She whirls an arthritic finger around her temple. "Not me. I'm sharp as a tack."

Anderson looks at her.

"You are, aren't you? I didn't think so when William showed up in Marjory's room with you. I thought he was nuts, trying to bring this slack-jawed drooling mindless zombie with us. He saw something in you."

"They kept us drugged. You know that, don't you?"

Anderson looks at Marjory for confirmation.

She nods. Marjory looks sad now.

"They kept everyone in there drugged, even the calm quiet ones. If you made a scene or were difficult, they drugged you more."

"Or if you tried to escape," Rose says. "They drug you into oblivion; into that slack-jawed drooling thing you saw."

Anderson looks back at her.

"Why were you in there, in the lockdown ward? You don't have dementia or anything like that, do you?"

"Like I said, I'm as sharp as a tack and I have a tongue to match." Rose taps her head. "My family dumped me there and never looked back. No doubt they sold and hauled off everything I had; cleaned me out of every penny, not that I had much."

"They are looking for you now."

"Let them." The glint in her old eyes is mischievous.

Soft guttural mewling comes from somewhere in the darkness. The sound resembles the cry of a weak low-voiced kitten. A dull scraping accompanies it and the mewling gains a small measure of strength.

The mewling becomes a stuttering sound as of throaty letters of the alphabet being repeated in a voice roughened by trauma.

Another dull scrape slides along the darkness. There is a rustle of movement.

The sound of something shifting or being shifted. Silence. Then the almost inaudible sound of something tilting and falling. The bang of impact is deafening in the otherwise silent darkness.

The mewling comes again with more scraping, as of something being dragged.

A small light blinks into existence, revealing the concrete floor with small cracks from the slab shifting and its own identity as a small reading light, the type you clip onto your book, and the gaunt bony hand gripping it, the curved wire making the light bow to the book it does not hold.

"Gghnnnnn."

The face shimmies closer to the light, shying from it as much as from the darkness.

"It lives in the light." The voice is low and guttural, clipped and hoarse, struggling to make the word sounds. "It lives in the light. It grows in the light. From the light. Light. Long light. Long night. Light. Night. Light. Night."

The hand gripping the small light snaps back, dropping the book light on the floor. The book light falls to land on its side.

The faint light spreading in the darkness reveals the sort of clutter one would expect to find in a basement, diffusing and weakening as it spreads out to cast feeble light that only gives shape to the mounds of clutter nearby. Boxes, old wicker hampers filled with junk, a rusted old bike, a machine that is old enough for its purpose to be a mystery to most people.

The odd sound comes again.

"Gghnnnn," repeating itself.

The hand snatches the light, revealing a flash of bruised cheek with dried blood crusting at the visible corner of the mouth. He clamps the book light to a box and grasps the wire, angling it to shed more light.

The light reveals the bottom jaw of a skinny man, malnourished and bony. That jaw is gnawing on the wrist of a hand, working to chew through the lamp cord tethering his wrists so tightly his skin is pulled in and slightly wrinkled, cutting off the circulation to his hands. The wrists are red and darkly bruised from the tight bonds and lack of circulation; his hands swollen, clumsy and pink tinged.

5   Informant

Lawrence paces in the dark. He hates being in the dark. He looks up at the unsubstantial street lights, his buzzard beak-like nose pointing to the sky, wishing they put off more light. The sound of cars in the distance is a dull rumble.

"Why do these guys always have to meet you in dark alleys and abandoned places?"

Lawrence looks around again.

"He should be here by now. Why can't informants ever be on time?"

He turns at the sound of a scrape of a shoe behind him. A dark shadow moves and breaks off from the rest of the shadows.

"Is that you? Hi, I'm Lawrence Hawkworth with the InterCity voice. My editor Paul Giovanni said you would talk to me."

The figure approaches, finally coming into the light.

He is conspicuously unimpressive; average in every way. The man is middle-aged with thinning hair cut in a business style. He is wearing a cheap suit jacket, trousers, and dress shirt with the top two buttons undone and no tie.

Lawrence looks behind him out of habit and back to the informant.

"You are the guy Paul sent me to meet? He said you know something about the elderly women who went missing from the Bayburry Street Geriatric Home. Who are you?"

The man steps closer into the light, revealing his face to show its lack of expressiveness and eyes sharp enough to miss nothing.

He is David's Anderson; the Anderson who sent David to meet Trevor as Mr. Miller in the rundown motel just to torment him.

"You can call me Graham," the man says, eyeing Lawrence as though he is weighing how much he can trust him.

"How much do you know?" Graham asks.

"Only what my editor, Paul, told me," Lawrence says.

Lawrence thinks back to his visit to the care homes with Jim McNelly. The image in his mind is pulled to the memory of looking into the open doorway of one of the rooms they were passing.

An elderly and very frail looking woman sat restrained to a wheelchair. She stared at him with fierce intelligence, not the blissful unawareness the Director implied all the residents have.

"Help me," she mouthed to him. "Get me out of here. They are trying to kill me."

It left him feeling disturbed.

And their next visit.

The same old woman, Mrs. Bheals, still looked frail sitting in a wheelchair in the same room. This time she was slumped and motionless. Her eyes were unblinking and dry looking. Vacant. Her head leaned limply to one side and thick strings of spittle hung down from her slack mouth. She was strapped to the chair, although in her state it was pointless.

He still cannot shake the image of her staring vacantly at nothing and the sickening feeling it gave him. The sharp intelligence was completely gone from her eyes.

Lawrence forces himself back to the present.

"Paul said there was an incident at the Bayburry Street Geriatric Home. One of the patients in the lockdown ward for dementia and Alzheimer's patients opened a door and let pandemonium loose. Fire alarms went off; the firefighters were there. In the midst of it all two elderly women walked out and vanished."

He looks at Graham.

"You think there is more to this story than that. Otherwise we would not be here meeting in the dark."

Graham smiles at him. It does not give Lawrence comfort.

"In a nice quiet facility where these women are carefully maintained, structured, and medicated," Graham begins. He breathes out his nose, not a laugh but more an expression of the futility of it all. He continues.

"And then one night it all goes to Hell. One woman, in a fog and lost to everyone including herself, opens a door and when the dust settles two old birds have flown the coop." He makes a fluttering gesture with his hand. "Gone."

Graham looks at Lawrence curiously.

"Do you know who the elderly ladies are?"

Lawrence makes a show of trying to remember, although he knows exactly who they are.

"Mrs. Bheals, and, uh . . .."

"Mrs. Rose Bheals and Mrs. Marjory McAllister." Graham looks almost triumphant.

Lawrence does not give him the reaction he craves to the name Marjory McAllister.

"The name is not familiar to you?" Graham says, cocking his head at Lawrence. "It should. You are the Lawrence Hawkworth of the InterCity Voice. The same Lawrence Hawkworth who helped the detective, Jim McNelly, catch Jason McAllister. You were there at the McAllister Farm."

Lawrence is guarded. *How does he know this?* He thinks.

"In case you don't know, Marjory is Jason McAllister's mother," Graham says smugly.

He shakes his head.

"Can you imagine it, being the mother of a monster, a serial killer of such renown? Jason T. McAllister is now the most famous man on Earth."

"You don't think Marjory just walked away from the home," Lawrence says.

"No, Lawrence, I do not. Marjory was drugged beyond comprehension after you and Detective McNelly visited her. She was agitated by your visit. They held that old woman down while she fought against them, large burly nurses against an old woman, and jammed a needle in her arm. She was a zombie. There is no way Marjory McAllister walked out of that home."

"What about the other woman?" Lawrence asks. "You think someone took Marjory from the home. What about Mrs. Bheals?"

"A distraction."

"A distraction." Lawrence is doubtful.

"Of course," Graham says. "Marjory McAllister, mother of the infamous serial killer, vanishes and people might wonder. If two women go missing, now it's just two women with dementia who got lost in the confusion."

"Who would take two old women?" Lawrence's look suggests he thinks Graham is playing him. "The InterCity Voice pays informants, but only if they have something worth paying for."

Graham grins.

"You think I am doing this for the money. That is good. Who would take Marjory? Her husband of course, William McAllister."

"So, this old man broke in, caused chaos, and kidnapped two old women who were drugged into oblivion." Lawrence shakes his head. "It sounds pretty farfetched. More likely they just wandered off and got lost with the doors open and people coming and going."

Graham chuckles.

"Perhaps kidnapping is not the correct term. After all, that would suggest she did not go willingly. The Bayburry Street Geriatric Home is not the only seniors' residence to lose a patient that night."

"Paul told me. The Cranbrook Nursing home."

"Yes!" Graham looks like he wants to clap for the victory. "And who went missing from the Cranbrook Nursing home?"

"Mr. Richard Andrews," Lawrence says hesitantly.

Graham nods, pointing his finger at Lawrence with a victorious grin.

The man in the dark gives up gnawing at the lamp cord and looks up to the world above, the stairs leading out of the place beneath.

"Ma!" His voice is raspy, hoarse, ruined from screaming earlier. "Mom! Ma! I'm down here! Ma, I'm stuck!"

He listens for the sounds of movement above. Footsteps. Anything. There is only the silence.

He moans, whimpering the name long and low. The sound is desolate, desperate. "Mommmmmiieee."

The moaning is stifled. He has covered his mouth with his hands, crying into them. The soft moaning sobs of the forever lost.

After a long moment of sniffling, he tries to wipe the sobbing away, wiping the tears and snot across his face, leaving it smeared wet.

He breathes a long slow desolate sigh. Then his breathing continues as a jagged pant, slowing, diminishing, until he lays silent on the cool concrete floor, the small reading light giving off just enough light to give away his location in the dark and little else.

6   Jim's Vow

Jim stares at the wall. Alone, but he is never alone. Guilt hangs with him every moment of every day. Failure; the failure to save every victim before they can be a victim.

He picks up his glass and sucks back the beer.

Old rock music plays in the grungy bar. The décor is eighties somber. It is no Peabody's pub. There is one bartender on, one tired looking waitress who seems to have no interest in serving drinks, and no pickled or jerked anything in jars on the bar.

Jim puts the glass down too hard on the table. He pulls out his phone, looking at the list of names Beth sent him again. aliases Michael Underwood used that she got hits on; working in police, fire, search and rescue, and even one military. There is even one listed working for a mortuary. There are large gaps between them and they are scattered all over the country.

The list also includes unsolved missing person cases his DNA is linked to. Those cases all have something in common. They are young women always around the same age as Jane Doe as she would have been at the time of their disappearances.

Jim enlarges the file on his phone screen, sliding it over to show the details on the right; ages, heights, weights, and their general descriptions.

Below each of these are details pulled from the crime files.

"That son of a bitch."

He takes another long swig of his beer.

"Michael Underwood." The name is just as foul on his tongue as it was the day he learned his ex-partner fooled them all. "David McAllister, Brian Downey, whoever the hell you are inside that twisted freaking head of yours. You were looking for her. All this time, you were looking for your sister, Stephanie Downey.

But you didn't know it then, did you? Or, did you? Do you remember your past? Your childhood before Jason McAllister kidnapped you, your sister, and your mother? Do you remember your parents?"

He shakes his head.

"No. Everything I learned on this job about victims surviving trauma tells me no. You were too young. You shut it out; most of it, anyway. You shut down. Maybe you don't even know that sick bastard is not your real father.

All those women, you killed them, didn't you? Alicia Long, found in a parking garage. Rebecca Shadway, the school teacher found buried in the sandbox in the playground of the school she worked at. Connie Wilson.

Katherine Kingslow, found alive in the root cellar under the McAllister farmhouse where you two kept her prisoner. Now missing; vanished with Michael after Jason McAllister's guilty verdict and, I presume, dead.

Our Jane Doe, found brutally beaten and tossed out with the trash, left for dead. Kidnapped again from the hospital where she was kept sedated with no memory.

These other women on this list, more potential victims of yours across the country. Where are they? Where are the bodies?

Why were you looking for your sister? How did you get separated? Why were you so obsessed with finding her, driven to the point that every woman who was not her had to die?

That has to be it. I know it. They match. Every one of them could have been her, Jane Doe. You are still looking for her, aren't you; your sister, Cassie McAllister, Stephanie Downey?"

He sighs heavily. His heartburn is rioting inside him and exhaustion is playing a cruel joke.

Jim rubs a hand roughly over his face.

"I have to get inside your head. I have to find out what happened, how you lost Stephanie, what happened to her.

To find out that, I need to get deeper inside the head of Jason McAllister, the man who raised you. But who will get me there? They are all gone; Jason, his sister Sophie, their parents William and Marjory. They have all vanished.

Who knows more about the McAllister family than anyone else?"

It comes to him. Something Lawrence said.

"Rick Dalton. The old Sheriff, Rick Dalton is alive. Lawrence found him.

Lawrence said Dalton did not believe William McAllister was the killer preying on young women in the area back then. He didn't peg him as the type. But he was convinced William McAllister was guilty of something. He just didn't know what."

Jim nods to himself, letting the idea flow.

"And then the McAllisters vanished, all those years ago, William leaving an anonymous note pointing Dalton in the right direction to catch the killer. The killer was caught and sent to prison for life. End of story.

Except Dalton could not let it go." He pauses. "Dalton showed Lawrence something he was sure was a treasure, an unidentifiable lump he found in the ashes in the wood stove. He never sent it anywhere for testing, never told anyone, but Dalton was convinced it was a trophy. He was convinced it was a bone fragment, a piece of Amy Dodds.

He didn't have William for that either, too clumsy. He thought William was too smart for that. He was convinced that was Jason's doing; probably his first victim and his mother tried to cover it up. That's exactly what we suspected too, that the girl, Amy Dodds, was Jason's first victim. His first taste of blood as a kid; his own friend.

Rick Dalton still could not let go of his idea that William McAllister was guilty of something big."

He is nodding his head again.

"Now history is repeating itself. The McAllister family has packed up and vanished again. Only this time there is no note."

"A retired sheriff has a lot of time on his hands." Jim stares at his empty beer glass. "I have to find out where Rick Dalton is."

He sneers.

"I am going to find you, Michael Underwood, David McAllister. I will find you and, if I have to, I will kill you. David McAllister, I will arrest you or kill you and I will find out where the bodies are.

I will find out where every last one of the damned bodies are."

7 Informant

"Why are you telling me this?" Lawrence asks.

Graham smiles. It does not make Lawrence feel any better.

Lawrence's nerves are jangling a warning.

"Who are you anyway?" he asks.

"Just an interested party," Graham says.

"You are familiar with the McAllisters."

"Very familiar." Graham's sly grin unnerves Lawrence more.

"All right then, I'll play. What do you know about the incident at the Bayburry Street Geriatric Home? Why do you think William McAllister liberated his wife from the nursing home?"

"I think you already know. You just are not seeing the big picture yet." Graham's eyes are unwavering on Lawrence.

Lawrence thinks.

"Where did it start?" Graham asks. "For you, I mean. Not the whole thing. Where did the investigation start for you?"

"It started with a Jane Doe discovered left for dead."

"Go on."

"She was badly beaten, thrown out with the trash in an alley."

"Good. And what did that say to you?"

"The attack was violent, merciless. I had a sense of rage, a deranged mind killing without purpose."

"And after that. Forget the other bodies, the women kidnapped, they are not important. You had a bad feeling about your friend's partner. You always had that unnerving feeling about him, haven't you?"

Lawrence is nodding without realizing it.

"Michael Underwood. I always got a bad vibe off him. He was watching Jane Doe in the hospital when she was taken from there. I followed the car, but I did not get to see the driver."

Suddenly an image swims into Lawrence's mind and through him, filling his world.

A man standing beside a car. He opens the back door of the car.

"Here, lie down here and go to sleep. When you wake up you will be safe."

Jane Doe, groggy and feebly crawling into the car.

The man helps her gently, laying her across the bench seat in the back of the car. Her eyes flutter closed.

Closing the door softly, the man hurries around the car to the driver's seat, getting behind the wheel and closing the door.

"Sleep now, sleep," he says softly.

The car drives away, sweeping around the driveway of a large building and past a sign with a large red H. As the car comes around the driver's face comes into view.

"Michael Underwood." Lawrence looks at Graham.

"We already know Michael Underwood was there when Jane Doe was kidnapped a second time."

"Yes, yes, and the other man at the hospital?"

"Jason McAllister. He was charged with the kidnappings of Katherine Kingslow and the others, and the murders, but now we know Michael was involved."

"And the connection?" Graham seems greedy for Lawrence to blurt it out.

"What connection? They know each other. That's the connection."

Lawrence realizes he is saying too much. He is trying to back out, to hold back information without being obvious. Everything about Jason McAllister is public knowledge. It has all been in the papers. But nothing about Michael Underwood has been publicized.

They are keeping that under wraps until they find Michael and he can break the story to the world.

"It's okay," Graham says, "you can say it. It was all over the news. It all happened at the McAllister Farm. That is where he," It seems he is going to say something else and changes his mind, "Michael Underwood, kept them, tortured them, and killed them."

A warning buzzes in Lawrence's head.

Michael didn't torture them, he thinks. He kidnapped them and beat them to death in a violent burst of anger or rage or some emotion. But they were not tortured. So why is he telling me they were? What does this guy know?

"What does this have to do with the old women?" Lawrence asks.

"William McAllister had to break his wife out." Graham is getting frustrated with Lawrence now. "Do I really have to spell this out for you?"

"Humor me," Lawrence says. "I don't like to make assumptions. I need to hear what you have to say from you."

The twinkle in Graham's eye shows he is playing with Lawrence. He is thrilling in the contest of minds.

"It all centers on the McAllister Farm. You and that fat detective are searching for Michael Underwood and Jason McAlister. And now the entire McAllister family has vanished."

"You brought up the other nursing home too," Lawrence says. "What does any of this have to do with Mr. Richard Andrews and the Cranbrook Nursing home?"

Graham puts a finger on the side of his nose with a wink and a nod. He turns and starts walking away, leaving Lawrence watching him go with a feeling he has just been taken.

Halfway down the alley, Graham pauses and turns to look at him. He turns again and continues walking away, laughing as he goes.

"That was really odd," Lawrence says.

He looks around, the uneasy sensation of being watched making his back crawl.

Lawrence starts walking away and realizes.

"He didn't actually tell me anything I did not already know and he knows what I know. Who the hell is that guy?"

His bad feeling about his informant, Graham, intensifies.

Graham stops against the wall of a brick building in the dark. He knows Lawrence can't see him here. He scouted the location before he set up the meeting through the reporter's editor.

He smiles, watching the ugly buzzard-like man bob in the darkness, and then start walking away. Lawrence hesitates, his walk slowing, and Graham nods.

"And he just realized."

He watches Lawrence walk away before turning and resuming in the opposite direction. Taking a corner and another, Graham gets into a car and sits there in the driver's seat in the dark.

From this vantage point he has a clear view between two buildings of where he met Lawrence Hawkworth.

Graham pulls out his phone and dials. After a few rings the phone is answered.

"Hello, Paul Giovanni."

"It's me," Graham says.

"How did the meeting go?"

"It went well. I think it will be a pleasure working with your reporter."

There is silence on the line. He can hear Paul's breathing on the other end. Paul's voice comes back, gruff and strained.

"Don't hurt him. He's one of my best reporters."

"That's the problem, Paul. He is one of your best. How he comes out of this will depend on how good he is."

He hangs up on the editor.

Graham dials again. This time it is answered on the first ring.

There is no greeting on the other end, just silence.

"I met the pigeon. More of a buzzard really, mindlessly circling carrion and waiting to pick off a few rotting scraps. The play is beginning and the characters are being set to their marks."

He pauses. "They will be easy to manipulate."

He hangs up, starts the car, and drives away.

The man in the dark wakes up. He looks around, blinking in the not quite total darkness.

"No," the sound is soft and urgent. "No nononnoonooo."

The light has faded; the small reading light grown dim on its waning batteries.

"No. Light, no. Don't go. Don't die. Don't leave Nathan in the dark."

His words devolve into the soft guttural mewling cry of a weak low-voiced kitten. He slides his tethered legs with a dull scraping sound on the floor.

Part Two
Ghosts

8   Marjory

Marjory moves around the motel room, pacing restlessly, her old legs moving stiffly.

"Marjory, come, sit down," Anderson says, trying to maneuver her to a chair.

She moves away, evading him and restlessly moving things around things that don't need to be rearranged.

"I need something to do," Marjory says. "I just need to keep busy."

Rose Bheals watches, making no effort to help.

"Please Marjory, sit down," Anderson tries again.

"Let the woman be," Rose says. "There is nothing worse than being an old woman and having everyone else think they know what is best for you. Everyone always tells you to sit down. If the woman wants to pace let her."

Anderson gives her a look.

"You are not helping."

"No, I am not."

Marjory can't stop feeling agitated. Her hands start going together, to grasp each other and start nervously wringing each other. She makes a conscious effort to stop them.

Every time I wrung my hands they gave me more medicine, she thinks. It's just a nervous habit, but they thought it was bad. They did not like nervous habits. Don't show nerves. Don't show stress or confusion. Be meek and quiet and calm. Manageable. That was how you survived the home.

That is what I have to be now, out here. Be strong. I don't want William and Anderson to worry.

Marjory glances at Rose as she turns to fuss with rearranging items on the small battered dresser. She takes the pad and pen, moving them to the desk and straightening them next to the phone.

"Marjory, you are making me nervous," Anderson complains.

Anderson watches Rose out of the corner of his eye.

How well do you know this woman, Marjory? He thinks. Do you trust her? No. A McAllister trusts no one. You don't trust me either, do you Marjory? I have to find out what I can about this Rose Bheals.

Nathan squirms across the dark basement floor, searching with the faint light coming from the small dying reading light gripped in his teeth.

He finds a toolbox and manages to open the hasps and lid. The inside of the tool box is coated with scraps of tinfoil and newsprint glued to the interior with the same paste he uses to coat the bedroom upstairs.

Nathan cringes with a moan.

"Bad tools in here. Tools with demons inside them. I don't like the toolbox," he hisses at the open toolbox.

Forcing himself to reach for it, Nathan tries to retrieve what he needs. A bad tool is on it and he pulls back. A green handled screwdriver, he can't make himself touch it. He kicks out at the toolbox and it scrapes loudly on the floor as it jerks back, dislodging the tools from their resting places.

Gingerly, he retrieves the wire cutters that are now free from the infested embrace of the green handled screwdriver resting on top of it.

Nathan looks around for some way to use the wire cutters to cut the cord on his wrists.

Carefully propping them between his feet with the cutting edges horizontal on the floor and the arms resting one on the floor and one up, he positions his hands to bring the cord inside the cutting blade. It is a difficult maneuver with the lamp cord tied so tightly on his wrists.

He tries to lower himself, twisting his body, to use one arm to press the handles together, closing the blades.

The cutters slip, falling to lie on the floor uselessly.

"The man becomes the boy. The boy becomes the man. The man becomes the boy the boy becomes the man. The man becomes the boy the boy becomes the man the man becomes the boy the boy becomes the man."

The words are a feverish whispered chant.

Dim light barely illuminates Nathan in the dark basement from the dying book light.

He is hunched into a sitting position, his tethered legs folded knees to chin and feet to floor against him, his arms hugging his legs and his hands still tethered. He is rocking and staring at something only he can see. His eyes are wild with fear.

His special suit is ruined. The suit is an old worn track suit the suit he got from a shelter when he was homeless. That was before Nathan's mother found him and brought him home.

His suit had newspaper and tinfoil stapled to it, covering every inch, and the rubber boots done to match with newsprint and foil glued to them, including the soles.

The foil and newsprint is torn and missing in places, his large silver oven mitts are missing, and his special hat ruined and left in the house across the street.

Behind him, the light barely touching it, the book light illuminates his ghostly apparition reflecting back at him in an old stained mirror door leaning against the wall with the far away dim beacon of light shining back at itself. Ghostly mirror Nathan has his back to Nathan on the floor.

"The man becomes the boy. The changer. He is a changer. I take the boy. Make him safe. Put him to his eternal rest. Safe. The changer is trapped and the world is safe. But the man . . .."

He shakes his head, a terrorized sick smile creasing his lips.

"The man is smart, but Nathan is smarter. I know. I am on to him. The changer is the boy is the man. Nathan knows. The man is the boy the boy is the man. The white van follows the boy. The white van wants the boy, the changer, the boy is the man the man is the boy. Follow the van find the boy. Find the boy find the man. Find the boy man find the changer. Nathan has to kill the changer to save the world."

Nathan struggles to pick up the cutters with his fingers again, working them into position, and trying again to cut the cord binding his hands.

It takes six tries repeating the process before the blades close together, cutting through the lamp cord tied tightly around his wrists.

9   Lawrence's Lock

Lawrence keeps looking over his shoulder as he walks up the sidewalk towards his apartment building, unable to shake off the feeling of being watched. It itches up his back like a sinister lecherous hand hovering a hair from touching him.

Every faint footstep echoes too loudly in the dark street with the distant traffic as a backdrop, amplified by his nerves. The sounds of lives within the apartments around him are oddly missing. No one is yelling at anyone tonight.

With the wet swish of tires on damp concrete, a car approaches from behind.

Don't look, don't flinch, Lawrence cautions himself. Act natural.

His nerves are screaming with the need to look by the time the car reaches him. It passes uneventfully and he sees it is no one familiar.

Lawrence tries to relax, but he can't. The feeling is still there.

He makes it to his apartment building and turns to go in. Just as he does, he thinks he catches a flash of motion in the street behind him.

Pausing to look, he sees nothing.

Lawrence goes inside and unlocks the inner door; making sure it latches securely behind him.

He ducks out of sight and watches the door.

No one comes to try it.

"You are being paranoid, old man," he mutters and goes to the elevator down the hall.

Lawrence rides up to his floor, walks down the hall, and stops before his door to pull out his keys.

Reaching for the door with the first key to the first lock, he stops, staring at the door. He studies it, bringing one finger and lightly running it over a small scratch on one of the locks.

"Was that there before?"

Lawrence looks up and down the hallway. There is no sign of life.

He studies the lock again, feeling the scratch again.

"I don't remember that scratch."

He examines all the locks, the door, the strike plate.

Tense and prepared, Lawrence cautiously starts opening the locks, taking special care to note the tension of the keys turning and the almost silent thud of the bolts moving inside the locks.

Lawrence freezes at the second last lock.

"Was it not locked?" he whispers. His hand shakes just a little as he turns the key, locking and unlocking it again, testing the resistance.

Ice slides down his back with the sudden certainty that the lock was not locked.

"I never forget to lock one," he whispers.

With a great feat of courage, Lawrence unlocks the last lock.

He grasps the door knob and turns it slowly, holding his breath. He pushes the door open just a crack, listening for any sound from within. There is no sound at first, and then the only sound is the humming of the fridge kicking in. It makes him flinch.

Ducking low, he pushes the door open a little more, peeking through the crack. When there is nothing, he opens it a little wider, revealing a little more of the apartment.

Lawrence pokes his head in and slides inside the apartment, staying low and against the wall. He looks and listens.

On first look the apartment is empty of intruders.

The living room with its couch and chair, low coffee table covered in piles of papers and files, stacked banker boxes, and lamps is visible. So is the doorway to the kitchen.

Lawrence delicately picks up the decorative bowl for keys off the small table by the door and sets it silently on the floor. He picks up the small table, brandishing it like a weapon.

Moving through the living room, he pokes his head around the kitchen doorway. The kitchen is clear.

Backtracking, he goes the other way down the hall.

A growing sense of presence grows in Lawrence, filling him with unease; a sense that someone has been in his apartment. The suspicion that someone was there hangs heavily on him.

Lawrence grips the table legs tighter and swallows. He stops at the open bathroom door, tensing and ready to leap back, and looks inside. It is empty. The bubbled partially frosted glass of the shower doors does not reveal the shape of an intruder hiding in the shower.

All that is left to check is the bedroom.

Moving cautiously, he takes the few steps towards the bedroom. The door is half closed. Pushing the door open, Lawrence steps inside, quickly looking around.

His eyes stop at the closet. The same old phrase pops into his head. *They always hide in the closet. In the movies they do.*

He opens the closet door quickly, brandishing the table at any attackers hiding inside.

There are only the usual clothes and boxes and bags inside. No burglars. No attackers lying in wait.

Feeling just a little foolish, after all it was only one of the locks on the door that was not locked; Lawrence straightens and returns the small table to its place by the apartment door.

He locks and sets the rest of his security devices on the door.

Lawrence cannot push away that uneasy feeling, though.

I never forget to lock a lock.

Trying to shake it off, Lawrence sits on the couch and looks at the piles of files.

"That strange meeting with this Graham guy is connected to the McAllisters in a way I am not seeing yet. I know it."

He picks up the file he pulled from the open banker box on the coffee table just before Paul called him, fingering it and flipping through it without reading it.

"Is it connected to this too? Are the McAllisters somehow connected to all this? All these missing persons. The mass graveyard in the woods behind the McAllister Farm. The bodies I'm certain the McAllisters have been hiding up there for generations."

He shakes the file in thought, bringing emphasis to it as if somehow the answer will drop out the bottom.

"All these missing person files you compiled over your career, generations of missing persons, generations of bodies in the hidden graveyard."

He looks at the file with renewed interest.

"Generations."

Lawrence looks at the time.

"It's too late to do anything else now."

He puts the file down, gets up, makes a pot of coffee, and looks at the new box of files on the coffee table.

"If only I could figure out how you organized these files. That would give me an insight on what you want to show me."

Lawrence looks at the box. He gets up, examines the lid and label. He does the same with the other boxes and the envelopes.

"It is your handwriting. But who is sending them?" Where are they coming from?"

Sitting down, he picks up the file again and starts examining it.

The file is organized exactly like all the others in the boxes sent to him. The first page contains a brief summary of the basic information and a photo of the missing person.

"Mr. Grant Cormer. Forty-seven years old when you vanished fifty-nine years ago. If you are alive somewhere today, that would put you at one hundred and six years old."

He looks at the notes jotted in the margins.

"It says here your address is an average middle class working family neighborhood. Now it would be an older neighborhood, maybe with small and tidy affordable homes, still maintaining the middle class lifestyle at below middle class incomes. You worked in an office as a low level accountant in an accounting firm.

Nothing about your life in this file stands out as anything but ordinary. What is it about you that caught his attention? What is special about you? Everything about your file is unremarkable."

Lawrence unclips the photo, examining it more closely.

The small photo of a middle-aged man was originally black and white, now faded to sepia-tinted with age, is not well focused. His hairstyle and clothing match the era and he is looking directly into the camera with a smile that is not quite there.

He stares at the photo, trying to imagine what the man may have been doing when the photo was taken.

"You do not look like you wanted your photo taken. Or perhaps you were troubled by something. Who is taking the photo? Why? Your eyes have a curious heaviness to them, the weight of something on your soul."

Lawrence clips the photo back in place and turns to the next page. It is the statement taken from the person reporting Mr. Grant Cormer missing.

He reads through the statement by Mrs. Mary Cormer, the missing man's wife. There was nothing unusual noted in his life or his behavior.

"Mr. Grant Cormer simply went to work as usual one day and never returned. They had no children."

The next page is jotted notes on the case. Research, impressions, questions asked and answered. He studies the notes.

"If only you were here to answer questions. Your notes leave me with more questions than they answer. Why is Mr. Grant Cormer important? Or is he? There are so many files across so many years. It's almost like you were searching for that infamous needle in the haystack, compiling files in the search of something you did not even know what to look for."

Lawrence stops. He looks at the box again. The other boxes piled at the door, on the floor, and filling a closet.

The one thing his predecessor had done was organize each file in an identical way despite the disorganization of the files themselves within the boxes.

"Knowing the man who left me the files, there has to be some point to their order. It's the key. What is important about their order? It's not date, location, or anything to do about the missing people. It is a secret that was taken to the grave with you."

There is a buzzing in Lawrence's head; distant, faint, deep inside.

He sets the file down, resting his open hand palm down on the files within the box.

The buzzing intensifies, still distant and faint, coming from someplace so deep inside him that it is as if it comes from some other place.

A voice, soft and very far away buzzes in his ear. He can't hear it, what the voice is saying. It is the sensation of someone who is not there, who is whispering so softly their breath does not quite reach your ear to tickle it, and yet they are.

Lawrence focuses on the voice. His head feels like it is slowly thickening, stuffed with something foreign; as if it is filling with cotton. The pressure intensifies. It turns to water, too heavy, freezing to ice, sending blinding hot agony through the center of his head.

His head falls and he closes his eyes, cringing at the pain. It takes a conscious effort to keep his hand on the files.

Lawrence feels powerless to move, to control his body. He feels like a scarecrow, hollowed out and stuffed with sawdust and straw, his skin pulled too tight, overstuffed to the point he might burst.

The room darkens and Lawrence swoons. He wavers in his seat, almost slumping. His fingers twitch.

The voice almost whispering in his ear is so soft, like the wind singing a low hollow mournful song of loss.

Find me.

His fingers move over the spines of the files, resting on one file.

He pulls it out, forcing his eyes open; his hands to move the file to rest it on top of the box, to open it.

The file is incomplete, holding only a handful of photos.

He fingers one of the two fasteners that would have held the pages in, the remnants of torn out pages still caught in the fastener. Those tiny paper scraps are yellowed with age, appearing brittle.

What is left in the file is a scattering of old photographs; black and white, sepia, all age-faded and of the poor quality common in cameras affordable to the average middle class working person. Aged pages of hand drawn sketches are there too beneath the photos, the pages yellowed along the edges and bearing the worn damage of pages that had been looked at many times.

Lawrence fingers the pages, spreading them across both sides of the open folder, revealing little of what lies beneath the top layers.

There are photos of trees, standing living trees and the remains of long rotting fallen trees. Photos of the ground. A dried brook, the rocks laid bare to the world. Dark photos of the interior of what looks like a long abandoned house, the house small and the furniture removed some time before the photographs were taken.

A window shines its poor light into the empty room, the wallpaper a ghastly flowered print stained with age and what may be water damage.

The window has a broken pane, the rotting stained sheer curtain is locked forever in its dance billowing in on the wind blowing through the broken window. The dance of a curtain whispering its secrets on the wind that refuses to let it escape its aging prison through that jagged cracked opening to freedom.

"What are you trying to show me?" he asks the photographs.

Darkness closes in further, pushing the apartment away from him, something else pressing in.

Lawrence looks around him. He is no longer in his apartment. The world has a lack of substance to it. Not completely there. The small home in the photos surrounds him. He is in the living room, looking at that same broken window with the curtain perpetually billowing on the wind.

The curtain hangs lifelessly, the glass behind it intact. The stained hideous flowered wallpaper is still a hideous flowered wallpaper, only the stains from age and possible water damage are gone.

Furniture from an age Lawrence is unsure the era of, only that it is long ago, fills the small room.

He lets the vision flow through him, its embrace an icy burning migraine pain in his head that leaves focusing on it difficult.

A woman swims into view, dressed in an outdated dress consistent with the old furniture, a worn house dress to match the worn furniture. These are people on perhaps the higher end of the poverty spectrum, straddling the border below what would be considered the beginning of middle income.

She paces the living room, returning to the window to look outside numerous times.

"This is not the house of Mr. Grant Cormer. The photos would have been in the same file. Who is this? Who is the woman waiting for? Who is missing?"

The vision fades with not enough to feed it and Lawrence's apartment swims back into existence, replacing the small home from the photographs.

He blinks, nauseated by the pain in his head, and looks down at the photos of the house.

"How am I ever going to find out where this is and whose file this is? There is nothing but these vague photos to go by. No name. No details. An empty house and some trees and ground."

He looks at the box.

"Why did you pull out these pages? This one is special, isn't it?"

10   Nathan

Nathan pulls the cord off his wrists, rubbing and kneading them against the pins and needles numbness slowly turning into a distant burning hot pain of circulation returning. He cuts his feet free, rubbing and kneading his ankles too.

Stumbling from having the circulation cut off for so long, Nathan manages to get to his feet and reach the cord for the ceiling light.

It clicks on and its bald light is glaringly bright after being in the dark so long. Nathan winces at the sudden light, shielding his eyes.

Among boxes, old wicker hampers filled with junk, a rusted old bike, and a strange looking antique machine, an old stained mirror door leans against the wall next to a cut out in the drywall. The hole in the drywall is half the width of a door and narrow enough a sizeable person cannot fit. Drywall is left at the top and bottom and the edges are roughly cut. The other side of the hole is black, the dim light of the single ceiling bulb making a rectangle on the floor.

Still unsteady on his feet, Nathan staggers to the hole. He stops and peers into the darkness. The light behind him splashes across his back, leaving a rectangle of light stretched across the floor with his slightly elongated shadow within.

He steps away, rummaging in the piles of rubble, and finds loose batteries in a box of random junk.

He goes to the battery powered lantern on the floor that Jason McAllister left Nathan in the dying light of after he rescued Billy from this basement.

Turning the lantern over, he unscrews the bottom, struggling with fingers that are still numb and tingling with returning circulation.

Replacing the batteries is harder. He fumbles with it, trying to pry the dead batteries out, and finally bangs the lantern on the floor, its noise too loud in the silence. He bangs it again, finally dislodging the batteries, and manages to push new ones in, screwing the bottom back on. Nathan holds his breath when he flips the switch, unsure if the batteries are good.

The lantern blinks on, adding its light to the bare ceiling bulb to send the shadows skittering in another direction.

Nathan sighs in relief, his eyes sliding around the room at the shadows still hiding behind the clutter.

"They were getting too close, those what live in the shadows. Too close. Too brave. Creeping closer, always closer." His voice is throaty and hoarse still, his throat sore from his earlier screams.

Taking the lantern, he steps through the hole cut in the wall to the space on the other side, bringing the dim circle of sallow light.

The room is a walled off section of the basement with no way in or out except the hole hacked roughly into the drywall. The window is boarded up; the cracks around sealed so no light can get in or out.

The only objects in the room are old steamer trunks of various shapes and sizes. The cracks around the lids had been sealed with thick layers of caulking. On top of each is what appears to be some kind of sick shrine to some strange god. No two shrines are alike. They are coated with dust layers of varying thickness, the dust having turned long ago into that sticky film dust will become, giving a rough determination of their age.

They are not padlocked, but the latches the locks would hold down are flipped down, the ring protruding through the eye. Anyone inside would not be able to get out unless they could push up with enough force to rip the riveted latch and hasp out of the box, or if they were lucky enough to knock the latch off the ring.

Except for one trunk. One trunk alone stands disturbed, its seal not caulked, sealing the air out, and the lid flung open.

Nathan approaches that trunk, looking in as if he half expects something to be there. The trunk is empty.

"He took the boy. But the boy is the man. The man is the boy. He took that part of him. But I know, Nathan knows. The white van follows the boy. Follow the white van and find the boy. Find the boy and find the man. Find them and kill them. Kill the changer."

He stops, tilting his head and listening. He winces.

"Sshh," he says to the voices clambering in his head. "I can't think when you all talk at once."

His legs still uncooperative, Nathan leaves the room of steamer trunks and stops at the bottom of the stairs, looking up. The door above is open and the house silent. Using the railing to steady himself, he advances up the stairs.

Nathan reaches the top. The house is dark. He goes to the living room doorway. The house is silent except for Nathan.

The heavy curtains are drawn closed, blocking out the dim light from the street lights outside, and the lights are all off. There is no sign of electronic life, the furniture worn and outdated. In the darkness there is a partial view of what appears to be the form of someone sitting in a chair.

"Mom."

The elderly woman sitting in the darkened living room does not answer.

"Mom, I have to do something. I will be gone a few days. You will be all right without me here to look after you?"

He darts out, rushing up the stairs, his boots clomping noisily, and rummages in a closet.

"Good thing I have a backup."

He pulls out a worn suit. It is outdated, the sort of cheap business suit a salesman with a poor sales record might afford, bought at a second hand thrift store. The suit hung in his father's closet since Nathan was a boy, never worn by him. The color would be ghastly if it were not completely hidden by the tinfoil and newsprint carefully stapled to it, covering every inch of the suit.

Pulling his boots off, he puts the suit on, moving slowly and carefully to not tear the newsprint and foil.

Inside the closet is a row of three pairs of rubber boots covered completely with newsprint and foil. He selects one carefully, and puts them on.

Nathan looks down at himself.

"The changer broke my helmet. I don't have time to make a proper helmet."

He looks up at the shelf. "The hat has to do."

He takes a hat from the shelf. The hat has foil and newsprint stapled to it, covering every inch of it.

Putting the hat on, he grabs another pair of large oven mitts made of a shiny silver fabric.

"Now I will be safe. My suit protects me from the beams, the rays, and the mind controlling wavelengths. It traps the monsters inside my head. It freezes them so they are quiet and I can think."

Nathan feels braver now that he is dressed in his protective suit. His boots clomping loudly, he runs down the stairs into the kitchen.

Rummaging in the cupboards, Nathan grabs at seemingly random things, tucking them in his arm; a box of baking soda, cereal, teabags, and a can of beans.

He turns to the fridge, opening the door. No light greets him. There is not much in the fridge. He pulls out a block of butter, an orange, and a piece of pie on a plate that has been there much too long.

Running to the dark living room, Nathan drops his treasures on a table near the chair.

"Here Mom, to look after you while I am gone."

Nathan pauses, looking around, and lunges at a book case. He grabs a couple of books and a basket of knitting on the floor next to it, taking those to the chair too.

He sets the basket on the floor next to the chair and the books in the basket.

"So you aren't bored without me."

He looks away, feeling a rush of guilt for leaving her.

"I'll be back as fast as I can. I have to do something important."

Nathan goes to the door, puts his large shiny oven mitts on, and looks at the door with a frown. He reaches for it and stops.

"My helmet worked better."

Nathan hugs himself and starts rocking. He starts his litany in a low voice.

"I can feel the sunlight burning my flesh when the sun is out. The stars shoot little pinpricks of light through me like little daggers, trying to kill me. I have to keep my body protected when the stars are out. I have a special suit for that. The moon is the worst. The moon talks to me. I don't like what it has to say.

I'm not sure if they control the sun and moon and stars, or if it's the extra-terrestrials trying to get at my demons from space.

They use the radio signals to try to control me, to try to talk to the demons inside me. The government wants my demons. They want them to escape from inside me so they can control them and do terrible things with them. The demons do terrible things when they get out and I can't hear them anymore. I know. They whisper to me about it inside my head when they come back."

He repeats it two more times.

Nathan reaches his hand out, grasps the door knob, and tries to open the door. He struggles with it, the large oven mitts making it difficult, and finally gets the door open.

He takes a deep breath. It takes all his inner strength to force himself to move and take that first step over the threshold.

Nathan looks quickly to make sure no one sees him, puts his head down, and jogs across the back yard to the shed. He pats the door and listens, then reaches up and around, touching parts of the rafters under the roof overhang. Finding the key, he struggles with it in his mitts, and finally has to take them off.

"Nngg," he moans, gritting his teeth, making a pained expression.

Hands trembling, he opens the shed and goes in, quickly jamming his hands back in the oven mitts.

He searches boxes until he finds what he needs; a device small enough to hide in his pocket. Scavenging batteries from another box, he puts them in it.

Nathan turns it on. The device blips. He smiles. It is the receiving end of a tracking device set he ordered online. Pressing buttons and reading the screen, it gives him a direction and distance.

He puts it in his pocket.

Walking to the front of the house, across the grass and to the sidewalk, Nathan starts walking.

"Looking at what lives beneath the ground makes Nathan invisible. No one sees Nathan when he stares at what hides beneath the ground," he mutters quietly. "That is how Nathan put the tracker on the white van. The white van sleeps. Nathan looks at what lives beneath the ground and walks to the white van. The white van does not see invisible Nathan. Look down Nathan. Keep looking down."

He forces himself to not look at the house across the street where the changer lived.

"The man is the boy," he whispers. "The boy is the man. The changer changes and takes the identity of others. Nathan has to stop the changer. The changer kills. Nathan has to kill the changer."

11　　Long Night

Startled by the opening motel room door Kathy turns and stares at it. She tenses more at the sight of Jason at the door.

Billy saunters in past him, trying to look like he is in his comfort spot, but unable to hide the nervousness that never goes away.

Out of habit, his eyes are surveying to room the moment the door opens, assessing, counting bodies in the room and where they are, determining where others nearby might be. He is already planning his escape route before his feet cross the threshold.

Jason comes in after him, the smell of burgers and fries clinging to the paper bags in their hands and wafting in with them.

"Supper is here," Jason says. "I wasn't sure what you would like, so I got regular burgers and fries."

He walks across holding one of the bags out to Kathy. She hesitates, reluctant to take anything from him.

David moves across the room quickly, taking the bag so she does not have to.

Jason ignores the slight, sitting on the stained couch.

Ravenous, Billy plunks down next to him and starts digging into the bag with their order, pulling his out and sliding the bag across the coffee table to Jason.

David gives a burger and fries to Kathy and they all eat in awkward silence.

A knock on the door comes just as they are finishing.

David gets up, looks through the peephole, and opens the door, letting Anderson in.

Anderson looks around.

"Good, you are all here. We will be here only tonight. Tomorrow we leave before the sun comes up. We will take turns watching the place through the night. I set up a discrete spot across the road. The car is parked there. David, Jason, you know the drill. The same as when you are scouting a motel on the job.

No lights, not even the light of your phone. No noise. You are watching for anything; someone acting suspiciously, a possible tail or stakeout, even a nosey motel clerk. Jason, you have first watch. Then Sophie, David, William, Cassie, and finally me."

"You gave Sophie one of the prime spots," Jason says.

Anderson nods. "I did. She is smarter at this than you are. We all know what times anyone onto us is most likely to put a tail or stakeout on us. Sophie, William, and I are covering those times."

Jason does not look happy. He is about to say something, and changes his mind.

"Get some sleep and don't make a mess. When we leave I want no sign left that you were ever here."

He looks pointedly at Kathy and then Billy. "Stay packed. Be ready always to leave immediately if anything happens."

Anderson turns his look on Jason. His eyes are cold.

"You should not have left the room. Everyone knows your face. Are you stupid? Next time send someone else."

Anderson leaves, closing the door behind him and moving on to Sophie and Cassie's room.

Kathy lies in bed next to David, unable to sleep despite the exhaustion. Her nerves are too frayed for sleep.

Next to her, David snores softly. Every now and then she can hear the movements of Billy turning restlessly.

He can't sleep either, she thinks.

Kathy keeps looking at the door. Waiting for it to open and willing it not to. She can feel Jason out there like a physical presence, watching as though he can see through the walls to see her.

The anxiety buzzing through her is a steady drone.

He can't see you. He isn't even looking at you. He is just on watch to keep us safe. How can I be safe? He was at the farm when the police raided it. He went on trial instead of David. For Connie, Alicia, Rebecca… the others. At the trial everyone said Jason is a killer; that he is the most prolific serial killer of all time. They said I was lucky to be alive.

I am alive, but it was Michael, David, who is guilty. What makes a man willing to take the fall, to go to jail, for another man's crimes? Some fatherly need to protect his son? David is not his son. He was his captive. Because he raised him to be just like him; to be a serial killer too, a monster?

Is it because of whatever happened to David's sister, Cassie? Is this Cassie even her? What if she isn't? She is with them too, as if all this is normal. As if travelling and living with serial killers is normal.

She swallows and blinks, feeling like she is going to suffocate. Kathy has to fight the urge to get up.

What am I doing with these people? Jason McAllister's family, David's family. They know they are both serial killers. They have to.

Kathy cannot take her eyes off the door. She is transfixed on it.

I could slip out right now and no one would know. I could sneak away while David sleeps. Run. Escape. She shakes her head. No. Who am I running from? David? Jason? I wouldn't get far. Jason is watching. Maybe they are watching as much to make sure I don't leave as to make sure no one comes to find us.

Kathy tries to push the thoughts away, to make her mind go blank. She lays there staring off into the darkness, staring at the door. She does not know the depth of depravity Jason is capable of.

Jason is sitting in the car in the dark, watching the motel.

A semi thunders past on the highway, its running lights casting a glowing pattern in the darkness that remains burned into his eyes behind the bright headlights for a second after it has gone by.

He fights the sleep threatening to close his drooping eyelids. He takes another sip of coffee.

Jason starts at a soft knock on the passenger window. The door opens and Sophie gets in, closing the door softly.

"You are early," Jason says.

He wants to ask how she got out of the room without his seeing, but does not want to admit he failed to see her or that she snuck up on him unaware.

"We need to talk," Sophie says. "I have a lot of questions."

"So do I."

Looking at Sophie, he still sees the little girl who was his sister in her creeping on middle-aged face.

"Fine," Sophie says. "But mine first. Why are you here?"

Jason smiles lamely.

"The police showed up. I didn't have much choice."

"You know what I mean."

His eyes and mouth show the weight he bears.

"I tried to do right by them. I really did."

"You would have done right by them by leaving them alone; by not kidnapping them and their mother, murdering their mother. You could have stopped there. You could have ditched the kids where they could not help the authorities find you. Hell, you could have killed them and been done with it. That would have been better."

"What did Cassie tell you?"

Sophie shakes her head.

"She doesn't remember much. She blocked it out mostly. She only knows what she was told by the people who finally adopted her. She was found wandering a road. She did not know her own name. They could not locate any family."

"Nothing about what happened before? The-," he can't say it.

"The blood? Whatever happened to her on that farm? Nothing. No one told her that part."

"So, how do you know about the blood?"

"She has nightmares. She was bounced around the foster system at first, family to family; probably because of the nightmares. Some families were not so good. Some hurt her. She remembers that. She finally ended up with the people who adopted her. The foster system tried to move her, but they fought to keep her, suing to adopt her. They won. I don't know how because the foster system always wins, but they won. They adopted her and she had a decent life after that."

"Until David took her."

Sophie nods.

"David has something missing inside him. He is sick, like you. Broken on the inside. There is something very dark in there and it scares the hell out of me."

"Sophie, that's not fair."

Sophie turns a steady stare on him. Cold and unfeeling.

"Amy Dodds. Do not tell me you are okay, because you are not. Tell me, Jason, which came first?"

"What do you mean?"

"The old Chalmers farm or Amy?"

Jason blanches.

"Yes, I know. You watched him torture and mutilate those girls. He was sick. It was the town secret no one wanted to admit to, so they blamed Dad. They came after Dad and tore our family apart. I was with Mom when the town women surrounded her and attacked her, us. She had to defend me. They wanted to hurt us both."

"You were just a little girl."

"You watched him and you liked it. You did the same thing to Amy Dodds and Dad had to clean up your mess. Only your mess got too big and we had to run away from our home. And now we can never go back, not in this lifetime."

"I did."

"That's because you are stupid."

"Sophie-."

She cuts him off.

"You don't know, do you? No, that's right, Dad never trusted you. You have no idea what secrets the McAllister farm hides."

"I know. I was the one Dad took on his trips. I was the one who had to follow him through the woods to hide the bodies, other people's victims. I know about the graves, all of them."

Sophie laughs. It is a soft sound coming more from her nose than her mouth.

"You don't know how long. You don't know how far this spreads."

Her mouth hardens angrily.

"You don't know about Mom finding your disgusting little treasure and trying to burn it in the wood stove to destroy the evidence," Sophie continues. "You don't know how it broke her to know what you did to Amy. What was she? Eleven? Twelve? Your own friend. You said you would marry her one day."

"Why are you telling me this?"

"Because you have to know what you are. What he is. You have to know the monster you created."

She shakes her head.

"I don't know which of you is worse. You kill for pleasure. He kills because he has to. You have to kill David and clean up your mess. If you don't, I will."

"What about his girlfriend?"

"She is weak. She will talk."

"And Cassie?"

"Cassie is one of us now. She is a McAllister. That monster you created never will be."

Sophie opens her door and gets half out.

"Get out. Go back to your room and figure out how you are going to clean up your mess. I'll take over the watch."

"Sophie, my questions…"

"Not this time. You haven't earned any answers yet."

Billy shifts restlessly again. It feels strange, being here with these people. Walking out in the open. Not hiding.

He hears Kathy shift too.

She can't sleep either, he thinks. No wonder. Something about that guy she is with is off. I can feel it. She must feel it too.

Billy looks around the darkened room, where each item he noted before still sits, untouched as if they had never been there. He runs through his checklist again.

The phone. Heavy enough you can hit someone hard in the head and stun them and get away. The ice bucket. It's light. If it had a handle it would be more useful. You could put something in it to weigh it down. The pen on the desk. You can stab someone with that, the eye is best, and escape. The window is sealed and won't open. The only escape is through the door. To the right is the office. You can go there for help, but they probably won't help. Nobody believes a kid. Left, you can duck between the soda and candy machines. There is just enough space for me to fit. Past that, if you can make it across the lot and the field, you can vanish in the trees.

Restaurants across the highway, if anyone is there. You can say a trucker kidnapped you and you escaped. They might buy it. If it's the same people who saw you, they probably won't remember you anyway. Hitch a ride on the highway if you can get picked up before anyone notices you gone.

It makes Billy feel better, knowing there is always a way out.

William's sleep is disturbed by someone moving around the room. He opens his eyes, blinking in the darkened room. It is not completely dark.

It takes William's old eyes longer to adjust than it used to, the images in the room swimming into fuzzy focus.

He finds the intruder faster because it is the only motion in the still room. The form is shuffling, more bumbling than moving, moving things around.

The bed next to him is empty.

"Marjory, what are you doing up?" His voice is hoarse with age, his whisper hoarse. He tries to speak softly, but it sounds too loud in the quiet room.

Anderson shifts where he is sleeping on the couch and William grimaces.

He is going to be right sore in the morning from sleeping on the couch, William thinks.

William focuses on Marjory again.

"Marjory, what are you doing? Come back to bed," he whispers.

"I have to find it," she mumbles.

"Find what? It can't wait until morning?"

William swings his legs over the bed, getting to his feet stiffly.

Anderson shifts again.

William hurries across the room to Marjory.

"Marjory, you are going to wake everyone up. Whatever it is, you can find it in the morning."

He looks around. "Look at the mess you are making. Marjory."

He takes her by the arm and she tries to ward him off, still moving things around.

"I have to find it," she says, her voice too loud.

"William, put your wife to bed," Anderson mutters.

Rose is moving in the other bed now.

"What is going on?" she mumbles, groggy with sleep.

"Nothing, just go back to sleep," William says irritably.

He turns his attention on Marjory, taking her by the shoulders and turning her to face him.

She looks at him in confusion.

William looks in her eyes and sees no recognition there.

12   Little Whispers

"David," the little girl voice whispers quietly. "Day-vid. Daayyy-vid." The voice remains quiet, a soft whisper only he can hear.

"Be quiet," David mutters under his breath.

"David."

He ignores the voice.

"You cannot leave me David."

He rolls over on the bed, facing the other way and covers his head with the pillow.

"You cannot forget me David."

"Shut up. Leave me alone," he mutters.

"You cannot escape me David."

Kathy comes out of the bathroom and looks at him on the bed.

"You can't hide from it, David," Kathy says. "It's time to get up and move on. They will all be waiting for us."

David pulls the pillow off his head and swings his feet over the edge of the bed, sitting up.

"I'm ready. Let's go."

He gets up and picks up their bags, heading out to the car.

Kathy follows, giving him a worried look.

"He is still talking to his ghost," she says so quietly David does not hear.

The others are gathering at the two vehicles, loading their bags in the trunk and truck box.

"We have a six hour drive," Anderson says. "Then we pick up a third vehicle. I don't like us travelling split up in so many vehicles. It increases the risk of us getting separated, but we need to change our travelling groups."

He looks at William.

"Everyone, get in. William and I will do one last sweep of the rooms to make sure we are clear."

"What are they checking for?" Billy asks.

"To make sure you didn't leave any save me notes," Ethan says. He gives an annoyed tug on the dog's leash, pulling him away from whatever he is trying to sniff on the ground.

"To make sure we left no evidence we were here," Lauren says.

"Knock it off you two," Sophie says. "They are just checking that nobody left anything behind."

Kathy glances at Cassie.

Cassie does not return the look, her look guarded.

Minutes later, William and Anderson return from checking the rooms and they are driving away.

Billy watches the motel vanish in the distance behind them.

13   Retired Sherriff Rick Dalton

Jim's ugly old brown Oldsmobile pulls into the parking lot of a small diner on the edge of nowhere. Finding a parking spot, he gets out, the springs on the driver side giving off a relieved groan when his weight is removed.

He looks around. There are only two vehicles in the lot, both old pickup trucks that look like they should not have been driven off the farm. The lot is dust and gravel and full of potholes resembling a cluster of mini asteroid hits that he suspects developed over a long time.

Jim walks across the lot to the diner. The bell over the door jangles an unpleasant sound that ends with a dull clunk.

He glances up at it. It is impossible to enter without everyone inside knowing the door had just been opened.

Stopping just inside, he surveys the diner, seeing no one at first.

Then he spots movement to his left; the top of a head just on the other side of a tall-backed booth seat, the head moving with the motion of sipping coffee.

Jim walks down the aisle between booths and stops to take in the only resident of the diner. The man is grizzled and thin in the way of an old man who has grown old on the range herding cattle or some other range-borne pursuit.

His skin is leathery and wrinkled from too many hours over too many years spent in the sun, and seems permanently tanned a darker shade than the small triangle of paler skin at the opening of his button-up shirt and circling his hairline just below the hat brim matted hair. Age spots mottle his skin. His hands have the thick corded look of a hard laborer's hands gone arthritic and knobbed.

Everything about the old man says, "Old and hard."

"Are you Rick Dalton?" Jim asks.

"I am. Have a seat." Rick makes no move to either look up at him or motion him to the seat across from him. He only casually lifts his coffee cup with one hand, taking another slow sip.

Jim looks around.

"I don't see anyone working here. What does it take to get a coffee?"

"Coffee pot is on the burner behind the counter," Rick says.

Jim grabs a turned upside down cup from one of the tables, goes to the counter and fills it, and returns, sliding into the seat across from Dalton.

"Rick Dalton, I am Detective Jim McNelly."

Rick nods a greeting to him.

"What can I do for you Detective Jim McNelly?"

"You are the retired Sheriff Rick Dalton?"

"I am."

"We have a case in common."

Rick breathes a low chuckle out; gritting his teeth in what Jim assumes is an attempt at a friendly smile. It looks more pained than anything.

"I'm retired," Rick says.

"You don't retire from a case like this."

Rick raises an eyebrow at him.

"The McAllister Farm," Jim says.

"You have my attention."

"I am hunting down the McAllisters."

Rick starts chuckling and it degenerates into a wheezing cough. He shakes his head, letting the cough work its way out.

"You are wasting your time. If they don't want to be found, they won't be found."

"I am very determined."

Jim leans forward.

"I need your help. I'm sure you saw the news. Jason McAllister was convicted for the disappearance and murder of multiple women; women he kept at the McAllister Farm. He vanished, along with the man I am more interested in bringing in, David McAllister."

He catches the spark of interest in the old retired Sheriff's eyes.

"There is no David McAllister," Rick says.

"Not on record, but he exists. You and I both know Jason McAllister is a monster. He kidnaps and murders women because he enjoys it."

Jim pulls an old photo out, placing it on the table between them. He taps the photo.

"This is David McAllister," he says.

The smiling faces of a little boy and toddler girl stare up at them next to the photo of a young woman whose smile is already too tired for her years.

"That is Madelaine Downey and her kids, Brian and Stephanie," Jim says. "Jason McAllister kidnapped Madelaine Downey in her own vehicle. We suspect the kids were a bonus, a surprise he was not expecting. Only, instead of leaving them somewhere or killing them he kept them. He renamed them David and Cassie McAllister."

Jim watches Rick for a reaction.

"The monster raised two children at that farm while he was still kidnapping, mutilating, and murdering women."

Jim's breath is coming heavier now with emotion, feeding his urgency to find and stop Jason and Michael.

"I knew Brian Downey as a man going by the name Michael Underwood and Jason taught him everything he knows," he finishes.

Rick just looks at the photos staring up at them.

"Michael Underwood, David McAllister, Brian Downey, they are all one person and he is a serial killer just like the man who raised him," Jim says. "I have to find him and stop him, and the only way I am going to do that is by getting inside his head."

"And without catching him the only way you can do that is by getting inside the head of the man who raised him," Rick says.

"Yes. The whole McAllister family has vanished. All I have left is you. I need to get into the head of the sheriff who quit his job, retired, to chase a ghost. I need you to get me inside the heads of the boy who grew up to create the killer, and the man who raised him."

"It makes sense," Rick says, finally looking up at Jim. "They keep it in the family."

"What do you mean?"

"The bodies. They hide the bodies."

"What bodies?" Jim feels a rush. *The old man knows something.*

"All of them."

14   Little Cassie

"She is not who you think she is, David." The voice is soft, quiet, whispered in his ear. The voice of a little girl, little Cassie.

David looks around. He is sitting at a picnic table. No one is close enough to hear. Her voice is all there is of her.

"Stop it Cassie," he says quietly.

"She does not act like a sister happy to have her brother back. I do not think she even remembers you. Your Jane Doe, she is not your sister. She is not Cassie. She is not me."

"She is so Cassie."

"She would remember you, David. Wouldn't she? If she is me? I remember you."

"Don't go there Cassie."

"I remember what you did."

He turns. Cassie is standing there. So little. The Cassie of so many years ago. Cassie of the barn, bloody, her hair mussed and full of straw and dirt and blood. Dead Cassie.

David closes his eyes to shut out the image.

"You have to find me, David. She is not me. You got the wrong one."

"No."

"Your sister is still out there somewhere. Find her, David. Find me. Save me."

David almost screams at her to shut up. He stops himself on the verge of the words exploding from him. His muscles are tense with anger. His jaw is tight. He gets up, his hands clenched into fists.

Kathy is walking towards him. She sees David get up, his posture and movements angry. She pauses.

He turns to face her, not seeing her, and she blanches at the rage she sees in his expression. She turns quickly, walking away.

15   They Hide the Bodies

"Yes, they hide the bodies," Jim says. "We found the graves in the woods. The McAllisters have been burying their victims there for generations. There are hundreds of bodies in the hidden graveyard in the woods behind the McAllister farm. It will take years to identity them. For most it will be impossible to determine a cause of death.

We started researching unsolved missing cases too. In every one of the historical missing persons cases that I think can be attributed to the McAllisters, there is no trace of the body. We might still find them among the hundreds of graves still being exhumed, but there is one thing they all have in common."

"If the McAllisters don't want the body to be found, it will never be found," Rick finishes for him.

"You ran into this, didn't you?"

Rick nods. "We had a serial killer. It shocked the community. We never had a serial killer. No murders. No one went missing who did not plan on going missing. Eventually they show up, alive."

Jim is nodding.

"Yes, I found that odd when I was researching the area. Everywhere is touched by the tragedy of murder at some point in history. Not that area."

"Like animals. They don't soil where they sleep," Rick says.

He looks at Jim levelly.

"What is the fastest surest way to get caught?"

"Committing the crimes in your own back yard."

"Right. First thing the police look at is who is around when a crime is committed. Who lives, works, and plays there. Who might be travelling through. Priors, arrests, anything on file on anyone suggesting they could be a suspect. Any potential witnesses, persons of interest, anyone who might know who could be a witness or person of interest."

"The bodies we found were dumped sloppily. There were clues everywhere. They were meant to be found. They were tortured and killed by the serial killer, Walter T. Olson, and he went away for it thanks to William McAlister sending me in the right direction.

"Only one," Rick taps the table, "only one body could not be found."

"Amy Dodds," Jim says.

"Amy Dodds," Rick repeats. "And the one victim we found no trace of. Amy Dodds is the only one I am sure was killed by a McAllister."

"By Jason."

"Jason is not as smart as his old man," Rick says. "The boy was always impatient, impetuous."

Rick fishes in his pocket, pulling out a cloth handkerchief.

The fabric is yellowed and brittle with age. He unfolds it carefully to reveal a misshapen greyish lump. It is unidentifiable.

"Jason likes to keep trophies."

"Is that-," Jim's breath comes quicker; he stares at it, unable to take his eyes away.

"Amy Dodds big toe."

"You had it tested?" Jim flashes him a look. Without testing, it is useless. Without a body to test against, testing is useless.

Rick shakes his head. "No need. I know."

"We found her. We found Amy Dodds," Jim says. "At least, we think it is. We can test that fragment against the body."

Rick carefully wraps it up again, putting it back in his pocket and shakes his head.

"There is no need. I know."

"If William McAllister is so careful, how did you find it?"

"He has a weakness." Rick smiles. The smile holds the promise of revenge. "His family. That is his weakness. William McAllister above all else is a family man. He protects his family above all else."

Jim nods towards the lump in Rick's pocket.

"Marjory is his biggest weakness," Rick says. "She was always a nervous little thing. I have never met anyone so frightened of the world. Shy. Always wringing her hands like she could strangle the fear out of herself. Couldn't stand for herself. I knew her growing up. Her family pushed her around, until she met William. From the moment he set eyes on her, William protected that frightened little lamb with every fiber of his being. And she found her strength only in protecting her children."

"She found the toe," Jim says.

Rick nods.

"William messed up. My guess, he was so shocked, so utterly destroyed by the discovery of what Jason did to Amy, that he missed that she was missing a toe. You see, William was a lot of things; a criminal, a man with a dark secret. That, I never doubted. He was not a killer. He was too strict with those kids, but that was to protect them. William never killed unless he had no other choice. He was sickened by what his own son was capable of."

"So, Marjory found the toe and tried to dispose of the evidence."

Rick nods.

"William was too smart, but his boy, not so much," Rick says. "And a stupid boy, who does not learn what his father teaches, who is willful and stubborn and impulsive, will take short cuts."

"So he did not train David as well as his father trained him."

"But William still trained Jason."

Jim's eyes widen.

"The bodies. The bodies we got Jason for. They had traces of dirt. We suspect they were buried and dug up."

"If William McAllister did not want a body to be found, it would not be found," Rick says. "Jason is not as smart, but when it comes to William McAllister's business . . .."

"You do not mess up," Jim finishes for him.

"You do not bring attention on yourself or the McAllister family."

"I thought Jason messed up. Or he changed his mind and dug the bodies up."

"They were left for you to find. Someone wanted them found," Rick says. "Probably Jason. He was always a reckless boy. I don't think William would do that. He would have made his problem vanish before he risked the discovery of their secret."

"They all match Jane Doe's description. They were all Michael's victims. David's, I mean. So, Jason dug up the bodies to get him caught. But why?"

Rick shrugs. "He raised the boy. What is one lesson every boy learns from his father?"

"How to raise his son. Jason had to stop him. He could not bring himself to kill his own son so he tried to get him caught. He dug up the bodies David hid and left them for us to find."

Rick starts chuckling again, and again it devolves into wheezing coughing.

"That must have right messed David up."

"It did. But that means Jason knew where David buried them."

Rick nods. "Of course he did. I am sure they all know where every body is."

Jim looks at Rick again.

"One thing is bothering me. If they don't mess where they sleep, then why the graveyard in the woods behind their own farm?"

Rick smiles.

"Because William McAllister is hiding a bigger secret. How does a magician keep you from knowing his trick? Smoke and mirrors, smoke and mirrors."

Jim stares at Rick in shock.

"William McAllister wanted us to find the graves." Jim's face is slack.

"To put you off the real secret."

"That seems pretty desperate. Not the act of a smart man who does not make mistakes."

"Maybe he is covering one up," Rick suggests. "Or maybe he did not intend the graves to be found at all and Jason is just that stupid."

He shakes his head, chuckling and wheezing.

"No, you are right. It does not feel right for William. Jason is just that stupid. He let the proverbial cat out of the bag. He blew up history's worst best kept secret. He let you find the bodies. He almost let you discover the truth."

"The truth. What is that?"

"I don't know yet, but I will not go to my grave without finding out."

"There is a bigger secret yet, isn't there?" Jim asks.

"You have to find them if you are going to have any chance of finding it," Rick says.

"We are looking in the wrong place. I need your help. Where could they have gone?" Jim asks.

He rubs his eyes wearily.

"We had it right," Jim says. "Right from the start, we had it right. There are more bodies buried in those woods than one man can kill and not get caught. More than one man in every generation can kill and not get caught."

"Now you understand," Rick smiles a grim smile.

"What did Beth call it? A murder club." Jim shakes his head. "A special club for serial killers. Whatever else the McAllisters are guilty of, they are making the bodies disappear. That's why so many killings go unsolved; why so many people just vanish and are never found."

He looks at Rick. His eyes are bloodshot and red rimmed.

"I have been so preoccupied with chasing down Michael, David McAllister, that I forgot."

"You won't forget again," Rick says.

"Will you help me?" Jim asks.

Rick stares down at the photos still on the table between them. He nods slowly.

"Give me two days."

"Thank you." Jim scoops up the photos, trying to hide the slight tremor in his hand, and pockets them. He nods to Rick and starts walking out, his untouched coffee cooling on the table.

"They are not their victims," Rick says to Jim's parting back, not knowing or caring if Jim heard.

After Jim is gone, Rick calls out.

"You can come out now."

A past middle-aged man in a cook's outfit comes out from the kitchen. The smock covering his large belly is stained from the day's work.

"Join you for a coffee, Rick? Or do you have someplace to be?"

Rick nods towards the counter behind him.

"Sure, grab a coffee. While you are doing that I need to get up and stretch these legs for a moment."

Rick eases himself to the end of the bench seat, grips the table top with one hand, and pushes off the seat with the other, groaning from the stiffness and pain of trying to move his limbs.

"Damn, this getting old is murder on the body," he grumbles.

The cook reaches out a hand to help him up and Rick looks up, taking it gratefully.

"Thanks Isaac."

"I don't know why you have this thing about anyone else seeing your weakness," Isaac says as he pulls him up. "You are an old man. It happens."

On his feet now, Rick starts stiffly moving his legs, using the seat backs to support himself and limping across the floor.

Isaac goes to the counter and pours himself a coffee while Rick walks back and forth, working the stiff pain out of his leg.

He looks at the old man, watching his limping movements and seeing the pain in his face that Rick tries to hide.

"How long has it been?" Isaac asks.

"What? Since I got shot? Long enough it should be healed by now."

Isaac shakes his head.

"It takes the body longer to heal at your age. How long has it been since you saw them?"

"Doesn't matter," Rick growls. Even that deteriorates into a coughing wheeze.

He stops, doubling over with the violent spasm of coughs and gripping the backrest of a booth seat for support.

"I will find them again," he finally manages when the coughing lets up.

"You don't have much time, old man," Isaac says. "You're dying."

Part 3
Moving On

16   Dealing

David is standing alone, watching the two kids play. The little girl; so small, her long hair soft with a slight wavy curl, her round cheeks, and pouty lips. The boy is older. He hasn't dared ask their ages. He would guess eight or nine years old for the boy.

Ethan throws the ball too hard and too far to the right, making it impossible for Lauren to catch it.

She gives him a disapproving look and scampers after the ball.

"Come on, Lauren, right here. Throw it right to me," Ethan calls after her.

Lauren returns to her position, sizes up the throw, brings her arm back, and throws. The throw is too high and it goes over his head.

Ethan jumps to catch it and misses. He gives her a look.

"You throw like a girl," he complains, walking to fetch the ball.

"I like being a girl," she naps back. "It's better than throwing like a boy."

Taking his place again, Ethan winds up and fakes a pitch, holding onto the ball.

"Just throw it, Ethan," Lauren says.

"I'm not going to throw it because you can't catch or throw."

Lauren puts her hands on her hips in a sassy posture.

"She looks so much like Cassie at that age," David says. "Acts just like her too. Sassy and not afraid to put her big brother in his place."

"Just throw it, Ethan," Lauren says again.

Ethan winds up and throws hard, again over her head and past her instead of throwing to her. It is obvious it is on purpose.

With a huff of frustration, Lauren stomps off to retrieve the ball.

When she is back in her spot, she eyes up the throw again.

"Come on, Lauren. Throw it like you mean it this time," Ethan sneers.

Lauren spots Billy behind Ethan and off to one side, watching.

Billy gives her a nod.

She winds up, sizes up her throw again, and gives the throw everything she has. The ball sails for him and Ethan has his hands out at his midsection like a baseball catcher, ready.

It sails high and he brings his hands up too late, the ball connecting with his face with a blow that makes him instinctively snap his neck back.

Ethan lets out a loud wail, bending over double and holding is hands over his face.

David shakes his head. "That's my Cassie. She never let me get away with anything either." He smiles.

Behind Ethan a door opens and Sophie comes out, looking around with a stern look. Seeing Ethan doubled over, hands to his face and crying, she walks purposely to him.

Kneeling before him, she takes his arms in her hands.

"Shh, Ethan. Is it really worth all this? What happened?"

He resists her attempt to pull his hands away to see his face.

"Lauren hit me in the face with the ball. She did it on purpose."

Sophie looks at Lauren, giving her a questioning look.

Lauren shrugs, her expression wide eyed innocence and full of concern for her brother.

"We were just playing ball," Lauren says. "Ethan even said I can't throw. I did not mean for it to hit him."

Hiccupping sobs, Ethan lets Sophie pull his hands away. She inspects his face.

"She did it on purpose. She aimed for my face."

Sophie looks at David for confirmation.

"It looked like an accident to me. Lauren's aim is pretty bad. I thought she was going to take out one of those second floor windows on the last throw."

Ethan flashes him and angry look, grits his teeth, and glares at his sister sullenly.

"We need to put some ice on this," Sophie says. "You already have a goose egg growing on your forehead. Come on."

Lauren walks over to them, looking at Ethan closely, inspecting the damage.

He waves her off with a vicious swing of his arm that just misses striking her.

"That's enough," Sophie says sternly. "Come on, Ethan. Let's go fix you up."

Sophie turns and goes back to the room for a cloth to fill with ice.

Behind her back, Ethan leans in to Lauren.

"You did this on purpose," he hisses at her. "I am going to make you pay." He follows his mother into their motel room.

Billy pushes off from leaning on the wall and saunters past Lauren.

"I won't let him hurt you," he whispers quietly as he goes past.

Alone, Lauren stares after the open door where her mother and brother went. She is frowning.

David walks over to Lauren.

"I had a little sister just like you when I was his age," he says.

"He is a jerk," Lauren says moodily.

"Sometimes older brothers can be jerks. But, you know what? Older brothers are supposed to protect their little sisters. Sometimes we forget that. He will come around."

Lauren looks up at him.

"Cassie is your little sister, isn't she? Did you ever forget to protect your little sister?"

A dark look crosses his eyes and he quickly tries to hide it.

"Yes. I did. But I'm better now."

David looks down at her and smiles. The smile is a little off. Forced. "I will protect you Cassie. I won't let anyone ever hurt you again."

Cassie? Lauren thinks. Did he just call me Cassie?

"You will see. Everything will be just fine. We are going to move on and we will find a nice place to live. All of us. You will like Sophie and her kids. She has a little girl just like you."

Lauren gives him an odd look, but he seems oblivious to it.

David turns and walks away like the peculiar conversation did not just take place.

She watches him go.

"That was odd. He is so weird. Maybe it is a game. Sometimes grownups play strange games. I don't think they know how to be funny anymore."

She says nothing about the strange encounter.

17   Rented House

"I don't think I can do this," Cassie says. She looks at Sophie. Her eyes are pleading.

They are sitting outside of a small rented house they are staying at now. It's another temporary stop, but more comfortable than the motel rooms.

Sophie gives her a level look.

"How much do you really remember?"

Cassie looks away, then down.

"I meant it when I said I don't remember much," she says. "I don't remember my birth parents. I have some foggy glimpses of memory, a farm. I remember a dog. I can't remember his name. I remember long grass. I remember a barn."

Cassie's eyes cloud over. She shakes her head.

"You will just have to endure it," Sophie says. "We won't be with them long. We can't all stay together. In the meantime, you just have to deal with them both being here."

She looks at Cassie. "Which of them bothers you more?"

"Both. I don't really remember Jason. The years I spent living with him, being raised by him. Just the little glimpses of memory. I don't even know why he frightens me. He just does."

"It's probably good you don't remember. What about David?"

Cassie shakes her head as if to shake out both the fogginess and the fear and pain welling up inside it and spreading through her whole body. She begins to shiver, the effect of shock on her nervous system from the dark memories now flooding her mind.

She rubs away the tears roughly with the back of her hand.

"I have no childhood memories of him. I don't remember the first time David kidnapped me. I don't remember being kidnapped. I remember going about my day, every day, everything normal. I don't even know when it happened. Just, I just-," she has to pause. Cassie swallows the lump in her throat. It feels like it will suffocate her.

"I remember hazy bits of dreams. Voices and people. They talked like I wasn't there. I shouted at them to hear me, but they couldn't, or just ignored me.

I just woke up and everything was strange and foggy. I remember being trapped up high with no way down. It was just in a hospital bed. But, I remember it was like I had to crawl to the end of this long narrow white cliff. Everything was white. I remember the disorientation of being so high and afraid to try to climb down."

Cassie has to clear her throat. Her voice is catching with the pain filling her.

"I don't remember getting outside or into his car. Not even the car ride, not really; just laying on some sort of couch and the world gently rocking and the steady noise. Faint glimpses that come and go of old shack walls, old furniture, and a rope ladder."

"The farm house," Sophie says.

"I was nauseous all the time. Weak. I remember that. The world slowly coming together in bits and pieces. Broken moments in time."

Cassie looks at David and Kathy sitting together across the yard.

"I remember Kathy. I'm pretty sure he almost killed her. She looked terrible. I think she was starving to death.

Kathy would not come with us, after he brought Connie there. He thought Connie was me too. It didn't matter that he already had me. He still took Connie, like he was looking for me still and did not understand that."

She looks at Sophie.

"We managed to escape, Connie and me, but Kathy wouldn't come. She chose him over us, over freedom. She trapped him in that damned cellar and then she just let him go. David killed Connie because of her."

"How does that make you feel?" Sophie asks.

"Angry. I want to kill her. I want to make her pay for Connie. But, I also feel sorry for her. She is a victim of the darkness in his soul as much as Connie was."

"As much as you are too," Sophie says softly. "They will get what they deserve. No more and no less . . . when it is time."

"You promised you would let me help you clean up," Cassie says.

Sophie looks down, then away. She looks back to her, meeting Cassie's eyes.

"Are you ready for it? It's easier when you know why you are doing it. They never tell us that. Only your handler and their handler will know. Sometimes you can have a pretty good guess. Sometimes you make up your own reason. Usually it seems pointless and the cleanup," she pauses for a moment, "pointless. It's harder when there is a family involved."

"How did you get into this field?" Cassie asks. "You know, instead of just hiding them after . . . you know?"

"It's all the same business really." The lie shows in her eyes. She shrugs. "I couldn't bring myself to do it." Sophie's look is haunted. "You don't walk away from this business. Either you do it or you find some other way to serve the organization. At least this way I can tell myself I am helping the innocent."

"Sometimes," Sophie adds.

"Who are you helping this time?" Cassie asks.

Sophie looks at the three kids in the distance. Lauren and Ethan are both playing and arguing with each other. Billy is on his own a little distance away, always the outsider.

Billy keeps his distance from the other two kids. He is that little bit older that if feels the age gap is larger. The life he lived makes him feel decades older.

He watches them play their childish game, Ethan not doing a very good job of tolerating his younger sister. They fight more than they play together.

"If I had a little sister like that, I wouldn't be so mean to her," Billy mutters.

The soft sound of a truck on the road in the distance pulls his attention. Billy watches the truck turn before it reaches them and continue on until it is out of sight, relieved it did not come their way.

"This place is pretty peaceful. Quiet. Out of the way. I like that."

He takes a moment to take it in, relishing the relative safety.

A dark cloud replaces the unaccustomed feelings.

"Don't get too cozy. No place stays safe forever and we are moving on again in a few days. These people are okay for now, I guess. In a while I'll have to move on too."

Billy scans the area, always watchful. He sees movement in the trees beyond the yard. He tenses, watching the trees warily. He shifts, ready to bolt, playing the action out in his head.

I will go for Lauren first. Take her with me. Keep her safe. We go past the house and duck down into the ditch there, moving as fast as we can.

The movement in the trees pulls his attention back with a sick feeling of dread.

A doe walks from the trees, her tail flicking nervously. Her head is up, alert. She stares directly at him. He feels frozen by her stare.

A fawn comes stumbling out of the trees, dancing in the long grass, ears bobbing over the stalks. Another follows and the two start playing in the long grass. He gets glimpses of them.

"I guess it must be safe enough if she brings her babies here. So why don't I feel like it is safe?"

A sense of unease makes Billy turn around. Sophie and Kathy are looking at him.

18   Disguises

They arrive at a discount outlet mall in three vehicles. Getting out, they congregate for a moment.

"Remember your groups," Anderson says, "and the plan. Keep to your group, ignore anyone not in your group if they end up in the same store, try to avoid each other, get what you need and what is on your list, pay cash, and do not ask for help. This isn't about fashion. Everyone gets a change of clothes. Something low key that will blend into any crowd and that is not a style you would normally wear. We want to be invisible and not easily recognized."

"I need sunglasses," Rose says happily. "Big ones and a big hat."

Anderson looks at her. "Low key. Invisible."

"And do not bring attention on yourselves," William warns.

"Why can't we go with who we want to?" Ethan complains.

"Because you don't want to get caught and have your mom taken away," Billy says.

Ethan gives him an irritated look. "I'm not that dumb."

"Do I have to repeat it again?" Anderson says. "They are looking for us as a group. In the event we split up, they are looking for us by group. Your mother, Cassie, and a boy and girl your ages. Your uncle Jason and Billy, if they know about him. David and Kathy. And the four of us together." He indicates himself, William and Marjory, and Rose. "We mix up the groups and it mixes them up."

"Let's move," Anderson orders.

"Come on Mom," Sophie says, leading Marjory away across the parking lot.

"Shall we?" Jason motions to Rose and Lauren to accompany him.

With a smile, Rose takes his offered arm and the three of them start off.

Cassie and Kathy walk away in another direction together, heading for a different store.

David watches them go for a moment.

"It's really nice seeing them get along. I knew they would like each other. They will be great friends."

William flashes him a look and Anderson puts a restraining hand on his arm. William looks at Anderson and Anderson shakes his head almost imperceptibly.

Oblivious to their exchange, David looks at Billy.

"It's you and me, kid. You too, Ethan. Let's go."

Billy follows him sullenly, unknowingly playing his part seamlessly with his moody look. Ethan looks at his mother's retreating back, shrugs, and follows David and Billy.

William and Anderson are left alone. They give each other a nod and set off in different directions. Along with their own shopping, they are watching out for the whole group.

Sophie glances at her mother, feeling the edge of anxiety.

Please don't let her make a scene, she thinks. If she starts wringing her hands or looking nervous people will notice.

But Marjory is holding her own at the moment and not showing any nervous signs. Marjory looks around the store wistfully.

"I used to like to have your father drop me off at the store in town. Not because I needed to buy anything. I just liked to overhear the gossip. It was the only thing that made me feel a part of the town, like our lives, our world, was more than just the little world of our farm."

A chipper saleslady sets eyes on them and starts in their direction.

"We don't need help, thank you," Sophie says before she asks.

Her spirit crushed just a little, the she turns in search of other customers.

Sophie scans the store and spots what they are looking for.

"Over here, Mom."

Inside another store, Kathy eyes the exit.

"Are you thinking of running?" Cassie asks, noticing where her attention is.

Kathy looks at her guiltily. "No, I won't run," she lies.

"We haven't had a chance to talk," Kathy says. "I'm sorry, you know."

"No, I don't know," Cassie says. She stops and looks at Kathy.

"Do you mean about coming with us uninvited?" Cassie asks.

Kathy's cheeks redden.

"I had no idea about that. I didn't know where we were going."

"Or," Cassie continues, "do you mean about siding with him?"

"Please," Kathy says quietly, "don't do this."

Cassie steps in, closing the space between them.

"Don't you feel strange, them pairing us together?" she says.

"It was probably David's idea," Kathy says. She can't look at Cassie.

"Why are you still with him?" Cassie asks. "After all this time, you must have had chances to get away. Don't tell me you love him."

She shakes her head. "I wish I could say that you don't know what he is, but you do. That's what I don't get. What could possibly be worse than that?"

"Please," Kathy's voice is barely a whisper. "I did not mean it. I mean, we were all in a very bad place. I couldn't think clearly. I don't think I really understood what I was doing when I did it."

Cassie moves closer, leaning in so no one will hear.

"You could have come with us, escaped," Cassie says softly in her ear. "Instead you chose him. You stayed. You let him out. You let him come after us."

She glances at another shopper looking at them with an odd look.

"Look, he thinks we're lovers," Cassie whispers.

Kathy glances at the man standing some distance away and quickly looks away, the shamed flush on her cheeks from his stare growing.

Cassie brings her lips so close they almost touch Kathy's ear.

"I do not forgive you," she whispers so softly Kathy almost does not hear.

Cassie turns away, taking Kathy's hand. "Come on, let's shop."

Kathy lets her lead her. Bewildered and overwhelmed, she can do nothing but follow meekly.

Inside, Cassie feels like screaming. She feels like slapping Kathy over and over until she knocks some sense into her. She feels like running out that door and away from all these people.

I need to escape. The thought is a silent whimper in Cassie's head.

Jason leads Rose and Lauren into a store. Rose looks around. Feeling shy, Lauren follows them silently, barely looking around.

"What kind of clothes do you like?" Jason asks, stopping to look at a rack of children's clothes.

Lauren looks anywhere but at the rack of clothes.

Jason sighs. "Are you this much trouble shopping with your mother? Come on, just look. You need some new clothes."

A woman shopping nearby overhears and smiles to herself. She pauses, and then turns to them.

"Let me guess, it's Daddy's visitation day and she's feeling a bit weird about it."

She turns to Lauren. "It's okay sweetie, it's always weird at first after Mommy and Daddy separate."

She gives Jason a look suggesting he should be grateful for her help.

Jason is on the verge of dismissing her help, but he stops and looks at her. He pictures her, her face, her hair, the buttons of her shirt and her legs under her skirt.

The woman blushes under his look.

Jason's fantasy moves on. Her eyes flash at him in terror and her mouth pleads with him. It twists into an ugly grimace of fear.

The woman is looking back at him, enjoying his hungry look. When the look continues without words, she starts to feel awkward.

Lauren tugs on his sleeve and the spell is broken. Jason looks down at her.

"You are supposed to be my dad, not her boyfriend," she says.

Feeling suddenly uneasy by his look, the woman makes a quick escape.

Jason looks up to find her gone, looking around the store in a moment of regret.

"Let's get you some clothes. Then we have to get the other stuff."

Lauren tugs his sleeve again.

Jason looks down. "What?"

"Where is Grandma?" Lauren asks, keeping in character for the pretend game.

Jason looks around in alarm, only now realizing Rose is not with them. Grabbing Lauren's hand, Jason rushes through the store looking for the old woman. Each heartbeat is more frantic.

"We can't have lost her," he groans.

People are looking at them, wondering at his anxious movements as he rushes around looking like he just lost the little girl he is dragging around the store by the hand.

Jason goes to the exit, looking outside.

"Did she leave?"

He looks back at the store, lost for where to search, and out the door, half jogging a number of paces out. Jason scans the stores, trying to catch a glimpse of her through the storefront windows.

"There," Lauren says, pointing, "Grandma."

Jason looks down at her and she winks up at him with a small shy smile.

"Let's go get her."

Still holding her hand, afraid he will lose her too, Jason half-jogs to the other store.

Being alone with the little girl brings with it a wash of memories. Cassie, sweet little Cassie, who he had to comfort through so many long nights of night terrors. Her large eyes staring innocently and unblinking up at him from the floor of the back seat of the car, so huge and round in her little round toddler face. David staring back at him with a fear that matched his own at finding them hiding crouched on the floor in the back of the car.

It takes Jason a conscious effort to shake it off.

They burst into the store to find Rose talking to a sales clerk. They rush up to her breathlessly.

"I want a wig," Rose is saying to the clerk, "a blond one. I always wanted to be a blond."

"There you are," Jason says. "You left us in the other store."

He realizes what she is saying and blanches.

"We are supposed to stay together," Jason says.

"You were too busy gawking at that woman," Rose says. "So I went off to do my own shopping."

Another clerk joins them. She is carrying three wigs.

Jason's stomach sinks.

"You aren't supposed to ask for help," Lauren says.

Jason tries to shush her. He turns to the old woman.

"You don't need a wig. We are only here to get what we need."

Rose looks at him pointedly. "And I need a wig."

She turns her attention back to the clerks, leaving Jason and Lauren to exchange a helpless look while the clerks fawn over her.

Finally, she turns away from them, beaming.

"I have my wig. Now what do you need?"

Jason looks around quickly.

"They don't have anything but lady stuff. Let's pay and go."

Rose looks around and turns to the clerks.

"Sunglasses. I need big glorious sunglasses and a large hat."

"Are you trying to look like a movie star trying to hide her identity from her fans?" one of the clerks teases.

"Who says I am not a movie star?" Rose winks at her.

In minutes they have found her a large hat and large round sunglasses. Trying them on, Rose nods approval and turns to Jason. They dwarf the thin frail looking old woman.

"You can pay now dear," she says.

He gives her a sour look as the clerk cheerfully rings up the purchase.

As they are leaving the store, Rose looking pleased with herself, Jason leans in closer to her.

"You are not supposed to ask for help," he hisses at her.

"Pooh on that," Rose says. "I'm an old lady; if I don't ask for help that will look suspicious."

"She is right," Lauren says, nodding agreement.

"Don't encourage her," Jason grumbles.

They head off to find another store.

David, Ethan, and Billy are looking through racks of boys clothes.

Ethan takes a shirt off the rack, holds it to himself, decides it fits, and tucks it under his arm to look for another.

Billy is showing no interest in trying to find anything.

"I'm not sure we will find anything your size on these racks," David says, sizing up Billy against the clothes. "You are small and scrawny, but I think these are all for smaller kids."

Billy gives him a sullen look without looking at him and moves away to look at another rack. His eyes scout the store, always on the watch for an escape and something to escape from.

David moves around the rack and looks up. Outside he sees Jason, Rose, and Lauren walking past the store.

"Cassie," he whispers. He takes a step forward, watching them, his heart suddenly racing in his chest.

Billy looks and sees who he is staring at.

"We have to go get her," David says urgently.

"Who? We are not here with anyone, remember?" Billy says low enough no one else will hear.

David is moving and Billy has no choice but to follow him out of the store.

"Where are we going?"

"To get Cassie."

"We are supposed to stay apart."

Billy stops and watches David go.

David moves urgently, following the other three.

"That's not even Cassie," Billy mutters.

He glances back at Ethan, who has so far been oblivious to what is going on, shrugs, and follows, catching up to David inside another store where he is surreptitiously watching Lauren.

Billy ducks behind the clothes rack with him, watching her.

"What are we doing?" he whispers.

"Watching," David whispers back.

"Why?"

"She is not supposed to be here."

"Why not?"

"She is supposed to be at the farm."

Billy gives him an odd look.

"What are you talking about? We aren't even staying at a farm."

Distracted by dealing with Rose, Jason does not realize that Lauren wandered a little distance away.

With the distance between them grown, David makes his move. He starts for the little girl, whispering.

"Cassie. Cassie!"

Lauren stops and looks around at the sound of whispering, not seeing where it is coming from.

"Wow, he actually thinks she's Cassie or something," Billy mutters. "He really does, like he's someplace else. There is something wrong with that guy. No, he must be just mixing up their names."

Billy is watching and it feels like watching the inevitable slow motion of a coming train collision. Unstoppable. You know it's coming, but know you are helpless to do anything to stop it.

I can pull her out of the way of the train, he thinks.

Billy makes his move. He darts the other way around the rack, and into another, moving quickly to get behind the little girl.

He reaches through the clothes to tug on the back of her shirt, his hand darting back out of sight.

Lauren turns in confusion and spots him through the clothes.

She smiles. "What are you doing in there?"

"You have to get back to them right now," he hisses, motioning towards Jason and Rose with his head.

Lauren looks, realizing how far she is, and nods. She turns and hurries to join them.

Billy slips back out and retraces his steps. He looks around for David, spots him, and sneaks back to him.

"David," he hisses to get his attention.

David is still transfixed on the little girl.

Billy grabs his shirt and tugs.

"David, let's go."

David turns to look at him. There is no recognition in his eyes.

It sends a cold lump growing in Billy's stomach.

"Cassie." The whispered name is barely a breath on David's lips.

"She is going to meet us there," Billy whispers. "Come on."

Billy tugs at him and David lets him lead the way, lost in another time and place.

William walks across the parking lot, aware of every person and vehicle in it, moving on to walk the sidewalk in front of the storefronts.

He makes a pretense of going into a few of the stores and walking around them, leaving empty handed.

Finishing the circuit, William does it again changing his route and going into different stores, on the watch for anything and taking mental note of every person and vehicle that comes and goes from the lot.

19   Moving On

In separate locations, Anderson and William check their watches and make their way to the vehicles. They both have a bag, having managed to fill their own lists while scouting the area.

Anderson arrives at his vehicle first, a dark newer model van with third row seats and tinted rear windows. Getting in, he flips down the sun visor to retrieve the keys, starts it, and pulls out.

He drives around, stopping in front of a store just as Sophie and Marjory are coming out. Sophie's timing is impeccable.

They get in and Anderson drives around to park out of sight behind a trash bin.

Just as they are gone from site, William arrives at the lot, walking across to the opposite side of the lot from where Anderson took the van. Going straight to a larger model car, he repeats the same process as Anderson, arriving at the front of a store and stopping there to wait.

William looks at the store front. The door does not open.

Some distance up, Jason and Lauren walk out of a store, turning and walking away from William. They reach the end of the stores and turn the corner towards the back, getting into the van parked behind the trash bin.

William looks at his watch impatiently.

"Come on, you're late," he mutters.

He looks towards the store again, trying to peer through the windows. He doesn't see them. He looks in the rear view mirror, seeing Cassie and Kathy walk out of a store behind him. They turn and go the other way, heading for their rendezvous point.

"Damn, they will get there and I'll still be sitting here waiting."

Finally, the door to a store opens and David and Billy come out. It is the wrong store.

William scowls at them, watching them.

Billy spots him and tugs on David, pointing towards the car waiting at the curb. Billy keeps his head down and his face hidden as they approach. They get in the car, David in the front and Billy in the back.

"What are you doing?" William growls at them. "You are supposed to walk around to the van. Where the hell is Ethan?"

Billy looks up and William sees his panicked look. David looks sheepish.

"We lost him," David says.

"What? You lost him?" William turns to him, glaring and his face hard. "What do you mean you lost him?"

"I don't know. We just got separated."

"You are an idiot. Get out and go to the van and tell Anderson what you did." William shakes his head angrily.

"Bloody hell, Sophie is going to be mad," he mutters.

He looks at the storefront again.

"Now where is Rose? This whole thing is falling apart. I told Anderson we should have left you all somewhere and do this ourselves."

"There she is," Billy says from the back seat, pointing.

William stares at the store window.

An old lady is approaching the door.

"Finally," he mutters.

A clerk rushes to open the door and hold it open for her, saying something to her. The old woman has unnaturally youthful looking blond hair. She turns and he sees her face.

Rose waves at him, smiling. She turns to speak to the store clerk.

"What the hell has that woman done to herself?" William complains.

He turns to David. "Get out, go, both of you."

Billy is quick to exit the vehicle, glad to escape the old man's anger. He can see it building, the raw red blush of anger creeping up the back of his neck.

He stops half out of the car, his attention on Rose and the clerk holding the door, more so on movement beyond the open door.

Ethan comes out of the store and the smiling clerk holding the door for Rose waves goodbye to him. He glowers at her, walking towards the car with Rose. He looks furious.

"It looks like we found Ethan," Billy says.

David takes longer to get out, waiting and holding the door for Rose as she slowly makes her way to the car.

William's jaw works, chewing on his growing anger. This is not how they planned this.

Ethan glares angrily at David as he approaches and gets in the back seat of the car.

Rose finally gets there and David helps her into the front passenger seat.

"Let's go, Billy," David says, closing the door.

They jog across the lot, walking swiftly up the sidewalk and crossing the street to another set of stores where they were supposed to rendezvous with the van.

William stares at Rose, scowling.

She turns to him, beaming.

"I got a wig, blond. I always wanted to be blond, just like Marylyn Munro."

William shakes his head and starts driving.

David and Billy are crossing the street when Billy sees it sitting in the parking lot of a coffee shop, the male driver looking directly at them with no expression.

Billy blanches and almost stumbles. He has to concentrate on making his feet obey him and keep walking.

A white van, Billy balks at even acknowledging its existence only to himself. *Okay, stop looking at it. They will know.*

He can't stop. Billy cannot take his eyes off it.

I have to know. It's probably just some guy. There are lots of white vans. But, what if it's them?

He stumbles along woodenly next to David, the white van growing closer with every step.

The driver is still looking directly at them.

Another man comes out of the coffee shop with two coffees and a small paper bag, getting in on the passenger side of the white van.

The van has not moved yet when David and Billy reach the other side of the street, turn, and leave it behind them.

Don't look back. Don't look back. Billy keeps repeating the words, fighting the urge to turn around and forcing himself to look straight ahead.

Once everyone is in the vehicles, they drive to an isolated rendezvous point to make sure everyone is accounted for and rearrange who is riding in which vehicle.

William helps Marjory into the front passenger seat and then gets behind the wheel of the car. He leans out the open driver's window, waving at Jason and Billy. Cassie is already waiting in the back seat.

"Let's go," William calls to them.

The others are trying to sort out who will sit where in the van.

Anderson wanders over to stand next to William's open window.

"All right, you know where we are going," Anderson says. "You know the drill. We will see you there."

William nods to him as Jason and Billy finally get in the back seat. He starts the car, gives Anderson a wave, and puts it in gear, driving away.

Anderson turns his attention on the rest, watching in exasperation as they quarrel over seats.

"It doesn't matter who sits where," Sophie finally says in exasperation. "Just get in."

With the last of them taking their places, Anderson gets in the driver's seat. He starts the van and pulls out, taking a different route from William.

The long drive is filled with awkwardness and angry silence interspersed with Sophie's moody comments directed at David.

Forced to be in the van with David, Sophie and Ethan both keep giving him angry looks.

"I can't believe you lost my son," Sophie mutters, repeating the words she has thrown at David repeatedly and giving him another hard look.

"That's enough," Anderson says, his irritation showing.

Sophie lapses back into her angry silence.

Glad to not be in the path of those looks, Kathy just stares out the window, wishing she were out there instead of in the van.

Lauren watches the world go by out her window, playing silent car games to make the time pass.

In the front, Rose keeps happily checking her wig in the sun visor mirror.

In the car, Marjory sits next to William in the front, trying not to anxiously wring her hands. William grips the steering wheel with angry fists, glaring hatefully at the road ahead.

No one in the car dares utter a sound. William's anger is a palpable force inside the car that everyone can feel.

Cassie, Jason, and Billy are crammed together into the back seat, Cassie trying to keep distance between her and them and unable to in the tight space.

She stares out the window, hoping to avoid having to make conversation. She feels Jason's presence next to her larger than life and more pronounced than the inevitable gentle pressure of their bodies forced to touch in the small space.

This is the man who murdered my mother, she thinks. The mother I don't remember. The man who kidnapped and raised me and my brother, which I don't remember. The stranger who picked me up on the side of the road when I escaped and fled from David and the farm, and left with me Sophie and the kids. The man who warned me that if I ran, if I tried to go home before he came back to tell me it is safe, the man who kidnapped me would find me again.

She forces herself to not look at him. The urge is there, to say something, to ask the questions filling her. And at the same time his presence, knowing what he did, sickens her. It fills her with a cold fear that knots her stomach and makes her want to open the door and leap from the moving vehicle to get away.

He is the only one who can tell me what happened. How he lost me and how I ended up in foster care. What kind of a life I had before. What Sophie knows and won't tell me.

Cassie pushes the thoughts away, forcing herself to think of nothing but the drone of the tires on the road and the passing landscape.

Billy keeps looking behind them for any sign of the white van.

20   Watching the Coffee Shop

Lawrence sits in his car waiting. He dozes and wakes, startled and looking around for whatever it is that woke him.

He is parked off to the side, hidden from the view of anyone coming or going from the little coffee shop.

"A lot of business seems to happen in coffee shops."

He looks at the man who spoke, seated next to him in the car. The man is old enough to be his father, if he had fathered him before he hit twenty.

"How are you here?" Lawrence asks. "You are dead."

The man winks. "Am I?"

The soft buzzing disturbs him again and he opens his eyes, looking around in groggy bewilderment.

"I was dreaming," Lawrence realizes.

The buzzing comes again and he fumbles for it, finding his phone and answering it.

"Hawkworth, you bury 'em, I dig 'em up."

"You should retire that phrase," Jim's voice says on the phone.

"Jim, how did it go with Rick Dalton?"

"He's old."

"I know he's old. Is he going to help?"

"I think so, if he can. He doesn't look so good."

"Jim," Lawrence pauses, unsure if the unease he felt meeting the witness earlier is fed only by his imagination. "I met with a witness who claimed he knows something about the old ladies escaping the nursing home," Lawrence says.

"Did he tell you anything that can help us?" Jim asks.

"No. He didn't tell me anything we don't already know. But I got the impression he knows a lot more than he is saying."

"Are you going to meet with him again?"

"I don't think I should. I've got a bad feeling about this guy."

"What kind of bad feeling?"

"Bad. Anything he does tell me, I don't think I should trust it. You know that feeling you get when you know an informant is playing you? Like he's just twisting things up in a big knot to mess with you? I've got that kind of feeling."

"So, he's a bust."

"Worse, Jim. I have the feeling he means to hurt us. I've been in some bad places and talked to some bad people, and I never had such a strong sense of danger."

"What's his name? I'll get Beth to check him out," Jim says.

"He only gave me one name and I'm sure it's made up."

"These guys often reuse an informant alias. It's still worth a try."

"Graham. He didn't give a last name." Just saying the name fills Lawrence with a vague dread.

"I'm meeting with Rick again," Jim says. "Then I have to move on. There might have been a sighting. I'm going to check it out."

"I have some things I'm checking out right now too. I'll keep you posted." Lawrence hangs up and looks out his car window at the small coffee shop. The shop is in darkness.

There is no sign of movement at the coffee shop yet.

21   Rick Dalton

Jim is parked outside the little diner on the edge of nowhere where he met Rick Dalton. He hangs up his phone and looks at the diner. It does not look any different than his last visit to meet the retired Sheriff.

The same two battered old pickup trucks are parked in the lot.

He gets out and enters the diner to the serenade of the sickly unpleasant jangle of the bell over the door ending with a dull clunk.

He makes a point of not looking up at it this time.

Stopping just inside, he surveys the diner, seeing no one at first.

No sign of a cook or anyone else again, Jim thinks.

Jim spots Rick Dalton in the same tall-backed booth seat, visible only by the top of his head moving with the motion of sipping coffee.

He pauses to pour himself a coffee and walks down the aisle, stopping in front of the booth. This time he takes note of something he missed until the old man's wheezing alerted him to it during the last visit. Rick Dalton looks like he does not have much time left to settle his affairs.

Rick doesn't look up. He just motions towards the seat across from him.

As he slides into the seat, Jim notes the redness rimming Rick's eyes the way it does a sick old dog. There is a slight tremor to his motions too. The sort of age tremor you can try to cover, but cannot always hide.

Either the old man is in worse shape today, or I'm not as observant as I should be. He looks grey and his skin almost papery, Jim thinks.

"Have you decided if you are going to help me?" Jim asks.

Rick looks at him.

"I'm an old man. How much help do you think I can really give?"

"You can't be much older than William McAllister and we believe he broke his wife out of a lockdown seniors' home."

Rick blinks at him in surprise. "They broke her out?"

Jim's grin widens.

"You are already helping me. I didn't say anything about another person. You already know about Mr. Richard Andrews. Who is he?"

He is Anderson, Rick thinks, William McAllister's Anderson. But I won't bloody well tell you that. Not until I know how far I can trust you.

"Who is that?" Rick says. "I just assumed an old man like William McAllister would not be able to pull something like that off without help. I figured he must have had his son help him."

Except that he hates that kid like no man ought to hate his own, Rick thinks. Something happened between them back when he was just a boy; something that eats at William's conscience. Something William can never forgive. It has a name. Amy Dodds. I bet the old man was a split hair from killing that boy for what he did to that little girl.

"You know more than you are letting on," Jim says, staring him in the eye.

Rick nods.

"Probably more than I'm willing to share. All right, I'll help you find the McAllisters."

22   Watching Graham

A car pulls into the empty lot of the dark quiet coffee shop. A plump woman past middle age gets out and walks to the front door. She unlocks it and enters, locking the door behind her.

The lights flicker on inside and Lawrence can see her through the plate glass windows, preparing the place to open.

The imperfect feed from the listening device he planted in the coffee shop the day before comes crackling too loud from a receiver on the passenger seat of his car, startling Lawrence. He turns the volume down low, letting the garbled crackling sounds play just loud enough to hear they are still there.

Lawrence sits; waiting and watching. Customers come and go, shifts change, and the morning sun moves across the sky to sit at mid dusk in the Western sky.

A car pulls in and a man gets out. Half dozing, Lawrence doesn't notice him at first. A sense of familiarity missed, of something on the verge of happening, makes him look.

Suddenly Lawrence is alert, sitting up and staring through the window at the man some distance away. He recognizes him instantly. He is unmistakable in his totality of being nondescript.

He is conspicuously unimpressive. Average in every way. The man is middle-aged with thinning hair cut in a business style. He is wearing a cheap suit jacket, trousers, and dress shirt with the top two buttons undone and no tie.

"Graham," Lawrence breathes the name. "The man must have a closet filled with identical outfits."

He blinks.

"The name of this diner was repeated in your notes on the files in that last box. From your grave you are still looking for whatever it is you were determined to find. Your notes on the files and a hunch I should check it out and we have found the witness who wanted to talk but had nothing to say. Who are you Graham and why are you important?"

As if sensing he is being watched, Graham pauses halfway to the coffee shop door, looking around.

Lawrence ducks down, breathing a sigh of relief when he does not look directly at him.

Graham continues on into the coffee shop.

Lawrence turns up the volume on the receiver and the coffee shop sounds fill the car at a level low enough it will not be heard outside the car. He settles in to listen and watch who comes and goes.

He watches Graham move to a booth at the back of the coffee shop, seating himself. It puts him just out of Lawrence's view.

As the waitress reaches the table, she starts rattling off the evening's specials and is cut off by the raise of Graham's hand in a stop gesture."

"Coffee and an apple Danish please," Graham says.

She opens her mouth to say something else and he cuts her off.

"That is all, thank you."

Lawrence cannot make out the expression on her face as she nods and turns away, but he gets a sense from her posture that she found her customer to be quite rude.

Graham sits there for some time. Other customers come and go, and he does not move.

"What is he waiting for?" Lawrence wonders. He checks the time. "I should move so I can see him. But if I do, I risk him seeing the car. If I walk and he leaves I might miss the chance to follow him."

Lawrence pays no attention to the vehicles and people coming and going; only watching Graham.

A man walks into the coffee shop, pauses to look around, and heads to the back booths. He stops at Graham's booth.

Lawrence perks up.

"Wallace," the man says."

"I knew it," Lawrence mutters. "Graham is not his real name. Wallace, huh?"

"Have a seat," Wallace's voice comes crackling through the receiver." It is garbled into the noises of the whole coffee shop.

"Who are you?" Lawrence asks himself of Wallace's visitor. He is suddenly alert.

The man sits in the booth and Lawrence can no longer see him.

"Damn, I have to move. I have to see them."

The waitress comes to the table with a coffee pot, fills his cup, asking if he would like anything else, and leaves.

He starts the car and eyes the coffee shop, deciding what to do. He smiles. There is a semi tractor with a trailer parked along the edge on the other side of the lot.

Lawrence drives around, trying to avoid going where his car can be seen from the front windows of the coffee shop, but it is inevitable. He has to turn next to the coffee shop.

He pulls in behind the coffee shop, parking in the no parking zone at its rear. Pulling out ear buds, Lawrence plugs them into the receiver, silencing it.

Taking the receiver with him, he gets out. He moves around the building, walking on the far side of the large truck and trailer. The truck is empty, the driver presumably inside the coffee shop. He stops at the front of the trailer.

Lawrence peers between the truck and trailer. He can see Wallace and his guest, although he cannot see his guest's face.

"I need a better vantage point."

Watching to make sure Wallace is not looking his way, Lawrence moves to the front of the semi truck and darts quickly behind a pickup truck parked close, ducking down between them.

He is looking at them dead on through the window.

He puts the ear buds in his ears, the sounds of the coffee shop suddenly coming to life. The sound quality is better through the ear buds than its small external speaker and he can better distinguish the sounds coming from inside.

Lawrence pulls out a small magnifying lens from his pocket, holding it up to one eye. The distant figures inside the coffee shop leap larger and closer. He studies the side profile of the man sitting across from Wallace, memorizing him.

"How did the trip go?" Wallace asks his guest.

"Uneventful," the man says. "Is that issue with Mr. Miller being resolved?"

"It has been handled," Wallace says. "Mr. Miller will not be a problem. A representative has spoken with him and he realizes his error. It will not happen again."

"I hope not. If it does, my man will resolve Mr. Miller's issue himself. This was a very close one. Mr. Miller does not have the capacity to follow instructions."

"As I said, Mr. Miller has been spoken to. He understands how important it is to follow instructions exactly. Is there anything else?"

"Nothing else has come up."

"Good. I will see you next time then."

The man puts money on the table, presumably for his coffee, and leaves the diner.

Lawrence watches him go, noting the make of his car and the license plate. He resumes watching Wallace.

Wallace casually sips his coffee and sits there.

The waitress comes, refreshes his coffee and moves away.

An hour later another man enters the coffee shop and joins Wallace. Like the other man, he waits to be invited to sit.

"Wallace," he addresses Wallace.

"Have a seat," Wallace says, motioning to other side of the booth.

The man nods and sits. They wait for the waitress to come with a fresh coffee cup and fill it. The man orders a sandwich to go.

They wait in silence until the waitress is out of sight.

"How did the trip go?" Wallace asks his guest.

"Uneventful," the man says, sipping his coffee. "Everything went smoothly with our new Mr. Miller. My man said he was eager, but reserved. As long as he can keep the schedule, we have no problem."

"Good," Wallace says. "We had a good feeling about this one."

"Are there any other items to discuss?"

"Nothing else has come up."

"Good. I will see you next time then."

The waitress comes at that moment with his sandwich.

"Here you go, Sir."

"Thank you," he smiles at her.

He pays her and leaves with his sandwich.

Again, Lawrence watches him go, noting the make of his car and the license plate.

The process is repeated with two more guests stopping to visit with Wallace, a woman followed by a man.

"Are they all working with this Mr. Miller? Who is he? It's like salesmen meeting their regional rep. Whoever he is, it does not sound like this Mr. Miller is management. A customer maybe? Different salesmen dealing with the same customer? I'm going to have to find out who this Mr. Miller is and who he works for. I will have to find out who Wallace and his associates work for too."

Another man enters the coffee shop and approaches Wallace's booth.

"Wallace," the man says.

"Have a seat," Wallace says, motioning to other side of the booth.

The man nods and sits. Lawrence notes this man's body language is different, tense. His motions are jittery.

"He is scared of him," Lawrence whispers.

Again, they wait for the waitress to come with a fresh coffee cup and fill it. The man orders a donut. They wait until she is gone.

"How did the trip go?" Wallace asks his guest.

"We are having a delivery problem."

Wallace raises an eyebrow. His face remains passive otherwise.

"What kind of delivery problem?"

"Our procurers have misplaced a parcel."

Wallace narrows his eyes, his mouth tightening into a grim line. He leans forward.

"What do you mean they misplaced a parcel?"

The man shifts nervously in his seat.

Lawrence watches them closely, paying attention to the cues their bodies are giving off.

"Was this before or after the parcel was added into inventory?" Wallace asks.

The man's eyes shift away.

Lawrence gets a sense there is something more going on behind this discussion.

"He is hiding something from Wallace. There is something he is afraid to tell him."

"Well?" Wallace asks, his eyes steady and cold. "Did they misplace the parcel before or after it was added into inventory?"

"After," the man admits.

Wallace's lips tighten.

"What is the status of the parcel? What are the specifications?"

"The parcel has not been located. Small, feminine, bipedal."

Something buzzes in Lawrence's ear. A sense of unease tingles at his nerve endings.

Wallace leans in closer, staring hard into the other man's eyes.

"Will she be able to talk?"

The man nods guiltily.

"How old?" Wallace hisses.

"Maybe eight."

A vision swims into Lawrence's head, a brief flash, a young girl with large dark eyes and dark bobbed hair. Her eyes are filled with fear. She is dirty, her clothes muddied.

"They are talking about a child," Lawrence realizes. A cold chill fills him.

"Find her before someone else does," Wallace says, his voice so low the listening device barely picks it up. "You can go now."

The other man gets up reluctantly, looking as if there is something more he wants to say.

Wallace waves him off with a dismissive gesture, not looking at him. The man puts money down to pay for his coffee and leaves.

Lawrence's focus is on this man as he leaves the coffee shop; his walk, his mannerisms, his face. They all scream that this man is under extreme duress.

I should follow him, Lawrence thinks. But if I follow him, I lose Wallace.

He watches his progress, itching to run to his car, but torn by the need to keep watching Wallace and follow him when he leaves.

"Hey, what are you doing?"

Lawrence straightens, startled, and turns to face the man standing behind him.

"What are you doing to my truck?" the man's face is hard and accusatory.

"Nothing," Lawrence says quickly.

The truck driver's eyes narrow.

"Are you spying on people?"

The denial is on Lawrence's tongue. He swallows and nods guiltily.

"That guy over there. I'm an investigative reporter and they are involved in something I am following a lead on."

"I hate reporters. Get the hell out of here and away from my truck." The driver takes a step towards Lawrence, his hands balled into fists and his stance forward and threatening.

Lawrence steps back, almost making the mistake of stepping into view. He glances at the restaurant and blanches.

Wallace is walking directly towards him.

In a moment of self-preservation, Lawrence darts past the trucker, leaving the man staring after him and wondering what is wrong with him. He jogs along the length of the truck and trailer, keeping them between him and Wallace, breaking into a run by the time he reaches the end of the trailer.

Wallace looks at the truck in time to see the driver come around from the passenger side. The driver climbs up into the cab to sit in the driver's seat.

Pausing at the rear of the trailer just long enough to take a quick look for Wallace, Lawrence darts across to the side of the restaurant; running down its side to the rear.

He is out of breath when he reaches his car and quickly gets in.

Just as Lawrence is closing the door, he spots a car come around the corner in his rear view mirror.

With a panicked look, he drops down out of sight.

It is the car the last man to visit Wallace was driving.

The car comes up from behind slowly.

Lawrence holds his breath, trying to make himself as small as possible, pressing against the door.

Please don't see me, please don't see me, he begs silently.

The car passes him and keeps going.

One, two, three... Lawrence counts slowly to ten in his head before he risks sneaking a look over the dash.

The car is gone.

Lawrence sits up, breathing a sigh of relief.

He starts the engine and pulls forward slowly, turning up the side of the building and stopping just before breaching the front parking lot. He scans the lot. The semi tractor is gone and so is Wallace's car.

"Damn," he mutters.

Part 4
Jobs & Plans Askew

23   William's Job

Anderson pulls into the motel lot, parking around back and walking to the front of the motel. He knocks on the others' doors on the way past.

Sophie and Jason both open their doors seconds after he knocks, looking out at him. David and Kathy do not answer theirs.

"Get them out here," Anderson says, motioning back to David and Kathy's door. "Meeting."

Sophie ducks back into her room.

"Cassie, come on. We are having a meeting."

Jason looks back at Billy in the doorway behind him.

"Stay here. This won't take long."

"Why can't I come?" Billy complains.

"Adults only," Jason says.

He goes to David and Kathy's room, banging on the door.

"David, open up," Jason calls through the door.

Go away; please just go away, Kathy pleads silently inside the room, staring at the closed door.

Anderson goes into the room he shares with William, Marjory, and Rose, leaving the door open behind him.

"Marjory, Rose, perhaps you should go for a walk and get some fresh air. It will do you both good. You look a little peaked from being cooped up."

Rose gives him a knowing look.

"I'm not naïve. You don't trust me, and you want to discuss things without me here. That's fine." She turns to Marjory. "Come on Marjory, let's go for a walk."

Marjory looks at Anderson and William and nods.

The two elderly woman leave for a walk.

Jason bangs again on David and Kathy's door while Sophie and Cassie are walking to the other room.

Inside the room, Kathy is sitting on the bed staring at the door, her eyes wide and afraid. She swallows.

They are not going away. I have to open the door.

She gets up, approaching the door slowly, jumping when the loud banging on the door starts again. It takes every ounce of control to fight the trembling of her hand when she reaches for the door knob.

Kathy opens it just enough to look out.

Jason tries to look past her.

"Where is David? Anderson called a meeting."

Kathy glances away, then up at him quickly, and away again.

"He's not here," she says quietly.

Jason's lips tighten into a line.

"No one was to go anywhere. Where did he go?"

Kathy shrugs, still unable to bring herself to look into the eyes of this serial killer.

"Stay in the room. When he gets back, you tell him to see me."

His movements are angry when he turns away.

Kathy closes the door, locking the deadbolt and latching the chain. She leans against the door, wiping away a tear.

"I can't do this," Kathy murmurs, her voice cracking with strain. "I just can't do this. It was hard enough being on the run with David. Now we are with all these people and some of them scare me."

Jason joins the others waiting in the other room, closing the door behind him.

Anderson, William, and Sophie all look at him, questioning.

"David went out," Jason says.

William juts his chin out, his eyes cold and angry.

"Leave it William," Anderson says. "It's just as well."

Anderson turns to look at each of the others, who all focus their attention on him.

"As you are all well aware, there is no out of this business. You can get old, you can try to run and hide, like David did, but you are never truly out. There is in and there is dead."

They all look at Anderson, their faces mirroring each other's expressions of concern.

"They think I'm just some old lady from a nursing home," Rose complains as the two elderly women walk. "That Anderson didn't even want to take me out of that home too."

"That was a bad place," Marjory agrees. "A very bad place."

"I'm glad your William saw fit to take me out of there," Rose says.

"You did not belong there," Marjory says.

"Neither did you." Rose looks at Marjory.

The woman is as lucid and smart as I am, Rose thinks. If she belonged in that care home with all the other crazy and infirm minded, then I am a bloody daft princess. So why was she really there? She wasn't dumped there by family. The last thought sits like the ruined ember of old anger that sat smoldering too long in her stomach.

Not Marjory, not with a devoted husband who visited her every day. I have my doubts her being there had anything to do with her mind. A lot of them were senile. Some of those dumped there deteriorated with the cocktails of drugs pushed on them and from being trapped in that hell hole full of crazy people and dementia patients. And some only pretended to be senile.

"Back at Bayburry, you were mostly off in some other world, lost and confused. Now, not so much," Rose says.

"It's not always obvious," Marjory says.

"Yes, you are probably right," Rose shakes her head.

Yes, I will be keeping an eye on you, you crafty old bird, she thinks.

"The way they kept everyone medicated, I wonder how you have any mind left at all," Rose says.

"I do too," Marjory says.

"So, they knew where David was all along," Jason says.

"Of course." Anderson looks at him.

"When he was a boy . . .."

"Yes," Anderson says. "They kept tabs on him to make sure he would not become a problem."

"They could have . . .," Jason starts, and stops. "No, of course not. They won't interfere. They won't help. They only remove a problem if it comes up."

Anderson nods.

Cassie looks around at them all, trying to figure out what is going on. She realizes and a cold dread fills her.

"All these years, since I was a little girl, they knew where I was?"

"Yes. They kept tabs on you. They keep tabs on every soul linked to the organization."

"David . . . when he . . .."

Anderson shakes his head. "They don't work that way. They would not have given him your location. They did watch to see if you would remember anything."

"In case I told anyone anything and became a problem."

"Correct," Anderson says.

"Let's get to business," Anderson says. "You may not be aware, being in my position I must maintain contact with the organization."

He looks around at them all to make sure they understand.

"If you think there is no out for you, that goes double as you move up in the organization. They left you alone, William, in your retirement, as long as you kept to yourself."

"Keep to yourself, mind your own business, and do not bring attention on yourself," he mutters under his breath. "That's what I always said."

He looks at the others, his eyes narrowed and full of anger.

"Now we have all got their attention, every one of us. Because you and that boy you raised can't control your bloody selves."

His eyes have stopped on Jason.

"I should have put the boy down all those years ago," he mutters so quietly that Cassie, who is closest to him, is not sure she heard it.

"They are putting you to work," Anderson says. "Not just Sophie, who is still active. She will continue to get her orders as normal. They are putting the rest of you to work. You could say they are testing you. See how you hold up on the run without a stable base."

He lets it sink in for a moment.

"If we mess this up, Sophie will be a lot busier," Jason says.

Cassie looks at Sophie with alarm.

Sophie lowers her head, looking at the floor.

I don't know if I can do what they expect me to do, Sophie thinks unhappily. I feel like they chose me because they are setting me up to fail. If I fail, I'm dead. If I don't fail, I might as well be.

"Are we breaking in a new Mr. Miller?" Jason asks.

"No. Miller is seasoned," Anderson says. "Miller is off schedule and their regular person is otherwise occupied."

"Where do we meet the Anderson?" Jason asks.

"This is William's job," Anderson says.

Jason looks at him in shock. "But he's- he is so…"

"Old?" William gives him a withering look.

"Look at him." Jason says. "How is he going to carry a package?"

William is glowering and about to say something, but Anderson cuts him off.

"You are right. He will need help. But you have to be invisible."

"But-," Jason starts.

"Your face is too known," Anderson says pointedly. "Did you not notice the looks you get when we are travelling? Everyone knows the face of Jason T. McAllister. You need to be a ghost. You need to no longer exist. Whatever we do from here on, no one can see you."

He looks pointedly at Jason.

"That means no going out for any reason unless I arrange it."

Jason does not look happy.

"Maybe you should send David then," he mutters.

"I don't trust that boy any more than I trust my own," William growls. "Less. There is something dark inside that boy. Dark and dangerous, and I don't think he can control it."

Jason flashes him a look and tries to hide it immediately, not wanting his father to see his fear of him and the worry for David.

"David needs to be reined in," Anderson says. His voice is low and level with an edge of threat to it.

"I raised him," Jason says. "I will keep him in line."

"You couldn't keep that boy in line when he was just a boy," William growls at him. "How are you going to control him now he's grown? Where is he? You don't know."

"We need to go find David and make sure he isn't getting into trouble," he says, "before he gets us all in trouble."

He meets Anderson's eyes. They exchange a knowing look. They both know more about David than the others know they do.

"You leave tomorrow," Anderson says. "I'll keep an eye on David."

Jason glances at the door, unable to hide the worry in his eyes.

"Nothing will happen to him," Anderson says. "Not yet. He will still be here when you get back . . . if he behaves himself."

"David, where are you?" Kathy can't help the distress she feels. "David is behaving strangely again. I thought it would stop now we are with is with his sister again. I thought he would stop talking to her. She doesn't even exist. She's a ghost of a memory of his sister when she was little. Whatever happened then, it haunts him so much that he can never let it go.

David will never stop trying to protect that little girl even though she is not a little girl anymore, even though she does not exist anymore. He can't separate that from what is real. He can't see that he can let go because his real sister is here, now, an adult."

Feeling like she is filled with a tightness that grips every fiber of her being, Kathy moves stiffly away from the door.

She looks at the offending door.

"I could open it right now. Slip out while David is gone and everyone else is in their meeting. If no one sees me go . . .."

She sobs, covering her face with her hands.

"Where will I go? How do I know they won't come after me and bring me back? I don't think they will ever just let me go."

Kathy thinks about her mother.

"I know Mom is still looking for me. She will never give up until they produce my dead body. Mom will never give up on me. I wish I could go back and tell her I'm okay. I want to go home."

Kathy looks at the phone sitting on the desk; a beacon of doing the damnable. It calls to her silently, its call a shrill and loud pulling on her nerves.

She moves to stand before the desk, feeling trapped in a world of unreality far from anything anyone would recognize as real. A world far apart from the real world.

If I just reach out . . . touch it . . . it will vanish like smoke.

Kathy reaches one hand out, stopping just short of picking up the phone receiver, and snatches her hand back.

The meeting is over. William is the first to move. He gets up, going to the door and opening it.

"William, a word," Anderson says, stopping him before he can leave. He motions the rest to go.

Leaning against the dresser, Jason stands and leaves.

Uncertain, Cassie waits for Sophie to move.

Sophie moves to start for the door.

"Sophie, you too," Anderson says.

Cassie looks from one to the other and Sophie nods her on.

"Go ahead," Sophie says.

Anderson nods towards the door and William locks it.

William and Sophie are both looking at Anderson, waiting.

Anderson lets out a slow exhalation of air as though what he is about to say weighs heavily on him. He rubs his eyes wearily.

"I'm too old for this," he mutters with a slow shake of his head. He looks up to meet their eyes, his gaze steady and holding a sadness.

"William, I know how you feel about Jason, but he is still your son."

William stiffens. He knows what is coming.

"He is my boy," he says, "but I knew a long time ago when he was just a boy that something inside him is wrong."

It is William's turn to shake his head slowly.

"I knew I should have put him down then. We do what we do, but it does not make us like them." The grim smile that curls his lips back from his teeth is one of loathing and pain. "He's one of them, a Miller. He just knows how to manage his own packages."

"He really messed up this time," Anderson says. "His attempt to have David caught; David's packages he dug up, leaving them where they will be found. He knew David had to be stopped, but he can't do it himself."

"That was pretty stupid," William agrees. "He was always a reckless boy, acting without thinking it through."

"I don't know if his intent was for the authorities or the organization to deal with David. It doesn't matter. Either way, the organization would have taken him out of the equation. But what he did . . .." Anderson pauses there before continuing.

"Jason caused the bodies behind the McAllister Farm to be found. Because of him we have one Detective who has gone off the grid hunting your whole family. He put the organization in danger."

Sophie nods understanding.

"So the decision on Jason is final then."

Anderson's eyes are apologetic when they meet hers. He nods once.

"And they are going to make me clean it up," Sophie says.

Anderson nods again, his frown deepening.

"It isn't right that they are making her clean up her own brother's mess," William growls, scowling with disgust.

"I knew you would feel that way," Anderson says.

Sophie looks at Anderson, her eyes steady and expressionless.

"What about David?" she asks.

"Him too," Anderson nods. "There was no walking back on that one and I didn't try. He is too messed up. He can't control the darkness inside him. I don't know how he hasn't been caught by the authorities yet."

"Dumb blind luck," William mutters. "Just like some of those fool Millers we deal with. I don't know how most of them don't get caught."

"Because the organization makes it so," Anderson says.

"Kathy?" Sophie asks.

Anderson's look answers the question before his words do.

"Her too."

"She can't just go home," Sophie says. "She knows too much."

"It's only a matter of time before she talks. She is a liability."

Sophie looks down. "It won't give her family closure. They will never know."

"It doesn't matter," Anderson says.

Sophie looks up at him quickly.

"She only has the mother," he says. "She won't stop looking for her, asking questions, demanding answers. She may have already been dealt with by now."

A shadow crosses Sophie's eyes and she closes them. *She was innocent*, she thinks.

"What about the boy?" William asks. "That mongrel Jason brought with him?"

Anderson shakes his head and William's eyes blaze angrily.

"So that fool son of mine destroys another life," he growls.

"He was lost before Jason ever set eyes on him. The boy is running from something, from someone. It's just his own dumb blind luck he is still alive."

Anderson looks at each of them.

"Someone has a claim on that boy and they want him."

"Who?" Sophie wants to take back the question even as she utters it. She knows better than to ask.

William flashes her a warning look.

"I don't know and it doesn't matter," Anderson says. "Even if I did, I would not say."

"No, of course not," Sophie says. "It was just a gut reaction."

"He's just a kid," William growls, giving Anderson an accusatory look.

"The kid has a past," Anderson says. "Maybe we can do something yet."

"What?" William's look is skeptical and still accusing.

"Find out who wants the kid," Anderson says.

A slow grin spreads across William's face.

"A man should never feel bad for putting down a sick coyote."

Anderson looks at Sophie. "You know your job."

Her eyes are steady, staring back. "When the time is right."

Anderson nods.

"You won't have to do it alone," William says, the growl of his voice heavy with more than anger.

Anderson moves to the door, unlocking and opening it.

"I have to check in. Get everyone ready to move. We won't be here for more than another day."

Sophie looks at Anderson, keeping the rest of her questions to herself. *I don't want to know if I will have to kill them all.*

They step outside.

"I have a truck for your job," Anderson says to William, "four doors with tinted windows. If Jason sits low in the back, nobody should see him. You two have half an hour to get ready. I will drive you to the truck. It's up to you from there. We will be gone from here shortly after. You know where to meet us."

William nods. "I'll get supplies on the way to the job."

William and Sophie walk away.

Anderson turns to return to his own room, and spots movement just off the back corner of the building. He stops and watches.

David comes walking around the corner, approaching him. He has not seen Anderson yet.

Anderson steps back out of his line of sight. He listens for the approaching footsteps.

The moment David reaches this corner of the building; Anderson steps out in front of him, causing David to almost collide with him.

David starts, his surprised movement awkward, and blinks into the angry rheumy eyes staring into his.

"You startled me old man." David grins, but it is a nervous grin.

"Where have you been?" Anderson asks, his voice calm and cold.

"I just went for a walk."

"You don't go for walks. No one goes anywhere that is not pre-planned. You got that?"

"Yes sir. Sorry."

"Get yourself in order. We are moving on as soon as I get word."

David nods and beats a quick retreat to his room. He can feel Anderson's eyes boring into his back.

"He is fidgety," Anderson observes, watching him go. "He was up to something."

Kathy looks up, startled when the motel room door opens.

"David."

He takes in her startled look and the tremor of her hands. She is packing her bag.

"Good, you are getting ready to go," David says, moving past her to his own. He opens his bag, taking a quick look around for anything to be packed.

He does not catch the hollow surprise that made her eyes widen, or her increased nervousness as she watches him.

"So," Kathy starts slowly, hesitantly, "you know?"

"Yes, I just saw Anderson. We have to be ready to go. We leave as soon as he gets word."

Sick relief fills her. She glances guiltily at the phone.

"Did he say how long?" she manages.

"No. But if we are ready, then we won't forget anything."

Anderson is waiting impatiently next to the van when William and Jason come carrying their bags, Billy tagging along behind. He looks at Billy then at the men.

"The boy stays here," Anderson says.

Billy's look shifts to him. He does not trust the old man.

"He knows," Jason says.

Jason stops, looking down at the boy.

"I will see you when we catch up with you."

Billy just looks at him blankly, hiding his thoughts.

"In the back out of sight," Anderson motions to Jason.

Jason nods, getting in the back. William gets into the front passenger seat.

Billy is left standing alone.

Anderson walks over to him, leaning in close and whispering.

"Don't go taking off," Anderson says. "I know running gets easier than staying sometimes. But staying with us is the safest place for you right now."

He turns and walks away, getting into the van and driving off, leaving a bewildered Billy staring after them.

Anderson pulls in behind an auto wrecker, the van bouncing over the rough pot-hole pitted yard to the far corner.

They don't see it until he pulls up and stops right in front of it. A truck similar to many trucks on the road is parked where a junction of building, fence, and trees block it from view at almost every angle.

"Keys are in the visor," Anderson says. "I'll see you at the rendezvous."

William nods, pressing his lips together grimly.

"Marjory will be fine," Anderson says. "Sophie is taking care of her and so will I."

William gives him a nod and gets out.

"Don't bring attention on yourselves," he says.

This time Anderson nods.

Jason and William get in the truck, Jason in the back.

Anderson waits for the truck to fire up before driving away.

William sits there letting the engine run, giving Anderson a head start. He looks at Jason in the rear view mirror.

"You know the drill. We will pick up supplies on the way to meet Mr. Miller and get the package."

"Free us." The whisper is that of multiple voices, barely a breath of a sound. It repeats itself. "Free us. We feel trapped. Free us."

"Fred," a woman in the store uniform is standing behind the store manager. Her voice is uncertain.

Fred turns around.

She looks uncertain, her eyes strained.

"What is it Maya?" he asks. "Is something wrong?"

"In the produce aisle. A man is behaving strangely."

"What is he doing?"

"I think you need to go look."

Fred sighs. With Maya following anxiously, he makes his way to the produce aisle.

He goes down the cereal aisle, passing a woman walking too quickly, pushing her cart ahead of her like a shield, two small children jogging to keep up and a toddler in the seat pointing behind them and crying.

"Banan," the toddler sobs. "Banan."

He turns his teary eyed round-cheeked distress on Fred as they hurry past.

Fred looks back at them curiously.

Following, Maya looks at them with a worried frown.

Fred turns at the end of the aisle, going past the meat counters, the milk and cheese, and reaches the other end of the store. He pauses before the last aisle, looks up it at the canned goods neatly lined up on the shelves, the boxes and packets of instant meals.

He sees an older woman go past the other end of the aisle, clutching her purse protectively to herself and looking back anxiously.

A man, presumably her husband and walking quickly, catches up to her. Taking her arm, they move for the exit.

Maya stops behind Fred, unwilling to go ahead of him. She looks up at him.

Fred turns towards the end of the store and takes those steps past that last aisle and stops, gaping.

"That is the strangest thing I have ever seen."

There, halfway down the produce aisle, is a man wearing a suit that appears to be made of tin foil and newsprint with boots to match. He has a hat pulled down low over his ears, bits of newsprint and tinfoil poking out from beneath it.

He is facing away from Fred, standing in front of the bananas. The floor around him is littered with pealed bananas and peals.

The man reaches for a banana, large shiny silver oven mitts on his hands, fumbling to pick it up and peal it. He drops the banana and peal on the floor at his feet.

"What the hell?" Fred is angry. He steps forward purposely towards the man.

"What are you doing?" he demands.

Maya stays a safe distance away, watching fearfully.

The man turns to look at him, picking up another banana and pealing it.

"Stop that," Fred demands. "Stop that right now."

"I have to free them," Nathan says. "They feel trapped. They want to be free."

He grabs frantically at bananas, trying to peel them faster now that he is caught.

Fred turns to Maya.

"Maya, call the police."

Nathan's eyes widen.

"No. NO. NONONOnoononnnoooo," he moans, gripping his head, imagining the wailing of coming sirens.

Nathan turns and bolts, running through the store and out the door.

"Hey, come back here!" Fred makes a half-hearted attempt to chase him, giving up the chase after a few steps.

24   Rest Stop

The group left the motel as soon as Anderson returned. After hours of driving, they are stopped at a roadside rest stop to stretch their legs on the way to their next location where they will meet William and Jason.

In the distance, Sophie is walking with her mother, Marjory wringing her hands anxiously. Behind them, Rose walks with a stiff limp that has been growing worse. The three kids and the dog chase each other through the long grass. David watches the kids play with an odd look, following Lauren's progress.

Anderson paces slowly near the vehicles, keeping watch over everyone.

Cassie and Kathy are sitting on a picnic table. Cassie looks at Kathy, breaking the awkward silence.

"Has David killed anyone since the two of you went on the run?"

The question startles Kathy. She has to force herself to breathe.

Why is she asking me this? Panic fills her and she hesitates before answering.

"No," Kathy says. Her eyes dart away quickly as if to avoid her lie being found out. She swallows. "At least, I don't think so."

She looks at Cassie to find her looking at her and has to look away again.

"You don't think so," Cassie says. "You don't know."

Kathy shakes her head guiltily, not looking at her.

"At first I was sure. He promised it was over, that he would never hurt anyone again. But he started acting strangely." Kathy stops, unsure how much to trust the other woman with.

Loneliness and the feeling of being trapped into something too big for her fills her. She can't take it anymore.

I have no one. No one to talk to. To confide in. To trust. Cassie is probably the only person in the world who might understand what I'm going through.

Kathy pushes herself to speak, almost breaking and staying silent. Her tongue is frozen. She is ice cold and feels her hands begin to tremble. Suddenly, she feels like she can't breathe. She needs to get up, to run. She falters, fumbling over the words at first and uttering nothing more than wordless sounds.

"David," the name comes out a croak from Kathy's dry throat, "his temper was getting bad. He would be okay one moment, then angry the next for no reason. He was being secretive and I would catch him talking to nobody like someone is there. I think he thought he was talking to you."

A flush rises in Kathy's cheeks with an embarrassed heat, expecting Cassie to reprimand her. To tell her how stupid it is.

Cassie only nods, waiting for her to continue.

"At first we were mostly together all the time. That was good at first until he started acting odd. Then he started going on trips. David said it was for business, but he didn't have any jobs that required travel."

Cassie nods. "He was trying to stay in the family business, or at least knew enough to know he can't get out. He had to check in and probably do some jobs."

"I got the feeling he was hiding something."

"He didn't want you to know what he was doing, of course."

"It was more than that. Almost like he was cheating on me, but I knew he wasn't. With him being gone for days, I don't know. I just don't know."

"He could have been taking more victims and killing them," Cassie says quietly.

Kathy looks at her and they exchange a look of understanding.

"You are afraid, aren't you?"

Kathy nods and a tear rolls down her cheek.

"You want out."

Kathy nods again.

25   Where the McAllisters Are

William pulls the truck into the parking lot of a small truck stop diner. He drives to the other side of the lot, parking where few vehicles park.

"Stay in the truck," William says. "Stay low and don't be seen. Stay down until we are gone and I say it's safe to sit up."

Jason smirks. "This is just like when you used to take me on jobs when I was a kid."

William scowls and gets out. His walk is stiff from the long drive, his legs paining him as he walks across the lot to the diner.

The feeling of déjà vu, walking up to the diner to meet Anderson before meeting Mr. Miller, brings home with a heavy grey pall the reality of just how infirm his once strong body has become with age.

This is not his Anderson, the old man he spent his adult life working and growing old with. This is another man.

He grips the door handle and pulls. The spring closure on the door, once a thing he barely noticed, now is a strain for his muscles.

The opening door triggers the merry jingle of a bell over the door, announcing a new customer to the woman waiting tables.

Bloody bells, William scowls inwardly at the unwanted noise bringing attention to his entrance.

The booths are to his left. William nods in response to the greeting smile of the waitress and makes his way to the fourth booth.

The man sitting there is half his age and dressed much like the truck drivers sitting at scattered tables and booths.

William looks down at him. "Anderson."

The man nods, motioning him to the seat across from him.

"It is a pleasure to finally meet you," Anderson says. "You are famous and respected, just like your father and grandfather."

His smile is too big, reaching his eyes with a happy shine. William nods without smiling.

The waitress is hovering before William can get himself seated. He nods to the coffee pot in her hand.

"Coffee please, and a blueberry muffin."

She expertly sets the cup down; already pouring coffee into it as she does so.

"Be right back with that muffin."

"Are you ready for this?" Anderson asks. The smile on his face is just a little forced now.

"I've never been not ready," William says.

Anderson nods.

"I don't expect you ever have. The details are waiting for you. You know where to get them."

"I do."

"All right then. We will see you when you are done."

The waitress arrives with the muffin.

William nods to her, puts down money for his coffee and muffin and an average tip, and takes the muffin, heading for the door.

"Where do we go from here?" Jim asks.

"We go where the McAllisters are," Rick says.

"How do we do that? We haven't been able to do more than get a few possible hits on where they have already been."

"We outthink them. William is smart. The only way to stop crafty old fox from eating your chickens is to outfox the old fox. William knows how the cops work, how they think. You are going to have to stop thinking like a cop and think like a man who will stop at nothing to protect both his secrets and his family."

"Like I said where do we start?"

Rick grins at him.

"How does the old fox lose the dogs he can't outrun? He backtracks, doubles back, leaves false leads, and knows when to hunker down and just stay put."

"Isaac, the maps", Rick calls out.

Jim looks up to see a man in a cook's apron materialize from the kitchen. Jim and Rick have to pick up their coffee cups as he spreads the map out on the table, its edges overhanging the table sides.

The map of North America is marked up with lines and markings in different marker colors spanning the entire map.

"The only way to catch a fox that won't be caught is to make him show himself. Know where he's been."

Rick points to a few of the markings on the map, his finger gnarled with age and arthritis and possibly a long ago break. The small city where the McAllister Farm sits just outside its limits, the city where William lived in a scummy little apartment building, and both the Bayburry Street Geriatric Home and Cranbrook Nursing Homes. The small town where Michael Underwood and Katherine Kingslow were living under assumed aliases is marked too.

"Do you think he will return to any of these places?" Jim asks skeptically.

"Not those ones. They are on the run, but they still have to check in from time to time." Rick levels his gaze at Jim. "If you are running a team of individuals working different areas who have to check in with you, how are you going to do it?"

"Have them come to you," Jim says.

Rick taps his head and motions to the cook. Isaac spreads out another map over the first. This one is of a smaller region.

Rick points to a marked location; Sophie's farm.

"They were here."

He moves his hand, pointing out two more locations.

"False lead." Rick points out another.

"That's our possible sighting," Jim says.

Rick nods. "They want you to think they are going here." He runs his finger along a highway.

He moves his finger to another point in another direction.

"They really went here. They will have to check in here." He taps a final marked location. "They will move on, move around, but they will double back to where they have been while you are looking forward and trying to figure out where they will go next."

"How do you know that's where they will check in?" Jim asks.

"That's where the others check in."

Jim just stares at the map, absorbing its details, the marked points that far outnumber the few Rick drew attention to.

He looks up at Rick. "The others?"

26   Dead Leads

Lawrence hangs up the phone and calls his editor. Paul's voice comes on the moment the phone stops ringing, impatient.

"Hawkworth, where are you?"

Lawrence looks around, sitting in his car at the junction of two gravel roads surrounded by farm fields.

"I'm not sure. I'm following a lead."

"I checked into those two names you gave me. Graham, the witness I sent you to talk to is a dead end. The other one, Wallace, is nothing. There is nothing there. Don't waste any more time on that. Lawrence, find another lead to follow. Drop this one. If I come up with any other leads I will let you know. Keep checking in. I want to know where you are on this."

"Right. I'll keep checking in."

Lawrence hangs up the phone, staring at the empty gravel road ahead.

"You are lying to me, Paul. Why are you lying to me?"

Lawrence looks down at the file folders on the seat next to him. The top file, Mr. Grant Cormer, has notes jotted on the front cover in Lawrence's handwriting.

"Let's hope someone remembers you Mr. Grant Cormer."

He puts the car in gear, turns right, and follows the road.

27   William's Job

William stops the truck on the side of the road. Ahead they can see the sign for an old motel chain that died off except for the odd motel.

"This is it. Stay down and out of sight in the back. I don't want Miller seeing you. You know how this goes. I'll get out and talk to him. We drive to the switch location, and go our separate ways. I will let you know when it's safe to sit up."

Jason grins. "Just like old times, going out on jobs with my dad."

William scowls, but he is feeling it too, the nostalgia of the days when he was young and strong, taking Jason on the road to teach him the business. Jason's eager young face looking up at him from where he is huddled out of sight on floor in the front.

It brings with it also the darker memories; Jason just a boy, shooting the coyote bitch, intentionally torturing the animal when he was a good enough shot to have killed her easily. The thrill he saw in his eyes, his enjoyment in the rabbit's slow panted terrified death at his hands. The barn. The blood. Amy Dodds.

William closes his eyes tightly against the unwanted intrusion of those dark memories from his past.

I should have put the boy down after the coyote. I should have put him down after the rabbit. Before Amy. The memories and the thought they bring is a physical pain that fills his whole being with a sorrow that cannot be denied; pain of loss and failure on multiple levels. It centers in his chest and sends a shooting pain down his left arm that leaves him momentarily breathless.

Jason watches his father's expression change. He sees the pain the old man can't hide and the color seeping from his face turning it grey despite the flush of anger rising up his neck.

Is he angry he has to bring me? Yes, he does hate me that much. Look at the rage having to spend even a moment with me is filling him with, Jason thinks. Dad, you've always been a hard unforgiving man. No matter how small the mistake I ever made; it just made you hate me more.

William pulls himself together with effort. *You are getting soft, Old man,* he thinks.

"Okay, let's go." William's voice is rough with the gravity of the moment.

He puts the car in gear and drives on. Jason ducks low in the back just before they reach where anyone at the motel might see him. Parking across the lot, William gets out and walks across the lot, his slow pained shuffle giving away his age-wreaked weakness.

William knocks on the motel door and it is opened almost immediately. He looks eye to eye with the man who opens the door.

"Mr. Miller?" William asks.

The man nods.

"Let's go," William says. "Drive out of the lot and turn left. Continue out of town and over the bridge. Turn left after the bridge and continue for three miles. I will pass you and then you follow me. Park back to back when I stop."

The man nods again.

William walks away, heading to the truck without looking back. As he is getting in, he sees Mr. Miller drive by in an SUV.

A thrill courses through William as he follows him out the parking lot. It is an undeniable excitement at being back doing what he has done his whole life despite the gravity that hollows him out.

He follows the SUV at a distance, accelerating to overtake it at the designated spot, and winds through country back roads with the SUV following until he finally pulls over. As instructed, the SUV does a three-point turn in the road, backing up with the rear bumpers facing each other and leaving room to stand between them.

"Stay down," William whispers to Jason and gets out of the truck.

Lowering the tailgate, William grabs rolled tarps and spreads one with some difficulty, his hands shaking a little with the effort. He silently curses his infirmity, hoping Miller did not notice.

Miller opens the back of the SUV to reveal a well wrapped and tied body-sized rug.

"Give me a hand with this?" Miller grunts, pulling one end towards the bumper.

William shakes his head, watching without moving to help.

"I don't touch the package."

"It's not going to bite," Miller complains, struggling with it.

William scowls.

"Moving your package is your responsibility. I don't touch it."

Miller grabs the other end, dragging it closer. He shakes his head at William as if in disbelief he refuses to help.

Miller struggles only a little to lift the package and shift his grip on it, turning and dropping it onto the tarp in the back of the truck, the shocks bouncing with the rough dropping of the package.

Miller turns back to his vehicle. "Oh yeah, there is this stuff too."

He grabs some scattered items from the back of the SUV; a purse and a few items of women's clothing.

"Toss it on the tarp with the package. You should have disposed of those already." William's voice is impatient with Miller's mistakes.

A seasoned Miller like he is supposed to be would already know these things. Do not ask for help because we do not touch anything to do with the package in his presence, William thinks.

Miller drops some of the items, kneeling down to pick them up.

William looks down. There is still a lipstick on the ground.

"You missed one," he says.

"Oh, can you get that?" Miller says casually, tossing the other items on the tarp.

"Pick it up yourself," William growls. "I do not touch the package."

"Touchy," Miller comments as he picks it up. "You are too old for this job if you can't help move a body."

William scowls.

"I don't know what your package is," he says, his voice gravelly with age but holding an icy calm. "I am only a courier. I transport packages from where I am asked to pick them up to where I am asked to deliver them to. I do not touch the package or anything to do with it." He pauses. "None of our couriers do. Union rules."

Miller laughs. "You are union now?"

He tosses the lipstick on the tarp and turns around, walking away to his vehicle. The lipstick hits, bounces, and rolls off back to the ground.

William clenches his fists at his sides, his face a careful emotionless mask, except he can't completely hide the hard glint of anger in his eyes.

Miller starts the SUV and drives away.

William stands there watching him go until he is long out of sight.

He looks around. His nerves are jangling a warning.

"This feels wrong. If Miller is seasoned like Anderson says, he should not have been trying so hard to get me to touch something."

William pulls a pair of thin rubber gloves out of his pocket. He puts them on, then pulls another pair out, putting only one on overtop the glove on his left hand. Using his left, he picks up the lipstick and puts it on the tarp with the other items. Peeling off only the extra glove on his left, he adds it to the items.

He carefully folds the tarp over the package and loose items, wrapping and tying it off to make sure nothing is lost. Then he pulls out another tarp from the truck box, unfolds it and secures it snugly over the box, hiding its contents.

William gets in the truck and sits there for a moment. He lets out a rough breath of air, then starts the truck and drives away. He is careful to keep exactly to the speed limit on the gravel road, the tires kicking up a cloud of gravel dust behind them.

Some distance down the road he reaches a crossroads. The gravel road continues on and the cross road is mud. Trees and brush in all directions partially hide the routes from view. William slows, stops at the intersection, and looks in each direction.

He continues up the gravel road, driving slowly to keep the truck from leaving a cloud of dust in its wake.

William pounds the steering wheel with one fist.

"You can sit up now," he growls.

Jason sits up, looking at him with concern.

"What's wrong? Why are you driving so slow?"

"So we don't leave a dust cloud. If Miller is trying to see where we went, I want him to think we took the dirt road. This whole job is wrong," William growls. "It feels wrong. Miller wanted me to touch the package. Dropped something and tried to get me to touch that. I have a bad feeling about this. I think we are being set up."

"Set up by who? Anderson?"

"I don't know." William shakes his head. "I trust our Anderson, but I don't know this guy. We have to ditch this truck. We are going to have to find another truck and swap the package. We make sure this truck will not be found. Then we deal with the package. We will change vehicles again before we meet with Anderson on schedule. We also need to contact Anderson and let him know."

"Our Anderson, right?" Jason asks.

"Of course our Anderson."

They drive on for some time, William taking random turns and speeding up when he feels they have travelled far enough.

"There," Jason says, pointing out the window towards a farm.

Parked out of sight from the house is an old beater farm truck.

"Let's hope the farmer leaves the keys handy," William says.

He drives past the farm, and turns into the access to the field just on the other side of the windbreak for the house.

"Don't-," William starts.

"I know, don't be seen," Jason finishes, getting out. He closes the door slowly so it does not bang, giving it an extra shove to make sure it is latched.

Inside the truck, William watches Jason go.

"Damn this old body," he mutters. "He better not get caught."

He watches Jason's progress until he cannot see him anymore. He turns the truck off and opens the window to listen. All he can hear is the wind rubbing the leaves, hissing ticking of insects, and the occasional low bawl of a cow somewhere in a field not far away.

Jason jogs along the tree line away from the road, cutting through it at the back of the neighboring yard. Keeping an eye out for any sign of movement, he uses whatever he can for cover until he can get behind the outbuildings and make his way unseen to the old truck.

He gets in and looks. A smile creases Jason's lips. The keys are conveniently left in the ignition.

"The trust these people have."

The truck engine chokes and struggles, but it starts, running louder than he would like. Someone might hear it.

Jason drives forward along the edge of the property where a rough two-wheeled path runs to the fields on the other side of the tree line. Keeping to the outside, he turns to follow the tree line, hoping the motion of the truck is not spotted through the gaps where he can see the farmyard. The truck rattles and bounces over the rough ground.

He reaches the end and there is no path through the trees bordering the two fields. Stopping, Jason looks around. He shrugs, turning to follow the edge of the field going away from the road.

Time drags and William's impatience grows. He shifts, fighting the urge to get out and go looking for Jason.

Finally, he hears the rough sound of a sickly engine.

William perks up; looking in the direction Jason went.

The loud engine and rattling of the truck bouncing over the rough ground alerts him before the motion does. William turns to see the truck coming from the other way.

Jason pulls up next to him, driver door to driver door, grinning.

"There was no path so I had to drive through the brush. I got stuck a few times, but we have a new truck." Arm hanging out the window, he slaps the outside of the door for emphasis. "I also happened to see a spot to abandon that one. It looks like an old abandoned quarry. A few other people had the idea too. There are a few smashed junkers there. Looks like someone tried driving them over the cliff to the quarry lake below and missed."

"All right. Let's take a look."

Jason turns the truck around and William follows him back across the field and through the brush. They make their way over some almost impassable spots and finally Jason stops and gets out.

William pulls up behind him, getting out and walking over to look over the edge of a cliff.

Some distance below is a crater dug out by man-made machines. Tracks creating well-travelled trails show where locals drive regularly.

"Looks like a busy spot," William says. "I can see at least three areas the locals probably go to shoot off their rifles at targets. Good spots for hunting blinds."

He points across one hilly section.

"I would bet there is a coyote den in there somewhere."

Jason squints and shades his eyes to see.

"How can you even see that?"

"You can see where people set their boats in too."

"So, it's too busy. We will just have to drive them both until we find something else."

"It's perfect," William says.

"What?"

"See the color of the water? How it changes in the different pools? I bet this one right below us is very cold and deep."

Jason steps closer to the edge, leaning and looking over. Directly below at the edge of the water are the mangled wrecks of two other vehicles likely driven over this very ledge. A third sits slowly rotting in the sun where there is only the sandy bottom of the quarry.

Looking at Jason teetering on the ledge, a thought comes to William. If he were a boy still, I'd be grabbing and yanking him back or his mother would kill me.

That is followed by the image of himself walking up and shoving Jason over the edge. Jason's startled look, hands grasping at air, and staring back at him with shock and confusion as he falls to his death.

The fall would kill him. Regret and sadness fills him, turning to anger. I failed to raise him right. Despite everything I tried to teach him, Jason turned out to be a monster. Something inside him is broken, dark. Bad. He's going to kill again. He can't help himself. Same with that boy he stole and raised, David. That one has a worse darkness inside him. I should have put Jason down a long time ago. Now I have to put them both down. It has to be done. It isn't right they put that on Sophie. A girl shouldn't have to kill her own brother.

"All right, let's get to it," William says, turning and walking back to the truck. Jason follows, opening the tailgate of the farm truck.

William unties the tarp and pulls it back. They each grab an end and transfer the package to the other truck. While Jason is transferring the tarp and tying it down, William goes over the truck thoroughly to make sure nothing of them is left behind.

He tosses a folded bag of tools to Jason, motioning to the back bumper. While William wipes down the truck for any traces of finger prints, Jason transfers the plates to the plate-less farm truck.

Finished, they look at each other.

"Let's do this," William says, starting for the truck they are about to drive off a cliff.

"Wait," Jason says. "Are you sure you can do this? I mean, you aren't as agile as you used to be."

"Neither are you," William says. "You are middle-aged."

"And you have gotten old."

William clenches his jaw. He wants to tell him . . ..

What? That I'm not old? I am, dammit. I can't do what needs to be done and I know it. That's why Anderson sent him with me.

William nods. "Don't get caught in it when it goes over the edge."

He sizes up the area.

"Those other fools didn't get enough head run and speed. You need enough of a run to get the speed up enough to sail it as far into that lake below as you can."

"And jump out without killing myself at that speed," Jason adds.

"Weight down the gas pedal. We have to find a good sized rock; something that will press it right to the floor. Tie off the steering wheel to keep it straight."

They scout the area, finding a rock mostly buried, and have to dig it up with their hands, using the tools they have to gouge out the hard-packed mud and clawing at it until they free the rock.

Jason lugs the rock over and they stand at the open truck door, the rock on the ground between them.

"How are we going to do this?" Jason asks.

"You get in. Start it, keep the brake to the floor, and put it in neutral. I'll set the rock on the gas."

"The rock is too big. It's going to press down the brake too. You won't be able to get it on the gas with my foot on the brake."

"We need a smaller rock or something to put on the gas pedal that we can put the rock on."

"Hey!" The distant voice is angry.

They turn to see a stocky man with a pained bow-legged walk and a hunting rifle in the crook of his arm walking purposely towards them from the trees across the field.

"Hey! What are you doing . . ."

They don't wait to hear the rest of what he is shouting.

William and Jason look at each other and bolt in different directions.

William leaps into the old truck and Jason dodges for the other one, starting them up and flooring the gas. Both trucks kick up dirt, grass, and rocks, grinding against the earth as they charge forward, racing across the field away from the drop off and the bewildered man they leave behind.

"I swear that looks like my truck," he mutters, watching them go. "Oh, damn it all to Hell." He turns and starts making his way back to his truck parked behind the hunting blind.

When William and Jason make the road, they surge to greater speed, leaving the farm and quarry behind.

Some distance down the road, William pulls over and Jason follows. Jason gets out and walks to William's window.

"I bet that was his truck," Jason says.

"Could be, or he's seen too many people try to put a vehicle over that edge."

"Damn. Now we have to ditch both trucks," Jason complains.

"We can't go far with this thing anyway. First police sees us will pull us over. There is no way this thing is road safe."

"Now what?"

"We transfer the package back and drive that one into the bush and leave it," William says. "I haven't seen any signs of farms for some time. First chance we steal another vehicle and lose this one."

Anderson pulls the van into the parking lot of an aged hotel ten minutes outside a city. Driving the car, Sophie parks next to him. There is nothing around except a few businesses and old homes across the highway.

"I still don't know why you won't let me drive," David complains in the back seat.

"Shut up. You haven't earned our trust," Sophie says.

Anderson gets out, entering the hotel office to check them into their rooms. Minutes later he returns, motioning them to come.

They collect their things from the vehicles and Anderson hands out the plastic key cards. The room assignments have not changed with them crowding into three rooms.

Full of pent up energy from the endless days of car rides, Lauren and Ethan are bickering, and Koda is bouncing and barking and lunging while Ethan tries to hold onto his collar.

"I can't hold him Mom," Ethan complains.

"Where is his leash? I told you to put the leash on him," Sophie scolds him.

Ethan loses his grip on the dog and Koda bolts off across the parking lot.

"Ethan!" Lauren shrieks at him. "You let him go!"

"Koda!" she yells after the dog. Koda!" She drops her things and starts chasing after the dog.

"Lauren!" Sophie calls after her. Leave him!"

"Koda! Come!" Sophie commands, whistling for the dog.

Koda is too in need of burning off the pent up energy and he ignores the summons, running out into the road ahead of a car that speeds by him without slowing down.

"He's going to get killed!" Lauren sobs. She turns on Ethan with a furious glare. "You did this. If Koda gets killed it's your fault."

Ethan gives her a hard shove, almost pushing her off her feet.

"That is enough," Sophie says sternly. "Apologize to your sister."

"Sorry," Ethan mutters moodily in a voice that is not sincere.

Annoyed and feeling the pent up frustration as much as everyone else, anger rises in Billy at Ethan's shoving Lauren roughly. He has the urge to lash out himself and strike the younger boy. Ethan's forced apology does not help.

Sophie calls and whistles for the dog again.

A second car swerves when the dog comes back into the road, narrowly missing him, blaring the horn at the dog. The car keeps going.

Billy looks down at Lauren to see if she is okay. Seeing the pain and fear in little Lauren's face, Billy knows he has to do something.

Stupid dog, he thinks, putting his stuff down and bolting off after the dog. He dodges cars in the road.

"Now we have two playing in traffic," Sophie mutters as Billy dodges cars to cross the road.

The dog looks back. Seeing Billy coming, Koda bolts the other way with a new burst of speed, eager for a game of chase.

With a low growl of frustration, Billy sprints after the dog. Koda is faster and the distance between them widens quickly.

"Let's get everyone in their rooms before we lose anyone else," Anderson says.

"But, Koda and Billy," Lauren turns a teary-eyed look on everyone, looking for someone to do something.

"Billy will get him," Sophie says. "Koda is smart. He knows how to stay out of trouble. Nothing ever got him on the farm, did it?"

"No," Lauren says in a small unhappy voice. "But he knew the farm. Koda doesn't know lots of cars. And if we go inside they won't know where to find us."

Cassie gets the leash out of the car where Ethan left it.

"You go get the kids settled in the room," she says. "I'll stay out here and watch for them."

"But what if Koda tries to cross the road?" Lauren asks.

"I will wait on the other side of the road," Cassie says.

Lauren nods and lets her mother lead her into the hotel to their room, looking back to see that Cassie really is going across the road.

Billy continues his pursuit, following the dog through the small grouping of streets where a few old homes and businesses have grown in the vicinity of the hotel in the middle of nowhere.

Koda slows and stops to sniff something interesting, giving Billy hope. Just as he is closing in, the dog looks back at him and darts off, renewing the game of chase.

With a tired growl of frustration, Billy pushes on.

The dog disappears around a corner behind a building.

Billy reaches the corner and stops. The dog is gone.

"Koda, where did you go?" he complains. "If I don't bring him back, Lauren is going to be heartbroken."

Billy walks forward slowly behind the building, watching and listening for any sign of the dog. Koda has completely vanished.

"He has to be here," he mutters.

Halfway up there is still no dog.

A door opens, startling Billy, and a man comes out with a large clear trash bag. He barely glances at Billy as he walks over to a large garbage dumpster and tosses it in, going back inside.

His heart racing, Billy forces himself to act casual, continuing his search for Koda. He reaches the end of the buildings and stops, surveying the area for any sign of the dog. There is none.

"If I was a stupid dog, which way would I go?"

Left is bush and long grass. Right is back towards the hotel. The scent of burgers wafts to him and Billy stares at the restaurant to the right.

"Nothing attracts a dog like food. Right it is."

He goes that way, past the front of the building and across to the restaurant. In the distance, beyond the few businesses and houses, unkempt wild grassy expanse and a gas station, is the highway they crossed, and beyond it the old hotel they are staying the night at.

He reaches the restaurant and looks for the source of the scent of food. His eyes settle on the dumpster behind the restaurant.

Billy heads for it.

He is almost there when a man's voice behind him stops him.

"Hey kid, you lost a dog?"

Instinct kicks in with a cold dread and Billy stops. He automatically considers his options for flight.

Don't bring attention to yourself. That's what that old man William always says. Running will bring attention.

He has to force himself to stand still and turn around.

A man is standing there, a little rough looking and probably between thirty-five and forty by his guess. One shoulder is slouched down, his hand gripping Koda by the collar.

Koda's eyes stare back at Billy unhappily, his skulking body language, ears down and back and tail between his legs, are all the signs of a dog who knows he was caught. The dog won't look at the man, instead moving his eyes away and back to Billy repeatedly.

Billy's senses jangle a warning. It does not feel right to him.

The dog is scared, Billy thinks.

"Yes sir." He manages to keep his voice mostly calm with just a trace of anxious quiver. "That's my dog. He got away."

He looks at the man for a moment, unsure if he should move to take the dog.

"Well, here you go," the man says, dragging the dog forward a step.

Koda has his stiff legs splayed to dig in, resisting the man's pull.

Every nerve is screaming at Billy to run.

Billy moves closer, reaching for the dog, his hand accidentally touching the man's hand as he slides his fingers under the dog's collar to grip it.

For just a moment his and the man's eyes stare into each other and it makes Billy feel awkward. The man releases the dog.

"Thank you for catching him mister." Billy gives him a nod.

"You don't want anything to happen to your dog, do you?" the man says.

"No sir. He won't get away again."

Billy wants to move faster, but forces himself to move at a measured pace, dragging Koda along by the collar. At first the dog balks, and then when he realizes they are leaving the man who caught him behind, he surges forward, almost dragging Billy off his feet before he can get his balance against the dog's pull.

He struggles with the dog, dragging him awkwardly by the collar while Koda tries to pull away and run.

They reach the other end of the lot and Billy turns, looking back. He freezes, almost letting the dog go. Across the lot and parked where he could not see it before is a white van.

An icy terror fills him. Panic makes him unable to move. Billy swallows the lump suddenly filling his throat. He feels like he can't breathe. He stands there blinking at it.

"They found me," he gasps.

Billy looks across the highway to the hotel. It feels very far away. He sees Cassie waving at him from this side of the highway.

"Can I make it? Can they help me?"

He looks around. The fastest way out is to bolt away from both the white van and Cassie.

Run. Let the stupid dog go and just run.

He looks at the white van again. He can see a man sitting in the driver's seat, older. He does not recognize him.

"Is it them? They didn't grab me. No, it must be a coincidence. Other people have white vans too."

He looks at Cassie again.

"Or, are they watching me? Why? Why just watch and not just grab me? They could have drove up next to me, dragged me inside the back, and gone. No one would have known. It has to be just some guy who happens to have a white van. No way they would just watch and not nab me. The guy who caught Koda is one of the truck drivers parked there."

He looks at Cassie again. She is waving with both arms now, holding up the dog leash to show him.

Billy forces his legs to move. They respond woodenly, feeling like they are not all there. He drags the dog along, making his way too slowly towards Cassie.

The man who caught the dog watches his progress for a bit, then walks over and gets into the passenger seat of the white van.

William leads the way through the woods. They are moving slowly, William struggling over the terrain on his age-ravaged legs, a pair of shovels over one shoulder, and Jason under the weight of the body-sized package.

"How do you know where this place is?" Jason asks.

"It's our job to know," William mutters, out of breath and trying to hide it.

William finally stops. He examines a tree, moving on to examine another."

"What are you looking for?" Jason asks.

"I'll know when I see it."

Four trees later William gives the tree a few pats. "This is it."

Jason starts dropping the package.

"Not yet," William says. "I have to pace it out first."

Jason struggles to recover, and loses it. The package hits the ground with a thud and an odd wet ripping sound.

"Oh," Jason gasps, backing off and turning away, gagging and covering his mouth and nose, waving at the air.

"Augh." He groans. "I think it just broke open. I can taste it."

William pulls a compass out of his pocket, gets his bearings, and starts counting and pacing. He turns, counts and paces more, turns counts, and continues in something resembling a macabre walking-dance to the dead.

Jason groans. "And I thought it smelled bad carrying it," he complains, still gagging.

"Here." William drops one of the shovels. He jabs the other hard at the ground, stepping on the top of the blade and bearing down with his weight, working the handle back and forth to break ground.

Jason retrieves the other shovel, digging next to him. Working together, they dig until William is satisfied with the hole.

They pick up the package slung between them, carrying it over, and drop it into the hole. The landing pushes another wave of gasses from the already decomposing corpse like an oily cloud of putrescence.

Jason gags again. "I never could get used to that smell."

"You made sure nothing was left where you dropped it?" William eyes Jason.

"I checked around carefully," Jason says.

William nods and starts shoveling dirt into the hole, covering up the body. They fill in the hole, carefully covering all traces of their ever being there.

"Let's go switch vehicles again and meet with Anderson," William says.

"You still have to tell our Anderson about the package swap," Jason says.

"Not until we are far away from the package. I will talk to him before we meet Anderson."

Picking up the shovels, they retrace their steps, walking past where Jason dropped the body.

Neither sees the lipstick nestled in the forest floor detritus as they pass.

William and Jason have disposed of the vehicle they last transported the body in, leaving it submerged in a pond. They are now driving another extended cab truck, the license plates switched with another truck to make it harder to trace. They are parked against the bushes behind the building at a highway rest stop.

"Go for a walk while I call Anderson," William says.

Jason gives him a look. *There is something he doesn't want me to hear.*

He gets out, walking away and wondering what the secret is.

Jason does not get far before his attention is drawn to a woman travelling alone who just pulled into the rest stop. She gets out, stretching from the long drive, and heads for the building and the rest rooms inside.

They are parked where she would not see them. There are no other vehicles. The woman would think she is alone at the rest stop.

Jason looks back at the truck briefly and heads for the doors of the building.

Using an untraceable disposable phone, William calls Anderson. Anderson answers after too many rings.

"What went wrong?" Anderson asks. William was only to call if there was a problem or they will be delayed making the rendezvous point.

"The whole thing is wrong," William says.

"How so?"

"It feels wrong," William growls. "Either Anderson lied about Miller's experience or something else is going on. Miller was supposed to be experienced. An experienced Miller knows we don't handle the packages."

"He made you handle it?" Anderson's voice has an edge of alarm. He pauses, thinking. "It happens. Maybe he was just nervous."

"He tried too much; tried to get me to help move it. Then dropped stuff all over and tried to get me to pick that up too. Miller wasn't bumbling. He seemed determined I touch something."

"Do you think he knew about Jason in the truck?"

"If he did, he did nothing to give it away."

"Even the seasoned Miller's don't always follow the rules. You know that. The guy was probably just trying to take advantage of your not being his regular guy. Go for the meeting with the Anderson. Be careful and play it cool. Meet us at the rendezvous. Call me if anything else happens."

"Will do." William hangs up.

He looks around, seeing no sign of Jason, and gets out.

Walking towards the front of the building, he still sees no sign of Jason.

The woman's car comes into view.

"He better be staying out of sight," William grumbles.

William continues around the building and finally enters it. He goes into the men's washroom. It is empty.

He turns his head, staring towards the women's washroom.

Moving like he has a weight hanging off his shoulders, William steps out, pausing at the door to the women's washroom. He listens.

There is no sound.

Pushing the door open, William enters cautiously.

If any women are in here they'll make a damned scene, he thinks.

William walks to the middle of the room, checking the stalls.

This bathroom is empty too.

A purse lies discarded on the floor. He stares at it. His eyes narrow.

"Damn you Jason."

Picking up the purse, his aged body making bending down difficult, William opens it, taking a quick look inside. He takes it with him, leaving the bathroom.

Stopping outside the door, he looks around. There is a room marked utility. He looks inside. Nothing out of place except a bottle of cleaner on the floor and a few empty pegs on the wall.

There is another entrance door on the other side of the building.

William uses it, stopping outside. He looks to the highway, the car parked in front, and towards the back. That way is a grassy area for walking pets, a play structure, and beyond that is nothing but fields and bushes and trees.

He looks down. There on the ground is a broken painted fingernail. Bending down stiffly, he picks it up, looks at it, and puts it in his pocket.

Eyes narrowed, he stares towards the trees. Shaking his head, he starts walking. He goes past the empty play structure and the grassy area where someone did not bother to pick up after their dog. At the edge of an age-crumbled cement curb stop where the trimmed grass turns wild, something at the edge of the long grass catches his eye. A set of keys.

William picks them up, looking at them.

"Ford. Like the car."

Walking with angry purpose, he crosses the grass to the trees.

Inside the trees he spots color that does not belong. Making no effort to be quiet, he heads for it, stopping when he comes upon a bound and gagged woman, her clothes and hair disheveled, shirt torn, and dirt smeared on her cheek is staring up at him. Her face is tear streaked and her eyes terrified and pleading for help. Blood is still running fresh from her nose and a bruise is already starting on her cheek. Her partially revealed chest is smeared with blood.

"Jason, come out."

Jason steps from behind a tree a little distance away. His face is flush with excitement.

"I heard you coming."

"Of course you did." William glares at him. "What the hell are you doing?"

"She saw me," Jason says lamely.

"Before or after you grabbed her?"

Jason looks away guiltily.

"What the hell is wrong with you?" William growls, his voice low and hard. "You stupid idiot. Low profile. Don't be seen. You just couldn't control yourself, could you?"

He shakes his head in disgust.

"Give me the weapon." He holds his hand out to Jason, staring at the woman staring back at him pleadingly.

The relief in her eyes that help is there, along with the terror and pain, is a physical pain in William's chest.

Jason steps closer, handing him a small box knife he found in the utility closet.

William walks to the woman, kneeling before her.

"I am sorry this happened to you. It's all over now," he says gently, kneeling next to her.

She nods, tears still running down her face, and a sickly smile of relief behind her gag.

She tries to talk, but her words are muffled and unintelligible.

William takes the back of her head in his hand and she leans her head forward to make it easier for him to remove the gag.

He curls his fingers into her hair gently, tightening them.

A new fear flashes in her eyes and she stares up at him in shock.

Gripping her hair firmly with a strength she did not think this old man capable of, William pulls her head back to reveal her throat.

She struggles, whimpering and trying to beg for her life behind the gag.

"It's ok," William whispers.

He rolls her head to the side and she wonders again if he is only trying to remove the gag. Her eyes widen, anxiously watching his other hand come towards her with the box knife.

William puts his free hand with the knife behind her head, running a gentle finger along the base of her skull. He positions the knife below the gag tied around her head.

Bowing her head forward, his other hand jerks towards him suddenly, jabbing it home hard up through the base of her skull in one quick sharp movement.

For just a moment her eyes stare at him in confusion, and then the life is gone from them and she slumps limply.

Releasing her, William stands up.

"Clean up your damned mess," he mutters roughly, walking away and leaving Jason and the woman behind.

William returns to the truck, sitting in the driver's seat. Pulling rubber gloves from his pocket, he puts them on and carefully wipes down the keys from the ground with a cloth. He waits until Jason finally appears carrying the woman's body slung over one shoulder in a fireman's carry.

William gets out, meeting Jason before he reaches the car, unlocking the car trunk.

"You need to deal with this. The car too."

"I know." Jason nods, dropping the body in the trunk.

William tosses the keys and the woman's purse at him.

"Follow me, after we make sure there are no security cameras."

After scouting the rest stop for cameras and finding none, they drive for the next six hours, putting distance between them and the last place the woman's vehicle may have been seen.

They dispose of the car first, careful to leave no traces of Jason in it. Leaving the car submerged at the bottom of a murky pond, the woman's body and purse carefully wrapped in burlap and placed in the truck box, they get in the truck.

"We are going to have to meet Anderson with the damned body in the truck," William says. "We will dispose of it after, far from the car. We are behind schedule. We are supposed to be meeting Anderson in an hour and we are hours from there. We are going to miss the rendezvous with the others too."

"Sorry," Jason says, looking apologetic.

They drive for some time with only William's heavy angry breathing to break the silence.

Finally, William speaks.

Jason isn't sure if his voice holds hatred and anger for him, or heartbreak and regret.

"Why? Why did you do it? You just had one job to do and that was to not get yourself into trouble."

Jason looks down, thinking how to answer. There is a long heavy silence between them.

"I like the way they look at me," he says in a small voice, "like I can help them." There is another pause of silence. "I like the way it makes me feel," Jason says softly.

William gives him a quick look, keeping his attention on the road ahead of them.

Nathan is standing on the shoulder of a highway looking down at the device in his hand. It is dwarfed in his large shiny silver fabric oven mitt.

He is still wearing the outdated thrift store business suit that was once his father's. The ghastly color shows where the tinfoil and newsprint carefully stapled to it, covering every inch of the suit, has torn away. The newsprint and foil that completely covered his rubber boots is now worn off on the bottoms. There is a tear on one side that he tried to fix and failed, the flap flopping loose. His hat is still covered with the foil and newsprint stapled to it, covering every inch of it, if a little worse for wear now.

Every shred of missing newsprint and foil is a physical pain to his being with the fear and stress it fills him with.

Nathan fumbles with the receiver for the tracker he put on the white van outside the house. The signal is weaker and the miles distance has grown.

"The white van is getting further away. Nathan needs to move faster."

He looks up, studying his surroundings. There is nothing but barren land and empty highway as far as he can see. Wires strung on poles snake off into the distance along the side of the highway.

Nathan looks up at them.

"Bad wire," he whispers. "They are trying to control me. To stop me. But I won't let them. The radio signals run on the wires and from the poles. They use the radio signals to try to control me, to try to talk to the demons inside me. The government wants my demons. They want them to escape from inside me so they can control them and do terrible things with them. I won't let them."

He pushes his hat down harder on his head to block out the radio signals.

"Nathan has to keep moving. Nathan has to find the white van."

He puts his receiver in his pocket, struggling to get it in with the bulky silver oven mitts.

"The white van follows the boy," he whispers. "The white van will show Nathan where the boy is. The boy is the man. The man is the boy. The changer changes and takes the identity of others. Nathan has to stop the changer. The changer kills. Nathan has to kill the changer."

Nathan attempts to fix his ruined suit, wincing at the whispers filling his head.

"My suit protects me from the beams, the rays, and the mind controlling wavelengths. It traps the monsters inside my head. It freezes them so they are quiet and I can think."

He focuses his attention on the ground at his feet. He needs another mantra. His ruined suit is not doing enough to protect him.

"Nathan is not invisible. Nathan needs to be invisible. Don't look at Nathan. Nobody look at Nathan. Nathan does not look at you, you can't see him. Looking at what lives beneath the ground makes Nathan invisible. No one sees Nathan when he stares at what hides beneath the ground," he mutters quietly. "That is how Nathan put the tracker on the white van. The white van sleeps. Nathan looks at what lives beneath the ground and walks right up to the white van. The white van does not see invisible Nathan. Look down Nathan. Keep looking down."

With his head down and his eyes staring through the ground beneath him, Nathan walks on, following the direction indicated on his receiver.

Seeing the strange looking man walking down the side of the deserted highway ahead, a semi tractor driver takes a double take.

"What the hell is that?"

Reaching the strange man, he slows, his brakes farting and belching as they release their air.

He stops next to the strange man, lets out a short blast of his horn, and rolls down the window.

"Wow, that's some getup you have. You on your way to some kind of geek convention? You've got a long walk. There is nothing out here for miles."

Nathan nods.

"Yes. Something like that." He makes himself look up because people don't like it when you don't look at them when they talk to you.

"Hop in."

Nathan hesitates. "It is a very long way and Nathan is very tired."

The interior of the truck looks darker than the world outside it. That helps make his decision.

Nathan nods and approaches the truck as the driver leans over, pushing the door open.

Fumbling in his oversized silver oven mitts and careful of his suit, Nathan has some difficulty climbing up into the truck.

"It would be easier if you took that shit off," the driver says.

"I can't."

"Staying in character, huh?" The driver gives him a shake of his head, thinking the guy is kind of loony. "I will never get what drives guys like you."

Nathan struggles with the door handle, manages to close it, and looks straight ahead.

The driver does not drive.

Nathan looks at him.

"Seatbelt," the driver says. "I don't want a ticket for that shit." He thumbs towards Nathan's seatbelt.

Nathan fumbles with it until the driver gets impatient, leans over with a curse, and buckles it for him.

The driver starts the truck rolling down the highway.

"So where are you headed?" he asks.

"Southeast."

"That's vague. I'm going in the right direction anyway."

William pulls in at a gas station, parking around the side away from the pumps, careful to avoid the security camera aimed at the pumps.

"Get in the back," William says. "We are almost there."

He gets out too.

"Where are you going?" Jason asks.

William glares at him, his expression seething with anger.

"I have to let them know we won't make the rendezvous." His tone is accusing.

Jason starts to follow. "Maybe I can . . .."

William cuts him off. "Stay with the damned truck and keep an eye on it," William snarls.

Jason sags and returns to the truck, getting into the back seat.

William waits until he is out of earshot before pulling out the disposable phone and calling Anderson.

"What happened?" Anderson's aged voice crackles into the phone after the second ring.

William's jaw tightens angrily.

"That damned Jason ruined everything. We are late to meet the Anderson, cleaning up his mess."

"What mess? What happened now? Wait, you didn't make your meeting?"

"Jason killed again," William growls quietly into the phone. "He couldn't resist the temptation." There is an edge of pain in his voice.

William paces, unable to contain his fury.

"I have to do it. Damn it, I should have put the boy down back then. I have to do it now. I am going to kill him right here and now."

Alarmed, Anderson grips his phone tighter.

"William, don't do anything you will regret, that we will regret. Just deal with your meeting and find your way to us. We will decide how to deal with Jason then."

"We won't make the rendezvous."

"No, but let's just deal with one thing at a time. You are late. Sometimes it happens. Just tell him what you told me before. Keep Jason's mess out of it. Start heading this way. We will talk again and figure out where to meet."

"I can't do this," William says. Anderson can hear his breath still coming angry and hard through the phone.

"I know you William," Anderson says. "You are stronger than anyone I have ever worked with."

William nods slowly. He closes his eyes for a moment then opens them.

"All right. We are almost at the meeting place. I will meet with the Anderson then we will get rid of the package and work our way towards you."

"Wait, you are meeting him with the package still in the vehicle?"

William scowls. "Didn't have time to finish cleaning up his mess."

"Do what you have to and get back to us," Anderson says.

William returns to the truck after hanging up. He gets in and sits a moment, the weight of it all wearing down his old body.

"All right, let's do this," William says heavily. "Duck down and stay low. Do not be seen."

He starts the truck and heads for the meeting with Anderson.

William pulls into the diner parking lot, not glancing back as he exits the truck and walks to the diner.

The jangle of the bell over the door has a sickly ominous ring to it this time when he opens it. William heads straight for the same booth, stopping to stare at the empty booth.

"Over here," a voice calls from behind him.

William turns to see the younger man sitting on the other end of the diner. He walks to stand at the table.

"I like to switch things up," Anderson smiles up at him. "Have a seat. You are late. You are lucky I am even here. Problems?"

William sits, giving him a cautiously expressionless look as a waiter comes and pours him a coffee.

"Nothing else," William says.

"Mr. Miller had a little trouble with his package," William says.

Anderson's eyebrows rise, questioning.

"It seems he could not handle it alone. He needed help moving it. The man was a clumsy fool too."

Anderson just continues smiling too casually.

"Did you help him?"

"I don't touch the package," William says in a low even voice, controlling his anger.

"There was no problem then. So, why are you late?"

William leans in, lowering his voice.

"I'm too old to play games. The whole thing felt off. If my gut doesn't trust it, I don't trust it. I had to take time to change vehicles a few times, and change my route."

Anderson chuckles. "You are too old for this world old man; old and paranoid. Mr. Miller is one of my more reliable shippers."

"Mr. Miller is a fool if he thinks he can trick me into touching his package in front of him."

"So everything is fine then" Anderson says. "No harm done."

"You need to screen Miller better," William scowls.

Outside, a woman walking across the parking lot pauses and stares. Her eyes widen and her mouth drops open. She hurries on, half running for the door of the diner.

The noise of the woman barging into the diner causes them both to look, drawing the attention of everyone in the place. She is worked up, looking around quickly with excitement oozing out of her and her voice shrill and too loud.

"Do you know who I just saw? Out there in the parking lot?"

She is pointing to the lot. People just look at her with expressions ranging from boredom to curiosity.

"I just saw him!" She points again.

When no one bites, the woman becomes more agitated.

"I just saw the serial killer, Jason T. McAllister! He is sitting out there right now in a truck."

Now she has their attention. She is repeating her story, telling everyone who will listen.

Anderson stiffens, giving William a cold knowing look. He knows William could not do this job alone. He is too old, his body giving out to infirmity with age.

Pressing his lips into an angry line, William nods goodbye, puts his money for his coffee and an average tip on the table, and makes his way out the door past the too loud woman.

Their eyes meet for a brief moment as he passes her and the look in his age-lined eyes sends a chill down her spine.

Shaking it off, she continues excitedly telling her story as though she just faced off against a dangerous creature. A few people look out, trying to see the infamous serial killer, while voices chime in shock that such a man could be released to roam among the public.

William's pace increases with his growing fury. He reaches the truck half expecting to find Jason missing.

He sees Jason's head move as he reaches the truck, getting in.

"Bloody hell, I told you to stay down of out sight," he snarls, jamming the key into the ignition so hard he almost snaps it.

Starting the truck, William puts it in reverse gunning the gas too hard, brakes, shifts it into drive, and roars out, driving too fast.

"What's wrong?" Jason asks.

"You were seen."

Jason pales. "Anderson?"

"Some woman came in all lathered up about seeing the Jason T. McAllister in the parking lot," William spits it out.

William takes a corner too fast, trying to put as much distance as he can between them the diner. His knuckles are white in their hard grip strangling the steering wheel.

Three days later they are back with the group. William and Anderson are sitting together on a bench outside a highway rest stop, the two old men looking like any other pair of old men.

"I am going to kill him," William mutters. "I should have done it a long time ago. I should have put that boy down then, as soon as I knew what he is."

"Don't do anything yet," Anderson says. "We still need Jason."

William looks at him balefully. "You know what he did. All he had to do was behave himself. Not do anything stupid. I let that fool out of my sight for just a few minutes." He lets out a heavy breath.

Anderson pauses. "Besides, he is your son. Your only son."

"My son is no killer," William growls. "My son died in that barn with Amy Dodds when he was twelve. That," he motions towards Jason across the lot, "is no man. That is not even an animal. Even an animal does not kill just for the love of it. That thing is sick up here, in the head." He jabs his temple angrily with one stiff finger.

"Well, you can't kill him. Not yet anyway. Jason and that woman are probably the only two people who can control David."

Around the corner, Billy turns away, quickly putting distance between him and the old men he was eavesdropping on.

Billy's face shows his shock and concern. He feels sick hearing what Jason and William did while they were gone.

"I always had a bad feeling about Jason, like he was some kind of creeper. Now I know. He kidnapped a woman and was doing stuff to her. Really bad stuff. But the old man killed her. Why? He could have saved her, let her go. Instead he killed her."

"He was protecting Jason, his son," he decides. Billy shakes his head. "No. He hates Jason. That is obvious. So why?"

The sound of Lauren playing with the dog drifts across to him. He watches them for a moment.

"To protect them," Billy decides. "And their mom, Cassie, and the old woman. Anderson too. He will do anything to protect them. He doesn't like me. Does he see me as a threat?"

He turns to look at the traffic.

"I haven't seen the white van in days. They are still out there. If William finds out, he'll kill me to get rid of the white van people."

Tears burn at his eyes and he wipes them away roughly with an angry motion.

"I'm not safe here with them. I'm not safe without them. I'm not safe anywhere."

David is sitting alone a little distance from the others. He takes a sip of his soda, looking off at nothing. He is thinking moodily about being made to stay behind with the women and children while Jason and William did the job.

A small voice whispers in David's mind. A voice only he can hear. Distant. A little girl's voice.

David closes his eyes, willing his ears to block it out, but the voice is inside his head. It continues whispering its unwanted words.

He kidnapped your mother and murdered her. He kept you and your sister. You grew up in terror of him. You ran away to live on the streets; just another street rat, just like the one he brought with him. Is he your replacement? Is Billy supposed to be you? Is he really you?

"Get out of my head," David growls, looking around quickly to make sure no one heard. The voice is persistent.

He has a new son. He does not need you David. He is going to kill you now.

"Shut up Cassie," David keeps the angry growl quiet. "Get out of my head!"

As if hearing him from across the lot where she is talking to Sophie, Cassie turns and looks at him.

28   Games

Lauren and Ethan are sitting at the little table in the motel room with three disposable paper cups and a small single-cup coffee carafe half-filled with a transparent golden liquid. They have changed hotels yet again and the kids are getting frustrated with the constant bouncing from hotel to motel.

The motel room door opens and Cassie walks in. She looks at the two kids, pauses, and goes pale.

Her eyes lock on the kids at the table. The small coffee carafe and the little paper water cups. Next to the carafe is an open box of tea. The string from a tea bag hangs from the mouth of the carafe and she can see the tea bag soaking in the puke yellow liquid.

Chamomile tea.

Sophie's suitcase is open and rummaged through. Koda is laying quietly chewing a bone on one of the beds.

The words are on her tongue. Where is Billy? She sees him before she can speak.

Billy is sprawled motionlessly on the floor, face down and head turned to rest on one cheek as though he fell and did not move again.

Lauren and Ethan are sitting at the table looking up at her with half smiles.

Cassie almost screams, clamping her hands hard over her mouth to stop. She rushes forward, filling with panic.

"Don't drink it!" Her voice is shrill as she leaps at the kids sitting at the little table. She swipes the paper cups up, juggling them and almost dropping them, grabbing the carafe.

She hurries to the bathroom, dumping the contents down the sink. She drops the carafe and it hits the floor with a dull crack and shatters.

"No," she moans.

Cassie rushes to kneel next to Billy, shaking him. He is limp and unresponsive.

"No, no, no." She is panicked.

Cassie hurries to the door and runs out, banging on the next door. It is taking too long to open. No one is there.

"Sophie! Sophie!" She bangs again, her face twisting with anguish.

"What's wrong?"

Cassie turns to find Sophie standing behind her with grocery bags. Her mind freezes in panic, the words there, but she is unable to utter them. She points to the open door.

"Tea. Chamom-." It is all she manages to get out.

Sophie looks at the open door and goes in, looking at the kids at the table, the boy on the floor, and her open ransacked suitcase.

Cassie stumbles in after her, tears in her eyes.

"They got into the Chamomile tea." Her voice is choked.

Cassie rushes to Billy, falling to the floor next to him and trying to shake him, slapping his cheek.

"Billy, Billy." She looks up at Sophie. "Help me. Do something. The tea…"

"Get up. Game's over," Sophie says, calmly moving to the small beaten desk and putting the grocery bags down. "And clean up your mess."

Cassie's eyes widen.

Billy's face twists into a grimace he can't hold back anymore. He starts laughing. He laughs so hard he rolls onto his side, clutching his stomach.

"Wow, you said she would think I was poisoned and you were right," he manages through his laughs.

Ethan joins him, doubling over with laughter.

Cassie looks from one boy to the other. She looks at Lauren. Stunned, it takes a moment for it to sink in that Billy is fine. Tears sting Cassie's eyes and her heart is still pounding, her chest filled with the lingering anguish of finding the boy dead on the floor, poisoned.

Lauren is sitting there, small and full of innocence and sweetness, like she has no idea what just happened.

"We were just having a tea party," Lauren says.

"Don't play with Cassie like that. She does not find it funny," Sophie says. There is no anger in her voice. She holds back the smile, keeping her expression mildly stern.

Cassie's mouth drops open. "You were playing me?"

She looks at Sophie, incredulous.

"They know about the tea? They were playing a joke on me?"

"Of course they know," Sophie says. "You don't think I would have something like that in my house and not tell them. They could be accidentally poisoned."

Behind Cassie's back, a small slow sly smile spreads across Lauren's lips.

"What's special about that tea anyway?" Billy asks.

"Never you mind. Just don't drink it," Sophie says.

"All right, clean this up and pack your things," Sophie says. "We are moving again."

"Again?" all three kids moan in unison.

"Yes, but the next place we are going to stay in for a little while."

"Yay!" they cheer. The dog barks approval with their cheer.

29   Investigating Grant Cormer

Lawrence arrives at a small town two hours from anything of significant size. He pulls into a diagonal parking spot on the street and turns the car off, looking around.

"Where in a small town do you find people old enough to remember a man who vanished fifty-nine years ago?"

The town looks pretty much how he envisioned the town the McAllister Farm sits near would have looked when William McAllister and his family still lived there; before it grew into a small city. The buildings are old, many appearing to have been built at the turn of the century and long overdue to be torn down and re-built. It feels the same size too.

"The old farmers hung out at the hardware store."

Spotting the hardware store, Lawrence gets out and makes his way up the street to it. He enters and looks around. The elderly clerk looks at him curiously, but makes no effort to offer to help him.

Taking a cursory look around, Lawrence leaves. He walks along the street, taking in the buildings, until he spots a legion.

"Old veterans," he says quietly, a grin that looks almost predatory in his pleasure creasing his lips.

He changes course, heading for the legion.

Relative darkness engulfs him when the door closes behind him, leaving him standing there letting his eyes adjust. The dim lighting, well-worn ambience, and few scattered grizzled patrons inside are reminiscent of Peabody's pub.

Lawrence sits at the bar between two old men who look like they have been there for a while.

"Good afternoon, what can I get you?" the man behind the bar asks the stranger who somewhat resembles a buzzard.

"Draft, whatever you have on tap," Lawrence says.

He waits for his first sip of beer, hoping to create a sense of camaraderie in his two seat-mates, before seeking answers.

"You lived here your whole lives?" Lawrence asks.

One old man just grunts.

"Not many leave this town and fewer move here," the other says.

"Do you remember anything about a man who lived here that vanished fifty-nine years ago?"

"Cormer," the old man who answered nods. "That was a while ago. Why are you asking about that now?"

"I'm investigating his disappearance."

"You a cop or something?"

"No. I'm investigating for the family," Lawrence lies. It's only a partial lie, so he hopes it rings true enough.

"You are lying," the old man says. "Judith would not have hired no investigator."

"The other family," Lawrence tries again.

The old man shakes his head, looking at him suspiciously. The silent one only drinks his beer.

"There is no other family. The only family left lives right here."

Not to be undone by this old man, Lawrence tries again.

"Not Cormer's family, the other family."

"What other family?" The old man's suspicion is growing, but now Lawrence has piqued his curiosity.

Lawrence turns his full focus on him with a feigned look of incredulity.

"You didn't know?"

"Know what?"

"Mr. Grant Cormer is not the only one who went missing. The family of one of the other victims has not given up hope. But, to investigate their missing loved one, I need to investigate the disappearances of them all. There is strong evidence the disappearances are tied to each other."

The old man's eyes widen. He bit Lawrence's lure.

"How many? Who are they?"

"I am afraid I cannot divulge the other names at this time, but there are three that we know of. So far."

The old man is nodding now.

"Everyone knows about Cormer."

"According to the report his wife filed, Grant Cormer just went to work one day and never came home," Lawrence says.

"Sounds about right," the old man says.

"Do you have any idea why? Were there rumors about why he might have vanished?"

"It's a small town. There's always rumors. Doesn't make any of them right."

"Right you are."

Lawrence turns his attention on the other old man. He looks older and more grizzled than the other.

It's usually the silent ones who have the most to say, Lawrence thinks. This fellow would have been just a kid when Grant Cormer vanished, maybe in his teens. But this old man would have been older. He probably knows things the other one doesn't.

"He doesn't talk much, does he?" Lawrence says to the room, talking loud enough to try to draw him into the conversation.

"He doesn't like strangers," the talkative old man says.

The man behind the bar nods agreement with the observation as he serves all three another drink without being asked.

The older man on Lawrence's left has already finished his beer, the other one on his right is not far behind. Lawrence looks down at his own, surprised to see how much he drank without realizing.

"Nobody knows why Cormer never came home," the old man on his right says. "Mistress, maybe. Some say he probably had an accident and someday they are likely to find his car down some ravine off the road. Nowadays everyone thinks serial killer every time a person just vanishes like that. They say he went to work, put in a full day as if nothing was going on, and just never came home."

"Who is Judith? When I said I was investigating for the family, you said Judith wouldn't have hired an investigator."

"Judith is his daughter; all that is left of Grant Cormer's family."

"The report his wife filed said they didn't have any kids," Lawrence says.

"I don't know about that," the old man says. All I know is Judith is his and Mary Cormer's daughter."

"Why would Mary Cormer tell the police they don't have a daughter?" Lawrence rolls the probabilities around in his head.

"She didn't know she was pregnant," he says.

"Mary told folks she found out after she went to the hospital for shock," the old man on his left says.

Lawrence looks at him, almost in shock he finally spoke.

"Grant Cormer was forty-seven when he vanished. Was his wife much younger than him?"

The old man on his left shakes his head.

"Mary Cormer was infertile. Wasn't supposed to be able to get pregnant. Grant and Mary learned to live with it and be happy childless. Though, I don't think Mary was ever really happy not being able to have kids."

"Yes, I remember some of that now," the old man on his right says. "My mother always said she didn't know why the Cormers didn't just adopt, since Mary couldn't have kids of her own."

Lawrence focuses on the old man on his left again.

"Mary said she found out after she went to the hospital for shock," Lawrence repeats back what he said. "You don't sound like you believe it."

The old man shrugs. "All I know is Mary couldn't have kids. Her husband vanishes, and then she's got a baby."

"Do you think he left her?" Lawrence asks.

"Maybe it was his kid, maybe it wasn't. Maybe he had an accident. I don't think he left her."

Lawrence considers the possibilities.

"There is no reason to lie if they adopted. Do you think she was having an affair? Maybe it was Grant who was infertile?"

The man on his right is nodding. "No man wants to let on he's shooting blanks. Could be he had her lie and say it was her that was the problem."

The old man on Lawrence's left is shaking his head.

"You don't think it's her baby," Lawrence surmises.

"All I'm saying," the old man on his left says, "is she was forty-six years old. She went away and come back with a baby." He shakes his head.

"It's not impossible for a woman to get pregnant at forty-six," Lawrence says.

"There was some talk," the old man says.

"What kind of talk?"

"People saw a car hanging around watching the Cormer place. When people don't know what a thing is about, they make up their own stories. Grant Cormer vanishes. Mary has a breakdown and goes away for a time. The car is gone."

"Then Mary comes back with a baby," Lawrence finishes. "You think the car watching them has something to do with it."

"Grant Cormer often went away on business, leaving Mary alone, but she was no home wrecker."

"His old man was in love with Mary," the old man to Lawrence's right chimes in. "That old buzzard," he indicates the other old man, "had to watch his mother suffer knowing her husband was in love with another woman."

Lawrence looks at him and back to the old man on his left.

"Yeah, the old man was in love with Mary. But she wouldn't have him. Might have been mutual too, but she was married to Grant Cormer. Mary wasn't the sort of woman to fool around."

"So you think Grant had an affair? A younger woman maybe? And for some reason she left Mary to raise her baby?"

The old man shakes his head.

"Grant Cormer wasn't the mess around sort either. Kept to himself mostly. Didn't want anyone in his business. Didn't like rumors. Keep to yourself he would say and mind no other man's business. Didn't like attention on him and Mary either. He wouldn't let no one take his photograph even."

Lawrence's senses jangle with a feeling of déjà vu.

"Do you know what kind of vehicle was watching the Cormers?"

"A white van."

The jangling of his senses ups a notch.

"Does Judith live in their house?" Lawrence asks. "Did it sell over the years? Do you know who lives there now?"

"No. The old Cormer place is abandoned now. Mary Cormer wasn't so good at keeping the place up after she got old. Then she had the first stroke and couldn't do the little bit she could before anymore. The second stroke put her in a care home. Mary and Judith weren't on good terms and Mary refused to let the house be sold. Judith wouldn't even visit Mary after they argued about that."

The old man snuffs out a sardonic breath through his nose.

"I never would have taken Mary for the sort that would hold on to an old house just because. Not as the sentimental type either. But for some reason, she just refused to let that house go. It's sat pretty much abandoned since she went in the care home. Even after she passed, Judith never bothered trying to fix it up and sell it."

"One would almost think she had something there to hide," he adds quietly after a pause.

"You two gents have been a huge help," Lawrence says. "Next round is on me." He motions to the man behind the bar, putting money down.

He serves them and they drink the next glass while discussing small town politics. Lawrence finishes his and turns to them.

"Where did you say the old Comer place was? I have the address from the file, but it I couldn't find it on the map."

"That's because they don't bother putting every small town road on those travelers' maps," the old man on his right says.

"I can't believe you got old Frank here talking to you," he says.

Old Frank just scowls at that.

"Head north," he continues. Turn left at the gas station. You'll find the street."

"Thank you," Lawrence says and leaves.

He starts out driving the wrong way, taking a short tour of the main streets of the town, exploring it to get a feel of the place.

When he passes the Legion again, Lawrence follows the old man's directions, eventually finding the street.

Lawrence half expects to see the scene from the old photos from the other file as he drives up the street looking for the house; standing living trees and the remains of long rotting fallen trees and a dried brook, the rocks laid bare to the world. He sees none of that.

The house itself is impossible to miss. It is the only house that looks abandoned. Unlike the house in the photo, the grimy front window does not sport a crack.

Lawrence pulls into the driveway and gets out, looking at the homes up and down the street.

His initial assessment was right. It is a short road off a street in what was an average middle class working family neighborhood back when Grant and Mary Cormer lived there. Now it is an older neighborhood with small and tidy affordable homes, still maintaining the middle class lifestyle at below middle class incomes.

A car drives past, slowing for the driver to get a good look at the stranger standing in front of the old Cormer place.

Lawrence walks to the front door and tries it. The door is locked. He walks around, trying the back door. The door is not locked.

He smiles. The trust of small town people. The smile falters.

"An unlocked abandoned house in a town with limited activities to entertain the teenagers. This place is going to be destroyed."

Opening the door, he walks in and stops. Amazingly, the kids have not touched the place. The small home is tidy except for decades of dust coating everything, cobwebs, and the inevitable littering of dead insects long agro dried to empty husks where they fell.

He walks further, wincing internally at the faint sound of one of those insect corpses crunching beneath his shoe, sounding too loud in the silence of the house.

Lawrence moves cautiously through the house, the floorboards occasionally groaning beneath his weight, exploring every room.

Upstairs, he looks past the age-stained curtain and grimy glass out a bedroom window to the front street.

He has an urge to duck back when an indistinct white van drives into sight, slowly passing the house.

His head is swelling and slowly thickening, stuffed with something foreign as if it is filling with cotton. The pressure intensifies. It turns to water, too heavy, freezing to ice, sending blinding hot agony through the center of his head.

His head falls and he closes his eyes, cringing at the pain.

Lawrence looks out and the van is gone before it could have finished its drive by past the house.

He is stuck in place, powerless to move, to control his body. He feels like a scarecrow, hollowed out and stuffed with sawdust and straw, his skin pulled too tight, overstuffed to the point he might burst.

Distant voices come on the silence filling the house. Almost too quiet to hear, the words almost impossible to make out. He can make out the tone though. A woman and man are arguing.

"I don't care," the woman is saying. "I don't want the baby."

"I got it for you," the man pleads, "to make you happy. I did it for you."

"Tell them no."

"They already have the baby. There is no going back. I can't have them get a baby and just give it back."

"That is someone else's baby!" There are tears in her voice. "Someone else is going to forever mourn the loss of their baby, just like I mourned ours since the miscarriage."

"That was years ago. You never let it go, Mary. But now you can. You can have a baby."

"It's not my baby! It's stolen from someone else! Make them give the baby back!"

"That's not how it works Mary. Shush, lower your voice. They are watching the house."

"Try. You have to try. Tell them to just give the baby back."

All right, I'll try. I will speak to Wallace. I have to go away for a few days next week for meetings with some of my people. He should have an answer for me after that."

"I hate the people you deal with. I wish you could just quit. I hate what they do, those Mr. Millers and the others. I shudder to think such people can live in this world. I don't even want a baby anymore knowing … knowing no one is truly safe."

"You are safe. The baby will be safe if we take it, him or her. We are above the touch of the Millers of the world."

"And the people who dispose of their mess for them," she says.

"Yes."

"I won't have that baby. But Grant, don't let them kill the baby."

"Anderson," the name is but a breath exhaled on the air; an impression that is not voiced.

The vision loses its grip on Lawrence, leaving him weak and drained.

"I feel like Death himself just touched my soul," Lawrence mumbles. He staggers forward, pacing the house and walking it off.

Feeling more himself, he starts methodically searching for evidence that might give a clue as to why Grant Cormer vanished without a trace fifty-nine years ago.

30   Regional Manager

"You aren't playing games with me, are you?" Jim growls.

"Absolutely not," Rick says. "Look at me. Do you think I have time to play games? Everything you think you know about the world is wrong. I've seen things you would never believe."

"We've been sitting here for two days. Who is this guy we are waiting for again?"

They are parked on a street with a lot of rundown buildings, many of them closed, a few permanently boarded up. One of the few open is a car wash a few buildings up the street from them.

"Anderson. Think of him as a supervisor. You have a guy on the road doing a job, he has to check in every once in a while. Get instructions; make sure everything is running okay."

"And this supervisor, he is going to show us how to find the McAllisters?" Jim is doubtful.

"Not knowingly," Rick says.

"How is he going to help us find them then?"

"His guys check in with him. The supervisors check in with theirs; let's call them a regional manager. From what I gathered, today is the day this guy checks in with his boss. We just have to follow him, find out where his regional manager meets with the supervisors under him. We stake it out and wait for an old man to show up, your Mr. Richard Andrews."

"And if Richard Andrews never shows up?"

Rick shrugs. "We are back to square one. Maybe we follow them all and see who each supervisor meets with."

"This supervisor has a name?" Jim asks.

"Not a name; a title. None of these people have a name. The victims, that's the package. Not even a person, just a package." Rick's disgust at the dehumanization of the victims is clear in his scowl.

"The killers are all Mr. Miller. Why? I don't know. I guess any name is as good as any other. It's nondescript, a safe sounding name, easily forgotten."

"And the regional manager?"

"Wallace."

"Wallace? That's one of the names Lawrence gave me to have Beth check out."

Rick's face drops into a mask of surprised concern.

"Where did he get that name?"

"He heard it staking someone out."

"Does he know how dangerous this is? Jesus, he's just a reporter."

"An investigative reporter who's gotten himself into more than his share of dangerous situations," Jim corrects him. "He's careful."

"He better be. Let's hope they didn't see him. If they did, then he's already dead. Did he give you any other names?"

"Graham."

"Doesn't ring a bell. Let me call my cook."

"He's more than a cook, isn't he?"

Rick just winks in response.

He dials, giving the cook from the diner the name. Just as he is hanging up, a car shows up, pulling into the car wash.

"That's the first customer they've had since we started watching the place," Jim says.

"That's him," Rick says, "Wallace. Now we watch and see who shows up to see him."

"We are almost there," Anderson says. "This is our last rest stop. After this we are at a safe house. It's too far to walk to anything."

He glances in the rear view mirror and Kathy has the unsettling feeling that last comment was for her.

He pulls into the rest stop and they get out. William pulls in behind them. They have changed the vehicles again.

Everyone wanders off, some to the washroom facilities, the kids and dog racing to burn off their pent up energy, and the four older people slowly hobbling the pain and stiffness out of their joints.

Kathy finds herself alone. She looks around. There are no other vehicles on the highway and nowhere to flag one down without being seen. She wanders around the corner of the building and finds herself staring at a pay phone. It fills her entire world.

I could call my mother. We won't be here long. We'd be long gone before anyone traced the call. And if they do find us... maybe I can go home.

Kathy looks around quickly, steps closer, and leans into the wall next to the phone as though it might hide her.

Her hand shaking, she picks up the receiver and puts it to her ear.

She is greeted by silence.

Kathy joggles the receiver cradle, wincing at the quiet sound it makes. Her ear is still met by silence. The phone is dead.

Her face twists into a mask of pain, her eyes and the edge of her nostrils redden, and she closes her eyes tight to fight the tears.

Opening her eyes and feeling like she does not have control of the pain filling her, Kathy gently replaces the receiver.

She stands there for a moment longer, trying to compose herself.

Kathy turns and freezes, staring in mute shock and fear at David.

"What are you doing?" David asks. His eyes move from her to the pay phone and back.

Part 5
A New Farm

31   Setting Up House

"This is it," Anderson says. The car and van are parked side by side so close the mirrors almost touch. The front windows are open so the occupants can talk without shouting between the vehicles.

They have pulled to a stop in the road. Up a long driveway reminiscent of the McAllister farm left behind so many years ago, a quaint farm house sits back from the road with a few acres of frontage.

This house is not as small or as old as the McAllister farm. It does have an old shed out back, visible beyond the house, and borders on the woods to one side and behind and fields to the other side.

A chill runs through Kathy as she stares out the window at it. The house, the barn, even a small gardening shed to one side; the fields and woods beyond, it all reminds her of the other farm.

She pictures the little room with the free standing storage cabinet, the trap door in the floor in the middle of the room, and a rope ladder beneath that door vanishing into the darkness of a dirt floor root cellar. She can even see the scratches in the floor around the trap door from an unknown number of victims digging their nails in as they scrabble to climb in or out of that cold dank root cellar.

Nausea suddenly lurches in her stomach. She feels like she is swimming in unreality.

Cassie stares at the farm with her own feelings of dread, all too aware of David's presence.

She remembers ghostly images of him; his face, his voice, his hand holding hers. Disconnected foggy memories of those brief moments she swam from nothingness towards the light above in the darkness of the abyss. The blinding antiseptic whiteness that she now knows was the hospital room where he kept watch over her.

Vague and disjointed memories of her escape from the hospital and a man putting her in a car.

Cassie remembers seeing Kathy for the first time. It took some time for her appearance to burn through the fog of the drug induced fugue state she was still coming out of. The petite woman who looked very sick and drawn, dirty tangled hair, and her dress and visible skin smudged and dirty. Her eyes staring blankly back at her, hollowed by trauma. Kathy looked near death there in that farm house where she had been kept prisoner.

Cassie remembers sitting in a chair in a haze of fuzz while David grilled her on the memory she does not have of their past; his sudden lunge at her. His hands around her throat, tightening, squeezing and choking off her air, painfully crushing her windpipe.

She remembers frantically clawing at those hands, his face, anything; thrashing and kicking at him, her still drug groggy body too weak and uncoordinated to fight back effectively.

Things were less clear after that, her air restricted and her attempts to fight back feeble.

Cassie remembers being yanked forward off the chair, helpless to do anything while he held her up, screaming at her.

"You are not her," he yelled, repeating the words in a mantra of words pouring out strung together in one endless rage-filled sound. "You are not her, not her, Youarenothernothernothernother."

Despite her mind growing dim from lack of oxygen, still in a fog from the drugs in her system, she had a strange clarity about that moment.

She fought frantically, his grip on her throat making it hard to breathe, her weakened body refusing to listen. She could do nothing when he dragged her across the room, throwing her down on the floor, screaming at her, his voice a frothing rage.

The blind fury in his eyes terrified her.

Cassie is not sure which came first, that he grabbed her again, shaking her, raging, yelling while she kicked at him, scrambling across the floor, trying to escape; or the frantic screaming coming from somewhere below.

Kathy's screams; choked with tears, desperate, pleading. Screams that eventually seeped through his violent rage, making him falter; his attack slowing and finally stopping.

That rage-filled terrifying mask swims before her now, twisted in abject misery and devastating loss. Cassie closes her eyes against it, but it does not help. The image is burned into her memory.

Cassie remembers being led down a hall, stumbling as she is dragged along and confused that he stopped killing her. She sees these images and more every time she looks at David.

She had watched him, feeling far away and numb as he pulled back the bolt and opened the trap door, releasing the frantic screams from below to fill the room with their deafening shrillness. She saw him wince as if someone struck a painful blow against him when the full force of those screams was released.

Cassie watched numbly as if from someplace else when he hooked the rope ladder on and dropped it down the dark hole, the darkness greedily devouring the rope.

He looked at her then and she saw pain, loss, and confusion in his eyes; eyes that begged forgiveness and understanding; eyes that only a moment ago were blinded with violent rage.

Cassie remembers the violent tremors that came over her as she looked down and wondered if the rope was still there in the blackness below. She trembled so violently she could barely control her limbs.

Knowing what was expected of her, she had looked at him, pleading silently. He only motioned again to the blackness below.

She approached the yawning opening cautiously, the frantic screams from below making her more afraid to go down.

He motioned again and she hesitantly got down on all fours, grasping the rope ladder and swinging a leg over the edge, feeling for the sagging braided rung. Ever so slowly she climbed down the rope ladder into the darkness below.

Cassie pushes away the dark memories that haunted her dreams every night since she escaped the farm. Memories that are rushing through her now larger than life as she sits on the cusp of setting foot on a farm that so eerily resembles the place she barely escaped alive.

Connie did not escape alive, she thinks. David caught her and shook her like a god damned dog shakes a rabbit. He killed her right there in front of me.

With a large effort of will, Cassie forces herself to push all thoughts out of her head. She feels weak and nauseas, her head swimming and filled with pain and fear.

Each of them is faced with their own inner demons as they look at the farm; each facing their own memories of the McAllister Farm.

Except the three kids and Mrs. Rose Bheals, who never set foot on that infamous farm.

"Did you have to find a farm that looks so much like that damned farm we left behind?" William complains, breaking everyone's reveries in the car.

Anderson does not look at anyone.

"I had no idea what the place would look like. Let's go. Like it or not, this is home for now."

They turn into the driveway, the passengers staring in uneasy silence at the approaching buildings.

"Damn, it even has the god damned hen house and goat pen," William growls when the small outbuildings come into view.

He glares at Anderson, even though he knows it was not intentional. The place brings back his own dark memories of the McAllister farm. Memories William would prefer to forget.

"Let's get unloaded," Anderson says, getting out and going to the back of the van, opening the tailgate.

The others get out, relieved to be free from the confines of the vehicles.

Ethan and Lauren immediately start running around, burning off pent up energy, the dog racing around them barking.

Billy stands a little distance away from everyone else scanning the area. He takes note of the places to hide, escape routes, and where he might get a good vantage point of anyone coming and going.

Rose gets out of the car with a little difficulty. She limps a few steps and stops. She watches the bags being unpacked for a moment and limps forward again, intent on getting her bag herself.

"I'm going to have trouble walking for days," she says, her breath wheezing a little with the pain and effort.

She starts bending over with difficulty to pick up her bag, Anderson handing it to her before she gets far. Taking the bag, Rose starts limping for the house.

"Why don't you take it easy," Jason says. He extends his hand, offering to help her walk. "Let me help you."

She waves him off. "I have never taken it easy and I am not about to start now," she says, stubbornly making her way towards the house without accepting his help.

Sophie is unpacking her things in the upstairs bedroom she now has to share with Cassie due to the extra people. Along with her clothes, she puts away her teas into the dresser drawers.

Cassie comes in with her suitcase, dropping it on the bed.

"You aren't putting those in the kitchen?"

Sophie stops, looking at the tea box in her hand.

"There are so many of us now, I wasn't sure that would be the right thing to do."

"If we are staying here for a while, shouldn't everyone else know about the code and the risks?" Cassie says.

Sophie frowns at the tea.

"You're right. If anything happens, they all need to know what to do. I'm just worried about what will happen if anyone forgets to not drink the Chamomile."

Cassie studies her for a moment.

Sophie puts the teas on top of the dresser.

"You are worried about your mom and Rose."

"We should all be worried about Rose. We don't know anything about her, her background. She is just some old woman Dad felt sorry for in the seniors' home and took along with Mom. He should have left her there."

They hear a sound in the hallway and pause, listening. They quickly identify Rose's shuffling footsteps.

Sophie and Cassie exchange a wary look.

Rose grunts and they hear her breath hissing like she has a slight wheeze. The hallway linen closet door opens and closes.

"Just looking for some towels," Rose says from the hallway, knowing by their sudden silence they know she is there.

They see her shadow on the wall lumbering as she turns. It vanishes with her shuffling footsteps retreating back to the stairs.

Her huffing breaths reveal her descent back down the stairs.

"Was she spying on us?" Cassie whispers.

"Or maybe she was just looking for towels." Sophie's tone suggests she believes the old woman was spying on them.

Sophie looks at Cassie. "Maybe we should make sure she is someplace else while I explain the teas."

"How will you make sure she doesn't drink the Chamomile?"

"I will have to think of something."

Supper is ready and Kathy, Cassie, and Sophie are in the kitchen setting the table for supper. The kids are hanging around, hungry and impatient.

The others are starting to file in for supper, chatting and helping set the table and put the food out with family dinnertime banter.

Billy watches. It feels unreal to him, the casual familiarity between people who do not all know each other, those that do having not seen each other for years, and seemingly oblivious to the invisible ugly weight of the truth that envelopes them all.

Sophie passes a look to Cassie, a silent signal.

Cassie nods almost undiscernibly and moves to intercept Rose.

"Rose, can you come help me with something in the other room?"

"With what?" Rose asks. "We have everything we need here."

Cassie gives her a sly wink that looks forced. She is not very good at being covert. She leans in.

"It's a surprise," she whispers in her ear.

A lover of surprises, Rose grins and winces, glancing at the others quickly, worried they might have noticed. She gives Cassie a sly wink back. She lets Cassie lead her out of the kitchen.

"What is the surprise?" she whispers when they leave the room.

"We made a special dessert," Cassie whispers. "But we ran out of time. It needs to be put together."

Rose hunches her shoulders in eagerness, thrilled to be part of the surprise.

In the kitchen, Sophie turns to the others, waving them over.

"Everyone, please listen."

She looks at Billy, debating sending him out, and deciding after the kids' trick on Cassie there is no point. He already knows.

She glances after Cassie and Rose, hoping they are out of earshot.

"I need to discuss something important."

She looks to each of them, making sure she has their attention.

Sophie turns to the counter, turning back with boxes of teas.

She sets them down on the table, one at a time, looking at the group staring at her.

"We need to discuss teas."

Kathy looks skeptical.

David smirks like it's a joke.

Jason almost laughs at Sophie's serious expression.

"You have always been so serious Sophie," he says.

"This is serious." Sophie gives him a level look.

She turns her attention back on the group.

"Our father raised us to always be careful. Never bring attention on yourself was one of his favorite sayings."

"I feel like this is my wake," William mutters under his breath.

Sophie gives him a look.

"We need a warning system," she says. "This is a system Cassie and I used. And before she came to live with us, this is a system the kids and I used."

She picks up the first box of tea, putting it on the table separate from the others.

"First, remember the code phrase is tea biscuits."

David snickers and she gives him a withering look.

"Tea biscuits is code for this is real. If someone says tea biscuits you had better be paying attention, because whatever tea was mentioned is what is really going on. Do not," she looks to each of them meaningfully, "use the words tea biscuits unless you mean it."

"But I like tea biscuits," David complains. "What if I just want tea biscuits?"

"Don't be an ass. Call them something else," Sophie says. "Nobody uses the term tea biscuits anymore. Call them sweet biscuits, soup biscuits, or just say you want a damned biscuit."

She taps the green tea box on the table.

"Green tea. Green for go. Green means safe. You talk about green tea and you are letting everyone know it is safe."

She takes another box, putting it next to the green tea.

"Orange Peko. Think amber light. Amber alert. Amber, orange, means caution. Be aware. Be on alert. We are not safe or we don't know if we are."

She sets the Earl Grey next to the Orange Peko.

"Black tea means run. If someone uses a reference to black tea and tea biscuits you drop whatever it is you are doing and you run. Just run. Don't think, don't question. Run. We will sort out finding everyone after."

Sophie holds the last box for a moment, hesitating to put it down. She puts it down.

"Chamomile. The Chamomile tea is special. Never ever drink the Chamomile. Chamomile is death."

She looks around at each and every one of them.

"If I say Chamomile and tea biscuits, you make the Chamomile, and that is the only time you will ever make the Chamomile tea. But only the intended target drinks it. I say it again, Chamomile is death. The Chamomile tea is poisoned. The Chamomile is for making problems go away."

Billy stares at her, stunned.

I thought they were just playing that it was poisoned. It really is? He thinks, feeling like the world just got a little less real, and a whole lot more real at the same time.

I can make this all go away with Chamomile tea, Kathy thinks.

At that moment Rose and Cassie come in.

Cassie gives Sophie an apologetic look that says, "I tried."

Sophie looks at the old woman, alarmed.

Rose sees the stunned looks of everyone directed at her and Sophie's almost panicked look.

She waves them all off, shaking her head and chuckling.

"It's okay. I know all about your teas and your little codes."

Sophie gapes at her. The others stare in stunned surprise.

Rose starts chuckling and it escalates into a full laugh.

"You people really are not very good at keeping secrets," she cackles. "It's not very easy to avoid hearing things in close quarters."

She looks at the mixed expressions on the faces gawking at her.

"Don't worry. I'm not going to tell anybody. Do you really think I want them to find me and put me back in that damned home?" She shakes her head. "I'm all in on whatever it is you people are up to. A co-conspirator, you can call me. I even have my disguise."

Rose pulls her blond wig out of her bag, plunking it on her head.

They just keep gaping at her in stunned shock, her disheveled wig sitting crookedly on her head making her appearance comical.

"And if anyone in my family does happen to find us and come around, you can feel free to steep them a nice big pot of that Chamomile tea."

She starts laughing again, unable to stop it cackling out, her laugh devolving to a wheezing guffaw.

"Hell, I'll drink it myself before I'll go back to that bloody Bayburry Street Geriatric Home," she mutters under her breath.

Lauren breaks first. Her shock turns into an uncontrollable grin. Looking around at the serious faces, she tries covering her mouth. She cannot stop her own laughter from bubbling up.

Sophie gives her a quick severe look.

Anderson gives William a "What did you do," look, still blaming him for bringing this woman along when he felt they should have left her behind at the nursing home.

"Let's just eat," Sophie says.

"If we are going to stay here for any length of time, we are going to need a plan," Sophie says.

"What are you thinking?" Cassie asks.

"We have to fit in. We can't have the people in the area looking at us curiously and wondering what is going on."

"How do we do that?" Cassie asks.

"We start with enrolling the kids in school," Sophie says.

Billy gapes at her, his mouth dropping open.

"That is too risky," Jason says, looking at Billy with a look bordering on panic.

"Nonsense," Marjory says, coming to Sophie's defense.

"How would they get to school?" Jason asks. "David and I are not supposed to be seen by anyone. Everyone knows my face; Kathy and Cassie too. All four of us have been all over the news."

"You grew up on a farm," Marjory says. "We managed. They will take the school bus, just like you did."

"They are just kids," Jason complains. "What if they talk?"

"He kept Cassie and me on the farm. Didn't let anyone see us or know we were there," David says, arguing Jason's side.

"Kids need an education and to be around other kids," Sophie says. "Where did you get yours? Are you saying my bother home schooled you?"

David looks away.

"That's what I thought," Sophie says. "My kids are going to school and so is Billy."

"How will we register him?" Jason asks.

"I am already working on that," Anderson says. "I pick up a birth certificate for him in two days."

"What name do I get?" Billy asks, suddenly interested.

Jason turns to Anderson, curious what he would come up with.

"Since you are already with us and it's a common enough surname, I made you part of the family. Benjamin William McAllister."

Billy makes a face, wincing at the name Benjamin.

"Apparently you don't like your first name, so you choose to go by your middle name or Billy for short."

William scowls. "This stray has my name," he grumbles under his breath. "You expect us to keep him?"

"It's too late for that William," Anderson says. "He's been with your son too long. The assumption would be there that he already knows too much, whether he does or not."

Billy gives Anderson an alarmed look.

"There is no going back for this kid. If we cut him loose, he's dead."

William shakes his head, unhappy with the situation.

Billy looks even more alarmed. He looks from Anderson to William to Jason.

"It's okay kid," Jason says quietly. "It means you can stay."

What if I don't want to? Billy thinks, the strain of the moment filling him up inside like a sticky sickness. What if I make a run for it? It's past time I move on. I can't be stuck staying with these people forever.

"We are on a farm," Sophie says, bringing them back to the discussion. "It only makes sense we farm it. We have good acres of pasture for cattle. If we don't farm while we are here, that will make people in the area start asking questions."

"I'm too old for this," William mutters, shaking his head again.

"Are you seriously thinking about this?" David gapes at them.

32   Rose Bheals

Rose is in the kitchen humming to herself. The boxes of tea are lined up on the table before her. She pulls a cell phone from her jacket pocket, looking around quickly to make sure no one is coming, and turns it on. She starts searching online.

Kathy walks into the kitchen and stops, staring at her in surprise.

The feeling of being watched makes Rose look up. She flushes guiltily, almost hiding the phone, and decides it doesn't matter.

"Anderson said no phones," Kathy says. "They can track us."

Rose gives her a cautious look.

"You aren't going to tell on me, are you?"

Kathy slips into one of the chairs with a sigh.

"No, I'm not going to tell."

She stares at the phone. I *could call my mother,* she thinks.

"What are you doing with it?" she asks. "Where did you get it?"

"While we were shopping for our disguises; it wasn't hard to slip away from Jason long enough to get a quick phone set up."

"I thought you didn't have any money. You came straight from that nursing home."

"I have my sources." Rose winks.

"Are you looking for your family?"

"Yes, but it's not what you think."

"They all say that," Kathy says with a small sad smile.

Rose chuckles. She looks at Kathy levelly.

"You and me are both here by accident, aren't we?"

Kathy nods. "Something like that."

Rose lowers her voice, leaning towards her and whispering.

"I don't think they will let us go. I think these people are not who they seem to be. I have the feeling they've done bad things and are on the run from the police."

It's so much bigger than that, Kathy thinks.

"What do you think they are?" she asks carefully.

Rose looks to make sure no one is coming or listening in.

"I think they are killers. I heard Marjory say things that made no sense in the home. She's smart that one, but I think the Alzheimer's has her in its grip. Sometimes she's confused, and sometimes she's only pretending to be. But, she's let things slip. I think that's why she was there. There are others in that home, like her. They keep them heavily sedated so they can't think. So they can't talk.

There are people there who don't belong, who have nothing wrong with them. It's a place to hide them so they aren't a bother anymore, to get them out of the way for one reason or another."

"Is that why you were there?" Kathy asks. "You don't seem like there is anything wrong with your mind. So, why were you locked in a facility for people suffering dementia?"

"My family put me there to get me out of the way. They wanted to shut me up and get rid of me. Murder is illegal. Locking someone up in one of those places and drugging them stupid isn't."

She looks intently at Kathy.

"Don't ever let anyone put you in one of those places. It's horrible, the way they treat you there. They don't treat you right. They abuse the patients, don't always feed them, and deny them water. And when they are so drugged into oblivion that they soil themselves, they don't clean them up. They just leave them to fester in their own mess."

Her eyes have a faraway hollow look.

"Why do you want to find your family if they put you in there and abandoned you to that?" Kathy asks.

"To make them pay."

Rose picks up the box of green tea and gives Kathy a wicked grin.

"The secret is in the teas."

She sets it down, moving the Orange Peko next to it, lines up the Earl Grey, and finally picks up the Chamomile and just stares at it.

Rose glances at Kathy, looking back at the Chamomile.

"You can make all your problems go away with the Chamomile."

Kathy looks at her in confusion.

"What problem do you think I would make go away?"

"Him." Rose gives her a sly wink. "I know you want to escape," she whispers.

She turns her attention back on the tea.

"When I find my family I think I will steep them a nice pot of tea with some fresh baked tea biscuits while we discuss why they locked me up in that shithole so they can steal everything I own."

Cassie walks into the kitchen and stops; staring at the two women sitting at the table with the teas.

Rose and Kathy both turn to look at her, Kathy's face flushing with embarrassment at being caught. Rose slips the phone out of sight into her sweater pocket.

"What are you doing?" Cassie asks, her eyes going to the Chamomile tea in Rose's hand with a flash of panic.

She steps forward, taking the tea. "You weren't going to drink this, were you?"

"It's okay, pet," Rose says, standing up and patting Cassie's hand. "I killed my husband once too." She winks at her, turns, and walks away, leaving Cassie and Kathy staring after her gape-mouthed and stunned.

Sophie is just walking into the kitchen and Rose gives her a meaningful look for Cassie's benefit as she passes her.

"She thinks Sophie killed her husband?" Cassie says quietly, shocked.

Kathy gives her a quick look.

"Why are all the teas out?" Sophie asks, looking at the boxes lined up and the one in Cassie's hand.

Just out of sight down the basement stairs where he just managed to scurry as Rose entered the kitchen, Billy is pressed against the wall listening.

The teabag gripped in his palm feels larger than life. His hand is getting clammy with sweat and he quickly lets it dangle by the string, afraid the sweat will make the tea leach into the skin of his palm.

Stepping carefully to not make the stairs groan; Billy retreats to the darkness of the basement to wait for the chance to go back upstairs unseen.

33   Old Ghosts

Lawrence has been at the old Cormer house for two days, sleeping in his car outside. When he isn't sleeping in his car he is slowly and methodically searching the house and yard. When he is not doing that, he is slowly walking or standing staring at nothing, trying to get a sense of the life that once lived within these walls.

He has disjointed glimpses of the broken ghost of a baby's memories. This is one of those moments.

Lawrence is standing outside. A car slows as it drives by, the driver studying him, and speeds up again.

Spastic flashes of infantile memories stutter. Insane.

"No one really knows what goes on in an infant's head," Lawrence muses. "If they think kids are not rational, the irrational insanity of an infant would shock them. It takes years to learn sanity."

Lawrence focuses on the breeze, feeling it. Nothing comes to him.

"This isn't getting me anywhere. It's time to visit Judith Cormer."

He packs up his things and leaves.

It doesn't take long to get to Judith's tidy little house.

Lawrence parks in front, studying the house for long minutes before getting out and going to the door.

He is ringing the doorbell for the third time before a woman answers. She would be pretty if not for the hollow haunted look to her eyes and unhappy downturn of her mouth into a permanent frown that suggests she does not have a pleasant side.

Lawrence looks at her hopefully.

"Miss Judith Cormer?"

"Yes, what do you want?"

He offers his hand for a handshake and she only looks down at it for a second, fixing her attention on reading his face.

"I am Lawrence Hawkworth. I am here on behalf of a family investigating the disappearance of their loved one in the area fifty-nine years ago."

"What does this have to do with me?" she asks suspiciously.

"That is close to the time your mother filed a missing persons report on your father, Grant Cormer."

"I was a baby," Judith says. "What do you think I would know about it?"

"It's a small town. People talk. They would talk for years about something like this."

"Then why haven't I heard about anyone else disappearing in the area?"

"The disappearance I'm investigating wasn't a local man. No one in the area would have even known. My investigation led me here to this town. He was passing through and never made it to his destination. You don't know about anything unusual at all around the time your father vanished? There is nothing your mother might have said over the years?"

Judith's face turns into an ugly scowl at the mention of her mother.

"All I know is my father left me with a mother who did not want me and she never hesitated to let me know that."

"She did not want you and she told you that?"

"She didn't tell me. Not to my face. But I would overhear her complaining to herself, complaining that my dad left me with her. That she never asked for me."

She looks at Lawrence, her expression less angry.

"I don't think she was even my real mother."

"What do you mean?"

"I think my father had an affair and brought me home."

"Did your mother or anyone else ever say he had affairs?"

"No. If anything they all thought my dad was a bloody saint. It's just a feeling I got."

"Your mom adopted you then?"

"Not so much. Not legally. I think whoever my real mother was; she did not want anyone to know. I don't know how they did it, but my birth certificate says that Mary and Grant Cormer are my biological parents."

"You don't believe it."

"He might be, but not her. I always felt it."

"What do you think happened to your father?"

"I don't know. Maybe he got sick of my mother and left us. She never forgave him for leaving her alone, but she never said he left. It was just her mourning. She was convinced something happened to him."

"Do you think he had an accident?"

"Maybe. It's possible. If he did, they never found him."

"You never took over the house. Why? Was it in that bad of a shape?"

"I don't really know. Maybe a part of me thought living there would make me crazy too."

"Crazy? How do you mean?"

"My mother was paranoid. She kept secrets hidden. Cryptic little notes. Every time she saw a white van she would go crazy moving and re-hiding them all."

Lawrence feels a sudden thrill rush through him.

"Do you remember where she hid them?"

"Sure. The old shed. Not in it, but under it. She'd pull out rocks and dead plants she kept shoved in to hide the hole. The back corner of the vegetable garden. She stopped using that one when she saw a man standing out there over the spot one day. In the basement rafters behind the furnace. There was even a spot behind the wall inside the bottom cupboard next to the stove."

"Do you think whatever she was hiding is why she would not sell the house?"

"Hell yes. And they were nothing. Really. Just cryptic little notes on paper."

"You looked?"

"I did. I had to know what was so important. I thought it might give me a clue what happened to my father." She sniffs. "It was just my mother being crazy."

"You mentioned a white van."

"She had an irrational fear of white vans."

"Did she ever say anything about the white vans?"

"Only that they were watching." Judith's expression changes. She looks at him curiously.

"You think there is something to it," she says intuitively. "You think there really was something going on, that the white vans had something to do with my father's disappearance."

"No, but it appears your mother did."

"You are lying," Judith says. "What happened to my father? Did the white van people have something to do with it?"

Her words ring far away in Lawrence's head, hollow and echoing. The white van people. He breaks the spell, shaking his head.

"I don't know yet, but I plan to find out."

The look in her eyes sends a sudden chill through him. Lawrence regrets his words as a warning jangles in his gut.

"I doubt it means anything," he tries to recover.

"You are lying again."

"Thank you Judith. I have to go. I have a few other people to talk to before I leave town."

"Are you going back to my mother's house?"

"No," he lies, turning and leaving.

She watches him go.

Lawrence glances back after he gets into his car. In her expression he sees that she does not believe him.

"Are you really Judith Cormer?" he asks.

Anderson drives into the farmyard and parks. The dog appears, letting out a few gruffs but approaching him with his tail wagging slowly.

"Dog," William says to him, getting out of the passenger seat and having to walk around the dog.

"Let's go break the news to them," Anderson says.

They go in the house to find Sophie, Cassie and the kids in the kitchen.

"It's all set up," Anderson says. "The kids are enrolled. The school bus will pick them up in the yard tomorrow morning."

"So soon?" Ethan complains with a look of horror on his face.

Lauren grins and claps her hands with a little excited jump.

Billy does his best to keep his face passive and fails. The idea of going to school terrifies him.

I haven't been to school for so long, he thinks. I don't even know what to do. I won't know anything.

Another thought sends a darker chill of fear through him. *There is a record of you in school. They will find me.*

Jason and David come into the house.

"Did we miss a meeting?" Jason asks, joking.

"No. We're just telling the kids they start school tomorrow," Sophie says.

David looks around.

"Where is Kathy?"

"Kathy is hiding in her room again," Ethan says. "She's been doing a lot of that."

David just gives him a look and leaves in search of Kathy.

William leaves the kitchen to find Marjory. Going upstairs, he opens their bedroom door and stops, staring.

"Marjory, what are you doing?"

Marjory turns to him, wringing her hands anxiously. Her eyes have a vaguely lost look.

"William will be home soon. I need to tidy up."

"Oh Marjory," William says softly.

On the bed behind Marjory is every piece of clothing they have carefully laid out flat edge against the next piece. The small spaces missed have unfolded socks laid carefully to fill them. There is not a stitch of the bedcover visible. On the floor are her two shoes carefully lined up with the insoles pulled out and lined up next to them.

William looks at her bare feet, her toes knobbed with age.

Marjory hasn't a shred of clothing on.

His eyes go to her nervously wringing hands again. She is not just wringing them anxiously, she is holding something too.

Marjory looks down at her hands, realizing he is looking at them, and quickly puts them behind her back like a small child trying to hide something.

"What do you have there Marjory?"

"Nothing."

She pushes whatever it is further behind her.

"Let me see Marjory."

William walks to her.

Marjory tries to hide it better, but he still takes it from her hand.

A cloth handkerchief is rolled up.

Laying it in his hand, William carefully unfolds it to reveal what is inside.

It is a small bird skull, clean of any flesh or feathers.

She must have found it on the ground, he thinks.

Lawrence goes back to the old Cormer house. He sits outside, looking at the house before getting out of the car.

"I guess I'll start in the back."

Walking around to the back, he goes to the old shed. The structure has a lean that makes him nervous about digging around its foundation.

He walks around the shed, studying it, opens the door, and looks in. Among the other tools, old cobwebs, and a scattering of dried leaves, are a couple of rusty shovels, their wooden handles cracking and splintering with age. The wood floor is soft under his weight as he steps in to take one of the shovels.

Lawrence moves around the shed, using the shovel to test for holes around its foundation. It doesn't take him long before the end pokes into a soft spot. Shoveling what he can, he scoops out some detritus of rotting leaves and what appears to be some sort of old nest along with a few loose rocks.

With a grimace of distaste, he has to resort to getting down on his knees and scooping out more with his bare hands. It turns out his large paws make good scoops and with just a few Lawrence has uncovered a hole large enough to fit his arm into.

Bending low to the ground, Lawrence peers into the darkness beneath the shed. "This is the part I don't like."

Holding his breath, he sticks his hand in, feeling around. Something small and hairy scurries over his hand, making Lawrence almost jerk it out. Forcing himself to ignore it, he presses on, leaning in to reach deeper.

Lawrence's questing fingers touch something. Touching it delicately, he feels around, working his fingers over it and grasps it. He pulls it out.

Standing up, he studies the old baking tin. The design is older than he remembers ever seeing in a store or in old advertisements. Much of the paint is rusted off.

He pries the lid off with some difficulty, and looks inside.

Inside is a torn piece of age-yellowed paper. He pulls it out.

The faded ink is barely discernible. It is a series of four groups of letters and numbers. Lawrence smiles.

"Was Mary Cormer so paranoid she kept notes in code?"

Shoving the paper back into the tin and closing the lid he moves on to the vegetable garden.

"Which back corner?"

Using the shovel, Lawrence starts digging in one back corner, then tries the other. After some digging, the shovel hits something with a dull clunk. He jabs the ground again and hears nothing. A third time rewards him with another dull clunk.

Digging it out, Lawrence is rewarded with another rust-eaten metal tin. This time it's an old coffee can.

"How old is this thing?" He turns it over to examine what little of the original paint is still intact. "Must be at a hundred years old."

He pries off the lid to find another torn piece of paper.

Lawrence pulls it out and studies it. The ink is faded like the other. The handwriting is clearly different.

"MM" is followed by three two digit numbers. Below that are numbers that appear to be a date.

"Fifty-nine years ago." Lawrence tries to picture the missing person report. "Is this the last day his wife saw him?"

He moves on to the inside of the house.

Starting in the kitchen, Lawrence gets down on all fours and opens the bottom cupboard next to the stove. Pulling the pots and pans out, his fingers leaving marks in the sticky dust coating them, he sets them on the floor. He runs his hands along the walls, looking for the hole that must be behind the wall.

Finding none, he pulls out his phone, using its lit screen as a poor imitation of a flashlight. The light reveals the line between the flat boards making up the wall in the back of the cupboard.

He reaches in, running his palm over it and trying to push on it at different angles. It shifts under his questing hand.

"Got you."

He pushes it again and it dips in on one side, the other pushing out. Pulling the loose board out, he stares into the whole behind it. Inside is an old small metal tea canister.

Lawrence pulls it out, looking it over, and pops the top off. Like the others, it has a single yellowed piece of paper. He studies it.

The faded ink handwriting is similar to the one under the shed. It is a different series of four groups of letters and numbers similar to the first.

He moves on to the basement. Stopping in the basement doorway the little late day light now coming in through the windows casts his shadow spilling down the dark staircase to be absorbed into the darkness below.

He pulls out his phone and awkwardly searches its buttons.

"Humph, I was told there was a button that turns this thing into a flashlight."

The screen lights up with his fumbling. Accidentally pressing the icon on the screen, the screen goes dark with what appears to be a switch. Lawrence looks at it, shrugs, and slides his finger over it. The flash comes on, lighting the wall.

He shrugs. "I guess that's it."

Using his phone as a flashlight in the darker basement, Lawrence descends into the darkness. The basement is unfurnished and sparsely filled with the old items that inevitably find their way to the basement. He finds the furnace without too much trouble.

Lawrence looks around for something to stand on, finding an old kitchen chair. Using it to give him added height; he reaches up, feeling around in the rafters behind the furnace.

He pulls out a small metal child's lunchbox. Opening it, he finds a trove of little torn slips of paper, all with varying groups of digits and letters in the same handwriting as the other two.

Lawrence stares down at the little box filled with slips of paper.

"Who wrote the one in the corner of the garden? Is it the man Judith said was standing there one day? What do they mean?"

He brings the lunch box upstairs, stopping in the living room.

Lawrence looks up at movement in his peripheral vision. He watches a white van drive by the house outside, going much too slowly. It speeds up once it is past.

34   The Farm

"What is this Marjory?" William asks, looking from the little bird skull to her eyes.

Marjory looks down, shifting uncomfortably.

"Look at me Marjory," he says gently.

She wrings her hands in agitation and he puts his free hand on them to still them.

Marjory meets his eyes hesitantly.

"Jason-," she starts, blinking tears away.

"What about Jason?" William tenses.

She looks at him imploringly.

"Amy Dodds," she manages, choking on the name. "Jason . . . he . . . he . . ." She stops, swallowing. "It was him."

She looks at the tiny bird skull he is holding in the open handkerchief.

Marjory looks ill, a gray pallor washing through her with the chill sweat and nausea of intense emotional strain.

"That's her toe. He kept a souvenir. He's sick, William. There is something very wrong inside Jason. He keeps souvenirs of them."

William feels like all the breath in his body has been sucked out, like he just got kicked in the stomach by a horse.

"William, we have to destroy it before the sheriff comes to search the house. It's only a matter of time before Rick Dalton comes to search the farm. The whole town thinks you killed those girls. They all think you are guilty and he does too. We can't let them find it. We have to protect Jason."

William feels weak like he has never felt in his life. Helpless. The world feels tilted and off.

Marjory, he thinks sickly. She knew. All these years she knew about Jason and Amy Dodds and never said anything.

The tiny bird skull in the handkerchief suddenly has the weight of a lifetime of worrying over his family's safety.

If she found Amy's toe, what did she do with it? She would have tried to destroy it. The wood stove? Did she succeed? If she didn't . . . if Rick Dalton found it . . . the sheriff would never let it rest. Dalton would spend the rest of his life hunting us down.

"Marjory put some clothes on. I'll go destroy this."

William walks out stiffly to find Anderson.

Sophie comes into the house looking anxious. She sees Rose sitting in the living room.

"Have you seen Lauren?"

"Not since first thing this morning," Rose says.

"Where did you see her?"

"She was in the kitchen having breakfast."

Marjory is coming down the stairs.

Sophie turns her attention on Marjory.

"Mom, have you seen Lauren?"

Marjory's eyes are a little clouded with confusion, but she seems to come out of it quickly.

"I sent the children outside to play," Marjory says.

"When? How long ago?" Sophie asks.

Confusion starts clouding Marjory's eyes again. She gets a little flustered.

"It's okay Mom. Was it this morning? After lunch?"

"I think after lunch." Marjory looks down, clutching her hands to keep from wringing them.

Sophie turns and hurries upstairs. She goes to the bedrooms, finding Ethan.

"Ethan, have you seen your sister?"

He looks up from the toys he is playing with, shaking his head.

"Your grandmother says she sent you two out to play after lunch. Where did Lauren go after that?"

Ethan looks at her with a confused expression.

"Did you two go out to play?"

He shakes his head.

"Grandma didn't tell you to go play outside?"

"That was yesterday." He resumes playing with his toys.

Frowning, Sophie hurries out, checking the other bedrooms. They are empty.

She searches the rest of the house, not finding Lauren. She ends in the kitchen, where Cassie has started preparing supper.

"Cassie, I can't find Lauren. Have you seen her?"

"Not since breakfast," Cassie says. "William told her to collect more eggs. Sometimes she hides when she has to collect them because of that one chicken that bites her. Have you tried her new hiding spot?"

"Another new one? Where is it?"

"Behind the fallen tree behind the barn."

Sophie nods, hurrying out to find the fallen tree. She walks purposely across the back yard, past the barn to the edge of the woods behind it.

She searches the woods with her eyes, seeing no sign of life other than the trees and a pair of squirrels chasing each other. One pauses long enough to chitter down at her angrily before resuming their game.

Picking her way through the growth that has not been cleaned up in decades, Sophie makes her way to where the fallen tree lays behind the barn out of sight from the house.

It takes a few minutes to find the tree. It had fallen, its roots likely weakened, in some storm long past, dying and slowly turning soft with rot. Large bushy branches stick up as though pleading with those around to lift their fallen brethren, the remaining leaves dry and brittle and brown. With the growth around it, the tree and bushes make a formidable fort for a child.

She walks around it, seeing no way past the tangled branches.

"She is not behind it, but is there any way in underneath?"

Sophie studies the back of the fallen tree and spots a possible way in. She goes to it, trying to see inside.

"Wow, if someone was looking for her and didn't know about this, they would never find her."

"Lauren," she calls.

There is no response.

She calls again, twice more, before getting down on all fours and crawling in. It is not an easy fit for an adult. If she were any larger she would not have been able to squeeze through.

There is no little girl hiding inside the fallen tree fort.

Sophie sits there for a moment, a surge of worry filing her, before she crawls back out again.

In the barn, she finds Anderson and William tinkering with an old tractor.

"Have you seen Lauren?"

"Not since I sent her to fetch some eggs this morning," William says.

"You can't find her?" Anderson asks.

Sophie shakes her head. "No one has seen her since just after breakfast. I looked everywhere."

Seeing how worried she is, William stars wiping the grease off his hands with a rag. "Have you asked everyone?"

"No. I haven't seen Kathy, David, Jason, or Billy yet."

"She's probably with Billy," Anderson says.

"I'm not sure I like the idea of those two being gone alone somewhere for hours," Sophie says. "He is too old to want to play with a girl her age. He's been spending too much time with her."

"What are you thinking?" William asks.

Sophie does not meet his eyes. "The boy is a runaway. Who knows where he's been, what he's done." She leaves off there.

William nods understanding.

"You think he did something to her," Anderson says. "You have been in this business too long. The kid is a runaway, but I'm not so sure he would hurt her. He doesn't seem like a bad kid once you look past the aloofness and always looking for an escape route."

"I still don't feel comfortable with it," Sophie says. Her lips press into a grim line. "If he hurt her . . .."

"Let's go looking," William says.

"If we find the others, I am sure one of them will know where she is," Anderson says. "She's probably with one or more of them."

They leave the barn, pausing before they split up.

Sophie looks at them.

"I haven't seen Koda either. I haven't heard a bark from him."

William nods.

"The dog is probably with Lauren. The McAllister dogs always seem more attached to the little girls in the family. Call the dog while you search. If he comes pay attention to where he's coming from. If he barks, follow it. I always said the dog was the best chance at finding a missing McAllister girl."

He turns away before he can see Sophie's look.

Her look is dark, clouded with memories of the past.

The McAllister dogs don't live very long either, she thinks. Zeke, who Dad put down after he saved Mom from the rabid raccoon. Boomer, who Dad was going to put down after he was injured saving me from the coyotes. He didn't last long after we had to abandon the farm. Max, she swallows, forcing the darker part of this last memory out of her mind. They had gotten Max later. That one too was injured, that time saving her from another kind of predator.

"Dad."

Sophie's voice stops him. The tremor of worry and pain in it. He does not turn around to look at her. William does not want to see the pain he knows is in her eyes.

"If you see him, no matter what, please don't put Koda down. If it has to be done, I will look after it myself." Sophie tries to sound strong and firm, but she cannot escape that waver in her voice.

William nods and walks on.

They each go their separate ways in search of David and Kathy, Jason and Billy, the missing girl, Lauren, and Koda.

Anderson goes East, past the yard towards the open fields. He sees a lone figure on the road in the distance.

He stops, shielding his eyes from the sun with his hand to try to get a better look.

"Adult," he mutters. He starts the low slow walk of the aged, detouring to the driveway to get one of the vehicles.

"These old legs aren't what they used to be," he says.

Getting in, he drives out to the dirt road, the windows rolled down. As he gets closer, the figure walking towards him in the road grows clearer to his age ruined eyes. It is Kathy.

When he finally reaches her, he stops.

"Kathy, where is David?" Anderson asks.

Worry tugs at Kathy's stomach.

Why are they looking for him? She can't help the doubt that creeps in. Did he do something? She pushes it away. No, they are just keeping tabs on where everyone is. Anderson is probably going to scold me like a child for going for a walk. But, I needed fresh air. I needed to get out of there, to be alone to think.

She is about to say he is back at the farm, but realizes. They would not be driving around looking for him if they didn't already look.

"I don't know," she says quietly, feeling the burn of guilt for betraying him. She tries to tell herself that telling the truth is not a betrayal. Not when he is not doing anything wrong.

"I thought maybe he went for a walk," she adds, shrugging to show how harmless such an act is.

Anderson's expression barely changes, showing only in the slight narrowing of his eyes and slightly harder line of his mouth.

"Have you seen Lauren since this morning?" Anderson asks.

"No."

"Get in. Sophie can't find Lauren. We need everyone accounted for and to plan a search if she isn't found by then."

Her brow furrowing in worry, Kathy gets in.

"You did not see David on your walk?" Anderson asks.

"No."

"He didn't say where he was going?"

She shakes her head. "He never said he was leaving."

Anderson drives on, planning to turn around up ahead.

"Keep your eyes peeled for anyone on the road, field, or along the trees."

Taking the other vehicle, William goes West on the road. The road does not go far in that direction before it winds towards the highway. That side of the farm is all bush for miles. The lack of neighbors is what made the location appealing.

Now, with a missing little girl, the forest is a threat.

William scowls, his jaw working and his eyes hardening as he drives, watching the ditch and the tree line for any signs of life.

The only thing he sees is a cow that does not belong roaming loose.

"Where could they have gone?" Sophie wracks her mind, trying to think. There are limited places to go.

She wanders the edges of the yard where the shorter grass butts against the longer grass of the field and the forest.

"Koda!" she calls. "Lauren!"

She keeps calling, cupping her hands to her mouth to make the sound travel further. There are no answering calls or barks.

Sophie is walking along the tree line when she notices a break in the brush, a deer trail.

"Maybe they went for a nature hike?"

She remembers her own tendencies as a little girl to go roaming into the trees beyond where she was allowed to go. A chill slithers down her spine with the memory that surges up of finding herself face to face with what was a very large coyote to her.

More afraid for Lauren, Sophie picks up speed, moving down the deer trail away from the farmyard. The further she goes, the more worry fills her. She keeps calling Lauren and Koda.

Some distance down the deer trail, Sophie finally hears voices ahead. She picks up speed, jogging down the path and then breaking into a run, and finally comes on them.

Jason and Billy look at her, surprised to see her and even more surprised by her out of breath red-faced appearance.

Sophie gasps to catch her breath.

"Where is Lauren?" she asks between panted breaths.

"She isn't at the farm?" Jason asks, looking confused.

Sophie shakes her head, still trying to catch her breath.

"No. We can't find her. Have you seen David and Kathy?"

"I saw Kathy earlier. I didn't see David," Jason says.

"I haven't seen them," Billy says, alarmed by her worried look.

"Maybe they are together," Jason suggests.

"Maybe," Sophie says, "but I won't relax until I find Lauren."

"Where have you checked?"

"The house, the yard, the barn. Dad and Anderson took the cars to search along the road. I checked her new hiding place in the trees behind the barn."

"We'll come back with you to help look for her," Jason says.

The three of them head back down the trail to the farmyard.

Off the path and hidden by dense trees and bushes, they don't see the partially collapsed old shed, larger than the usual hen house but smaller than a barn, as they pass it.

They arrive at the yard to see that Anderson and William are back.

Sophie jogs over to them. "Did you find her?"

"No," Anderson says, looking past her to see Jason and Billy following her.

Sophie looks at Kathy. "Did you find David?"

"Kathy thinks he went for a walk," Anderson says.

"Has anyone checked the house?" Jason asks, joining the group. "Maybe she came back."

Sophie nods, jogging to the house. She runs through the house calling Lauren, finding Cassie still in the kitchen preparing supper. Rose is there helping her.

"Has Lauren come back? Have you seen her?"

"No." Cassie shakes her head, feeling worried now too. "What about the others?"

The others are filing into the house through the back door off the kitchen.

"Everyone is accounted for except David," Sophie says.

Kathy's cheeks feel the flush of the burn of embarrassment.

I should have said something sooner about him being gone, she thinks. If anything happened, they will blame him. They will blame me by association.

They are all talking over each other with their theories of where the little girl could have gone.

"Maybe she went exploring in the woods. You used to do that all the time as a little girl," Jason says. "Mom was always sending me out to find you."

Cassie has shut off the dinner by now.

"We have to find her before dark," William says.

"She doesn't know the area," Sophie says miserably. "She knows better than to be out wandering the woods alone. She wasn't allowed to do that at home and she was familiar with that area."

Tears are beginning to burn at her eyes with worry over Lauren.

"Get some paper," Anderson orders. "We will draw a sketch of the area and set up a search pattern."

Ethan is on it and quickly produces some sheets of drawing paper and pencils.

With the help of the others adding in every detail they can remember, Anderson draws up a quick sketch of the area. They start with the farmyard and it's out buildings down to the smallest shed and the larger barn on the other side of the narrow strip of brush before it thickens into a forest. They sketch in the roads, service roads, what is farm field, fields left to go wild, and what they can remember of the woods surrounding the farmyard.

They add in the little brook running though the pasture to one side, and mark where they remember there being culverts a little girl might hide in.

"There," Jason points to the page, "an old barn rotting in the bush."

Anderson pencils it in.

"Don't forget her new hiding spot," Ethan says, pointing to the area of the fallen tree behind the barn."

They examine the map, satisfied that everything they know of is there.

Anderson splits them into search grids.

"Sophie, you and Ethan search this area. Cassie, you take this section. Jason, you have this area. Kathy, you are in this section. William and I will take these two areas. We can drive them. Billy, you search here."

"What about us?" Rose says, disappointed to not be given a search area.

Anderson glances quickly at William. He had not intended on giving the two elderly women search areas.

William looks at Marjory.

She is looking down at the map with a worried look.

"Marjory had a lot of practice finding Sophie when she used to hide and roam off into the woods. I can't think of anyone better to search all the buildings. If there is anywhere in any of them for a little girl to hide, Marjory will find it."

Anderson nods.

"Marjory and Rose, you have the house and outbuildings in the yard. Look for anything, anyplace, she could be hiding."

Satisfied, Rose smiles and nods.

"Search your area and then we all meet back here to reassess. With luck we will have found Lauren. If not," he hesitates, "we will discuss expanding the search area."

"Koda is probably with her," Sophie says. "No one has seen him. So call them both and listen for any barking too."

They all set out to their search areas, moving through them and yelling Lauren and Koda's names as they search for any places they could be hiding. The afternoon wanes on and the sun begins its slow descent in the West.

Billy is the first to finish, returning to find the farmyard empty. He jogs to the house, going room to room, and finding no one.

He steps out the front door, staring off across the yard to the road beyond.

"Maybe she had the same idea. Maybe she made a break for it. No. Little girls don't just run away for no reason."

He stares off into the distance.

"I could go now. Run. I would probably get away. Everyone is busy looking for Lauren."

He takes the stairs down, going a few steps towards freedom. Billy stops and looks back.

"What if something happened to her?" He frowns, thinking.

Looking disheveled, Marjory and Rose are hobbling across the yard on their old lady legs, looking like they find walking difficult.

I can outrun them easily. The thought comes unbidden to Billy.

Sophie comes around the corner, her eyes and face filled with worry, Ethan tagging along.

She looks hopeful the moment she sees Billy and it sends a strange feeling surging through him. Almost a sense of belonging, but it is a foreign feeling for him. Billy never felt like he belonged.

"Did you find her?" Sophie calls out before she can get close enough for conversation.

Billy shakes his head. "No," he calls back.

Sophie's look falls, caving into a crestfallen worry.

Billy looks up at the gathering dusk. He starts for her, joining her at the side of the house.

Across the back, Kathy and Cassie are returning from different points. Jason appears from another direction, crossing the yard to them. The same question is on everyone's lips.

"Did you find Lauren?"

"No." The answer is uniform and they all look at each other with a growing sense of unease.

"That leaves Anderson and William," Cassie says hopefully. "They aren't back yet. Is that a good sign or bad?"

Just then one of the vehicles turns in, coming up the long drive towards them. Anderson pulls to a stop, looking at the group.

"No Lauren?" he asks.

"No." Sophie is growing more worried.

"That just leaves you, Dad," she says quietly.

Ten minutes later William returns. He pulls in, parking next to the other vehicle, his face hardening as he studies the group."

"No one found her?" he asks as he gets out.

Sophie pushes back the tears suddenly burning at her eyes. Her chest is filling with the tightness of fear and loss.

"No one has seen David either?" Anderson asks.

They all respond in the negative.

Billy is a few paces away, looking at the ground feeling that tension a boy will get when he feels like he is going to get it for doing something very bad, but has no idea what he actually did wrong.

Everyone is discussing options to expand the search.

He looks at them, looks away, and stiffens.

I have to tell them, he decides. It could be nothing. I could just be making trouble for nothing and that will have everyone mad at me. But what if. . .?

Billy approaches the group, clearing his throat and trying to make his voice not quaver.

"Um, I have to tell you something," he says. No one is paying attention. They did not hear him. He moves closer, raising his voice.

"I have to tell you something."

Sophie looks at him, alarm bells ringing in her nerves at the anxious edge to his voice.

Everyone else is still talking.

Billy meets her eyes and she does not like what she sees in his.

"Hush," Sophie says sharply.

Silencing them with a look, she turns to Billy. "Billy, what is it?"

Billy swallows the lump in his throat, unsure if his voice will work. He feels put on the spot with everyone looking at him now and just wants to vanish.

They stare at him expectantly, waiting for him to speak.

Sophie nods at him, urging him on.

"It's about David," Billy finally manages.

Kathy's knees feel suddenly weak at the fear in his face and voice.

Cassie glances at Kathy, noticing the change in her. *What does she know?* she wonders.

"Go on," Anderson urges, his voice level with a deadly calm.

Ethan looks at Billy with a look bordering on both amusement and panic.

Billy glances at him. You know, the thought directed at Ethan is accusatory. You know and you didn't say anything. She's your sister. This is your family. I'm a stranger to them, an outsider. No one wants the outsider butting into their family business.

Billy looks at Anderson and then at Sophie's worried face. She looks stiff, like she is ready to wail in despair or attack anyone who messed with one of her children, whichever the situation calls for.

"David has been acting kind of," Billy hesitates, "weird."

"Weird how?" Anderson asks.

"I thought it was just some dumb game at first. You know, the kind of thing where someone thinks they are being funny, but no one else finds it funny."

Sophie moves closer. Her hands are fists. She is almost standing over him.

Billy looks at Cassie sheepishly, almost apologetically. He avoids looking at Kathy.

"He keeps calling Lauren Cassie," he says.

Cassie blinks in confusion, looking quickly at Kathy. She looks just in time to see all the color drain from Kathy's face.

Kathy blanches, feeling sick. The icy shock of sweat drenches her, making her feel clammy.

"Kathy, what is going on?" Sophie asks.

She shakes her head. "Nothing. I- it could be just a game," she lies.

Billy looks at her, unsure if anyone will believe him now.

Jason's eyes widen almost imperceptibly and he stiffens.

"Billy," his eyes are on Billy, taking in every nuance of his body language.

Billy turns to him, his eyes flashing with the fear of a boy about to be called out on a lie. Only it is not a lie. But they have no reason to believe him. He forces the words out.

"David keeps calling her Cassie. He talks to her like that's her name. I thought he was just playing at first, but then I didn't think it was a game anymore. It's like he thinks she is someone else."

He looks at Sophie, his eyes begging her to believe him.

"I think there is something wrong with him" Billy says quietly. "In here." He points to his head.

Sophie looks past him, glancing at her father's shocked expression, and moving on to meet Jason's eyes.

"What do you know?" she asks, directing the question at Jason.

Jason looks at Kathy. "Tell them Kathy."

Kathy looks away, mute. She can't. Tears come to her eyes and she rubs them away.

Jason meets their looks, Sophie, William, and Anderson's. Marjory is wringing her hands again and Rose seems preoccupied.

"David never got over what happened when they were kids." He glances at Cassie and looks back at them all. "This is not the time or place to talk about it. Not here. Not in front of everyone, the kids. After . . . what happened, David ran away. I tried to find him, to keep tabs on him, but he would always run again. There is something very dark inside David. He gets. . . angry."

"What does this have to do with Lauren?" Sophie demands, staring at him. "Do you think he got angry at her?"

"No." Jason shakes his head. "But he can't let go. After. . . what happened. We lost Cassie. He could never let go of what happened, of what he did. He could never let go of losing his sister. A big brother is supposed to protect his little sister, keep her safe."

Emotions well in Jason, his own failure to protect Sophie all those years ago reflected in David's failure to protect Cassie. Only David's failure was so very much worse.

"He could not let go of searching for Cassie."

It's Cassie's turn now to pale, the color washing from her as a weakness seeps into her, making her feel weak and woozy. She wants to ask what David did to her, but can't make her mouth form the words.

"He talks to her when she is not there," Kathy finally says, her voice so quiet they almost did not hear her speak.

All heads turn to her, all eyes staring at her.

Kathy does not like being in the spotlight. Now she feels trapped into speaking. Her voice cracks.

"David talks to Cassie when there is no one there. He thinks I don't notice."

"He is talking to the ghost of the little sister he lost," Jason finishes for her.

"When did this start?" Anderson asks, leaning forward, grim and serious.

"That day at the prison," Kathy says quietly, "when he visited Jason after the trial. The day we went on the run. That's the first time I noticed it."

William's jaw is working, his eyes beady and hard with anger.

Marjory keeps looking at him. Her hands go together automatically, wringing each other.

Jason pales, looking around at them.

"Ethan, go in the house," Sophie says, her voice deadpan and her eyes hollow.

Ethan opens his mouth to object, but the look on his mother's face frightens him. He turns and runs to the house.

Jason motions Billy to go.

Casting a petulant look at him, Billy moves off, walking as slowly as he thinks he can get away with and trying to listen as he goes. He does not make it out of earshot before he hears Jason's ragged voice.

This is not good, Billy thinks, the moment he hears that heavy desperate tone of voice, before he even hears what Jason has to say.

"I think Lauren is in real danger of him harming her," Jason says. "Just like he did Cassie when he almost killed her when she was little."

Jason looks at them frantically. "We have to find them now."

Sophie's face fills with the loss of a thousand mothers; fear, anguish, and an anger that has no limit.

William's reaction is an explosion of furious rage. He shakes his fists, his face twisting into a frightening scowl, as he turns without direction.

"That bastard, if he touched. . . if he. . .," he growls in frustration at his aged limbs and failure to be there in the moment David took his granddaughter. "I am going to put him down," he snarls.

The barking of a dog followed by the sound of a little girl's voice is carried on the wind. They all turn to see first Koda come bounding out of the deer trail, and then Lauren and David walking out.

Billy turns to look, having not quite reached the house, feeling the burn of shame in his cheeks.

They'll all think I made it up now, even though what Kathy and Jason said supports my point.

Relief floods through Sophie and she runs to meet Lauren.

"Lauren, where have you been?"

Lauren is uncertain, wondering why everyone looks like they should be crying.

"We went for a walk," Lauren says. "David wanted to show me a special place he found."

Sophie scoops her up, glaring at David over her daughter's head; a look warning him to stay away from her daughter.

Kathy turns away. She can't look at David, feeling like she just betrayed him again.

David looks at them in confusion.

"Why are you all looking at me like that?"

William is on the balls of his feet, filled with the explosive urge to tear David apart with his bare hands.

"It's Jason's problem to deal with," Anderson mutters a warning to William.

Marjory puts a hand on William's arm, looking up at him.

"William," she says. "The boy means well."

He looks at her, patting her hand. "Let's go inside, Marjory."

He gives Jason a baleful look as they go.

"Do what you have to or I will," he mutters quietly to Jason as they pass him.

The others are heading inside and leaving them alone.

David looks at Jason innocently. "What's with them?"

"You don't just take someone's kid somewhere without telling them," Jason says, his voice as angry and cold as his face. "We've all been searching for her."

"I'm sorry, I didn't think. . .."

"No, you didn't." Jason gives him a hard stare.

David opens his mouth to speak. He almost says it, catching himself and correcting it the moment he starts uttering the first sound.

"Ca-Lauren is safe with me. I would never hurt her." He blinks at Jason, unnerved by his own mistake.

"Like you would never hurt Cassie, your own sister," Jason says, his voice so low it is almost inaudible.

David looks at him, unsure if he heard right.

"Tell Sophie I'm sorry. I won't do it again."

"Tell her yourself." Jason walks away, leaving David alone in the early evening gloom.

David follows him inside where they have begun warming the supper they abandoned.

The hostility in the room is thick.

Sophie gives David a cold hard look, feeling a surge of violence towards the man who had them searching for her daughter, who had her terrified something bad happened to her, and who she now suspects even more may be a danger to her daughter's safety.

Unsure what is going on, Lauren looks at her mother's angry face, feels the rage flowing from her, and looks guiltily at David.

I did something bad, didn't I? Lauren thinks. I don't know what I did bad, but everyone is mad at David. He didn't do anything. He just wanted to show me the special place. I knew I shouldn't go. Now David is in trouble because of me.

"Sophie," David starts. "I am sorry. I didn't mean anything."

"You took my daughter without telling anyone."

David takes a step towards Lauren.

"I wouldn't hurt her, if that's what you think. You don't know me, but I wouldn't. Not ever."

He moves to put a hand on Lauren. To put his arm around her to show he means her no harm.

Sophie has the urge to leap on him and tear her daughter away from him; a man who showed up at her home with one of his victims in tow. A man she turned away when he showed up as a boy.

That last memory almost deflates her anger, but it flares up again bright and hot.

Sensing Sophie's antagonistic distrust of David, everyone's stress levels boiling high, and Lauren's frightened confusion, the dog reacts protectively to David's attempt to touch Lauren.

With a snarl, Koda lunges at David.

David pulls his arm away quickly as the dog's teeth clamp down. Pulling his arm free, he rubs the painful spot, looking sullenly at the others.

Sophie has to fight the smirk that threatens to turn the corners of her mouth up.

Marjory pulls William aside after supper.

"William, I have to tell you something."

William glances at her, seeing uncertainty and confusion in her eyes. He is impatient, still upset over David and Lauren.

"Not now Marjory. We have to figure out what we are going to do about David. Here, sit. We'll talk later."

He tries to direct her to one of the living room chairs.

"I don't want to sit," Marjory complains, wringing her hands.

"Oh Marjory, you are getting yourself all worked up again. Just sit for a while. We have things to deal with right now. Maybe Rose can come sit with you."

"William, I need to tell you something," Marjory insists.

"Come on Marjory, stop this," William growls in frustration under his breath.

She finally sits, wringing her hands. She looks up at him, her eyes clouded with confusion and with something else. There is a lucidity in there too, if only partially.

"Will you listen to me now William? It's Rose. I have to tell you something about Rose Bheals."

"Just sit Marjory and calm yourself. You've worked yourself into a state. You have to stop doing these things."

"But she needs to believe. William, she needs to believe."

He looks at her and she meets his eyes, her own steady and clear.

"She has to believe," she repeats.

"You don't trust her," William says, sitting next to her.

"I do and I don't. She has her own skeletons in her closet, just like us. She isn't who she pretends to be. There is something about her that is just off."

Marjory leans closer to him, whispering.

"I think she's one of them."

William puts an age gnarled hand on hers.

"I'll look into it. Anderson is already working on finding out who she is."

"Ask him why he's having so much trouble. Why it's taking so long." Her eyes shift to the other room. A tear rolls down her cheek.

"You have to do it William. Jason and David, they both have something broken in them, a darkness, an ugliness they can't stop. They both won't stop killing."

William looks down. He can't look at her.

"I know," he says heavily.

He stands, his hand sliding off hers, and walks unhappily out of the room to find Anderson.

Marjory just sits there staring after him.

Rose finds Kathy folding laundry in one of the bedrooms. She enters and pulls the phone out of her pocket, showing it to Kathy.

"I think I found them, my family."

"What are you going to do?" Kathy asks.

"I have to find out what they did with all my stuff. I have to retrieve something important."

"How are you going to do that? They won't let you just go."

"I haven't figured that out yet," Rose says.

Rose looks at Kathy levelly.

"I know you want out. We can go together. I'll let you know when."

She puts a hand to her mouth indicating silence.

Billy walks into the living room to find Marjory sitting there staring out the window. He looks around to make sure no one is around before nervously approaching her.

"Mrs. McAllister," he starts.

She looks up at him. "Marjory. There is no need to be so formal."

Billy swallows and almost runs out of the room.

"Marjory."

Don't do this, he thinks, then changes his mind again. She's crazy, dementia. She won't remember the conversation anyway. She didn't remember any of the others.

He swallows again.

"Do you know anything about the white van?" he asks.

Marjory looks out the window and back at him.

"Is there a van out there? Do we have company?"

He shakes his head.

"No, the white van. The one that takes people and stuff."

"Everyone has heard those old stories. It's not real, you know. It's just urban legends."

Something in her eyes tells Billy the old woman doesn't really believe that.

"It's real," Billy says. "They are trying to get me. I ran away and they won't stop hunting me until they get me."

Marjory reaches out and pats his hand.

"You just stay right here next to old Marjory McAllister and you'll be safe. They won't touch you with my William and Anderson around." She smiles at him.

It's hopeless, Billy thinks. At least she won't remember I said that. Her brain is gone.

35   The Kids Hide from David

"Hi," David says, walking up to Lauren, who is sitting on the ground playing with a doll.

She looks up at him. "Hello."

"What are you doing?"

"Playing."

"Would you like to go for a walk?" David asks.

"Not really," Lauren says, still focused on her doll. "I'm not supposed to go for walks with you anymore. Mom said."

"Come on, I have something I want to show you."

Lauren looks up at him skeptically.

"That's what you said before."

"And it was pretty cool, right? This is even better."

"Okay," she says, leaving her doll reluctantly.

David leads her around to the back and through some thick undergrowth there.

They stop and Lauren looks up at him.

"Okay, so what do you want to show me?"

"This." He takes her hand, pulling her closer.

Lauren pulls back a little, but she is not strong enough. An uneasy feeling fills her.

He turns her head with one hand, making her look.

"Shh, you have to be quiet," David whispers, "or you'll scare them away Cassie."

Lauren pulls her head away, looking at him.

"I'm Lauren, not Cassie." She is getting tired of this game.

He pushes her head to look again.

"Just look and be quiet," he whispers.

"What am I looking at?" she whispers back.

"There." He points.

Lauren strains to see it, David steadying her with a hand on her back. His hand feels warm on her back and sends a tingling of nerves through her. Something about his behavior makes her feel off.

Then she spots it and her face lights up. She turns to him, glowing with happiness.

"They are so cute," she murmurs and turns to watch.

Three little baby bunnies, old enough to start venturing from their nest, are cautiously picking their way around a clump of wet dead leaves.

Tapping her shoulder, he points to something not far from the babies.

Lauren takes a moment to see it and her eyes widen.

A thin tomcat is slowly stalking the babies, his focus solely on the little rabbits as he silently moves forward in slow motion, getting into position to pounce.

"You leave them alone you big old ugly tom!" Lauren yells, looking for a rock to throw at the cat.

Startled, both cat and bunnies scatter.

David starts laughing.

Lauren turns to him angrily and hits him.

"It's not funny! He was going to eat them!" She stares him down moodily.

"Calm down Cassie. I know how to love baby bunnies. I would have stopped that old tom before he could do it. I wouldn't have let him hurt them with you watching."

She glares at him. "Stop calling me Cassie. It's not funny."

He gives her a weird smirk. "That's your name. What else would I call you?"

"My name is Lauren. I don't like your game pretending I'm Cassie."

David's smile falters. "Stop play games Cassie."

"I'm not Cassie," Lauren stomps her foot at him and starts to walk away.

David grabs her arm, stopping her.

"I said stop playing that game Cassie."

"She's not me, David," a little girl's voice whispers in his ear. "You can't replace me with her. Not like this."

David turns, but she isn't there.

"How are you doing that Cassie?" he demands. "How are you in front of me and whispering in my ear from behind?"

Lauren gives him an odd look, a flash of fear going through her.

"You are going to hurt her David," little Cassie whispers in his ear again. "Just like you did me."

"No, I didn't hurt you Cassie. He did. Jason did."

"Let me go," Lauren says, trying to pull free. She is scared now.

Jason pulls her closer, talking into her face.

"Stop saying I'm going to hurt you."

"I didn't say that," Lauren sobs, pulling harder.

She manages to pull free and darts away through the bushes.

"Cassie! Come back!"

Lauren can hear him chasing her.

David breaks through the trees and stops, not seeing her.

"Cassie, come back!" he shouts. He looks around with a growl. "Where are you? It's not time to hide."

He spots her. His longer legs move him much faster than her short ones and he catches her easily. David grabs her by the arm, his hard grip all that stops her from falling with the sudden stop.

"Cassie, we have to get back to the farm now. He's going to be mad." He looks around nervously. "If he catches us out here we are going to get it bad."

"Who? Who is going to catch us?" Lauren sobs, trying to pull free again.

"Our father. Now stop fighting with me. Let's go."

He starts dragging her off.

"She still isn't me," little Cassie's voice croons in a sing song in his ear. "You are going to hurt her. You are going to kill her just like you did me."

"No!" David shouts, stopping short and spinning to face her, still gripping Lauren's arm hard.

"You're hurting me," Lauren sobs, struggling against him.

David faces down little Cassie. It doesn't occur to him to wonder how he can stare at her while gripping her arm behind him.

"Stop it Cassie, just stop it," he hisses, taking a step towards her and loosening his grip. "Stop saying I'm going to hurt you. I won't."

Lauren pulls free again and runs, sobbing. She runs down the path to the chicken coop and around the corner, running into Ethan.

"What's the matter with you?" Ethan asks, taking in her tear streaked face.

"David," she gasps. "He's acting weird. He thinks I'm Cassie and he's getting mad. He says I keep saying he's going to hurt me, but I never say that."

"Is he going to?"

"Yes, I think so," she nods.

Ethan laughs. "You and your stupid games." He shakes his head.

They can hear David calling.

"Cassie, where are you? We have to get back to the farm now before he finds out we're gone."

Ethan gives Lauren an odd look.

David comes around the corner and they both jump. He stops, looking at them, then advances on them.

"Cassie, there you are. Come on. We have to get back to the farm. He's going to be mad."

Ethan almost laughs. He stares up at David and uncertainty washes through him.

"Who's going to be mad?" Ethan asks.

David barely gives him a glance. "Our father."

He is reaching for Lauren and she backs away.

"Lauren's father isn't here," Ethan says.

David pauses to look at him now. He turns his attention back on Lauren.

"This game you and your friend are playing isn't funny. You know we aren't supposed to have friends, Cassie. He's going to be so mad. I won't tell, but we have to go now."

Ethan takes a step back with Lauren.

"See," Lauren says, her voice shaky. "He thinks I'm Cassie. He thinks Uncle Jason is my dad."

Ethan makes a grossed out face at the thought.

David's face is twisting with anger.

"Cassie, let's go," he snarls, lunging and reaching to grab her.

Lauren squeals and darts away, Ethan running with her.

"Faster Lauren!" Ethan urges, his voice cracking with fear.

They can hear David pursuing them.

"Cassie, stop! Come back! I mean it!"

Ethan and Lauren run as hard as they can, but are no match for the man's longer legs. They dodge around the barn and through the man door on the side, letting it slam closed behind them. Their feet pound the ground as they race through the barn.

They hear the door open before they duck through a stall to a livestock door, darting back outside.

Billy is there. He turns to see them, noting Lauren's tear streaked cheeks and frightened expression, and Ethan hot on her heels.

"Lauren." he steps towards them, his hands balling into fists and stance aggressive.

Lauren runs in his direction.

Billy is ready for it as they approach. His arms are coming up to hit Ethan.

"Ethan, leave her alone," he starts and is cut off by Lauren.

"It's David," she gasps, sobbing. "He's chasing us."

Billy looks past them to see David coming through the open door.

"This way," he waves them urgently to follow.

Billy leads them, ducking through a fence. They run around the barn, breaking for the woods and racing down the path. They crash through the thick undergrowth to another path, stopping at the lopsidedly leaning outbuilding.

Going inside, they huddle in a dark corner, Lauren and Ethan gasping and out of breath. Ethan is looking in open-eyed shock. Lauren sobs into her arms, her body shaking with her trembling.

"Why is he chasing you?" Billy asks.

"He's bloody weird, that's why," Ethan says, still gasping to catch his breath. "He thinks she's Cassie and Uncle Jason is her dad. He's trying to take her to some farm. It's like he thinks they'll get in trouble, like he thinks they are both just kids, not just her."

Billy is shaking his head in disbelief.

"He was acting weird before too. I saw it."

Lauren leans into him, hiccupping sobs making her shoulders jump, and Billy puts a comforting arm around her.

"It's okay Lauren. I won't let him hurt you."

"It's not the first time he called me Cassie," she sobs. "I thought it was a game before."

She looks up at them with her tear-streaked face.

"I don't think it's a game."

"It's not a game," Billy says seriously. "There is something wrong with him. Something bad."

"Maybe it is just a game and he pushed it too far?" Lauren says hopefully.

"You always want to see the best in people," Ethan says. "It's gonna get you hurt, Lauren."

"How long should we hide?" Lauren asks.

"Until he remembers who he is," Billy says, his voice cold with anger.

Jason walks out of the house to see David pacing and looking around agitated.

"David," what are you looking for?" he asks.

David stops, staring at him. He pales and flushes with a sickly fear sweat.

"What's wrong, David?" Jason walks to him and stops, looking at him with concern.

Cassie is coming from the side of house with a laundry basket and stops out of sight around the corner, watching and listening.

David starts gushing out excuses like he did as a kid.

"We weren't doing anything wrong. There were baby bunnies and a cat. Nobody saw us or anything. I was taking her back to the farm and we got split up. We weren't doing anything, really."

"What are you talking about?"

David ducks his head, toeing the grass. He can't quite look at Jason. "I can't find Cassie," he admits, his voice small.

The spectacle makes Cassie feel sick. Making herself move, she continues walking, coming to stand behind Jason, keeping him between her and David.

"She's right there," Jason says, glancing back at her and turning his focus back on David.

David looks at Cassie, his face reflecting confusion.

"No, that's not her. She's a little girl."

Sophie comes out of the house. Seeing them, she heads straight for them. "Have you seen the kids? I can't find them."

A hot flush rises in David's cheeks and he just stares back at the three of them.

What have I done? He thinks, feeling panicked. I showed Lauren the baby bunnies. A stray cat just happened to be there; about to pounce on them. I was going to stop it before it could, but Lauren yelled first, getting angry.

Sophie stiffens at the tension between the three, realizing she just walked into a standoff. Cassie's stricken face sends a thrill of fear through her.

"Where are my kids?" She looks at David suspiciously.

Jason looks at her, sees the worry in her eyes, and looks at David.

"David," he says sternly, "Where are Lauren and Ethan?"

David half turns, looking around the yard.

"Somewhere in there I think." He points towards the woods.

"You think? Did you see them or not?"

"I think he was chasing them," Cassie says, her voice tight.

David flushes with guilt.

"Why were you chasing them?" Sophie asks, staring at him hard and making him cringe.

"She was mad at me and running away."

Sophie glowers at him. "What did you do?"

David looks away guiltily.

"You don't let him anywhere near my kids," Sophie warns Jason, her eyes blazing dangerously. She turns in the direction indicated, going in search of the kids.

36   The Network

"We've been watching this car wash for days," Jim complains. "Are you sure this isn't a dead lead?"

Jim and Rick are sitting in his ancient Oldsmobile just inside an alley across the street from the car wash where they have a view of the wash bay door exit and the front door.

"It's not a dead lead. Just watch and wait. He will come."

Rick's phone rings and he answers it.

"Dalton."

He listens, nodding.

"Got it."

He hangs up and turns to Jim.

"Your other name is nothing. Graham is probably just some random name he came up with to talk to your reporter friend."

"I'm not surprised."

"There he is," Rick says, indicating a man getting out of a car and entering the car wash front entrance. "Your Wallace. I'm sure of it."

"You're sure? You don't sound sure."

"All I have from you is the name, Wallace, and a few details. It's not a lot to go on."

"How many Wallaces can there be?"

Rick looks at him. "A lot."

"It's not a common name," Jim says, surprised.

"It's not a name," Rick says. "It's a title."

They are watching the man. He is as ordinary as it gets. The sort of man a witness would not notice in a crowd. He is tie-less and wearing a cheap business suit.

He is the same man who Lawrence met, and who set David McAllister on his jobs before he fled to Sophie's farm. The same man Lawrence watched as people came to see him at the diner.

When he disappears inside, Rick turns to Jim.

"You really don't know yet, do you?"

"Know what?"

Rick blinks at him in surprise. "But, you found the graveyard, all those bodies. You don't understand how big this is, do you?"

"At first we thought it was the two of them," Jim says. "But the graveyard goes for generations. Now we know there is a group of serial killers working together to hide their bodies."

Rick chuckles at his naivety.

"It's bigger than that. It's so much bigger than that. I've been hunting these people ever since I found Amy Dodds's toe in the wood stove at the McAllister farm."

"Explain it to me," Jim says. It feels unreal even though he knew the old sheriff would know more than he was letting on. He spent the last decades dedicated to this case.

Rick lets out a slow sigh before he starts, as if preparing for a long boring lecture he already recited too many times to count.

"It's a network like you wouldn't believe. You've got your McAllisters, people like them. They are nobody. They have no names, no title or identities. They don't exist. They make problems go away; problems as in dead bodies. The victims are just gone, never to be found again.

The Millers are the people with the problem. They have a body to get rid of, they hand it off to your McAllister, and their problem is gone. I've learned that the Millers can be just about anyone; serial killers or one time killers. Some of them are what I call couriers. The couriers pick up someone else's dead body, ones that need more distance from themselves and their crime. They move the body, sometimes across borders, and hand them off to the McAllisters for disposal. Hell, I've caught wind of some that smuggled the bodies overseas."

Jim is shaking his head in wonder.

"We suspected we would find something like this; murder tourism. But, you are saying it's human smuggling, except they're corpses when they are smuggled out."

Rick nods.

"Your McAllisters, the body disposal guys, they answer to a guy called Anderson. They all have an Anderson who manages a stable of these disposal guys. And each Anderson has a boss, a regional manager if you will. Wallace is your regional manager with a dozen or so Anderson's working under him. But that's not the only people he gets to do work for him."

"Who else works for him? What is this place? Where this Wallace meets his boss?"

Rick smiles and it's a sickly look of contempt.

"You could call what they do here procurement specialization."

Jim blinks at him. "Procurement. . .."

"It's a seedier side to the business, if it could get any worse."

They watch the wash bay door across the street rise. A white van exits, turning and driving away down the road, the door closing in its tracks behind it. The van is a solid box van with no windows outside of the windshield and two front doors.

Jim stares after the van.

"They get their victims for them."

"Only a small percentage of them," Rick says. "Here he comes. Get ready to follow him."

Wallace exits the building scowling, gets in his car, and drives away. Focused on his anger, Wallace does not notice the ugly rusting brown Oldsmobile parked in the alley across the street.

Jim puts the car in gear and follows at a discrete distance.

Wallace grips the steering wheel hard, his focus only partly on the road.

"Damn it," Wallace mutters. "He was supposed to get William to touch the body, something. This was a special order, kidnapped and killed just for this purpose. He failed."

Wallace shakes his head in frustration.

"Those old men think they are so clever, William McAllister and Richard Andrews. But I'm smarter. They are digging their own graves and they don't even know it. They will mess up again and soon I will be able to send the kill order and have the whole lot of them cleaned up.

McAllister and Andrews are preventing the boy from getting picked up, but that won't last. It won't be long now and the van will deliver him to me."

He smirks and the smile twists his face into a vile caricature of hate.

37   Lawrence

Lawrence is sitting on the living room floor of the Cormer house. The moon is high in the sky and glowing in through the large picture window, giving the room its only light.

Spread out around him are the little slips of paper like an impossible jigsaw puzzle whose pieces he is attempting to sort. He sat here for hours staring at them, moving them around and trying to make some sense of Mary Cormer's code.

The pile had grown, a more thorough search of the house produced more slips of paper hidden through the house; inside ducts, taking apart ceiling lights, pulling up aged carpet, and peeling back wallpaper that didn't seem to sit right.

One slip sits apart, the one from the back corner of the vegetable garden, singled out by its being penned by a different hand.

"Fifty-nine years ago. What was going through your head Mary?"

The papers vary in more than the numbers and letters written on them. The yellowing of the paper, shape of the tearing, fading and color of the ink, and even the direction of the characters in relation to the torn sides; these are all things that set them apart.

"It's almost like someone tore up a piece of paper to make the little slips to write on, then tore up another page when they ran out."

He stares at the papers, blinking.

"Or…"

Lawrence reaches for two slips, comparing them side by side. He starts moving quickly, determinedly sorting the pieces by age-yellowed hue, matching them age for age.

Finished, he studies the new piles. He starts sorting each by the tone of the ink. There seems to be no rhyme or reason to the combinations of letters, numbers, or both on the pieces. Some slips of paper have the characters scrawled across them to fill the small paper. Others have only a character or two.

He now has smaller groupings of the slanted characters written in Mary's scrawled handwriting, some only containing two or three pieces.

He focuses on two pieces.

OT MY

BA

Lawrence looks over the pieces of another grouping, the blue ink paler. The edge of one tear has darker ink.

He picks it up, focusing on it. Picking up 'OT MY', he puts them together, now seeing there is a partial letter before the O. The ragged tear on both pieces matches.

"Not my." He looks at the other pieces, finding a match.

BY

"Not my baby."

Lawrence leans in, working feverishly to piece the rest of the puzzle together.

When he is done, the torn slips of paper are put together roughly in the shapes of the original pieces of paper.

They are filled with Mary's slanted handwriting scrawled as if she were quickly jotting down notes on a hastily snatched piece of paper, reusing the same pages again and again until they are full. They are haphazard and not always going the same way. The ink of the jotted notes on each page varies, coming from different pens.

"She tore the pages into pieces after they were full and hid the mixed up pieces around the house."

He stares at the strange codes of varying combinations of letters and numbers. Some now reveal themselves to be dates, times and addresses or names of places. The same phrase repeats itself haphazardly. Not my baby.

There are still the others, combinations of letters and numbers.

"License plates," Lawrence breathes, remembering the white van that drove by earlier.

"Judith said she was obsessed with white vans. I need to visit Judith again."

He looks at the darkness outside, then at his watch.

"It's too late," Lawrence says resignedly. "I'll get some sleep and see her tomorrow."

A draught ruffles a few of the papers and he can hear the wind picking up outside.

Pulling his camera out, Lawrence snaps a few pictures of each shredded page, the flash piercing the darkness with a momentary brilliance for each one. It's an old school camera with a roll of film he will have to develop later.

He pulls out his phone.

"This thing is supposed to have a camera on it too. One I can see the photos on the screen."

He finds it quickly, snapping photos of the pages with the phone too. He studies them on the screen.

Satisfied, Lawrence puts away his equipment, scoops up the torn paper slips, and shoves them into one of the metal tins he found them in. Returning to his car, he starts it, moving it around behind a partially collapsed fence out of sight, and settles himself in for an uncomfortable sleep in the back seat of his car. He can see part of the front of the house and the street from where he is, but no one driving by or entering the yard will see him unless they come around to the back side of the fence and bushes.

In the morning, Lawrence stretches stiffly. He sits up, blinking.

"The door to the house is open. I don't remember leaving it open. I must have not quite closed it."

He drives to the main street, looking for someplace to get coffee and breakfast. Lawrence is rewarded with a small mom and pop restaurant with reasonably edible food. After eating, he returns to Judith Cormer's small house.

Moments after ringing the doorbell, he is staring into her displeased face.

"What do you want now?" she asks, not offering to invite him in.

"You said your mother wrote little cryptic pieces of paper and hid them," Lawrence starts. "Did you ever see her write them? Did she talk about that they were for?"

"I didn't bother much with what she did. I tried to stay away from her as much as I could."

"Did she write anything else? Dates, times, places to go, anything like that?"

Judith puckers her lips at him in distaste.

"Is that what they were? You pieced them together, didn't you? It figures. As I already told you, my mother was obsessed with white vans. Any time she saw one, she was frantically looking for paper to write on. Every time she saw one, she jotted down the date, time, place, and license plate if she could. When she couldn't she got hysterical over the need to write it down."

She looks at him levelly.

"I hope this is all. I have nothing else to tell you. I hated my mother, if that's who she was. I hated that she refused to sell that house after her stroke. All the years she was in the care home; that house just sat there and rotted. Goodbye Mr. Hawkworth, and don't come back."

She closes the door, leaving him staring at it on the front porch.

Lawrence pulls out his phone, pulling up the photos of the torn sheets of paper and looking at them again.

He notices now one thing that stands apart from the other notes jotted haphazardly on one of the torn pages; an address that does not have a date, time, or anything else with it.

"Hello there," Lawrence says, focusing on the address. "I have another place to visit."

Getting back in the car, he calls the office, hanging up just as someone answers.

"Something didn't feel right about that last witness and I have a feeling someone in the office knows about it."

He dials again, waiting for the answer.

"Hello," a woman's voice answers.

"Beth, don't hang up. It's Lawrence."

"What do you want Lawrence?" She sounds less than happy to hear his voice.

"I need a big favor."

"I'm a bit busy with something right now."

"I have an address. I need to know where it is and anything else you can dig up on it. It's related to Jim's case."

"All right, what is it?"

He gives her the address and hangs up, thanking her.

Lawrence starts the car and puts it in gear, pulling out.

"I hope she gets back to me before I get far. I'd hate to waste time turning around."

He thinks about what Judith said.

"What is it about the house? Is it the notes? Why did Judith refuse to sell it? That has to be it. I can get why Mary wanted it sold. She probably didn't want to live in the house she grew up in if she hates her mother that much. It can't have been a good childhood."

38   Sophie's Job

Cassie stops in the living room doorway looking at Anderson anxiously. He is sitting reading a newspaper and seems oblivious to her presence.

I've wanted to talk to him for a while, but it's impossible to get anyone alone with so many people in this house, she thinks.

"What's on your mind," he says not looking up from his paper.

Cassie falters, clears her throat, and steps into the room feeling awkward. Sitting in one of the chairs, she fidgets before speaking.

"Anderson, Sophie says she is taking me on a job, but I'm not sure I'm ready for it." Cassie is not sure if she is hoping he will confirm or deny her readiness.

"This is your first job?" Anderson asks, putting the paper down and looking at her.

Cassie nods.

"Her father trained her. William is a thorough man and Sophie has always been smart and level headed. If she believes you are ready, then you are ready."

"I don't feel ready."

"No one ever feels ready," Anderson says. "You just do it."

He studies her, taking in her nervous motions, her tight posture and the anxious and defensive position of her legs, her hands in her lap gripping each other.

"If you ever think you are ready, then you are not ready and you should not be doing it."

"What do you mean?"

"It means don't get cocky. Ever. You should be nervous. Not too nervous, but some anxiety will keep it real. It will keep you thinking on your feet. Sophie's is a dangerous job; one of the most dangerous jobs in the organization. The McAllister family," he motions in their assumed direction, "is traditionally a different sort of cleaner. On every job they risk being caught. They risk the client panicking, speaking, telling someone, breaking down and telling the authorities. They risk being pulled over and discovered; someone noticing the smell, coming across them when they are doing their job."

He shakes his head.

"That job was not for Sophie. She has always been sensitive, bothered by the innocent victims. There are innocents in her job too, it's inevitable. People make mistakes. Sophie's job is far more dangerous. You can never forget that the problems you make go away are people of a different sort. They are problems for the organization, not helping killers not get caught. You are hunting the hunter."

They are interrupted by a noise at the doorway. They both look to find Sophie standing there.

"Cassie, let's talk."

Cassie gives Anderson a thankful nod and reluctantly follows Sophie out. Sophie leads her outside and they walk across the yard to the trees, walking along the edge of the woods.

The branches above sway in the wind, dancing leaves on dark limbs against the slowly darkening deep dusky blue sky in the early evening. Soon the lowering sun will bring layers of crimson and orange staining the clouds across the horizon to herald the coming night shadows.

Sophie waits until she is sure no one is around before she speaks.

"Are you sure you are ready to do this?" Sophie looks at Cassie with a worried look. "We only talked about the possibility of you coming with me on a job. Actually doing it is very different."

Cassie looks uncertain despite her attempt to look confident.

"Anderson thinks I'm ready."

"I'm not sure how I feel about that. Anderson has been this figure who has always been a part of our world, but not there. I was told I met him when I was very young. I don't remember."

Sophie looks at her parents across the yard. Her father is helping her mother hang laundry. She laughs a soft sound through her nose.

"He's helping her with laundry. I never thought I would see my frightening father, the man capable of only one emotion, anger, doing something so domestic, or her to let him help."

She pulls herself back to the conversation.

"Mom met Anderson. She went on jobs with Dad before Jason was born. Can you believe that? The ever timid Marjory McAllister moving and burying dead bodies. I remember her always wringing her hands, always fearful and nervous."

She looks at Cassie.

"I also remember my mother standing up to a group of town women who surrounded us. Mom was frightened, wringing her hands, until one of them touched me."

Tears come to her eyes at the memory and she pushes them back.

"Mom was terrified. I was even more. They had us surrounded and were yelling at Mom to take us and leave town. Then one of the women grabbed me. She was shaking me hard and screaming in my face, saying the most horrible things, accusing my dad of doing them to the young women who were found dead. That was the first time I ever saw my mother stand up to anyone. It was beautiful."

Sophie smiles through her tears.

"She hit me. It was so hard my head was ringing and my face burned with her hand print. The woman's hand was about to strike me again and Mom caught it and held it. Just like that. I will never forget the words Mom said.

Keep your hands off my child. That's what she said. And then she tore into each and every one of them, telling them their own families' dark secrets; each and every one of those women.

I was never so proud of her. At that moment I decided I wanted to be just like her. Before then, I always thought her weak. At that moment I knew my mother always had a strength I never saw. I wanted to raise my own kids some day with that same strength.

I also learned that day that knowledge has its own special power. When you know people's dark secrets, you hold a power over them."

"You changed the subject," Cassie interjects. "Anderson thinks I'm ready, but I don't feel ready."

"Did he really say that?"

Cassie forces a smile.

"He said no one is ever ready, but you just do it."

Sophie nods. "What else did he say?"

"He said if I ever felt like I was ready, then I'm not ready and I should not be doing it."

"He has that part right."

Sophie is thoughtful. "Once we start there is no going back. You cannot undo something like this."

"I know."

"It's not always clean and it's never pretty."

"I understand." Cassie is starting to doubt, but she is not willing to acknowledge it. Not yet.

"It's not like the tea and some hypothetical situation. This is real people, hands on. Depending on the size of the problem, it could be a simple in and out; dealing with a single person, or it could be a big job."

"I'm ready." Cassie's voice has the slightest tremor, but she nods as if that will somehow convince both Sophie and herself.

Sophie looks at her. "There could be innocents involved. Kids."

Cassie swallows her bile, nodding hollowly.

"Okay. We leave tomorrow at first light," Sophie says.

Sophie pulls the van over, parking on the side of the highway. It is a white nondescript panel van, a utilitarian vehicle with only the two plastic covered seats in the front and the windowless back barren except for its painted steel shell.

Ahead is a gravel road.

"That's it?" Cassie asks.

The world feels like it is encased in an invisible thick cocoon coating everything with sound-dampening silk webbing. Everything feels muffled and distant as if she has been transported to a world that is just a bit off from the real world.

We will never make it to that road. The van can't move; the air is so heavy, like swimming through water the consistency of jelly, she thinks. If we do make it, we won't make it down that road. We will never make it to that farm. We will be stuck on that road forever.

Wistful or wishful, it does not matter. Cassie is trapped in a forward motion she now cannot stop. There will be no going back and undoing this. It's already too late to turn back the clock.

"It's up that road," Sophie says. "Does it help to know that he is a pedophile?"

Cassie's head swivels to look at her. It feels to Cassie like that simple movement takes minutes stretched eternally long instead of the mere second it really took. She feels her stomach filling with a hard lump of hollowness she cannot identify.

"He hurts kids?" Cassie asks. "Is that why we are here?"

"Yes and no. We wouldn't be here if he did not know about the organization's existence, so yes. But we are not here to kill him for the sickness rotting inside him. We are here because he asked for a delivery and then refused it when it was to be delivered. He was warned. He failed to heed that warning."

"What kind of package?" Cassie feels sick just asking.

Sophie's look is answer enough.

"So, he is a risk?" Cassie asks.

"Yes. There is a potential he is going to talk."

"But not for sure."

"It doesn't matter. We don't gamble on the risk."

"This is just him we are cleaning up, right? I mean, if that is what he is, he won't have a family or anything." Cassie stares at Sophie, willing her to say yes.

Sophie's face is devoid of expression; her eyes, her mouth.

"That will depend on our friend."

"What do you mean?" Cassie feels the alarm, but it is far away. The cold hard lump in her stomach grows, twisting inside her like some alien creature.

"Our friend is a family man. He has a wife and kids."

"But," Cassie is dumbfounded. "If he is a pedophile, how can he have a wife?"

Sophie lets out a short humorless laugh, the single syllable sound expressing the ridiculousness of these people's pretense.

"You want to say she isn't his type. No, she isn't, not when this bastard's real taste runs so much disgustingly younger. These sick monsters can play a decent game of pretend. They marry, have kids, work, and even go to church and volunteer in their communities. They are not all so ugly on the outside that the ugliness inside shows. It would be easier if that were true."

"He has a kid?" Cassie feels ill.

"Two, a boy and a girl," Sophie says. *Just like mine*, she thinks, pushing down the white hot hatred that surges inside her for this creature who preys on the young and innocent.

"So, we might be saving his kids from him," Cassie says with a small edge of hope in her voice.

"Maybe. Remember the plan, what we talked about. We will try to get our friend alone and find out who he told, if he told anyone. We will try to keep it to just him. If we have to, we widen the sweep to include everyone necessary to clean up his mess."

"The kids." Cassie feels hollowed out now, filled with empty sickness.

"If we have to." Sophie starts the van rolling forward. "Let's go."

We would be releasing them from a life of abuse, Cassie thinks, trying to convince herself she is not about to do something so mind-numbingly horrible that she will not be able to live with it. It doesn't work.

The gravel road is rough and dusty, and in need of repair from the most recent heavy rains that dried up weeks ago. The van rattles over it with a vibration that feels like it will vibrate their fillings out of their teeth.

It is not helping Cassie's sudden urgent need to urinate that hit her the moment they turned onto that gravel road.

The dust from the tires rises up in a heavy cloud that hangs chokingly in the air, only slowly drifting off across the fields. Some distance up the gravel road, Sophie turns up a narrow road leading to a farm house in the distance. She slows as they get closer, the sound of the gravel crunching beneath the tires growing softer.

She turns into the wrong side of a strip of trees planted to provide the home and yard with shelter from the winds. The ground is clear of bushes next to it, filled with grass in the space between the trees and the neat border of a grain field.

The van rocks on the uneven ground along the line of trees, the long grass whispering against the undercarriage as if to reveal the dark secrets it has witnessed. She drives to the back of the yard, parking behind a large tractor barn and out of sight of the house.

Cassie looks around them numbly. The farmyard is surrounded by acres of crop fields and a swath of woods on one side. The nearest neighbor is more than a mile away.

"It's so isolated," she says.

"That's good," Sophie says. "Less chance of any witnesses."

A dog barks somewhere.

"Let's scout the area and see if we can spot our friend alone," Sophie says. She gets out, softly closing the van door.

Cassie is slower to get out, hesitating. Her feet touch the ground and she is filled with the urge to flee.

Sophie looks at her across the hood of the van.

"You got this," she says. "We practiced. You know what to do."

Cassie nods.

I don't have this, Cassie thinks. I don't know what to do. I can't remember anything we talked about. A surge of panic fills her.

Sophie starts for the barn, walking around it and careful to not step into the view of anyone at the house, searching for a man door.

A dirty brown dog comes trotting around the corner of the barn, panting heavily under the weight of its coat and the filth matting it.

Rufus's replacement.

The dog is young enough to be too stupid and too friendly.

Cassie stops in her tracks, scared the dog will give them away.

Sophie reaches into her jacket pocket, pulling out a small wrapped bundle. She unwraps it, eyes on the dog.

"Here boy, come here boy," she says softly. She lowers herself to the dog's level and holds out one hand, waving the treat enticingly.

Smelling the strong odor of the chunk of liver, the dog sniffs the air and wags his tail. He approaches trustingly and eagerly takes the meat.

"Good boy," Sophie says, "that's a good boy."

The dog lets her pat his head. He quivers and lets out a small whimper, Sophie still petting him.

He turns to leave and she grabs him gently by the scruff of the neck. The dog tries to pull away, suddenly feeling less trustful, but she does not let go.

"Stay here boy," she says, holding him by the scruff and rubbing his ears with the other hand.

The dog wavers on his feet, his tail drooping, and he sinks to the ground.

Sophie continues to hold him, petting him. He struggles to get up and she holds him down. His head lolls limply, his tongue hanging out his open mouth, his eyes glazing over.

She moves her hand, closing his eyes, and looks at Cassie.

"He's only sleeping," Sophie says. "He is innocent and he won't tell anyone. Let's go."

Sophie is on her feet, rubbing her hand on her pants. "He stinks." She makes a face.

They find the man door to the tractor barn and go in. There is no one inside.

"I was hoping we would not have to go to the house," Sophie says. "Wait here and watch for my signal. Try to not be seen. If I can get inside without anyone seeing me, maybe I can get him to come out and meet us in the barn."

Sophie goes out the door, crossing the yard, and approaching the house warily. Reaching the back door, she presses herself against the house, kneels, and carefully peaks into the window.

There is no sign of movement.

Grasping the doorknob, she turns it slowly. As she expected, it is not locked. She opens the door slowly, pausing and cringing when the hinges begin to groan on the verge of letting loose a full blown squeal of un-oiled hinges.

She pulls a small can out of her jacket pocket. Careful to not let the door move, she raises up and stretches her arm out, spraying a small hiss from the can into the crack between the door and frame, targeting the upper hinge. She does the same for the hinge below.

The door opens soundlessly under her hand, the fresh smell of lubricant hanging on the air. Sophie enters the house slowly, listening for the sound of anyone inside. She still sees no movement.

The sound of water running somewhere is muffled. She hears the creak of weight shifting on the floor.

Pressing herself against the wall and lowering herself below the level of an adult's eyes, she listens, locating the direction of the sound. Staying close to the wall to minimize the chance of the wood floorboards creaking, she moves down the hallway.

Sophie stops outside a bathroom door. A man is standing inside the bathroom, the door open, shaving in the mirror.

Maneuvering behind him, she slowly rises to stand.

It takes him a moment to realize the face of a woman is standing behind him in the mirror. He turns in surprise, staring at her, his face half shaven.

"Mr. Black Donald," Sophie says quietly, her voice and face void of expression.

The man's face goes pale and sickly looking. His mouth claps open and closed a few times, lost for words.

"M-my family," he finally manages weakly.

"Will be fine if you cooperate. Are they here?"

He shakes his head. "They'll be back at any time." His voice is as sickly as his face.

Sophie nods. "Wipe your face. We are going to the barn."

He blanches, staring at her hollowly, and moves with wooden movements, reaching for a towel and wiping the white shaving lotion off his face.

He follows her out the back door and Sophie looks at him. He is looking across the yard to where a truck is parked in the wide gravel parking pad.

"Don't even think about it," she says. "You won't make it."

Defeated, he follows her to the barn.

Outside the man door, he looks down at the motionless dog on the ground a little ways ahead of them near the wall of the barn.

"Damn. They killed the dog the last time too. That was the warning. First the dog, then the family."

He looks at her, his face paling further and turning waxy and grey. "You are here to kill my family."

"Not if I don't have to," Sophie says.

They step inside and he is surprised to see another woman there.

"I guess I should have known you would not work alone," he says.

"Over there," Sophie motions towards the tractor looming inside the large overhead door.

He goes as directed. Waiting, Cassie nervously motions him to move closer to the tractor.

She loathes the thought of touching him, forcing herself to take his hand and raise it to the handle meant to help the driver climb into the tractor. She zip-ties his hand to it. She takes his other hand, zip-tying that one with the first and steps back.

"Why are you doing this?" His eyes are pleading and his face pasty and pale with sickly fear sweat.

"You know why Mr. Black Donald. You made a special request and when it was to be filled you backed out. There is no backing out. You know that."

"I-I changed my mind. They could let the kid go or give the kid to someone else." The simpering pleading in his voice sickens both Sophie and Cassie.

"You know it does not work that way. You were warned. You failed to heed that warning."

Sophie steps closer to him, showing no emotion.

"You have been determined to be a liability Mr. Black Donald."

Tears spring to his eyes. "I don't want to die. I'll be good. I'll take the kid. Please, don't do this. I will disappear. I won't say anything."

Sophie stops inches from him, looking up at him.

"Who have you told Mr. Black Donald? Your wife? Does she know about the sickness rotting you from the inside? Does she know what kind of a sick fuck you really are?"

She walks past him and fingers one of the tools hanging on the wall.

"Do your children know? Have you-," she pauses looking up at the wall of tools and farm implements hanging in neat order on the wall. She pulls down a shovel with a rounded blade that ends in a gentle point. "Ruined your children with the sickness festering inside you?" She turns to look at him.

He is shaking his head. He looks like he is going to throw up.

Sophie walks back to him with the shovel, pointedly putting it down, standing it leaning against a work bench.

"This will be easy to dig a hole with." She looks at him again. "How large do I need to make the hole?"

"Please," he is sobbing openly now, his face a twisted mask of fear.

The sound of a vehicle comes through the door.

Sophie, Cassie, and Mr. Black Donald all look at each other.

The back door of the farm house opens and a woman enters, pausing to look back at the door in surprise at the unexpected silence of the hinges.

"Ben, did you oil the back door finally?" Leslie calls out through the house.

She can hear the kids outside looking for the dog, who uncharacteristically failed to greet them when the car pulled into the yard.

"Ben," she calls again, walking further into the house.

There is no answer.

"He must be out in the barn."

"Stay quiet and your family may live," Sophie says.

He looks at her.

"If you are going to kill me, at least say my name. I'm a person. Say my name."

"Are the children you hurt people?" Cassie asks bitterly. "Do you say their names when you molest them? When you torture them with your disgusting body?"

He blinks at her as if he does not understand what she is saying.

Her eyes are angry and she is fighting back tears at the thought of what this monster does to helpless children.

"Did you rape your own children?" she is about to demand, but Sophie silences her with a look.

Sophie walks back to the wall, taking down a saw and walking back across the barn to him, pausing in front of him.

"Did you tell your family? Did you tell a neighbor? A friend? The police?"

"No," he shakes his head emphatically. "I didn't tell anyone. You can let us go; me and my family. You don't have to do this. I didn't tell anyone. I won't tell anyone. I promise."

"For their sake, I hope you are telling me the truth."

She walks to the bench, putting the saw down.

They can hear the kids outside calling the dog.

"I am going to need you to be very quiet," Sophie says. "This is what we are going to do. When we know your family won't see, we will walk out this door. You will not utter a sound. We will stay against the barn wall and walk behind it. We have a van there. We will all get into the van and drive away, and if you are not lying to me your wife and kids will be allowed to live."

He looks at her and a new look of desperate defiance joins the fear in his eyes.

"Say my name," he says. "My name is Ben. Say it. Say my name." He is angry and sobbing wretchedly, feeling the rush of all the emotions of a man unwilling to meet his fate.

Ben raises his voice, spittle flying. "Say my name!"

"That won't do," Sophie says softly. She starts walking towards him, pulling a gag out of her jacket pocket.

They hear his wife calling him.

His head turns towards the door. His eyes are filled with a wild desperation.

"Don't," Sophie warns him, shaking her head.

Ben looks directly at her, staring into her eyes. There is a glint in his eye. Evil? Some sort of twisted revenge? Sophie would like to think of it as fear. The weak simpering sickness-infested fear of a man without spine or the capability of compassion for anyone but himself. A man too afraid to die alone and so others must suffer his fate with him.

He opens his mouth and screams his wife's name. "Leslie!"

Cassie's eyes widen and she lunges at him, clapping her hands over his mouth as hard as she can, trying to stop the sounds pouring out of his disgusting mouth.

Sophie is in motion, rushing at him.

Ben screams his wife's name again, and the names of his kids, calling them

"Leslie! I'm in the barn! Kate! Henry! Leslie!"

They hear the soft footsteps of a running child approach outside, stop, and a gasp.

Sophie stares at him hard. "You just killed them."

A little girl appears in the doorway of the barn. Her eyes are huge and full of tears. She looks at the two women.

"Daddy?" She looks around then spots him with his hands zip-tied to the tractor. She does not understand yet, his predicament not sinking into her young mind.

"Daddy, Rusty is dead. It's just like Rufus. Someone killed Rusty," she sobs.

Cassie is about to say something to reassure her, to tell her Rusty is just sleeping, but Sophie flashes her a warning look.

The little girl finally notices the zip-ties. She looks at the two women suspiciously, then at her father.

"Daddy, why are you tied to the tractor?" She walks into the barn, stopping before him and looking up at him.

"Baby, I need you to run outside. Scream. You remember 911? I need to call like it is a fire or a tractor accident."

"You had a tractor accident?" She looks him over. "You don't look hurt."

"Yes baby. I need you to run out and scream. Tell your mom to run in the house, lock the doors, and call the police."

It is too many words for her young mind, but she remembers tractor accident and police.

Behind her, Cassie is shaking her head, her eyes pleading with him to stop.

"You don't call police for an accident," the little girl says. "You call an ambulance."

She looks at the two women and is suddenly afraid.

Blond curls bouncing, she turns and runs, dodging past Cassie for the open door, her little face twisted with fear and tears filling her eyes.

Sophie darts toward the door, just managing to catch the little girl by one hand and yanking her back.

She looks at Ben solemnly. "I did not have to do this."

Holding the girl firmly by the chin and pressing the back of her head to her stomach, she shifts her grip up to cover the child's mouth and nose tightly.

The little girl struggles, unable to breath, her eyes widening in terror. Sophie deftly spins her around, pressing the child's face to her stomach and pinning her head tight against her with her arm.

Sophie produces a sharp blade in her other hand and with one swift motion jabs it at the base of the little girl's neck.

The blade penetrates and the child jerks, a trickle of blood running down the back of her neck to stain her shirt, her blond curls soaking up the blood. It penetrated her spine at the base of her skull, severing it and the spinal cord and all the nerves from her brain.

Sophie lets the girl slump softly to the floor like a rag doll.

Ben stares down at his little girl in shock. He looks at Sophie, flapping his lips while trying to think of something to say.

"You-you killed her," he finally sputters in shock, his face twisting with agony and loss.

"You killed her," Sophie says to him emotionlessly.

They hear more footsteps running towards the barn.

A boy, older than the girl, appears in the doorway staring in at them in wide eyed surprise. He sees his dad tied to the tractor, the two women, and his little sister slumped motionlessly on the floor.

"MOM!" He screams, darting away.

Cassie and Sophie both break into a sprint, chasing him.

He races for the front of the barn, into the open.

Sophie and Cassie follow, skidding to a stop with the boy.

A woman is standing in the driveway before the barn staring at them in surprise.

"Henry," she says, blinking at the three panting from running.

"Mom." Henry's voice is choked.

His mother's eyes flash to the barn they just came from.

"Leslie! Run!" Ben screams from the barn.

She moves, undecided, flight or go for her son.

"Where is Kate?" She looks at Henry, the two women behind him.

"I-I think they killed her," Henry chokes out.

Sophie moves fast, darting ahead and grabbing Henry by the throat, pinning his head to her. She has the knife pressed to his throat with the other hand.

Leslie almost cries out, staring at her in frozen shock.

"Don't try anything or I will slit his throat right here," Sophie says coldly.

Leslie looks at them, pleading. "How can you? You are women, nurturing."

"There is nothing nurturing about who I am right now," Sophie says emotionlessly. Inside she is being ripped to shreds over being forced to kill the kids. "Start walking to the barn. No sudden moves."

Swallowing, Leslie starts moving. She walks forward stiffly, staring straight ahead, afraid to even look at the women as she walks past them.

"Mom," Henry chokes, swallowing and staring at her as she walks past him. Tears are streaming down his face. "Mom."

They walk back to the barn and in the man door.

Leslie looks at her husband tied to the tractor, and then her eyes find her little girl.

She sobs a guttural animal sound of loss and despair, rushing across the barn and falling to the ground, pawing at her daughter and wrapping her arms around her, lifting her and clinging to her as if she can somehow put her back together.

Leslie pulls her hand away, feeling wetness, and staring at the blood in horror. A scream tears from her throat followed by another and then a long keening wail.

Cassie follows her in, looking down at her with pain filled eyes.

Sophie comes in last with the boy. She looks emotionlessly at the woman.

"Did you know?" she asks.

"Know what?" Leslie sobs, broken.

"What he is? What he does?"

"He's a farmer," she spits the words out at them. "He's just a god damned farmer."

"Is he really married to you, or does he only pretend? Where does he fill his needs?"

"Are you?" Leslie looks to Cassie and then back to Sophie. "Which one? Which one of you is his mistress?"

Her eyes fall on Cassie accusingly.

"It has to be you. They always go for the younger ones. But why? Why are you doing this? Why kill us?"

Cassie shakes her head slowly.

"I'm not his type. I'm too old."

She nods towards the dead little girl in answer to Leslie's confused look.

"Or maybe he prefers boys," Cassie says.

The woman looks down at the motionless little girl in her lap, realization dawning. She looks up at her husband with disgust and hatred.

"You don't seem surprised," Sophie says.

In one deft motion she spins the shocked boy, jabbing at the back of his neck with the blade, severing his life. She lets go, letting him slump limply to the ground.

Another scream tears from Leslie's throat, and another, ending again in a high keening wail of loss and heartache.

Sophie walks to the woman on the floor, kneeling down behind her. Leslie does not resist.

Taking her by the chin firmly, Sophie raises her chin so that the woman is looking up at her. She meets the woman's tortured eyes and then turns her head to make her look at her husband, to force him to look into his wife's face.

Sophie looks at him watching from where he is forced to stand, impotent and unable to do anything but watch.

In one fluid stroke Sophie cuts deep and cleanly, slicing through his wife's throat. The air gurgles, sucking in and out the slash sliced in her neck, blood running down her esophagus as she gasps for air, choking on her own blood. It runs down her chest, sputtering and bubbling through her throat, filling her lungs and drowning her.

Sophie lets her go and Leslie falls sideways onto the floor. She gets up, walking to Ben. She stops in front of him, looking up at him.

He is panting, shivering with shock, his eyes glazed with it.

"Mr. Black Donald, you have become a liability. Your mess has been cleaned up."

He kicks out at her savagely a moment too late.

With a sweeping motion, Sophie's arm flies at Ben, slicing through his throat to release a splash of blood as she steps aside.

His savage kick misses, weakened mid kick by the shock of pain and sudden gush of fluid filling his mouth and running down his esophagus and filling his lungs.

Ben blinks at her, sputtering and spraying foaming bloody spittle.

Sophie watches him die expressionlessly.

Cassie wavers on her feet, feeling weak and nauseas. A cold sweat fills her, making her skin clammy. The world starts to spin.

"Don't faint on me Cassie," Sophie says, her voice commanding like she is scolding a child. "We have only started."

Ben is dangling weakly from the zip-ties lashing him to the tractor, his legs buckling and his head lolling. His eyes are glazed and delirious.

"I will give you a moment to get yourself together," Sophie says. She picks up the little girl, carrying her outside.

Cassie can't help it. She stares at the blood splattered on the floor where the girl laid.

Sophie carries her to the van, juggling her like her own sleeping daughter, and opens one of the rear doors. She gently lays her on the tarp spread there, and then opens the other rear door.

She wraps the girl carefully like a macabre present, tying the bundle securely. She pushes her across the back of the van against the back of the front seats.

Pulling another tarp from a large bag hanging from a hook on one side of the ceiling, she spreads it out and returns to the barn for the boy. After wrapping him the same way, she goes to the barn again. She spreads a tarp on the floor next to the dead woman.

"Cassie, grab her feet," Sophie commands, going to her head.

Cassie blinks at her and finally moves, rubbing away her tears angrily before bending down to take her feet.

"On two. One, and lift."

They lift her, swinging her onto the tarp and dropping her.

Together, Sophie making sure Cassie is doing it right, they wrap her, wrapping and tying the bundle securely with strong twine.

"Okay, grab an end."

They lift her, struggling a little with the weight, and carry her out, tossing her in the back of the van.

Sophie grabs another tarp and they return for Mr. Black Donald. She lays the tarp on the ground beneath him and slices the zip ties. He falls onto the tarp.

"Our friend, our business is done," she says.

Grabbing and rolling him into place, they wrap and tie him, struggling to carry him out and toss him in the back of the van.

Collecting cleaning supplies from a box one side of the van's cargo area, they return to the barn one last time.

Sophie splashes chemical over the blood. The chemical turns it first purple, then blue, and finally clear, eating the blood and breaking it down.

She finds the hose the farmer uses to clean the floor, spraying it down. Cassie takes chemical wipes, wiping down everything they touched.

"Get the doorknob on the back door of the house too," Sophie says.

Cassie nods, stepping outside and going to the house.

Sophie splashes the chemical on the blood soaked into the gravel driveway, dissolving it too. She kicks at the gravel with her foot, scraping it around with the side of her shoe, covering anything remaining to be found.

She puts the cleaning supplies in the back of the van, closing the doors, and returns to the house. She steps in, using a rag to open the back door.

Looking around, she spots the woman's purse, her keys next to it. She grabs the purse and keys and searches for the farmer's wallet and keys. Finding them, she takes them too and leaves, meeting Cassie outside.

"Take the car. We will have to make it disappear too. They will be looking for it along with the family. It will draw attention away from the house."

Cassie nods, swallowing and taking the keys. "What about the dog?" she asks. "There is no one here to look after him now."

Sophie looks at her levelly. She sighs. "Fine, take the dog. We will drop him somewhere someone will find him."

Cassie jogs back, lifting the dog and carrying him to the car.

He is starting to wake up and wags his tail at her weakly.

She puts him in the back of the car. He licks her hand when she pets his head.

"You know where to meet me," Sophie says.

Cassie nods, getting in the car and driving out.

Sophie returns to the van, turning around and driving out back the way she came in along the wrong side of the trees.

David looks at his watch impatiently.

"Where is she?"

"She will be here," Jason says. "Don't get impatient. You will botch the job."

They are barely visible in the dark, the truck turned off and the headlights dark.

"There," Jason says, pointing.

David looks, squinting to see in the darkness, and finally spots a ghostly pale phantom approaching on the road.

It grows at is comes closer, becoming a white van, running dark with no lights in the night. The van passes them and stops, turning in the road and coming back to pass them again. It pulls over and backs, angling to meet them back bumper to back bumper.

The motor cuts and the door opens.

"Let's get to work," Jason says.

They get out, meeting Sophie next to the van.

"We had to clean the whole family," she says, opening the back of the van. Her expression is stony and angry with the attempt to hide the pain filling her.

Jason and David get to work, pulling the wrapped bodies out of the van and putting them in the truck box.

"Don't forget the purse," Sophie says, grabbing the purse and handing it to David.

"We will see you at home," Jason says. They get in the truck and drive away.

Sophie gets in the van driving off, not turning the headlights on until she is close to the highway.

Cassie sits in the car waiting. She sees the van approaching only as the ghostly image of something pale moving in the dark.

Sophie pulls up and parks, getting out.

"Ready?"

"Ready," Cassie says. She gets the dog out of the car, putting him in the cargo area of the van.

The dog, Rusty, starts sniffing the cargo area with a vengeance.

She closes the door.

Sophie is already setting the car up. Sitting in the driver seat with the door open, she sets a heavy brick down on the passenger seat and makes sure the wheel is straight. She starts the car, presses the brake to the floor, and slips the car into neutral.

"Wouldn't the emergency brake help?" Cassie asks.

"No. At the age of this car, the E brake would have seized a long time ago. The cable is probably rotten through too. Get behind and be ready to push."

Sophie takes the brick, wedging it on the gas pedal, pinning it to the floor. The fumes of gas flooding the engine are thick inside the car. Keeping the brake pedal firmly pressed to the floor with one foot, she slips out, grasping the car by the door frame.

"Push!"

Her foot coming off the brake as she gets out, the car starts rolling down hill. They both push, accelerating the car's momentum.

Walking faster with the rolling car, Sophie leans in just enough to reach the gear stick, slipping the car into drive and ducking back quickly. The car just misses taking her with it as it leaps forward, the drive shaft suddenly lurching it ahead with the full gas coursing through the lines to feed the engine.

They watch the car's bouncing progress, the car accelerating quickly as it charges downhill. The hill ends suddenly with a sheer drop off and the car flies out over the cliff from its momentum, soaring gracefully, its weight bringing its trajectory down.

The car bows; the weight of the engine pulling its nose down and its momentum pushing its rear end up. It does a slow somersault mid air, splashing down on the water below, hitting it upside down and partially crushing its hood with the force.

The car sinks beneath the surface, vanishing in the depths.

"They will never find it," Sophie says. "That quarry lake is miles deep."

Little is visible beyond the headlights slashing through the dark night, the highway rolling beneath the truck tires with a steady drone.

"I never had an inside job before," David says.

"They have a special division for that," Jason says. "Anderson said we are doing it only because we are already involved."

He glances at David and back at the road.

"We really messed up," he says. "We were never supposed to know what Sophie does, what she is."

"What is she?" David asks.

Jason shrugs.

"I don't know what to call her. She's like us. She has no title, no name. She is nobody. She does not exist. If you would call us disposal experts, I guess I would call her a clean up expert."

Hours later, after the bodies are buried where they will never be found and with the morning sun rising on the horizon, they are on their way home.

39   Abandoned House

Lawrence is stopped at a crossroad in the middle of sprawling fields in both directions. Behind him, the highway is a ribbon cut through the fields of crops. Ahead of him, the strip of land bordering the cross roads is more or less untouched, long stalks of flowering plants indigenous to the area waving in the wind to the cultured stiffness of the farm grown plants to either side.

"Right, I go to the address on Mary Cormer's note. The address that I believe is the house where Judith Cormer's real birth mother lived. You were smart, Mary Cormer. You found her. You found the mother whose stolen baby Grant gave you, and you kept it secret."

He looks at the left fork. The file folder on the seat next to him is a physical presence pulling at him.

The file is incomplete, the pages torn out. All that is left in the file is a scattering of old photographs; black and white, sepia, age-faded and of the poor quality common in cameras fifty-nine years ago.

There are also pages of hand drawn sketches, yellowed deeper along the edges and bearing the worn damage of pages that had been looked at many times.

There is a buzzing in Lawrence's head. Distant, faint, deep inside, coming as if from some other place.

A voice, soft and very far away buzzes in his ear. The sensation of someone who is not there, who is whispering so softly their breath does not quite reach your ear to tickle it, and yet they are.

Lawrence's head feels like it is slowly thickening, stuffed with something foreign; filling with cotton. The pressure intensifies. It turns to water, heavy, freezing to ice, sending blinding hot agony through the center of his head.

He closes his eyes, gritting his teeth against the pain. Lawrence feels hollowed out and overstuffed with sawdust. His fingers twitch.

The voice almost whispering in his ear is so soft, like the wind singing a low hollow mournful song of loss.

Find me. It is the whispered voice of a little girl.

Find me. The whisper fades and is gone.

Lawrence can see the photos in the folder next to him in his mind's eye. Standing living trees and the remains of long rotting fallen trees. Seemingly random photos of the ground, as if snapped by mistake. A dried brook, the rocks laid bare to the world. Dark photos of the interior of what looks like a long abandoned house, the house small and the furniture removed some time before the photographs were taken.

A window shines its poor light into the empty room, the wallpaper is a ghastly flowered print stained with age and what may be water damage.

The window has a broken pane, the rotting stained sheer curtain is locked forever in its dance billowing in on the wind blowing through the broken window.

Feeling weak, Lawrence starts driving, taking the left fork. He follows the winding road without knowing where it is taking him. He drives on instinct, turning when it feels right to turn.

After some time, he pulls into a gravel road on a strip of land nestled between two farms as if it were plopped there by mistake. It's a funnel shaped strip spreading wider as he goes. The road turns to aged concrete and breaks into a cross-patch of little roads.

It could almost be called a town.

Lawrence turns up one of these roads and stops in front of a small older house. The layer of dust coating the windows suggests it has been abandoned for some time.

Getting out of the car, he walks up the cracked sidewalk to the front door. Hesitating a moment, he grasps the knob and tries it.

The knob turns and the door opens to the cry of un-oiled hinges.

He steps inside, closing the door behind him. The heavy dust assaults his nose, making him want to sneeze.

Lawrence walks into the middle of the living room, leaving his footprints in the dust behind him.

The small home in the photos of the cracked window and billowing curtain surrounds him. The curtain hangs lifelessly, pushed open to the outer edges of the curtain rod, the glass behind it intact. The stained hideous flowered wallpaper is just as ugly. The stains from age and possible water damage are faded with age.

Lawrence half expects furniture to fill the small room just like in his vision of days ago. The furniture is conspicuously absent from the empty room.

He walks through the small single-story house. The kitchen is empty, a lone pair of cupboard doors left open to show the barren shelves behind them. Even the fridge and stove are gone, leaving the stain-ruined floor to show where they once sat.

The bedrooms are empty also. One closet has a single empty wire hanger hanging in it, slightly twisted from the weight of something that once clung to it.

He returns to the living room and stands there; trying to bring up the memory of the vision he had in his apartment.

A woman dressed in a worn house dress to match the worn furniture, both consistent with the style fifty-nine years ago or so. He pictures her pacing the living room, returning to the window to look outside numerous times.

"Who are you mysterious woman? Who are you waiting for? Who is missing?"

He shrugs.

"I should do a more thorough search."

Lawrence looks at the coat closet by the front door. One door hangs off kilter, sagging on its hinges. He walks over, opening both doors. One side of the closet has a rod for coats, the other a narrow row of shelves spanning one third of its width.

An envelope sits on one dusty shelf.

He frowns at it, picking it up and examining it.

On the front a name is scrawled. Lawrence.

He opens it, pulling out a single folded sheet up paper and unfolding it.

RUN!

He looks at the note in confusion. "It's his handwriting."

Lawrence looks up. He sees a white van pulling into the driveway.

He turns to the kitchen doorway, seeing the back door.

Gripping the note in his fist, he sprints for it, fumbling to open it and running out through the back yard away from the house.

"Why am I running?" he pants as he continues to run away across the back of the houses.

Lawrence ducks down; hiding behind an old junker car abandoned at the rear of one of the back yards, panting to catch his breath. Staying low, he looks past the bumper to see if anyone is pursuing him. He sees no one.

He can see the abandoned house from here and only part of the driveway in front. It does not look like the white van is still there.

"Are they gone? Maybe they were just turning around. I don't even know why I ran."

He chuckles humorlessly. "Some old note left on a shelf years ago says run and like some idiot I run."

Feeling ungainly, awkward, and looking around quickly to see if anyone notices, he stands up and starts making his way back to the abandoned house.

He enters from the back, retracing his steps to the front coat closet.

On the floor are more than his single footsteps in the dust entering the house. He looks down at the prints.

"They came in and left."

Lawrence looks around him. The house does not feel right.

"It's the wrong house. The front window should be cracked."

The ringing of his phone is startlingly loud in the quiet house, making him jump. He grabs it, pressing to take the call.

"Hawkworth, InterCity Voice. You bury 'em, I dig 'em up." His voice is shaky.

"Lawrence, Jim," Jim's voice says into his ear. "Where are you?"

"Some abandoned house."

"Of course you are. Beth got another hit. We are on our way to check it out. We are going to blow this thing wide open. There's a whole damned network of these people."

"Which people?"

"The McAllisters; all of them. Beth was right. It's like some kind of organization for serial killers. People living ordinary lives."

The thought hits Lawrence like a physical blow.

Ordinary lives. Nothing about your life stands out as anything but ordinary. Everything about your file is unremarkable. But you, Grant Cormer, caught his attention. Something is special about you.

"Jim, do you know anything about white vans? You know, the old urban legend of white vans taking people?"

There is a heavy silence on the line.

"It's not just an urban legend," Jim finally says.

Jim looks at Rick sitting next to him in the car. Rick is nodding his head slowly, his expression grave.

"Lawrence, what do you know about the white vans?" Jim asks.

"One of his files, a Grant Cormer, vanished fifty-nine years ago at the age of forty-seven. His wife was obsessed with white vans to the point she had to note down the date, time, place, and license plate number every time she saw one. Neighbors reported seeing them around the Cormer house often."

And I think one just followed me here. He keeps this thought to himself.

"So what is this abandoned house you are at?" Jim asks.

"I don't know. It's another of his files, but most of the file is missing. There's just pictures."

"Give me the address. I'll get Beth to see what she can dig up on it."

Lawrence gives him the address.

"So what else?" Lawrence asks. "I get the feeling there is more you aren't telling me."

He can hear Jim breathing into the phone.

Jim looks at Rick, unsure if he should say it.

"Lawrence, be careful. That informant for Marjory McAllister and Rose Bheals's disappearance isn't an informant."

Tension fills Lawrence. He grips the phone tighter.

"What do you mean?"

"The name you gave, Graham, is bogus."

"I already figured that."

"You can call him Anderson or Wallace."

"Who is that?"

"Trouble. He sets up the serial killers to meet McAllister to hand over the victims so McAllister can make them vanish."

It's Lawrence's turn to be silent.

"Jim, did you find this guy?"

"I found where he meets his boss."

"I followed him. I know where he lives." He gives Jim the address. "I need to follow up on this Grant Cormer. I think he's linked to this abandoned house somehow. I think Mary and Grant's daughter Judith isn't their real daughter either. That could be the link. Maybe they adopted her from whoever lived here, only it wasn't a regular adoption. Grant and Mary Cormer are listed on her birth certificate, but Judith Cormer thinks it's a lie."

"Sounds like denial," Jim says. "I'll get Beth to check into that too. I want you to meet us. We think we know where the McAllisters are going."

A warning bell rings in Lawrence's head.

"All right. Where?"

Jim gives him the location and hangs up.

"He's coming?" Rick asks.

"Yes," Jim says.

40   Questions about The Past

Cassie finds Jason at the chicken coop repairing the fence meant to keep chickens in and predators out.

She stops, watching him work for a moment, trying to get the courage to speak.

"I don't remember you raising me," she starts finally.

He glances at her and focuses on the fence again, continuing to work.

"It's okay you don't remember. I wasn't the best father. I had no idea how to look after a couple of little kids."

"I don't remember David, except glimpses until I came out of the drug haze from the hospital. He kidnapped me, didn't he?"

"He did."

"He hurt me. They say he almost killed me."

Jason only nods, pain catching in his throat. He doesn't trust his voice to speak.

"I know you kidnapped our mother and killed her, that you raised us. And I know David ran away. But what happened to me?"

Jason looks at her now.

"How did I end up in foster care instead of with you?"

"You got lost. Someone found you on the road."

"Why didn't to try to get me back?"

"How could I? You didn't belong to me."

Cassie looks away.

"Foster care was terrible. Whatever life we had, I had, before had to have been better than foster care."

"It wasn't safe for you with me."

"Because of David. Why? What really happened to me? Why can't I remember anything?"

"David ... he hurt you. You were very little still." He looks away guiltily. "It was my fault really. The things I did. I had no one to look after you. I had to take you both on jobs. The bodies, I think it messed David up."

"You killed women too," Cassie says. "Did," she almost can't say it, "we witness that?"

"I tried; I really tried to protect you from that. To keep you separate from it." Jason says. His shoulders slump.

"You both saw. I chased you out of the barn a few times when," he chokes on the words, making himself continue, "I had someone in there, while I was, you know. And after, when I had to clean it up."

"And David?" Cassie looks at him searchingly.

"He saw more than a boy that age should."

Cassie nods solemnly.

"I know David is wrong inside. He's all broken, damaged. There is a darkness in him that can't be fixed." She pauses. "He almost killed me, didn't he? When I got lost as you say and ended up being picked up on the road."

Jason looks at her, his expression bordering panic.

"Don't worry," she says, "I don't remember it."

She can see his relief.

Jason nods, unable to respond.

Cassie nods understanding.

"That's all I need to know . . . for now."

She walks away, leaving him there feeling hollowed out like his world just dropped away.

"I'm so sorry Cassie," Jason manages to whisper to her departing back. "I never wanted you to get hurt."

Part 6
Everything Ends

41   Goodbye Kathy

"Kathy," Rose comes into Kathy's room urgently, closing the door behind her. "You have to see this."

Rose's alarmed attitude puts Kathy immediately on edge.
"What is it?"
Rose pulls her cell phone out of her housecoat pocket, holding it for Kathy to see.
"That's your mother, isn't it?" Rose says.
Kathy's eyes widen. She grabs the phone, skimming the news article, her mouth opening into a shocked oh.
She looks at Rose, her expression matching Rose's alarm.
"My mother, she's missing! Rose, I have to go home."
Kathy rushes to the dresser and starts pulling clothes out.
"Kathy, stop," Rose says urgently. "They won't let you."
She grabs Kathy's clothes, shoving them back in the drawer.
"You have to play it cool. They won't let you just take off."
"But . . .." Kathy's eyes fill with tears. She is beside herself with worry.
There is a noise outside the door and they both look at it, startled. Rose quickly shoves the phone in her pocket.
The door opens and David is in the doorway. He looks at Rose, surprised to see her. Then he takes in Kathy's strained look.
"What's wrong Kathy?"
Kathy looks at Rose, who gives her a warning look, and back at him.

"My mother, she's missing. I have to go home."

David shakes his head at her. "You know you can't do that."

"But, my mother."

He looks at her sorrowfully, unhappy about her pain.

"If you go, they will catch you. It could be a trick to lure you back and use you to get at me."

"I can't . . . I have to go." Kathy's eyes are pleading with him.

"If she really is missing then she's already dead," he says, regretting it even as the words come out.

"The organization," he says apologetically.

Kathy feels faint, the world spinning like a wildly out of control merry-go-round.

David catches her before she falls.

Weak and sick with grief, she lets him lead her to sit on the bed.

Kathy looks up at him, tears falling. Her voice croaks, choked by her sorrow.

"I have to go."

"You can't. Kathy-."

Kathy pushes herself up, trying to get past him. He grabs her arms, holding her there.

Kathy stares into his eyes defiantly, filled with agony and fear for her mother. "Let me go. I want to go. I have to go."

"Kathy, don't make a scene," he warns her.

"Yes, calm yourself down," Rose says, trying to help. "Don't make a scene."

David glares at her. "You did this. You told her, didn't you?"

Her expression is answer enough.

"Get out."

Rose leaves, closing the door behind her. She can hear David trying to talk sense into Kathy through the door.

She hesitates outside the door and finally goes back to her own room.

Kathy is lying awake in bed next to David, listening to his snores. The moon is putting off enough light to outline the furniture in the dark room.

She moves slowly to not disturb him, putting her legs over the bed and standing up.

Going to the dresser, she opens the drawer slowly, cringing at the soft sigh of sound it makes. Grabbing the clothes she had ready on one end, she pushes it almost closed and slips out of the bedroom, closing the door softly behind her.

Walking against the wall and taking soft steps, she creeps to the stairs and down them. In the living room, she slips out of her night clothes and quickly dresses.

Moving to the kitchen, Kathy picks up her shoes at the back door and stops when she hears the clicking of the dog's nails on the linoleum.

She looks at him alarmed; worried he will give her away.

He only stares at her, slowly wagging his tail.

"Stay," Kathy whispers, motioning at him.

She fists a set of keys hanging at the back door to stop their jingling as she takes them off the hook and slips outside, closing the door softly and putting her shoes on now that she is safely outside.

Staying close to the house to reduce the chances of being seen, she slips around to the other side.

Kathy looks across the gravel parking area at the vehicles.

"I can't move fast enough on foot, but if they hear the engine they will come after me."

She looks back at the house.

"I should have grabbed the other keys too, then they wouldn't have a vehicle to come after me with."

She almost goes back, but is afraid it will mean being caught.

"I have to stay off the road."

With an unhappy frown, she drops the keys in the grass and runs across the yard to the trees.

Using the trees as cover, Kathy runs for as long as her legs can, trying to put as much distance between her and the farm as possible. Finally, she goes across the field towards the road, hoping a car might come along and give her a ride.

The door of the house opens and Sophie comes out, dressed.

"Good boy," she says, petting the dog on the head.

The dog follows her outside, sniffing around, and trots around the house. He stops, nosing at the keys abandoned in the grass.

Sophie jogs over, patting him again. "Good boy."

Taking the keys, she gets in the car and drives out of the yard, turning into the road. She does not turn the headlights on until she has gone some distance down the road. The twin beams point the way, the car following as she accelerates.

Kathy is exhausted. She has been walking for hours. In the distance to the East, she can see the glow of the sun about to come over the horizon.

Her feet are almost dragging with exhaustion as she forces herself to keep putting one foot before the other, step after laborious step.

She hears the crunch of tires on gravel a fraction before she hears the engine. Kathy turns, hope soaring and then souring. She recognizes the car.

"Crap."

Kathy stops to wait. There is no point trying to run. She can't outrun a car, and in her exhausted state she has no chance even outrunning whoever is behind the wheel on foot, even if it's one of the old men.

The car stops next to her, Sophie looking at her levelly through the open window.

"Get in Kathy."

Kathy's shoulders slump in defeat and she gets in.

Sophie starts driving.

"You aren't turning around?" Kathy asks, her voice dead.

"Where are you trying to go?" Sophie asks.

A tear rolls down Kathy's cheek, followed by another.

"My mother," she croaks.

"You need to see her, don't you?" Sophie asks. "You miss her."

"I have to make sure she's okay."

Sophie nods, her expression grimly calm.

"I'll take you to where she is."

Kathy blinks at her in surprise. "Really?"

Sophie nods.

They drive for some time, moving to a concrete highway, then another, then back to gravel, and finally Sophie turns down a mud road.

"Where are we?" Kathy asks, her growing unease now screaming fear.

"Where you can see your mother," Sophie says matter-of-factly.

Sophie stops the car and gets out, taking the keys with her.

"Come on, just around these trees."

"Is she in hiding like us?" Kathy asks uncertainly.

"Something like that."

Kathy gets out, following Sophie reluctantly, keeping at a distance. They walk around the trees and she sees nothing, just more trees and a creek running through them, ribboning its way across a field beyond.

Kathy looks at Sophie. An indefinable sadness fills her and she knows.

"My mother isn't here."

"She is," Sophie says, "in a way."

Moving faster than Kathy can react, Sophie charges at her, grabbing her by the hair in both fists, and pulling her off balance.

All Kathy can do at first is instinctively windmill her arms trying to get her balance. She grabs at Sophie, trying to fight back, crying out and screaming.

Sophie drags her to the stream, pushing her down on all fours and falling on top of her, pressing her into the rocks and mud of the rough bank with her weight.

Kathy flails, trying to claw at her, tear her hair out, anything. She twists her body, trying to writhe free.

Still gripping Kathy's hair tight in both fists, Sophie forces her head into the water, pressing down, mashing her face into the bottom of the shallow stream.

Kathy can't help the screams that force the air from her lungs even as she tries to clamp her mouth shut and hold her breath. She struggles as savagely as she can while Sophie continues to bear down her weight on her head, holding it to the bottom.

Water gushes into Kathy's mouth with her body's automatic inhalation of air, the body gasping, choking, her lungs filling with putrid water.

Her struggles weaken, her movements becoming sluggish, her drowning body trying to save itself by becoming immobile, and she finally stills, lying limply beneath Sophie's grip.

Sophie holds her there still, counting quietly. Finally, she gets up, dragging Kathy's lifeless body with her. It sags limply and she drags it from the edge of the stream, letting it fall to the ground.

Sophie returns to the car, opening the trunk, and pulling out tarp and ropes.

Returning to Kathy, she spreads the tarp on the ground next to her and rolls her onto it. Carefully wrapping and tying it, Sophie picks up the tarp-wrapped body, slinging it over her shoulder in a fireman's carry. She carries her to the car, dropping her into the trunk and closing it.

Sophie gets in and drives on. Hours later she parks the car in a lone garage on the edge of a vacant piece of land. Inside, she swaps the body to a white van.

She drives the van for hours more, finally stopping and checking herself in at a roadside motel in the middle of nowhere.

Letting herself in the motel room, Sophie sits on the bed. She checks her watch and waits.

An hour and a half later there is a knock at the door.

Getting up, she peers through the peephole before opening the door to a strange man standing on the other side.

"Mrs. Miller?"

"Yes. Let's go."

Sophie walks across the parking lot to the van, ignoring him. He goes to his own vehicle, a truck with a covered box.

She pulls out of the lot, the truck following her down the road.

42   A Walk in the Woods

The road before Lawrence swims, becoming hazy as exhaustion fills his head with liquid cotton, making it heavy. He tries to focus on the road, but his concentration keeps drifting.

He blinks to clear his eyes. His focus keeps being pulled by the file on the seat beside him. There are a handful of files, but it is this one in particular, the one with the missing pages.

Lawrence passes a sign marking the highway number. Something jogs at him.

The car starts drifting across the center line and he slows, directing the car back to his lane and pulling off on the shoulder.

He tries to think of the highway number.

"Where the Hell am I?" he mutters. "That's not the highway I'm supposed to be on."

Lawrence tries to concentrate on the directions Jim gave him.

"I swear I followed the directions exactly, but I'm on the wrong highway. I need some sleep. I'm driving on auto-pilot and I must have taken a wrong turn somewhere."

Taking the whole road to maneuver a U-turn, Lawrence starts trying to retrace his path to get back on track.

Being lost has him feeling out of sorts. He focuses only on the road and his surroundings, not paying attention to his dash.

After some time, the car starts making an odd noise, kind of chugging. He looks down at the gauges on the dash and is greeting by the alarming sight of the needle resting on empty.

"Bugger."

The car coughs and dies. He lets it coast as long as he can, steering onto the shoulder as it slows to a crawl. Lawrence sits there for a bit in silence.

"Now what?"

He picks up his phone, trying to call for help, but the phone cannot complete the call.

Lawrence looks at the bars of service. There are none.

"That's just great," he mutters.

He puts his head back against the head rest and just sits there.

A couple of hours waiting provides not a single car driving past for him to flag down for help.

He sits up; looking at the folders next to him. Lawrence starts examining them, page by page, folder by folder. He studies the scrawled notes in the margins left by his predecessor.

Finally, he returns to the folder with the missing pages. He examines the photos and sketches one at a time, giving each a more thorough look than he did before. He examines every detail down to the smallest, pulling a handheld magnifying glass out of the glove box to go over those details again.

He goes back to the photos of the house, studying them again.

"It's not the same house. It's similar. Even the ugly wallpaper is similar. But it's not the same. Why didn't I see this before?"

Lawrence jumps, startled by a rapping on his driver's side window. He stares out in shocked surprise at the rugged face of a heavyset man in his mid forties.

Pushing down the unwarranted urge to flee, Lawrence rolls down the window.

"Hey, you broken down mister?" the man asks. The unfortunate odor of gas, oil, and sweat is emanating off him into the confines of the car through the open window.

"Yes," Lawrence says, wondering if he should trust this man.

This is how it always goes in horror movies. Stranded out of gas on a lonely deserted highway and out of nowhere comes some local guy to rescue you. He gives you a lift, often driving a tow truck, or just happens to have what you need to get you going to the next fill station or landmark. But then he kills everybody. I swear, if this guy is driving a tow truck . . ..

Lawrence looks in the rear view mirror.

Shit. He's driving a tow truck.

"You are in luck mister, if that's all you need. I can tow you back to the nearest station to fill up. Don't have anything else to be doing right now."

I'm dead, Lawrence thinks. He forces a smile on his face that looks more sickly predatory on his face that does not know how to make a proper smile.

"That would be great. Thanks."

Lawrence gets out, standing on the side of the road while the guy hooks up to the car. He has the sudden image of the guy taking off with the car hooked to his tow truck, leaving him standing there scratching his head.

"All done. Let's go," the guy says.

They climb in the tow truck and he starts driving, Lawrence having that awkward feeling that he should make conversation, but not knowing what to say.

"I've been sitting there for a long time," he finally says. "Not a single car came until you. I guess I'm lucky you came along."

"Nobody much goes this way. I take a drive out here once in a while just because we get the odd driver who gets lost out this way. It's a long way back to a gas station if they go too far. Lucky for you, you didn't get that far."

"Yeah, lucky for me."

They drive on in awkward silence for a long while.

When he finally leaves Lawrence and his car at a gas station, Lawrence giving him what little cash he has for his trouble, Lawrence watches him drive away.

"I guess the next step is I fill the tank and start driving only to find out this guy followed me and kills me in the next town."

He fills the tank, pays with his credit card, and starts the car, pulling out to the exit. Lawrence looks left and right, pausing.

"Continue to meet Jim and the retired sheriff, or go back and see if there is another house that matches the photos?"

He looks at the photos left on top of the folder next to him and turns to go back to where he found the wrong house.

Some time later, Lawrence is back where he was when Jim called. He parks in front of the house. He looks at the photos and at the house. The differences are too obvious to miss now that he knows they exist.

"It has to be in the area. I know it. But what about the note telling me to run? That was weird."

Lawrence pulls the note out, looking at it again. Now he sees the yellowed state of the paper and the fading of the ink.

"That it's old doesn't make this any less weird. Now how am I going to find the right house?"

He considers the options.

"I always seem to be going to the older generation for help. It's an old house and they are my best odds finding someone who knows an area's past."

He starts driving around; looking for anyplace he might find locals who could point him to a house matching the description. Seeing an older man dressed in jeans and a work shirt pumping gas, Lawrence stops and gets out, approaching him with the photos in hand.

"Excuse me, Sir. I was wondering if you could help me out."

The older man looks at him with a hint of suspicion.

"I'm looking for a house, but I don't have the address."

"That makes it harder," the man observes.

"Yes, it does. I know it's around here somewhere. An older house, small."

"That describes most of the houses around here. You got anything else?"

Lawrence nods. "I have pictures. They don't show much."

He shows him the photos.

"Those are some pretty old photos," the man says. "What reason do you have to be looking for this house?"

He steps back, looking at Lawrence levelly. Lawrence can see his distrust has grown.

Lawrence steps back into the lie he told looking for the Cormer house. He nods.

"I get it. Lots of people don't trust strangers coming around asking questions. I'm an investigator hired by the family of a man who vanished fifty-nine years ago. My investigation led me to a Mr. Grant Cormer a few towns over who disappeared around the same time. He was forty-seven when he just didn't come home one day. He left behind a wife and a new baby. Now it's led me here to find this house."

The man is nodding slowly.

"Makes sense, we had a disappearance some time ago too. Maybe sixty years ago? Maybe a few years less. It's been pretty much forgotten by most people now. I can tell you what house that is by that tree there. No one lives there now, so I don't know what answers you expect to get from it. There are a lot of abandoned houses around here these days. Less folks want to live out here I guess."

He points to the picture on the top of the pile.

Lawrence is filled with a sinking feeling and elation all at once.

The man gives him directions and he thanks him, getting back in his car to search for the house.

Minutes later, Lawrence is sitting outside another small abandoned home left to slowly rot back into the ground it sits on.

He holds up the picture with the cracked window. The camera is looking at the window from inside the dim interior, but he can see that the unnatural bend in the tree seen through the window matches the bend in the tree in the yard. The tree is larger, having years of growth on the photo, and now barren of any sign of leaves. The tree died some years ago and still stands.

Lawrence focuses his attention on the window behind the tree. The crack is still there, a piece of the window missing altogether.

"This looks like the right place."

He gets out, walking up the walk to the house with an eerie feeling of déjà vu.

Like the other house, the door is not locked and he walks in, leaving a trail of shoeprints on the dusty floor into the living room. The dust grime on the window diffuses the light coming in.

Standing in the middle of the living room, Lawrence takes it in. He holds up the photo, comparing it to the house. The ugly wallpaper looks the same, and the water damage that is different from the other house, but the contours match the photo. He can see where there was more water damage over the years.

"The roof must leak."

He studies the curtains. Even they match. The house is absent of furniture.

"This is it. This is the house."

A breeze picks up outside, blowing leaves across the yard and coming in the broken window, dancing the rotting sheer curtain in a dull movement weighted down by years of dirt stiffening the fabric.

He starts moving through the house, searching it thoroughly room by room.

Finished, Lawrence stands where he did before, surveying the emptiness around him.

"There is nothing here. The other photos were taken outside."

He goes out, walking around the house. The overgrown yard behind hides the remnants of a ruined swing set, the metal bent and rusted so that one end bows to the ground. He thinks he can see where there may have once been a vegetable garden. The clothesline is little more than a pole with empty umbrella-like spikes and a few straggling remains of rotted chord dangling where clothes would have once hung. Beyond that is nothing but bush and trees.

"Great. I hate the woods."

Taking his bearings and looking for any sign of a path through the trees, Lawrence sighs and moves through the long grass, pushing his way to vanish in the trees.

It is not easy going, but he pushes on, swatting at a faint buzzing in his ear.

It is not an insect.

Find me. The voice is the distant indistinct buzzing.

It pulls him. Lawrence presses on through the thick growth. He finds what might have been a path once, overgrown now, but easier to follow. He pushes on, stumbling over the rotten remains of a downed tree.

Lawrence stops. He pulls out the other photo and studies it; standing living trees and the remains of long rotting fallen trees, comparing it to the trees around him.

Then he sees it. The trees, standing and one fallen where one in the picture stood before. The remains of the long rotting fallen trees are almost indiscernible now, except for the remnants of moss that once covered them and the elongated mound of slightly raised ground.

He looks up, staring through the trees.

"He was here, right here. For whatever reason he took photos of the way. The way to what?"

The knowledge spurs him on, pushing him to go faster. Branches catch at him, scratching his face and hands.

Lawrence doesn't know how long he pushes on through the trees, following a trail that is barely there and sometimes not.

His foot catches, he stumbles and falls. He pushes his hands out in front of him instinctively to brace himself from the fall. They hit the ground hard and so does his knees. He sits there for a moment, hands and knees stinging, before trying to get up.

He sees it, what tripped him. Lawrence looks around in wonder at the long dried up remains of what used to be a brook. Rocks poke up from the ground, but the bushes and trees have grown in to reclaim the ground the water once owned.

"Am I close?"

Lawrence studies the long dried up stream, trying to imagine the feet that walked this route before. He pictures the shoes. They are not shoes meant for hiking through the woods. Slacks cuffs and shoes ruined.

He walks on, not watching where he is going, following the footsteps in his imagination. His head gets heavy, stuffed. An incessant buzzing irritates his ears.

Lawrence doesn't know when she appeared or from where, a little girl with the familiarity of a recurring dream. Her pig tails are off, as if she had done them herself. She leads him on through the woods. She stops to wave him on when he falters or takes too long to climb over a tree.

"I've seen you before," he says. "Where?"

She does not answer.

Finally, she stops and stands there just looking at him.

He stops, looking down at her.

"Why did we stop? Is this what I'm supposed to find?"

He looks at the ground, then looks around. Finding a thick stick, Lawrence starts clawing at the ground with it, digging the hard ground in little stick trenches.

When the stick breaks he finds another, digging on, sweat dripping after a while and the hole slowing growing larger and deeper. He unearths a rock. Stopping to pick it up, he is about to toss it away but something stops him. He looks at it again. It isn't a rock.

"It's a bone."

Lawrence drops to his knees, attacking the ground with the stick and his hands, digging frantically and unearthing more.

When he is done, he is kneeling staring down at it, wavering.

It is what is left of the bones of a child.

Lawrence fumbles for his phone and dials. A woman's voice answers, tinny and far away.

"Beth," he manages, "I found something."

"Who is this? I can barely hear you." The voice is cutting in and out.

"Lawrence. Tell Jim and call whoever the local police are."

She hesitates. "Where are you and what did you find?"

"Bones. I think it's a little girl." He gives her the coordinates.

Beth feels sick at the thought.

"You know it's a little girl? Is it the clothes? Can you give me a description?"

"I can't tell by the clothes."

"Then how do you know?" Somehow the thought it is a little girl makes it worse for Beth.

"She told me."

Beth pauses. "Lawrence? You are cutting out. Did I hear right? She told you? Who? What did she tell you?"

"The little girl. She told me to find her."

Beth blinks at the phone, unsure what to say.

"Why are you calling me directly with this?" Beth asks, looking at the coordinates she jotted down. "You should be calling Jim."

Lawrence's head snaps up. He looks around for the source of the noise he heard.

"Beth," he whispers urgently into the phone, "get this information to Jim. And tell him I think I'm being followed. It's a white van."

"Do you have anything more? A license plate, description of the driver?"

There is only silence and the line goes dead.

"Jim," Beth's voice on the phone is high and fast. He can hear her breathing heavily as if she just ran.

"What is it Beth? From the excitement in your voice, you must have found something."

"I didn't, your reporter friend, Lawrence Hawkworth, did."

"He called you directly?" Jim can't hide the surprise in his voice. Not only is that highly unusual, it also breaks a serious unspoken rule. Reporters do not call the civilian office staff.

"Jim, you need to check it out. You also need to find him." The urgency in her voice sets Jim's nerves ringing and his heartbeat racing. His palms are suddenly sweaty and he has to rub them on his pants.

"I'll give him a call," Jim says.

"No," Beth's voice is unusually forceful. "Calling him is not enough. You have to find him Jim. I think something happened to him. I think he is in trouble."

Alarm bells are ringing in his head.

"What happened to him?" Jim asks.

"I don't know that anything did yet. But, he sounded strange. I'm sure something is wrong. Jim, just make sure you talk to him in person so you can make sure he is okay."

Jim is nodding even though she can't see it through the phone.

"I'll check on him. What did he find?"

"He found a body in the woods," Beth's breath comes faster with the renewed excitement the words stir up.

"Is anyone on it?"

"Yes, I contacted the local authorities. They have a team out there."

There is a long pause on the phone.

"There is more, isn't there?" Jim asks.

"Jim, it's big."

"Big. Big how?"

"It is another hidden graveyard in the woods."

Beth's words are coming to Jim from far away, muffled and echoing with that unreality that distance gives a thing.

"It's hundreds of miles from the one behind the McAllister Farm. Early indications suggest it has the potential to be just as massive."

Jim almost drops his phone. He looks at Rick.

"It looks like Lawrence isn't going to make it."

43   Found

"Why are we making a side trip?" Jim complains. "We need to get to the last sighting that could be the McAllisters."

"Because Isaac says we need to check this out," Rick says, staring urgently at the map. "Turn up here. We're almost there."

"Who is Isaac really?"

"He's a lot of things. Was a lot of things; ex-police, ex-fed, ex-private investigator, among others. Now he's just a cook trying to live a quiet life."

Jim drops it, staring at the road ahead. The road is filled with scattered emergency vehicles. Straddling the road is a tow truck with water still leaking out of the pickup truck it dragged from a large swampy pond.

They park, getting out and approaching the scene, Jim leading the way and already pulling out his badge. A suited man with an air of authority meets him and Jim shows his badge before they can start the formalities.

"I'm Detective Jim McNelly with the-,"

The man looks past him. "Hello Rick. This will definitely interest you."

Rick steps past Jim, taking the lead.

"What's important about this truck?" Jim asks.

"A farmer reported two men with a truck matching this one stealing one of his old farm beaters. He said it looked like they were about to send the truck off a cliff into the quarry lake adjacent to his property," the suited man says, looking at Jim.

"Now why do you think they would do that with a nice truck just to steal some old farm beater? They need to get rid of it, that's why."

Rick grins at Jim.

"The two men were middle-aged and elderly," the man says.

"Jason and William McAllister," Jim says.

Rick points at him with a triumphant look.

"They must have split from the rest of the group to do a job."

"They will meet up with them again," Jim says. "We need to follow that lead to the last sighting of the rest. William McAllister will go back to his wife."

We should be looking for Lawrence, Jim thinks guiltily. But I can't let this lead slip away.

44   Nathan

The semi tractor hauling a trailer pulls over on the side of the road, stopping. There is nothing but farm fields in every direction, the highway and a few roads ribboning off through them. The passenger door opens and Nathan carefully climbs out, fumbling with the door in his large silver oven mitts. His out of fashion suit and boots has had some of the newspaper and foil repaired. It is not the same tractor that picked him up earlier.

"Are you sure this is where you want off?" the driver asks. "There's nothing around here."

Nathan tries to give him the thumbs up, but with the big silver oven mitt it's just a wave.

Pushing his hat down further on his head, Nathan lowers his head to stare at the ground, hunching into himself as the semi drives away.

"Nathan is close. The white van is close. The van follows the changer, Nathan follows the van. The changer is close."

Leaving the road, Nathan sets out across the field, vanishing in the trees on the other side.

Sophie is driving back to the farm, the gravel of the road crunching under the car tires with an incessant roaring. She spots a head ducking down in the ditch.

Hitting the brakes and gripping the wheel, she lets the car skid to a stop, sending plumes of dust in the air.

Turning to watch out the back window, Sophie guns the gas, backing up and stopping where she saw the head.

Taking the keys with her, she gets out and walks around the car. The ditch is empty.

"I saw you, Billy. Just come out."

She is answered only by the sound of insects and the car engine cooling.

Sophie steps down into the ditch. It runs along the road, between it and a farm field, the open maw of a culvert showing where water drains from one side of the road to the other to reduce spring flooding. Crouching down, she looks into the culvert.

Eyes stare back at her from a smudged face in the dimness inside.

"Don't make me come in there after you."

Billing reluctantly crawls out to stand before her. She stands up as he comes.

"You would too, wouldn't you?" Billy mutters.

"I would."

She looks at his face. There is a wildness to his expression, fear in his eyes.

"Why are you running away?"

Billy swallows.

"You know I can't let you go," Sophie says.

She steps towards him and Billy moves back, keeping enough distance so she can't lunge and grab him. He is eying escape routes, tense and ready to run.

Sophie looks at him levelly.

"I'm not going to bother talking to you like a kid. You've been on the street too long, seen too much." She sighs. "Everything is falling apart, isn't it? You see it too and that's why you are running."

Billy just eyes her warily.

"Look kid, you don't like me and I don't like you and I'm okay with that. But I've seen you with Lauren and I need you to keep watching her until we can split this group up permanently. There is something wrong with David. I know you've seen it. I don't trust him either and I need to know someone is keeping Lauren safe when I can't be there."

Sophie frowns. "I don't like it, but you are the only one I can trust; a street rat with an unknown past."

"What did you do with Kathy?" Billy asks quietly. His eyes shift away, unable to meet hers.

Sophie looks at him with a new interest, trying to read him.

"I just came back from running an errand," she says.

Billy is shaking his head, looking at her with suspicion.

"I saw her. Kathy ran away and you followed. She's not in the car with you. What did you do with her?"

"Kathy wanted out. Now she's out," Sophie says carefully.

"Cassie will be mad. She wanted to kill her."

"I never said I killed her."

"You didn't say you didn't kill her."

"Just get in the car," Sophie says. "You can tell me why you are running away on the way back."

Billy shifts, taking another step back, preparing to bolt.

"Why are you afraid, Billy? Because you think I could have done something to Kathy?"

Billy shakes his head. "I know why you had to kill her. I just don't know why you haven't killed David. He's going to hurt Lauren."

Billy shifts awkwardly, looking down. "I was going to take her with me so he can't hurt her."

"But you didn't," Sophie says. "You are a mess. You aren't just running away, are you? You are running from something."

Alarm flashes in Sophie's eyes and she pales almost imperceptibly.

"What happened at the farm?" she asks.

Lauren looks to make sure no one is watching before going around the corner of the barn. She goes to the fallen tree behind it and studies it. It is one of her secret forts.

Large bushy branches stick up from the fallen tree, its leaves dry and brittle and brown in the green growth filling around it to intertwine with the fallen tree.

She turns at the sound of branches breaking, looking through the trees. Her eyes go big.

It comes from the trees, stopping before her and staring at the ground standing perfectly still as if that will make it invisible.

Lauren blinks. "Do you think I can't see you?" she asks.

It does not respond, just standing motionlessly.

"I saw your eyes blink."

It closes its eyes.

"I see your big silver mitts."

It puts its hands behind it, hiding the mitts.

It is tall like a man, standing on two legs, and seems to be made of mud, leaves, and sticks patched together with ruined newspaper and tinfoil.

Lauren steps closer, looking up into its face. With its eyes closed, its face is dried and cracking mud.

"I see you," she says.

It opens its eyes, looking at her in wide eyed fear.

"It's okay. You don't have to be afraid."

"Look down Nathan. Keep looking down," it whispers hoarsely. "Looking at what lives beneath the ground makes Nathan invisible. No one sees Nathan when he stares at what hides beneath the ground. What lives beneath the ground. Nathan. What lives beneath the ground."

"Is your name Nathan? Do you want to see what lives beneath the ground?" Lauren asks.

"What lives beneath the ground."

"I can show you. This way."

Lauren reaches for a mitted hand and it backs away.

"You don't like to be touched. That's okay. Come, I'll show you what lives beneath the ground."

Lauren goes around the fallen tree and it follows at a distance.

She gets down on all fours and crawls into a hole in the bushes that is almost invisible, pushing green growth of bushes and weeds aside.

It stops and stares at the little girl who just vanished into the ground.

Lauren's head pops out along with an arm and she waves it to follow.

"It's ok. It's safe in here. Nobody will see you. You can be invisible."

She retreats and it gets down on all fours, crawling in. It has trouble fitting, snagging on the branches and tearing its muddied suit.

Inside, it sits and looks around in awe.

Lauren points to the rip. "Oh, you are hurt."

It looks at the rip, then at her.

"This is my tree fort," Lauren says.

She pulls back a wad of browned long grass tangled into a nest to reveal a hole.

"Look, what lives beneath the ground."

She smiles up at it as it leans forward to see.

Inside the hole, little pink bodies huddle together, their eyes almost purple blue through the thin bald skin of their eyelids.

"They're babies," Lauren whispers, putting a finger to her lips signaling silence. "They are sleeping."

She carefully puts the grass back.

"Now you know what lives beneath the ground," she says.

"I like you," Lauren smiles at him. "You're quiet. You don't say much. My brother, Ethan, he talks too much. Do you want to be my friend?"

It blinks at her.

"I bet you're hungry. Stay here. I'll get you a snack."

It stares after her as she crawls out of the fort beneath the fallen tree.

"The man is the boy," Nathan whispers softly. "The boy is the man. The changer changes and takes the identity of others. Nathan has to stop the changer. The changer kills. The changer kills. Nathan has to kill the changer."

"Nothing happened," Billy says, looking at his feet. "I just got to go."

"You are running away from something," Sophie says. "I get that. Whatever or whoever it is, trust me; you are not safer anywhere than with us."

Billy looks at her uncertainly.

"Come on. Get in. You don't think I've seen your panicked looks? That you are constantly looking for an escape? You aren't running from us and can't run anywhere that we won't find you, so you might as well just make the best of it for now."

Billy reluctantly follows her, getting in the car. Sophie starts driving.

"What are you running from anyway? Your parents? It must be a pretty bad home life."

She glances at him.

"No, I think it's bigger than that. You were a ward of the government, weren't you? Was it a group home? A detention facility? Those places can be pretty bad from a kid's perspective."

"They want me," Billy says quietly, looking down at his hands.

"Who?"

"The guys with the van."

Sophie stiffens. "What van?"

"The white van."

Her lips tighten into a hard angry line and her eyes narrow.

Bringing this kid in was a mistake. If they are after him, that puts us all in danger, including Lauren and Ethan. They will stop at nothing to take him. If they don't know who we are . . .. No, they have to know.

Her eyes blaze with anger that makes Billy shrink into his seat.

"Have you seen this van hanging around?"

Billy nods. "Everywhere we go."

"At the farm? Have you seen it at the farm?"

"Not yet."

Sophie glances at Billy, seeing the terror in his eyes.

"I despise the people running the white vans," she mutters under her breath and floors the gas pedal.

Lauren comes around the side of the barn to see David.

He stops, looking at her in surprise.

"I was looking for Kathy," he says. "I can't find her anywhere. Have you seen her?"

He looks down at her. His mind says, *Lauren*. The words that come out of his mouth say different.

"Can you help me look for her Cassie?"

Cassie? That's Lauren, David thinks.

"I haven't seen Cassie either, or Sophie. Do you think they all went somewhere together?"

"Cassie was in the house," Lauren says.

"Do you think she knows where Kathy is?"

"Maybe. I don't know." Lauren moves to go past David and he steps in her way, blocking her.

She looks so much like her, like Cassie did.

David feels the pull of the barn next to them, drawing him to it.

He's probably in there. He's always in there, working on those old tractors that don't need any work.

Inside the barn, William is tinkering with the old tractor, trying to keep busy.

The need pulls at David again; the need to find Kathy, the worry that she might have run away.

She's not happy here. She wants to go. What if she ran away?

"If you see Kathy, can you tell her I'm looking for her?"

"Sure," Lauren says. She slips past him and he watches her go.

"She left you David," little Cassie says.

David looks down at her and she is frowning up at him.

"Everybody is going to leave you because you are bad."

"No. She didn't leave me. Where would she go?"

"Home to her mother."

David blanches. He runs to the house, passing Lauren on the way.

Lauren stops and watches him go.

"He's acting weird again," she says, feeling a cold dread in her stomach.

David is yelling as he enters the house. A sense of unease deepens and Lauren takes a step back and then another.

"Kathy! Cassie!" David yells, bursting in the back door into the kitchen.

Jason steps into the kitchen. "What's wrong David?"

The words are on David's lips, but the look on Jason's face stops them. *I think she left me.*

Jason is angry.

"I-I'm almost finished my chores," David manages, retreating back out the door. The vision of Jason's angry expression urges him to walk quickly.

Jason goes back to the living room to face down Anderson.

"No, we are not doing it," Jason says, his eyes blazing.

"We don't have a choice," Anderson says. "They are coming for the boy and they won't take no for an answer."

Jason shakes his head, his expression deadly.

"They will have to. They are not handing Billy over to one of those monsters. We know what they do to kids."

Anderson can't hide the pain in his eyes. He knows all too well what Billy's fate will be.

"Does my father know?" Jason asks.

"Yes. He's been hiding in the barn since I told him."

Outside, David walks purposely, head down and staring at the ground in front of him, little Cassie jogging to keep up.

"Slow down David," she purrs beside him. "You can't run away from it. They are all going to leave you."

"Shut up," he mutters.

David stops and looks up.

Lauren is still standing not far from the barn, staring at him and unsure if she should go to the house. Now she wishes she had.

David focuses his attention on her and walks quickly to her.

"He's angry about something again," David says. "Did you get your chores done? He'll be mad if you didn't."

Lauren just stares at him mutely, his words confusing her.

David closes the gap, grabbing Lauren's hand.

"Come on, we have to hide you. I've never seen him so mad."

Lauren tries to dig her feet in as he pulls her along, trying to pull her hand free.

"Let go, David," she complains.

"Cassie, come on. We can hide until he calms down."

"I'm not Cassie. Let me go."

He has dragged her past the side of the barn, out of sight of the house.

"Stop playing with me Cassie. I'm serious. He's going to punish us."

David keeps dragging the struggling little girl on past the barn, past the fallen tree, and down the path through the trees.

Lauren keeps dragging her feet, trying to dig them in and stop, trying to wriggle her hand from his tight grip.

"Ow, stop David, you're hurting me. I'm not Cassie, I don't want to play this game," she keeps complaining.

Little Cassie skips along after them, David ignoring her.

Inside the barn, William looks up from the tractor, hearing David's voice. All he makes out is the name Cassie. He goes back to tinkering with the tractor.

Marjory is watching out the bedroom window upstairs. She watches David leave the house, grabbing Lauren and dragging the struggling girl past the barn to the woods.

She puts her hand to her mouth, her expression fearful. Bringing it down, she wrings her hands.

"Something is wrong. I always knew it. Something is wrong with that David. Like Jason."

She goes looking for Sophie and finds Cassie making one of the beds with clean laundered sheets.

"Where's Sophie?" Marjory asks.

Seeing her distressed look of confusion, Cassie misinterprets it.

"It's okay Marjory," she says, going to the old woman. "Why don't you just go have a lie down? I'll see if I can find Sophie."

Marjory lets her lead her back to her room and settle her on the bed with the meekness she learned as a necessity of survival in the care home.

"Find her, hurry," she says as Cassie leaves the room.

"He has Lauren," Marjory says to the closing door, unheard.

Cassie closes the door and goes back to making beds.

After a while Marjory gets up, going to the door and opening it. She peeks out, seeing Cassie in one of the bedrooms down the hall.

She wrings her hands.

Avoiding Cassie, she makes her way downstairs to the living room.

The tension in the room is strong. Marjory looks from Anderson to Jason.

"What has our boy down now?" she asks Anderson shakily.

They both look at her, wanting to continue the conversation without her.

"Nothing," Jason says. "It's okay Mom."

"He's not going on a job now," Marjory says to Anderson. "We have to find Sophie."

Thinking she is lost in some long ago memory, Anderson tries to hide the sorrow it fills him with. I hate to see her like this. Marjory, who has always been so meek but so strong when she needs to be.

"I think she's in the kitchen," he lies. "Find Rose. She'll help you look for Sophie."

He watches Marjory go.

I saw Sophie leave last night, following Kathy. I know what she's gone to do. When she comes back, the scene will be ugly. I wish I could keep Marjory from that. Maybe William can take Marjory and Rose for a drive to spare them being here for it.

"Find William too," he says to her retreating back. "The three of you can go looking for Sophie. Tell William I said so."

Marjory goes to the kitchen, finding it empty. She looks around as if Rose might suddenly materialize, her eyes stopping on the back door. She goes out and across the yard, going past the barn following David and Lauren.

David drags Lauren to the older abandoned barn hidden in the trees where the woods had been allowed to grow back in decades ago. The structure is leaning, its wooden boards shrunken and separated with time, turning grey-black and spongy with rot.

"We'll hide here until he has time to calm down, Cassie."

Lauren is still struggling to break free from his grip, holding his arm with one hand for leverage while trying to pull her other hand free.

"She isn't me, David," little Cassie says, standing just behind him. "Let her go David. You are going to hurt her like you hurt me."

David shakes his head, trying to block out Cassie who is not there and focus on Cassie who is.

"I am not Cassie! I don't like this game. Let me go," Lauren demands.

Lauren's fear has turned to insolent anger. She knows what her parents do, who they really are, despite their efforts to keep it a secret from her and Ethan.

Planting her feet defiantly, she glares up at David, an angry gleam in her eyes. The smallest of smirks turns up the corners of her mouth.

"I am not Cassie. Cassie wants to kill Kathy," she says.

"No," David says. "You and Kathy will be friends. You will be sisters-in-law when we get married."

"You can't have her," little Cassie says in a soft sing-song behind him. "You can't have Kathy because of what you are. You are a monster. You scare Kathy. You are going to kill her just like you killed me, David."

David squeezes his eyes closed, trying to block her out.

"No. Stop saying those things, Cassie."

Lauren thinks he is talking to her.

"My mom hates her too. She knows Kathy has to die," she says.

"We don't have a mom," David says. "You are just trying to be mean now. We just have him."

David's breath is coming faster, his grip on her wrist tighter, more painful. He is stiff with anger.

He actually thinks I'm Cassie. A sick feeling slithers around in Lauren's stomach. She knows she shouldn't, but she pushes it anyway, fighting to not visibly cringe from his painful grip crushing her wrist.

"My mom probably took Kathy away to kill her," she says cruelly.

"Kathy is gone David." The voice behind him is grown up Cassie now.

David turns to look at her. She is standing there, arms crossed over her chest and looking defiant.

"No, she's not gone," David says.

"Kathy and I can never be friends David," grown Cassie says. "She let you escape the basement. We left you down there to die. I will never forgive her for that."

"I never meant to hurt you, Cassie," David growls.

Lauren is staring up at him, watching him talk to empty air behind him, the icy chill of fear freezing her.

David closes his eyes against the dark memories pushing up inside him. Flashes of a barn like this one. Musty old straw. Dim light filtering in between the wood slat walls. Cassie, so little.

He opens his eyes. He needs to see grown up Cassie right now so he knows the memory is false.

There is no one there.

"Day-vid," little Cassie whispers in a taunting sing-song. "Day-vid. Why did you hurt me David?"

David looks straight ahead again. Little Cassie is standing there across the barn. Her hair is a tangled mess with straw stuck in it. Blood soaks her dress hanging limply down and plastering wetly to her legs, the dress that moments before danced around her legs as she hopped and played in the sunshine in the yard. A bloody hand-print is smeared across her face; the hand-print of a boy.

She stares at him with vacant eyes, the light of life extinguished.

"Cassie, I didn't. I didn't hurt you. He did. He killed you."

"No David, you did. You did it," Lauren says, trembling with fear, hoping to make him let go.

David looks down at her. He looks at bloodied little Cassie standing feet away, and back down at living little Cassie standing right before him.

"You are Cassie," he says. "It didn't happen yet, the bad accident. I can keep you safe."

"No, you can't keep me safe," Lauren yells at him.

David's eyes cloud over, darkening, his jaw working as a surge of anger fills him.

"She is not me David," little bloodied Cassie whispers. "You have to find me David. Keep me safe."

"You are Cassie," David says more forcefully.

"I am not Cassie," Lauren yells. "I will never be Cassie! I would never want to be your sister! You are bad!"

"You are bad David," grown Cassie whispers in his ear from behind, her breath chilled like the air from a freezer.

"Find me David," little bloodied Cassie taunts. "It's like hide-and-seek."

"I know you did something bad to her," Lauren yells.

"You killed me David." Grown Cassie's whisper is so quiet he barely hears it.

Darkness is closing in with the rage filling David's head. He can smell the sharp coppery cloying stink of blood. It is all over him, filling his nostrils and making him gag. His hands are wet with it.

"I'm right here David," little bloodied Cassie sings softly.

He reaches his hand out to her, past Lauren's head.

Lauren looks at the grasping hand reaching for her, cringing away and moving sideways, her wrist still in the steel-like grip of his other hand.

It's like he can't see me, she thinks. Lauren can't stop the words already coming out of her mouth.

"You hurt Cassie when she was little! You tried to kill her!"

The three Cassies's words are jumbling together in David's head. Flashes of memory continue to come. Little Cassie looking up at him, so trusting. Then hurt. Crying. Begging him to stop. Don't, David, don't. Her shrill screams.

David is unaware of grabbing Lauren with his free hand and wrapping his hands around her neck and squeezing with the black rage taken over, pushing out all conscious thought.

Marjory is moving with trembling motions, wringing her hands as she moves down the trail beyond the barn and the fallen tree.

She hears the shrill scream of a terrified little girl. She envisions her own little girl screaming in fear face to face with the coyotes.

Her feet move faster, thudding dully on the ground.

Another shrill scream comes down the path.

Marjory is running, her aged legs making her gait awkward.

The chuffing of panted breath comes from behind with the faster dull beat of multiple feet.

Koda brushes past her, racing towards the sound.

"Boomer, no," Marjory tries to call after him, but her words are choked, her age ruined voice crackling. She tries to run harder.

Barking furiously, Koda bursts into the abandoned barn, not slowing his charge as he leaps at David.

David releases Lauren as he dodges the dog just as he did so many years before, only this time he is much larger.

Koda bites his hand as he grabs the dog by the neck, strangling off the dog's yelp as his smaller and weaker hands were unable to before. Kicking at the dog savagely, he shoves him into a stall and wedges the broken door closed before the dog can turn and rally to attack him again.

"Koda!" Lauren screams through her choked sobbing, struggling to breathe with David's crushing grip taken from her throat. Her throat holds the marks already of his strangling grasp.

Koda throws himself at the door, biting at the wood slats and trying to pull them off, trying to wedge himself and squeeze between them.

David stomps across the barn, fumbling blindly, snarling in his blind rage.

"Stop Cassie! Just stop saying those things!" he growls.

Lauren tries to dodge him, but doesn't move fast enough to escape his reach.

"You are wrong David," little bloodied Cassie says. "You are going to kill me just like you did before."

Lauren is screaming. "You are going to kill me! Don't kill me!"

"Don't kill me David," little bloodied Cassie mocks him.

Marjory stumbles into the darkened interior, looking blindly at the moving shapes. Her eyes adjust, bringing the horror of the scene to her.

"David, no!"

She runs at him, flailing at him with her withered fists, trying to pull Lauren away from him.

He swings at her, a fist landing against her jaw and making her head ring as it snaps back.

Lauren manages a louder blood curdling shriek as David's grip on her loosens and his attack turns to the old woman.

William looks up from tinkering on the tractor.

"Did I hear a scream?"

He goes to the barn door, opening it and stepping out, listening.

He hears another scream. Distant.

William is halfway across the yard moving towards the house when the car pulls into the yard; driving up the long driveway towards the house.

He reaches the house as the car does, waving at Sophie to hurry.

She parks, getting out and looking at him questioningly.

Billy gets out, staying back. *Something is going on. Something bad,* he thinks. He looks around, seeing nothing out of place. No white vans. No one who doesn't belong. He is already planning his escape.

"I heard a scream," William says urgently. "Lauren." His look is stricken.

They charge into the house together.

"Where is Lauren? Where are the kids?" Sophie demands.

Anderson and Jason come from the living room, looking at them in confusion.

Rose and Ethan barge into the house, looking at them anxiously.

"We heard screams," Rose gasps.

"Where is Lauren?" Sophie stares at them fearfully.

Cassie is coming down the stairs to investigate the commotion. She pauses, blinking at them.

"Marjory," she says, her words stilted. "She was agitated. I told her to lie down. She was looking for you Sophie, but you were out. I didn't think anything of it, but she said something about Lauren. I didn't hear what."

They all stare at her transfixed.

"Where is David?" Sophie asks, her voice strained.

Cassie turns, racing back up the stairs, her feet stomping on the ceiling above as she races from room to room.

Jason charges to the basement, stopping in the middle looking around.

"He's not upstairs," Cassie yells as she runs down the stairs.

"He's not in the basement," Jason yells, racing back up.

"He wasn't in the yard," Ethan says, looking at Rose for confirmation.

"We have to find them." Sophie's voice is shrill with fear.

Nathan stands in the doorway of the abandoned barn. He gasps a sharp intake of air.

"You are the changer," he hisses in shock. "The changer has changed. The man is the man."

David does not notice him at first. He is shaking Marjory violently, her limbs flapping limply, pulling her up from the floor to smash her against it again with a dull wet thud repeatedly.

Lauren is standing in the corner behind him, frozen with terror and unable to move past him.

David drops the old woman's limp body, turning to Lauren. His eyes are crazed and his muscles hard knots of violence.

"Stop saying those things, Cassie." His voice is low and hoarse.

Lauren blinks at him, her throat too constricted to scream, and tries to dart past him. David rises, lunging, and has Lauren in his grip again. The construction in her throat breaks and she is screaming and trying to fight him off.

Marjory is motionless on the floor.

Koda is a frantic flash of hair and teeth attacking the slats of the stall door that he could not fit between. He is lunging and jumping, trying to scrabble over it. He is not as young and limber as he once was. He would have been able to do it in a few jumps before.

"Look at me Cassie! See me! Recognize me!" David is bellowing.

"I see you David," little bloodied Cassie says with a mischievous smile. "I see you killing her like you killed me."

David glares at her.

"Stop saying those things!"

He shakes Lauren again, hard, holding her up to stare into her eyes. Her eyes are rolling in her head and she is dangling limply.

"Look at me! Cassie!"

Nathan advances purposely on David and Lauren.

"Do not hurt her. She looks after what lives under the ground. She makes them sleep so they are quiet and don't talk to Nathan."

Something that does not fit is pushing its way into the black rage engulfing David. He falters just a little, looking for it.

Little bloodied Cassie is still there, so small and ruined, staring at him.

Something else is staring at him. Something of mud and newsprint and ruined once-shiny foil, with large fat silver paws that are scuffed and dirtied. One has a tear in it. The hair is wild and the eyes in the cracked mud face wilder.

"What?"

David stares at Nathan in terror. He is a boy again, locked in the dark nightmare that revisited him in his sleep so many nights as a child. One of the many dead Jason made him help bury has come back for him.

The desiccated corpse is staring at him. He can only stare in mute terror at the monster. Mud and leaves hang off it, its bony limbs shriveled and dried, not the fat bloated puss-filled gangrenous monster it sometimes is.

Nathan starts chanting, his voice low, staring savagely at David.

"The man becomes the boy. The changer. He is a changer. I take the boy. Make him safe. Put him to his eternal rest. Safe. The changer is trapped and the world is safe. But the man is smart, the changer is smart, but Nathan is smarter. I know. I am on to him. The changer is the boy is the man. It comes back as the man. Nathan goes there, tries to stop it. But the man catches Nathan. Makes Nathan show it the boy. The man takes the boy and leaves Nathan in the dark. The dark. But Nathan knows. The man is the boy, the boy is the man. The white van follows the boy. The white van wants the boy, the changer, the boy is the man the man is the boy. Follow the van find the boy. Find the boy find the man. Find the boy man find the changer. Find the changer find the man. Find the man find the man. The man is the changer the changer is the man. The changer kills. Nathan has to kill the changer to save the world."

With a bizarre shriek that echoes in the abandoned barn, Nathan launches himself at David. The hit is solid, at his mid-section, and knocks the breath out of David.

They fall, hitting the floor hard, David's grip on Lauren lost as his hand opens on impact with the floor.

The hard impact with the floor jogs Lauren back to hazy consciousness, her breath raspy through her partially crushed windpipe. She looks at them, her head lolling and eyes half closed. It takes a moment to sink in.

She rolls, scrambling away weakly. Lauren is trembling and staring at them struggling on the floor. She realizes she peed herself.

Lauren rises slowly to her feet, wavering and staring mutely at them.

"Run keeper of what lives under the ground," Nathan yells. "They are getting through! I can hear them, inside my head, too many, too many toomanytoomanytoomany. Make them sleep!"

Lauren breaks her paralysis and runs out of the barn and down the path back towards the house. She can hear voices calling her name.

They are searching everywhere in the yard for Lauren, every outbuilding and possible hiding spot, calling her, getting more worried by the moment.

"Check her forts," Sophie says urgently.

Ethan darts away to the fallen tree behind the barn. He makes it to the side of the barn when he sees Lauren running to him on the path. She is disheveled, her hair a tangled nest following her, her clothes dirty and face smudged with dirt. Tears streak the dirt on her face, giving it a patchy look.

"Lauren! It's Lauren!" Ethan yells.

The others run towards them, Lauren running past him to the yard and Ethan following.

Sophie scoops up Lauren, holding her tight and trying not to sob.

"Are you okay Lauren?"

She puts her down so she can check her over for injuries.

"What happened Lauren?"

"The mud man saved me," Lauren says, looking up. A sheepish look sneaks in with the fear and trauma.

"The mud man? What is that?" Sophie looks to the others for help, then back down at Lauren.

"He is like a man, but like he is made of mud."

"A man can't be made of mud, honey. What did he look like?"

"Mud. He looked like mud. No." She looks down, thinking. She shakes her head and looks up at them. "Not mud. Paper Mache. He was a Paper Mache man. He was made of mud and newspaper and foil."

They all stare at her in stunned shock.

"What did he save you from?" Cassie asks cautiously.

Lauren looks around at them all before answering. "David."

William and Sophie lock eyes over her head.

Jason looks pained. Anderson looks angry. The rest are in confused shock.

"Where is he?" Sophie asks, her voice deadly. She puts Lauren down.

Lauren points at the path. "That old building."

Sophie is running.

"Sophie, no!" Jason yells. He looks at William and Anderson.

"He'll overpower her. She doesn't have a chance."

He bolts after her, chasing her down the path.

"With Cassie and Grandma," Lauren says, staring after them, but no one hears her.

Locked in the nightmare, David fights frantically, wanting only to escape.

"Cassie, I have to save her," he hisses through gritted teeth.

Nathan and David are struggling, David's greater strength fuelled by a child's nightmare terror winning, and then Nathan's deranged frenzy taking the upper hand.

Grabbing an old hay pitchfork he spots, David swings it wildly at Nathan. It connects with his head, a solid blow that snaps his head back. Nathan falls to the straw littering the floor in the dark corner of the barn.

Still trapped in the stall, the dog continues lunging at the door and barking, chewing on the wood and trying to pry boards off to break free.

David staggers back, looking for Cassie.

"Cassie, where are you?" he hisses.

"You killed me, David," little bloodied Cassie says, her face and voice full of innocence.

He starts kicking at the straw, still unable to find little live Cassie.

"What the hell was that?" David mutters, turning at a sound coming from the corner where his worst childhood nightmare vanished into the blackness it came from. "It's coming back," he whimpers. "Cassie, where are you?"

"I'm right here," little bloodied Cassie says, "where you killed me."

"I'm right here," big Cassie says.

David staggers, turning to look at them both. Little bloodied Cassie is looking at him with quiet seriousness, a secret on her lips.

Big Cassie looks like she is in shock, her eyes staring at him with a wild blankness, her mouth twisted in a grimace of fearful determination.

"I had to get here first," big Cassie says.

"You came to hide," David says. "Good. He's mad again."

Big Cassie's eyes flash confusion, widening with fear. She narrows them at him, trying to steel her resolve.

"I said I was going to kill you, David," big Cassie says.

"I said I was going to kill you, David," little bloodied Cassie mimics.

"For what you did," big Cassie continues.

"For what you did," little bloodied Cassie copies her words almost as soon as they are out of her mouth.

Big Cassie takes a step closer and so does little bloodied Cassie.

"To Connie," the Cassies say almost in unison, taking another step forward. "To Kathy."

They step closer again, still almost in unison, "To the others."

Big Cassie brings a trembling hand up to draw a strand of hair from her face. She glances around, looking for a weapon, and spies the pitchfork lying on the floor.

Her legs are like sticks of wood with no feeling. Cassie forces them to move with all her willpower, slowly moving past David and putting him between her and escape.

David watches her, trying to keep an eye on both her and little bloodied Cassie.

"You hurt me, David," both Cassies say in unison as big Cassie continues slowly inching towards the pitchfork. "You hurt others. You tried to kill me and you won't ever stop."

"Stop saying those things," David growls, clenching his fists, his face twisting into an angry mask.

Cassie dives for the pitchfork, the motion spurring David to rush her. She falls to the floor, gripping it and bringing it up just as he lunges down towards her.

The collision of flesh and rusting metal almost wrenches the pitchfork from her hands. Cassie grips tighter, trying to not lose it.

The tines pierce David with a feeling of unreality for them both, his ribcage resisting and then giving with a pop-like feeling. Blood begins to stain his shirt.

David blinks down at her in surprise and stares down at the pitchfork protruding from his chest.

Little bloodied Cassie snickers at him.

"You killed me David. Now I killed you."

He blinks at her and coughs, blood spluttering from his mouth.

Cassie is staring at him in disbelief.

David grabs the tines protruding from his chest, giving them a tug. He looks at Cassie and at the tines again, giving them a second tug. The third try pulls them free with a wet sucking sound.

He is breathing heavy, his breath gurgling with the blood filling up his lungs, the wet air making sucking noises through his chest.

Sophie and Jason arrive at the abandoned barn to find David staggering out of it. The dog is still trapped in the stall, barking unhappily.

Sophie glowers at him. She realizes his condition, staring at him in mute shock.

David blinks at her and Jason in confusion. His shirt is torn, his hair messed, and his face bruised. Blood from his nose and split lip has dripped to his ruined shirt. His shirt and chest are full blood.

"Cassie . . .," he manages. He looks at Jason forlornly. "I'm sorry. I didn't mean . . . little Cassie . . . she's-." He breaks off, unable to continue. He coughs and splutters, blood spraying from his mouth.

Jason and Sophie exchange a look. Hers is seething with fury, his pained.

"He's mine," Jason says softly. "My mess to clean up."

"He hurt her," Sophie says, her voice hard and low.

Jason approaches David.

"I'm taking you home now David."

"We are both taking him home," Sophie says, stepping forward.

They move quickly, grabbing David and walking him back into the darkened interior of the abandoned barn.

Taken by surprise, David tries to fight back weakly.

"Kathy. Where's Kathy?" he chokes, coughing more blood.

"I took her home already you sick piece of shit," Sophie growls.

The dog in the stall is barking frantically, scrabbling and trying to claw and chew his way out.

Jason manages to pin David's arms, Sophie maneuvering around behind him. She grips David's shirt, pulling it tight around his neck, wrapping her fists in it and pulling it tighter, cutting off his air.

David struggles feebly, kicking, his arms flailing, trying to suck in choked breaths. He weakens, his motions becoming sluggish, his breath little more than a wheezing whisper.

Sophie tightens her grip, wrapping more shirt around her fists, the fabric pressing in against his neck like a garrote and crushing his windpipe, closing off the little air he is getting.

David's face is red, his eyes bulging. His now collapsed lungs are in agony in their need for oxygen. His eyes redden, going bloodshot with the pressure building. He feels like his eyes and lungs are going to explode.

David needs to cry out in the agony of suffocation, but cannot make a sound past his strangled throat. The only air he is getting is what wheezes through the hole in his chest, blood bubbling on his chest with each exhalation and sucking wetly in with each inhalation, prolonging the torturous death.

His lips turn purple and his mouth foams. His feet dance a final tattoo on the ground and he goes limp in their grip.

Sophie continues the pressure, the shirt digging painfully into her hands, counting silently.

Finally, she releases the pressure on his neck, unwinding the shirt twisted around her hands, leaving indents on her hands.

Jason slumps to the floor, holding David, the only son he knew.

They look at each other, Jason's eyes hollow with sorrow and Sophie's cold and empty.

Sophie goes to the stall, wrenching on the door and finally opening it.

Koda bursts out, charging David and biting him aggressively.

"Get off him," Jason snarls, lashing out at the dog, trying to protect David's corpse from the dog.

"He's only doing what he's trained to do," Sophie says. "Protect us. Koda, off."

The dog backs off obediently, circling them and finally sitting next to Sophie.

"Let's clean this up," Sophie says, walking out of the barn.

Jason sits there for a moment, just holding David. His body is still warm as if he could take another breath right now. His slack face and blankly staring eyes give away the truth.

He rubs angrily at his eyes, fighting the tears.

Cassie steps from the corner where she watched. They didn't see her. They didn't expect anyone else to be there.

Jason looks up at her in surprise, his face pained.

"Cassie-," he tries.

"Don't," Cassie says, her voice stricken and her face the bland expression of one who has gone long past shock a long time ago.

Jason takes in the blood splattering her and looks down at David. He lifts David's shirt to reveal the ragged holes in his chest.

"He was already dead," he says.

"I had to," Cassie says.

45   Little Girls Change Everything

Sophie steps from the path, walking across the yard. Everyone is fussing over Lauren. The little girl would be soaking in the attention if she had not just escaped being beaten to death.

Already Lauren seems barely affected by what happened to her.

Koda runs ahead of Sophie, straight for Lauren and giving her wet kisses as she wraps her arms around him in a hug.

Sophie reaches them and reassures herself again that Lauren is okay.

"Take the kids into the house Rose," she says.

"Let's go inside Lauren, Ethan. You too Billy," Rose says.

They wait until they are gone, leaving only Sophie, William, and Anderson.

Anderson looks at her intently, staring into her eyes.

Sophie nods, meeting his look.

"David has gone home, Kathy too."

"Jason?" William asks.

"He's back there, grieving."

They look to stare down the driveway at the sound of an approaching vehicle. A white van turns into the driveway, heading towards them. The van stops, two men getting out. They take a moment to take in the group of people.

Anderson and William give Sophie guarded looks.

She nods at them. "Let me talk to them."

One of the men walks over to stand before her. She meets his steady stare, her own unwavering.

"Geoff," Sophie says.

Inside the house, Rose looks out the window.

"Someone is here," she says. The kids join her to look out.

All color washes from Billy's face. He feels sick, his body too weak to move.

"White van." The words hiss from his mouth.

Lauren looks up at him, a shock of fear filling her at his terrified expression.

Billy comes running from the house, darting to run the other way across the yard.

"Don't, Billy," Sophie yells. "Don't run. You have nowhere to go."

Billy stops, his head dropping in defeat. He slouches over to them, his eyes filled with terror. He looks up at William and Anderson's hard expressionless faces, taking no comfort in them and feeling that no one is on his side.

I'm dead, he thinks, feeling hollow and lost.

"You know why I'm here, Sophie," Geoff says. "I have to take him. I have orders."

Billy gapes at him, his eyes round and large with terror. His worst fear is realized.

Sophie moves to put herself between Geoff and Billy.

Billy moves back, standing between William and Anderson. He realizes his mistake, it makes him easier to grab, but is feeling too lost to fight it and move.

"I can't let you do that," Sophie says.

"Sophie, please," Geoff says. "Don't do this. You know I have to do as ordered at all costs."

"They can't have him," she says.

"I will have to kill you."

Sophie stands her ground firmly. "I'll kill you first."

"Who is that?" Billy whispers, his voice quavering.

"That is Sophie's husband," William says.

"Daddy!" Lauren comes racing from around the house; charging fearlessly at him with a squeal and oblivious to the tense standoff.

Billy almost cries out, one hand moving to stop her although she is too far away. He starts to move to stop Lauren and is stopped by William's grip on his collar.

Lauren throws herself into Geoff's arms.

He looks at Sophie over the little girl's head.

"Why you?" Sophie asks. "Why did they send you?"

"Because they know no one else would be able to take the boy from you. Why are you protecting a street rat?"

"He saved her life."

Geoff shakes his head at her, a small smile curling up the corners of his mouth that does not reach his eyes.

"You are too soft Sophie. You always have been."

He looks past her to see Cassie standing uncertainly a short distance away. He keeps looking at her as he says it again.

"You are too soft. You always have been. They won't always look the other way. This time they are not going to."

"Why don't we have some tea and talk about it?" Sophie says. She turns away, walking to the house, leaving them to watch her go or follow.

"We are having tea and tea biscuits," she says to Cassie as she passes her."

Cassie watches her as the others move past.

"Don't run," William growls under his breath at Billy before they move to follow.

Billy follows woodenly.

Sophie walks into the kitchen.

"Put the kettle on Rose, we are having tea and tea biscuits."

Flustered and thrilled to be part of the game, Rose hurries to put the kettle on.

"Orange Peko," Sophie says.

Rose nods, fumbling in the cupboard for the teas. She turns to them, looking at Sophie all flustered.

"I'm afraid we don't have any tea biscuits."

"That's all right Rose," Sophie says. "Just make the tea."

Ethan and Lauren move to stand next to Billy, the three of them watching the adults in their strange dance of word games.

"Have a seat," Sophie offers their guests chairs in the kitchen.

"We'll stand," Geoff says. He looks at Sophie, his look guarded.

"You have some cleaning up to do. Have you started?"

"Two have been taken care of."

Geoff looks around the room, taking stock of who is present.

"Where's your brother?"

"Tidying up." Sophie gives him a steady look. "You are here to check up on me."

Geoff offers a forced grin that does not reach his eyes.

"I knew this would be a hard one."

"Wallace didn't send you?"

His eyes shift away for a moment, but he meets her look. His nod is almost imperceptible. It's enough. Sophie gets it.

"It will be taken care of," she says. "Jason is just wrapping something up for you right now."

Geoff nods. "David has gone home."

Geoff's partner has been watching Rose.

"Who is this?" he finally asks, indicating her. "That's not Marjory, is she?"

"Nobody," Sophie says.

He smirks at her.

"You people really have a knack for taking in strays, don't you?"

Sophie doesn't like his tone or his look. She gives him a hard look.

"The tea is ready," Rose says, pouring the boiling water into a teapot and adding the tea bags.

Cassie is setting teacups on the table. It feels surreal; everyone talking like everything is normal and no one noticing the blood splattered on her shirt, flecks of it dried on her face.

"That won't be enough tea for us all," Sophie says. "That's okay. I have a special tea for you, Geoff, your friend too. Chamomile."

Sophie moves to the cupboard, taking out the box. She sets it down to open it.

Geoff walks over, putting his hand over hers on the box.

"We won't be drinking any Chamomile tea Sophie."

She meets his look, looking into his eyes.

"Let this go, Geoff. Let us go. The problem is gone."

He shakes his head. "You know I can't do that. You know what the cost of that is."

"Where is Marjory?" William asks. The others look at him.

The door is knocked open and Jason stumbles in carrying Marjory, his face twisted with pain. He stops, looking at the faces all turned to him now in shock.

"Mom," he manages, his voice choked.

Anderson's eyes and expression harden, keeping the pain inside.

William stares at him in disbelief, then suspicion. It quickly turns to anger then fear. He rushes forward.

"Marjory! What have you done?"

Jason can only stand there, looking around at the room for help.

"David-," he says simply, the name trailing off.

Cassie stares in shocked disbelief and Sophie's eyes burn with the hot agony of loss and knowing that which you don't want to know.

Marjory is staring sightlessly ahead at nothing, her body limp in Jason's arms. She somehow looks thinner than before, frailer.

William is trying to pull her away from Jason now, but he is staggering under the weight of devastating loss.

Lauren looks at them, stricken, while Ethan stares in stunned surprise, trying to decide what is going on and if it's true. Billy is blinking back tears. He forgot to take the opportunity to run.

Lauren moves closer, staring at Marjory. She looks around at the adults with a look of pain.

"Grandma tried to make David stop hurting me. He hit her. Then the paper Mache man came and saved me."

Tears are slipping down her cheeks.

"He was too late to save Grandma." The words come out now shaking through hiccupping sobs.

"Stop it Lauren," Sophie snaps at her, fighting for control against her own agony and loss. "There is no paper Mache monster. It isn't real."

Lauren backs away, looking at her mother with a hurt look. She runs out of the room crying.

Seeing her pain, Sophie regrets her words and harsh tone. She has to force herself to not look at Geoff.

Sophie steps in, checking her mother for any signs of life, desperately willing to make there be one.

William is lost. He puts his arms in the air, sobbing loudly, unable to either walk away or stay.

"She's gone," Anderson says. "Set her on the couch."

Jason stumbles woodenly to the living room, gently setting her down.

"This doesn't change anything," Geoff's partner says. "Let's get this done."

Sophie gives him a hate-filled glare. Her voice is dangerously cold when she speaks. "You son of a bitch."

Geoff nudges him, a caution to cool it. He turns to Sophie.

"I'm sorry about your mother. This is a bad time, but we can't go without all the packages we came for."

William has fallen to the floor in front of the couch, sobbing and moaning and hugging Marjory while clutching her hand.

Sophie gives Geoff a hard stare and motions everyone out of the living room to leave William to his mourning.

"Jason," she says, her tone hard to break through his misery.

He looks at her with pain-filled eyes.

"We have to show them where David took Lauren."

Jason nods numbly, turning and stumbling back out the door.

Sophie nods to Geoff and his partner to come. They follow Jason out and Sophie moves to follow.

Anderson grabs her arm as she pushes past him.

"I'm coming with you," he says quietly.

Sophie nods.

They go past the barn to the abandoned one leaning haphazardly and nearly hidden in the trees, Jason leading the way.

When they file into the barn, they look down at the carefully wrapped body on the floor.

Geoff nods to his partner and they take positions at each end, kneeling and lifting David's body.

Sophie, Anderson, and Jason watch them carry the body out. They look at each other.

Jason tries to stare into Sophie's eyes, but she looks away.

"They gave you orders to kill me." There is no question in his voice.

"They were more concerned with David and Kathy. They were the big problem."

She looks at him now.

"Do you think you can learn to control yourself?"

"I'm not like David. He can't stop."

"No, but you don't want to stop. Maybe you can't."

"I control it. I always have."

"Amy Dodds. You were in control then?"

"I was a kid."

Sophie shrugs. "They might let you go. David and Kathy were firm. And they want the boy, Billy. That is not negotiable."

Jason looks stricken. "He's just a kid."

He bolts, running for the house.

"Jason, you can't stop them!" Sophie calls after him. She starts running after him.

Anderson shakes his head and does his best to walk quickly on his aged legs.

Geoff and his partner load David in the back of the van.

Billy is watching from the window, looking ill. *I'm next.*

Geoff gets on his phone as they start walking back to the house. It is answered on the first ring.

"Yes," Wallace says. "Have they been dealt with?"

"We picked up the second package. David and Kathy have gone home." Geoff hesitates. "She doesn't want to give up the boy."

He can feel the anger he is sure is on Wallace's face.

"You get that boy and bring him to me. I don't care what it takes. Send every one of them home. Do it. You clean this up."

Wallace is pacing angrily, clutching the phone so hard his knuckles are white. He is wearing his usual nondescript cheap suit jacket, trousers, and dress shirt with the top two buttons undone and no tie. He runs his hand agitatedly through his thinning hair.

He stops pacing, staring straight ahead.

"You know the price of failure. It's not just your wife you will lose."

Geoff's eyes narrow and his mouth tightens into a thin line. He stops, working to compose himself, to stop the trembling starting in his hands.

Anderson is standing before him, looking at him levelly.

"That's him, isn't it?"

The look on Geoff's face is all the answer he needs.

Anderson's hand lashes out, taking Geoff by surprise, the speed of the motion unexpected from this withered old man.

Anderson has the phone, quickly placing it to his ear before Geoff can snatch it away again.

"You know who this is," Anderson says into the phone.

"I do," Wallace says, recognizing the aged voice.

Anderson holds a hand up, motioning Geoff to wait.

"This is a lot of effort for a street rat," Anderson says.

"That is not your concern," Wallace says. "Nothing is your concern anymore. I've called you all in. You are all going home now."

Geoff is trying to warn Anderson off.

"William's wife is dead," Anderson says. "If you think he is going to let this go, you are mistaken."

"He's so old. What is he going to do?" Wallace barks a laugh into the phone.

"He is going to clean up his mess," Anderson says. "William McAllister always cleans up his mess." He hangs up the phone with a small hard grin.

Geoff is staring at Anderson with alarm. All he can see is the faces of Lauren and Ethan, Sweet little Lauren, staring sightlessly at him.

"He's going to kill my family."

"He's my son, you bastard," Wallace says to the dead phone, seething with rage.

46   Rick Dalton is not all good

Jim's ancient brown Oldsmobile is racing above the speed limit, its engine straining under the pressure. The area around them has been growing more desolate with the miles put behind them.

"You are sure this is the place?" Jim asks. "It doesn't look like there will be anything out here. I haven't seen a farm for over an hour."

He glances down at his gas gauge with a frown.

"I haven't seen a gas station either."

"There should be one in a few miles," Rick says.

True to his word, a gas station appears as if from nowhere in the distance. They pull into the station, the overheating Oldsmobile engine ticking away, and Jim pounds the steering wheel.

"Damn it, it's closed. We aren't going to get far."

"That's all right," Rick says, getting out of the car. "Come, I want to show you something."

Jim gets out, panting with the stress he is under, and follows.

"What do you want to show me all the way out here?"

He looks grumpily back at the gas station building.

"This place looks like it hasn't been open for a long time."

Rick is leading him past it to the back of the building.

"This gas station is abandoned," Rick says.

Jim pauses, looking at him. "Then why the Hell are we here?"

They are walking through the wild bush behind the station now, the branches pulling and snagging on their clothes as they push their way through it.

"For this," Rick says.

It takes Jim a moment to see it. The trees and bushes have overgrown it, engulfing and growing around and through it, or rather what is left of it. It is a small house, abandoned long before the gas station and left to return to the earth it stands on. Part of the roof is caved in and the walls are crumbled at the top. A section of wall on one side is mostly gone. The window they can see has only remnants of broken glass in the sill. A single strip of curtain can be seen hanging rotting and forlorn at the edge of the window on one side.

"What is this place?" Jim asks. "It must be a couple hundred years old or more."

Rick is staring at the ruins and beyond it.

"Older. It's one of McAllister's secrets. Beyond this is a graveyard that is so old you likely won't even find remnants of bones. No one has been here in so long," Rick pauses, "it's so far off the beaten track of anything, you can bring a man here and no one will ever find him."

Jim stares at him, feeling uneasy.

"I have to ask you again, Rick, why the Hell are we here?"

Rick turns to look at him.

"You have to give this up, Jim. Drop it. This secret does not belong to you. This is bigger than you and your friend, Lawrence."

"You know where Lawrence is, don't you?"

"I do. Yes, he is in trouble. The sort of trouble you don't come back from. I know about a lot more than you can imagine. I lost everything, you know, chasing down William McAllister. My wife, kids. They don't like anyone getting their nose in their business."

"So, I'm right. The McAllisters, William, his son Jason, they belong to some kind of organized group."

"It's not like you think. It's not like organized crime. They just tidy things up, keep some semblance of control. You can't control these monsters, you know. The serial killers, people like that. They don't think like you and me, like civilized society. They can't just be locked up and they can't be just killed."

He studies Jim for a moment.

"Have you ever wondered why serial killers exist? Why some people for reasons they don't understand themselves are driven to kill again and again? Why people are driven to do such disgustingly horrid things to each other?"

"Every day."

"I learned the secret." Rick taps his head. "Think about it. We are at the top of the food chain. The alpha species.

Every species has its place and they all know where they belong. The rabbit will give up to its fate once caught because it knows that is its place. The lion sees all creatures within its domain as food because that is its place. We hunt the lion. When the rabbit population booms, so do its natural predators. It's just nature's checks and balances. It's just nature looking after itself. Even the beasts at the top of the food chain have at least one natural predator, us.

What happens to the species at the top? What happens to the one species that has no natural predator?"

"What?" Jim is increasingly wary.

"Us. We are our own predator. It's just nature, natural selection. With no true predators, we evolved to be driven to prey on our own. It has to be allowed or we will overwhelm the world. That's why there is such a high rate of people needlessly victimizing people; war, murder, on scales small and large.

It can't be stopped. Every predator you take down only creates another. Check and balance. The best we can hope is to manage them. That's what it's about, managing them. Allow nature to run its course. Allow the predator you know to do what it's driven to do so that we are not overrun with predators we cannot control. It's just business."

"You are crazy asshole."

Jim stares at him, realizing.

"You found him. You tracked down William McAllister years ago. He got into your head, didn't he?"

His heart is pounding in his chest and his breath comes faster. He hesitates before he can say it.

"Are you . . . are you working with him? Oh, shit. You brought me here to get rid of me."

Hearing the noise in the woods, Lawrence hangs up on Beth and runs blindly; sure whoever is driving the white van is there. His own large feet trampling the dead dry leaves and branches mixed with the vibrant living plants, his body tearing through the trees and bushes; drowns out any real sound of pursuit. Still, he hears it in his head, feet pounding after him and breath huffing behind him.

And then the ground beneath him vanishes with the dry soft cracking of old rotting boards and the earth swallows him up. His forward momentum bounces him off the side of the hole, pounding him against the dirt and roots. He continues falling, hitting the ground some distance below hard. He lays there staring up at that square of light, the ruined jagged teeth of the boards making it look like a mouth that swallowed him whole. As the world above fades and closes with consciousness seeping way, Lawrence thinks he sees the hazy image of people looking down the hole.

Words far away and barely discernible echo down. Or it could just be the echo of clattering falling boards or the birds above, or just his imagination.

"If he's fallen down there, he's done."

The dull scraping sound as of something sliding roughly as the square of light above shrinks and goes out.

He succumbs to the nothingness enveloping him.

Blinking his eyes, Lawrence is disoriented. He has the sense of time passing, but the last thing he remembers is falling.

Lawrence is in darkness. His own breathing is loud in his ears in the enclosed space.

He moves cautiously, feeling himself over for injuries. He is sore but there seems to be no broken bones. He reaches out with shaking hands, feeling out the dark space he is trapped in.

"It must be some kind of old mine shaft."

Lawrence fumbles in his pockets. He finds his phone and sits back with a sigh of relief.

Turning it on, its faint light reveals that he is in some kind of mud hole cut into the ground.

Lawrence tries dialing for help. He has no signal. He looks at the phone with a frown.

"Looks like I'm on my own to get out."

Using the flashlight app to look up, the poor light reveals darkness; mud and roots making the walls, and a dark flattish ceiling. The roots do not look like they will help him climb out. Examining the ceiling shows it is not completely flat. Boards were pulled or fell across to cover the hole.

He examines the dirt floor. A round rock is barely sticking out of the ground. There is nothing else he can use.

"I might need a weapon if I can climb out."

Lawrence starts digging at it with his hands. He gouges the mud around it, revealing more of the round rock. Finally, he starts rocking it and working it out.

Lawrence holds it up, looking at it. The rock proves to be a skull. He drops it as if it is hot and digs beyond it, revealing a partial bone.

Scurrying back as far away from the remains as he can, Lawrence stares at them.

"I have to get out of here."

Standing up stiffly, using the wall for support, he holds the phone high, looking for a signal to call for help. Finding none, he tries anyway, getting a connection error.

Lawrence presses send again.

"Help. Hello," he yells at the phone over and over as he keeps trying.

He tries climbing the wall, pulling himself up with a thicker root and gripping the phone, trying to hold it as high as he can, trying again to call for help.

"Help! Hello!"

47   Breakdown

Geoff's partner goes into the house to get Billy. He stops, staring at the boy. His phone rings and he answers it. He listens for a moment.

"Yes sir," he says. He looks at the two boys. Billy and Ethan are staring back at him. Lauren is somewhere in the house.

"Let's go kid," he says to Billy, hanging up the phone. "Stop running, it's not doing you any good."

Jason bursts into the house, making him turn to look. Seeing it coming, he braces as Jason charges straight at him.

"Ethan, Billy," Rose tries to urge the boys away from the grappling men.

Billy uses the distraction, darting towards the front door. The door bangs closed behind him and he sprints across the yard to the trees.

Geoff reaches to take his phone away from Anderson when his head explodes with brilliant and black light and pain. He drops to the ground. Sophie is standing behind him looking down at him.

She looks at Anderson.

"They ordered Geoff and his partner to clean us all up," Anderson says.

They look at the house.

"Jason went inside," Sophie says.

Cassie grabs a large kitchen knife and approaches the fighting men warily, keeping her distance.

They bang against the wall, each trying to throw the other off balance, kicking savagely at each other's legs to bring the other down. They fall heavily to the floor,

Billy is pulled up short suddenly by something grabbing him. His momentum whirls him around, ripping him out of his attacker's grasp and sending him tumbling to the ground.

He looks up to see the terrifying sight of what appears to be a man made of mud, newspaper, and tin foil.

"Changer," it hisses at him. "The changer is the man is the boy. The man is the boy. The man becomes the boy."

Billy blinks up at Nathan in shock. Nathan is staring at him with wide wild eyes. There is a familiarity. Then he remembers. The crazy man who grabbed him outside the rooming house and zip-tied his wrists and ankles. He carried him across the street. Struggling as he carried him down to a basement and forced him into a trunk. Blackness. Hours spent trapped in the dark in that tiny trunk.

His mind is whirling desperately through thoughts.

He kept saying weird shit like this. Talking about whispers and them talking to him, whoever they are. Chanting and talking about a changer, something he thinks I am. Changer. What is a changer? Something that changes. The man becomes the boy. He was watching Jason. He thinks Jason turned into me. If I can make him think I'm me . . .."

"Hey, no, the changer, he changed again," Billy shouts.

Nathan is reaching for him and he falters, looking down at him. The boy is on the ground and he looks terrified.

"I hear them too," Billy says urgently. "I hear them all the time. They whisper."

Nathan is reaching for him again and Billy turns, burying his face in the ground. He screams when he feels Nathan grabbing at him, shrill and loud.

"I see them," Billy manages through his screams. "I hear them. The changer is at the house. He's inside. Inside the house!"

Nathan falters again, staring down at Billy.

It sees them, Nathan thinks. It stares at the ground and sees them. It hears them. It is not the changer?

"You are lying," Nathan says. "You are the changer. The man is the boy is the changer. The changer devoured the boy and became the boy."

"No, nobody ate me," Billy cries, keeping his face buried in the ground as if not looking will make the crazy man less real. "It-it tried to. I got away. Yes, the man in the house, the man in the house is it."

"The man in the house is the changer."

"Yes, yes," Billy sobs, "it ate the man in the house. It's there."

Nathan looks at the house through the trees uncertainly. He stumbles away, towards the house. He runs low across the yard, coming to the house.

Looking in the window, he sees Jason and Geoff's partner wrestling, bouncing off the wall, and falling to the floor. Jason is on top, and then the other man is, rolling as they struggle against each other.

In his mind they are melding, becoming one. Nathan gasps.

Cassie pounces at them, slashing with her knife. They come apart, rolling away from each other.

Geoff's partner staggers to his feet, awkwardly staggering to the front door and out, almost falling as he staggers down the steps.

Nathan looks in the window again and Jason is lying motionlessly on the floor, Cassie standing over him clutching the knife. Blood drips from it to splatter on the floor.

He looks at the man staggering away, blindly.

"The changer devoured him," Nathan whispers. "It left the empty husk of what it was. It became the man. The man became the man."

He follows, closing in, and pausing with a frightened whimper.

"The man is the changer the changer is the man. The changer devours. Nathan has to kill the changer."

He staggers after Geoff's partner, catching up to him and knocking him down. Nathan straddles him and he tries to fight back, but he is losing blood and weakening. Nathan presses down with his oversized silver oven-mitted hands around his throat, trying to strangle him.

The man on the ground claws weakly at him, gasping and trying to suck in mouthfuls of air, but he is not dying.

Nathan realizes his mistake.

"It is trying to suck out Nathan's soul. The changer is trying to devour Nathan. Nathan has to stop it sucking out what lives inside Nathan with the soul."

He shifts his hands, covering the prone man's mouth and nose and pressing down with all his weight.

The man struggles, feet kicking uselessly against the ground, trying to pry Nathan's hands away from his face.

William breaks from the dark haze of mourning. The shouts and cries were distant background noise to the devastation of his loss.

"Marjory, my Marjory," he moans desolately, sobbing.

He staggers to his feet and towards the kitchen in time to see Cassie plunging the knife into Geoff's partner.

The prone man and Jason are still clutching at each other and rolling on the ground, each trying to get on top.

Geoff's partner puts a hand out too late to stop the knife coming at him, feels the unreality of the white hot agony of the blade slipping into his body and the sticky warm wetness of his blood leaking out.

He pulls away and Jason lets him go, laying in limp exhaustion on the floor.

William watches the man stagger through the living room and out the front door, Cassie standing over Jason and the bloodied floor in shock. A large bead of blood drips from the knife, splattering on the floor.

"Let him go," Jason gasps without moving. "He won't get far."

Sophie kneels beside Geoff, looking down at him sadly. He landed half on his side, one arm splayed out in front of him. She gently touches his hair, lovingly caresses his face. A tear rolls down her cheek.

"Goodbye," she whispers hoarsely.

His eyes open, looking at her blurrily. He fumbles his arm towards her.

"Sophie, I'm sorry. I have to. The kids."

"Shh," she whispers to him. "I know; they'll just send someone else and kill me and the kids if you don't. They will kill you and the kids if I don't."

She looks up at Anderson, blinking through her tears.

"He played us. He played us all. Wallace. There is only one way Lauren and Ethan can live."

"No, don't do it," Anderson says, knowing it's useless. He doesn't finish. What's the point? He can say there is a way out, to keep them all alive. It would be a lie.

Steadying Geoff's head with one hand, Sophie jabs hard and quick at the base of his skull, severing his spinal cord. Blood sprays on both her hand and the knife, she drops it on the ground. She stares down at Geoff.

"You have to do it Anderson, so Lauren and Ethan can live. Do it and make them disappear. Don't make my dad have to do it."

Choking down the emotion filling his throat like a wad, Anderson steps forward. Stooping down, he picks up the knife and walks around Sophie.

Gently taking her head in one hand to steady it, he plunges the knife home with a quick stab to the base of her neck. There is resistance on the knife, and his aged hand trembles, Sophie jerking in a reflexive attempt to live, and he pushes harder. His age-withered muscles make it harder, but the knife pushes through, blood spraying his hand.

Sophie slumps to the ground and he lets her fall.

Carrying the weight of what he has done, Anderson starts walking to the house.

He walks in to fine Rose and Cassie standing over Jason with William standing on the other side.

William and Anderson look at each other and Anderson gives him an almost imperceptible nod.

"Wallace ordered a full cleaning," Anderson says.

"You talked to him?" William asks.

"Yes. I told him you will not let this go; that you always clean up your mess."

William's eyes water. "Sophie. . .."

"She followed Geoff home."

William nods awkwardly, trying to push down the pain filling him.

Cassie looks at them, realizing, and wails in anguish.

William's eyes blaze with fury, his face twisting in agony.

"My Marjory . . . Sophie."

He looks around and spots Ethan.

"Where is Lauren? Somebody find Lauren."

"I'll find her," Rose says, moving past them up the stairs to search.

"Where is Geoff's partner?" Anderson asks.

"He ran outside," Jason says. "Cassie stabbed him."

Anderson nods. "We have to find him and make sure."

William and Anderson exchange another look, both trying to weigh how much further this will go.

"Cassie, go with Anderson," William says. "Jason, you are with me. Let's go."

They head out in different directions, searching for Geoff's partner.

"There, blood," Jason points to the ground.

Jason and William follow the blood across the yard. They find him before the trees, splayed out on the ground staring sightlessly at the sky.

"Just what I thought," Jason says. "Cassie got him good. He didn't get far."

He looks around.

"Billy took off. We have to find him and make sure he's safe."

"Billy!" he shouts. "Billy!"

"Check him," William says gruffly.

Jason looks at him and William motions to the dead man on the ground.

"He's dead," Jason says.

"Check him anyway. This isn't the time to get sloppy."

Jason kneels, checking him. The blow comes as he realizes. He turns to look up at his father as the blow is coming down, taking it in the side of the face. He didn't see William take the heavy little clock that probably sat on top of the small china hutch in the living room for decades.

Jason falters, falling to support himself with one arm, trying to bring up the other as William strikes him in the head again.

"I should have put you down after the coyotes," William says, his voice low and rough with the unbearable agony of what he is doing. "After the rabbit." He strikes him again. "Before Amy Dodds. Before the others."

William stands over Jason's motionless form, blood dripping from the clock. He lets it slip from his fingers to thud on the ground.

"I knew I had to put you down and I couldn't do it. You drove your mother into that despicable place with her keeping your ugly secret all these years. You drove your sister into this business. We all kept your secrets. That woman . . . her kids. You shouldn't have kept them. They were not yours to keep. Look what you did to them. Look what you did to them."

William staggers off into the trees looking for Billy, sobbing out his grief, moaning Marjory's and Sophie's names.

Ethan stands alone staring down at the blood on the floor where Geoff's partner was stabbed. He starts shaking with shock. He stumbles through the kitchen and out the back door.

He stops. Two prone figures lay sprawled on the ground next to each other.

Walking to them, Ethan stops, standing over them staring down at Sophie and Geoff. They each have a hand reaching towards the other, almost touching. Their eyes stare blankly at nothing. He knows his parents are dead.

Ethan just stares at them, his face void of expression.

"What happens now?" Cassie asks, looking at Anderson walking beside her. "Everyone is gone, aren't they? William is going to kill Jason, isn't he?"

Anderson just walks, stone faced and looking ahead, putting distance between them and William and Jason.

"I knew them growing up," Anderson says, finally speaking. "Jason and Sophie. I knew Marjory before the kids came."

"Sophie is dead," Cassie continues, as if he hadn't spoken. "Her husband, David and Kathy, Marjory. That just leaves Rose, me, and the kids. Are you going to kill us too?"

"Do I need to?"

"No. David was sick. He had a dark sickness inside him, and Kathy was too broken. Jason had a sickness too. Sophie told me what he did, about Amy Dodds and the other women."

She looks down, struggling with her words.

"My mother."

"Wallace won't be satisfied unless he thinks we are all dead," Anderson says.

"What do we do?"

"We split up and try our damnedest to disappear. We won't succeed. Nobody does. But maybe it will give William a chance to finish."

"Finish what?"

"Cleaning up his mess."

Anderson stops and looks at her.

"That's been long enough. Let's go back. We have to leave now."

"We weren't really looking for him?" Cassie asks, looking at him.

"No. We were giving William time to do what he has to," Anderson says gravely.

Billy is hiding. He holds his breath, listening. He hears the footsteps crunching through the bushes, coming closer. He shifts, trying to flatten himself and be invisible.

Something grabs him, yanking him roughly out of the bushes he is hiding in. He cries out, but it is choked off with fear.

"Stop yelling, it's me," William snarls gruffly.

Billy stares up at him, his heart pounding wildly in his chest.

"You're strong for an old guy," he manages.

"You don't hide good for a street rat," William complains.

"It's over kid," he says.

"The white van-," Billy starts. He is shaking so hard he can barely speak.

"Gone. They went home. We have to go now."

"Come on Lauren, come out of there," Rose pleads, trying to coax Lauren out from under the bed.

Lauren blinks at her, face streaked with tears, and finally starts sliding out. She stands up and rubs the tears with her sleeve.

"Here now," Rose says, gently dabbing at her tears. Taking her hand and leading her to the bathroom where she washes her face with a warm washcloth.

"That's better, isn't it?"

"Are they all gone?" Lauren asks.

"Only for now," Rose says. She leads Lauren downstairs to the kitchen, trying to block her view of the blood when they pass it.

She fails and Lauren stares down at it, leaving a partial shoe print in the edge and tracking it with her into the kitchen.

"Let's sit down while we wait," Rose says.

"Grandma is in the living room," Lauren says.

The door opens and a disheveled man covered in mud, newspaper, and ruined foil comes shuffling it, struggling with the door in his oversized ruined silver oven mitts.

Rose stares at him in open-mouthed shock, her eyes widening with fear.

"That's the paper Mache man," Lauren whispers to Rose.

"This looks like a good time for some tea," Rose says, flustered, turning to the cupboard and reaching for the Chamomile tea box with a trembling hand.

"I think he would like some green tea and tea biscuits," Lauren says, beaming up at Nathan.

Rose turns to stare at her.

"It's okay, this is just Rose," Lauren says.

Nathan is frozen, staring at the old lady.

Lauren frowns.

"I don't think you should be here when they come back. I think you should go," she pauses, choosing her next words carefully, "back to your mom."

"Mom." Nathan blinks at them.

"It's okay to go now," Lauren says.

"Nathan goes to Mom."

Lauren nods.

He looks uncertainly towards the back door. *There are dead people out there.*

"They are out there," he whispers.

"I know they are out there," Lauren says. "It's okay. They are sleeping."

Nathan nods, putting a different meaning to her words.

"Keep what lives beneath the ground sleeping," he whispers and stumbles back out the door, struggling with it with his oven mitts.

"That was very peculiar," Rose says, staring after the strange man.

Jim eyes Rick warily, taking in the signs of exhaustion from the long hours driving and the hike, his wheezing breath.

"You are dying, aren't you?"

"I am," Rick says. "I'm sick. I don't have more than a few months. Looking at you, you don't look like you are doing much better."

Jim shifts his stance, edging away. Rick follows him.

"Where are you going to go, Jim? You wanted to know the secret. You wanted to find the McAllisters. This is it. You are here."

Rick's arm shifts towards his waist and Jim bolts as well as he can with his obese weight, dodging just as he hears a pop behind him, the crack echoing off the sky.

"Oh, shit," he puffs, dodging trees and trying to zigzag as he runs.

He hears Rick mutter behind him.

Rick stumbles, limping after him and unable to run. He points the handgun and pulls the trigger, another pop cracking off the sky.

"This is bigger than you, Jim. You know it," he calls after him, firing another round at him.

The bullet hits a tree beside Jim's head, sending splinters of sharp bark shrapnel stinging his neck.

Rick keeps limping after him, handgun held up and looking for a clear shot through the trees.

Jim feels like his heart is going to explode by the time he sees the gas station through the trees ahead. His breath is wheezing so hard he can barely get any air.

He stumbles against a tree, his phone falling out of his pocket to the ground.

Jim looks down at it, about to stoop down to pick it up, but another bullet whizzes by too close.

Pushing himself on with effort, he runs, breaking from the trees and cover to run across the open lot to the pumps.

The car groans and shifts with his weight as he throws himself into the driver's seat, fumbles to shove his keys in the ignition and start it, the engine choking before it catches.

Jim presses the gas pedal to the floor, the tires shooting gravel out behind them as the car surges forward. Pulling into the road he tears off as fast as he dares push the ancient car.

Anderson and Cassie arrive at the house moments before William and Billy come from the woods.

Rose and Lauren look up at their entrance.

"Have you seen Ethan?" Rose asks, concerned.

"No," Cassie says. "He isn't with you?"

"I can't find him in the house."

Cassie turns to the door to go searching just as it opens and William comes in, the two boys ahead of him.

"Found a couple of street rats," William mutters.

"We have to go right now," Anderson says.

Anderson looks at the phone in his hand, realizing he is still holding Geoff's phone. He hits redial and send. It's answered on the first ring.

"You need to send a pick up crew to the farm," he says and hangs up. He turns to the others.

"Let's go. It's time to disappear. We'll split up as soon as we put some distance between us and this place."

He leads the way out the back door, dropping the phone on the ground next to Geoff on the way to the vehicles.

Lauren and Ethan stare down at their parents as they walk past.

"Wait," Lauren says, stopping. "Koda."

"He's gone," William mutters. "We'll get you a new dog."

Lauren looks at him with large unhappy eyes.

"Get in," William growls.

They get in, driving down the long driveway to the mud road, Anderson driving and William riding shotgun. Turning at the road, they start down it.

"Stop," Lauren cries, pointing. "There he is."

The car stops and William gets out, looking into the distance. He whistles shrill and loud. Something in the distance comes bounding towards them, picking up speed as it comes.

Koda races to them, tail wagging.

William opens the back door, motioning.

"Get in, dog."

Koda jumps in on top of everyone in the back seat and he closes the door, getting back into the front passenger seat. They drive on.

The ugly brown Oldsmobile's engine clunks again, chugging roughly and losing power, slowing despite Jim pressing the gas pedal harder. He rocks in his seat, gripping the steering wheel as if that will somehow make it keep going.

The Oldsmobile coughs and dies, coasting to a stop in the road. From the sound of the clunk the engine makes, Jim knows this is the end of it.

The over-heated engine ticks and hisses and smoke starts rising from under the hood.

Jim just sits there, not moving.

Finally, he looks around. There is nothing of consequence as far as the eye can see.

"I'm done; in the middle of nowhere. They'll never find me. No one even knows I'm here. There is no way I can walk out of here alive."

Lawrence

Lawrence is submersed in the boxes left to him by his mentor, his obsession now taking over Lawrence. The apartment is littered with piles of files lined up along every wall. Each pile marked with color coded sticky notes on the walls above them with virtually illegible scrawls.

On one wall is a large poster board set up with boxes and a left and bottom graph axis. Each of these boxes is split into small ones like a Sudoku puzzle, and those color coded to match the sticky notes on the walls.

Lawrence looks disheveled, like a man who has not changed, showered, or slept in days. His hair is askew, his clothes wrinkled, and his face a washed out stubble-infested mask of fanatical exhaustion. Mud is caked in the wrinkles and seams of his clothes, under his nails, and dusts the lines of his face. His eyes are heavy with sagging bags, glassy, and stained red with bloodshot lines tracing in from the corners in a spidery web of veins.

END

Other books by L.V. Gaudet:

<u>The McAllister Series:</u>

Where the Bodies Are

Are you ready to step into the twisted mind of a killer? What kind of dark secret pushes a man to commit the unimaginable, even as he is sickened by his own actions?

A young woman is found discarded with the trash, left for dead. More bodies begin to appear.

The killer's reality blurs between past and present with a compulsion driven by a dark secret locked in a fractured mind. Overcome by a blind rage that leaves him wallowing in remorse with the bodies of victim after victim, he is desperate to stop killing.

The search for the killer will lead to his dark secret buried in the past.

The McAllister Farm

Take a step back in time to meet the boy who created the killer and learn the secret behind the bodies in Where the Bodies Are.

William McAllister is a private man who does not like to have attention on his family. His family history is as dark as the secret hiding in the woods.

Just as he begins to bring his troubled son into the family business, a serial killer starts preying on local young women. The McAllisters quickly find themselves drawn into the spotlight when the town decides William McAllister is the killer.

The attention is a threat to both William McAllister's profession and his family. He has no choice but to find the killer himself.

He might not like what he learns.

Hunting Michael Underwood

Step deeper into the twisted mind of a killer as he slips further into madness.

Hunting Michael Underwood follows on the heels of book one, Where the Bodies Are, bringing the first two stories and their characters together as the search for the killer continues.

Michael Underwood has vanished and Detective Jim McNelly will not stop until he finds him. Working with the detective, Lawrence Hawkworth is still chasing the bigger story he knows is behind the bodies.

Jason McAllister knows he must stop the killer he created before he goes too far. He may be the only one who can stop him.

Unable to let go of his barely remembered past and the search for his sister, the killer goes looking for Jason McAllister's past and his family.

Killing David McAllister

Sometimes the only way to stop a monster is to kill it. He has gone by many names, but he was raised as David McAllister, and finding what he is looking for is not enough to quiet the darkness inside him.

Other Books:

Garden Grove

Who wants to stop construction at the new Garden Grove residential development? Garden Grove is a hotbed of complications from costly mistakes and vandalism to sabotage and the poisoning of the work crew.

While the construction crew struggles to stay on schedule, they face growing problems and, with them, a growing sense of unease.

A group of local housewives drawn into the growing mystery uncover a secret that brings Garden Grove deeper into a new mystery connecting all the suspects.

The mystery deepens with the discovery of old human remains that have their own dark past recently planted at the jobsite.

When all attempts to shut the site down permanently fail, two long time elderly residents step up their own efforts. Each with their own family secrets, the pair of quirky old birds are pitted against each other and their longstanding family feud is brought to the boiling point.

The Gypsy Queen
(1952)

When a young man with an enthusiasm for get rich quick schemes discovers a rotting abandoned paddle wheel river boat, he has dreams of the riches and glamour she will bring rebuilt as a floating casino. His best friend and unwilling business partner sees only rot, decay, and their ruination in the old boat.

Struggling to rebuild her, they are pitted against everyone from the Shipbuilders' Union to the local casino boss. Meanwhile, strange accidents and a sense of dread falls on those who enter the boat as she awakens with a hunger for her ounce of blood.

The Gypsy Queen's dark past will not be forgotten.

Old Mill Road

Twelve years ago four kids found something in the woods that tore their innocence away. They made a vow to keep it secret. Now, impossibly, someone found it again.

The abandoned mill off the old Mill Road has a dark history that has been told for generations, a story about something sinister haunting the woods.

Unable to remember the events of twelve years ago and troubled by the haunted look he sees every time he looks at his sister's eyes, Nick has returned to learn what happened when they were kids.

Still obsessed with Felicia and Nick's family suddenly vanishing in the night after their childhood discovery, David is determined to get answers from Nick, while his brother Ian tries to temper his obsession.

Felicia's return to help Nick will trigger new revelations about the mummified bodies of children appearing in the woods decades apart.

About the Author

L.V. Gaudet is a Canadian author, a member of the Manitoba Writers' Guild, the Horror Writers Association, and Authors of Manitoba.

L.V. grew up with a love of the darker side; sneaking down to the basement at night to watch the old horror B movies, Vincent Price being a favorite; devouring books by Stephen King, Dean Koontz, and other horror authors; and has had a passion for books and the idea of creating stories and worlds a person can get lost in since reading that first novel.

This love of storytelling has this author working writing and editing into a busy life that includes work, family, and supporting the writing community. L. V. Gaudet volunteers with the Manitoba Writers' Guild, is the editor of the MWG newsletter, proofreads for the HWA newsletter, and visits schools for I Love to Read month.

L.V. Gaudet currently lives in Manitoba with two rescue dogs, spouse, and kids.

Follow L. V. Gaudet:

Facebook: https://www.facebook.com/LVGaudet.Author/
Instagram: lv_gaudet
Twitter: @lvgaudet
Wordpress: https://lvgaudet.wordpress.com

Killing David McAllister
The McAllister Series Book 4

Sometimes the only way to stop a monster is to kill it. He has gone by many names, but he was raised as David McAllister, and finding what he is looking for is not enough to quiet the darkness inside him. David McAllister must die.

While the McAllisters move into hiding, Detective Jim McNelly and his reporter friend, Lawrence Hawkworth, continue to pursue them. Jim and Lawrence split up to follow their own leads, routes that will take them each on their own path to discover secrets behind the McAllisters.

Anderson and William are trying to keep the group together and ahead of the detective hunting them while trying to resolve the issue of what to do with David, Kathy, Rose Bheals, and the boy Jason brought, Billy.

Kathy is becoming increasingly fearful both for and of David and wants out but feels trapped. She is certain death is the only way out.

Cassie swore to kill David for what he did to Connie and the others. Torn by memories she does not have and the knowledge of the dark hole this life will bury her in, she needs to escape.

Sophie has been ordered to kill David and Kathy. She may have to kill her own brother, Jason, too. When the time comes, she's not sure if she can do it.

With Marjory's lapses into the foggy confusion of Alzheimer's, nobody believes her when she really needs them to, when Sophie's little girl's life is at stake.

David is slipping further into madness and, convinced she is the little sister he lost so many years ago, he is going to take little Lauren with him. Having his now adult real sister, Cassie, there is no help.

Will someone reach David and Lauren in time as the blackness closes in and rage takes over?